HE CHOKED BACK A SOB. THERE WAS A FAINT SCRATCHING.

"No," he whispered.

(when he was five his father took him into the mountains and showed him how he could stand flat against a high rock and look up at the clouds moving in his direction, look up and suffer the illusion the rock was falling on him)

Don't look up, he thought, and the sky won't fall.

Scratching.

He backed away from the boulder on hands and knees, and saw it perched above him, red eyes watching.

He screamed and jumped to his feet, his arms pinwheeling helplessly, and his legs out of control, paying no attention to the trail he'd been following. He knew only to head for the trees.

Lifting from the boulder, climbing, furling its wings. It was still hungry . . . and now it was ready.

The Nestling

Charles L. Grant

PUBLISHED BY POCKET BOOKS NEW YORK

This novel is a work of fiction. Names, characters, places and incidents are either the product of the author's imagination or are used fictitiously, and any resemblance to actual persons, living or dead, events or locales is entirely coincidental.

Another *Original* publication of POCKET BOOKS

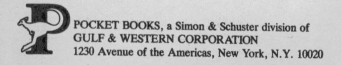

POCKET BOOKS, a Simon & Schuster division of
GULF & WESTERN CORPORATION
1230 Avenue of the Americas, New York, N.Y. 10020

ISBN: 0-671-41989-7

First Pocket Books printing June, 1982

10 9 8 7 6 5 4 3 2 1

POCKET and colophon are trademarks of Simon & Schuster.

Printed in the U.S.A.

For Stephen and Tabitha,
who know the fun of conjuring a nightmare,
and know the thrill of riding a scream;
with friendship, and love,
and a scratching at the window.

Author's Note

Though the Wind River Reservation and the Shoshone who live there, and Ft. Washakie and Pinedale and the Wind River Mountain Range, are all factual, I have taken some liberties with the geography of the area to give the Wind River a new, secondary bed, and add a plateau, a village, and a town that do not exist, save in my imagination. The Shoshone Nation offshoot is also fictional, and its beliefs and legends should not be confused or connected with any that have existed or do now exist. And the beauty of Wyoming would defy any man's words.

Ah, sir, you dwellers in the city
cannot enter into the feelings of
the hunter.

BRAM STOKER,
Dracula

To run forever through the endless
   woods and fields
Beneath the festering fullness of
   the moon:
The case, the hazard, the quarry
   and the blood.
Oh, the blood! Oh, the blood!

AVRAM DAVIDSON,
"Loups-Garous"

Prologue
THE TEACHING

ONE

In the beginning was the Teaching. A chanting for evocation, a summoning from the time when the bison were plentiful and the eagle was king. A Teaching conceived by a woman without names, though the others called her Dark Moon in the shadowed safety of their lodges.

In the beginning was the Teaching, and from the Teaching came the pain. Nothing else existed save that nugget of agony, and its layers of scarlet fire that hardened to become crimson. That grew to become saffron. That expanded to become sun. That exploded into a whirling that became, at last, calm. That became soaring. That became peace.

And in the beginning the pain might have been unendurable if it had not been for the words that had once been the source, the words that dampened the scarlet and tamed the crimson and guided through the sun and the soaring to the inevitable peace.

The words were the saving; in the language from the time when the bison were plentiful and the eagle was king, they made it worthwhile.

And in making it worthwhile they made it easier, far easier

3

*with each summons until the pain was little more than a prick
upon the soul.*
   It happened that fast.
   A prick upon the soul.
   *In the beginning was the pain . . . and in the end was the
dying.*

(1)

David Carosa's combination welcome-home and twenty-
fourth birthday party was held in his father's backyard,
behind the building that housed (in front) the barbershop/bar
and (above and in back) the family's residence. Like most
other yards and streetsides in Windriver the grass was rich
and fully green, the pine and hickory, birch and oak high and
richly crowned, as though lawns and trees alike drew water
continuously from the river that flowed on the town's south
side. The temperature had dropped considerably since sunset, but not nearly enough to spoil the summer-picnic cast
Anthony Carosa had worked to give his son's celebration;
just biting enough to remind those who thought about it how
high this part of Wyoming was held in the Rockies' relentless
arms. Chinese lanterns had been strung in rainbow profusion
from the lowest branches, folding tables had been set up to
hold trays and platters and bowls of food and a dozen or more
folding chairs had been hauled from the Methodist Church
for the guests to rest on when they grew tired of singing, tired
of dancing.
   The noise was considerable, but no one complained.
   They quieted only once . . . to hear a train's passing.
   And by night's end—which would be far too soon for most
of the young—nearly everyone in town would have dropped
by at least once to say a few smiling words to Anthony and
Mary Carosa and spend a few nervous minutes standing by
David's rocker, trying desperately not to stare at the red
tartan blanket covering his legs or the hardwood canes
propped carefully by his side. If they felt any pity, they would
keep it to themselves; sympathy would be expressed in
doleful whispers on the way home. However David felt about
his crippling, Windriver expected him to be grateful he was
still alive, that his fall across the tracks had not included his

torso as well, that Sheriff Harmon had been riding nearby and had seen him and had streaked him to Doc Vance's before the bleeding killed him.

And David was indeed grateful, and thankful, and filled with pious prayers . . . though none of it stopped him from swearing now and then.

Set in the yard's back corner was a low wooden platform not an inch above the grass; on it, four local musicians played guitar and fiddle, Jew's harp and electric bass for those who wanted to do more than listen to gossip or wonder how soon Mary would come to term with the Carosas' third child. The tunes were loud, the melodies sprightly, and the only breaks came when a deep breath was needed.

Jake Harmon, wearing a shimmering dark blue shirt with matching string tie, creased black trousers and highly polished boots, stood behind one of the larger tables with Carosa. They said nothing to each other, eavesdropping instead on conversations darting past them, nodding when they were acknowledged, shrugging when they weren't. Then Carosa took Jake's arm lightly, led him through the screened door into a spacious, glaring white kitchen.

Jake waited silently by an oval butcher-block table while the barber rummaged through an overhead cabinet. A moment, and the portly Italian turned with a green-necked bottle clasped to his chest. His hands were massive, but his fingers held the container as if it were a holy relic.

"Been saving this for three years," he said, yanking out the cork with thumb and forefinger and pouring them each a full measure of the wine. "The family already had its share. Now it's your turn."

Jake accepted the glass without speaking. He stared at it, swirled it, looked at the ceiling, looked at the floor. "I didn't save his legs, you know," he said quietly.

Carosa cleared his throat. "No, but he's still alive. He'll learn to walk again. And you helped him, god knows, with all them letters you sent him." He grinned and scrubbed at the tight black hair curled about his scalp. "You thought I didn't know that, right? You thought maybe . . . ah, never mind. He appreciated them, Jake. We all did. Your health, my friend."

He drank, and Jake drank with him, not hesitating at all when the man offered him more.

"I heard," the barber said as he replaced the bottle in the cupboard, "that Billyboy took a shot at Aaron Sweetwater today."

Jake nodded, daubing at his chin with a fine linen handkerchief. "Word gets around fast."

"Perkins told me so himself. The fool bragged about it."

Jake shook his head with a mischievous grin. "You mean he actually came to town alone? All by himself? You sure Gloria wasn't all trussed up in the back of the pickup?"

Carosa's curiously high laugh filled the room. "For sure, Jake, I don't see why he married her. Don't see it at all. She's been nothing but trouble from the moment they come out of the church. Trouble is, she's too damned beautiful for a town this size."

"Tony, a woman cannot be too beautiful—it's against the law of nature." He set his glass on the counter and sighed. "Sweetwater called me about it. I called him a damned fool for shortcuttin over Billyboy's land like that. He didn't even seem concerned, just wanted me to know Billy was gunnin again. I tell you, friend, them Indians better be more careful or one of these days one of them's gonna be dead."

Carosa nodded, scratching at the back of a hand so covered with hard hair it seemed gloved. "Some people wouldn't mind that, y'know."

"Tell me about it," Jake said, with sorrow and acid.

"But I've heard stories about Sweetwater's temper, too."

"Yeah," said Jake, opening the door and stepping aside to let his friend through. "But then, I've heard stories about Gloria, and I ain't never had any of her, either."

They stood for a moment on the back stoop, their eyes readjusting to the dim light outside. A comfortable silence, then, while they scanned the milling crowd and listened to the music.

"Don't see Carole," Jake said. "She got a date?"

Carosa scratched at his stomach idly. "You could say that."

Jake noted his sudden discomfort, then kicked himself mentally. "Hey, Tony, I ain't mad or anything."

"I know, I know. It's just that your Ellie used t'go to the MacKenzie ranch all the time, y'know? Now my Carole goes out to read to the old woman and I kinda feel bad about it. Like I was movin in on Ellie or something."

Jake shook his head quickly. "Don't be foolish, man.

Ellie's got a ton of studyin to do, she just ain't got the time anymore. I'm just glad Mrs. MacKenzie found someone she likes. Carole's a good girl."

"Yeah," Carosa said. "Most of the time."

Jake ignored the reference to Carole's summer humiliation the year before, the preaching from the pulpit Reverend Thornton did; he never did like the minister and figured there was more to the situation than anyone knew—anyone, that is, except Tony and his daughter. And he'd never pried. He'd just let it go, and hoped Carole was over most of the shame.

There was laughter, sudden and shrill, and Jake turned his gaze toward the girls hovering around David's chair. He poked at his friend's side with an elbow and nodded. "He may have to sit, but he ain't lost his touch."

"Then you'd best watch your daughter, lawman," Carosa said, grinning broadly. "We may be relatives yet."

"Nope," Jake said seriously. "With that scholarship she's got, Ellie goes straight to college in the fall if she knows what's good for her. After she graduates she can have a million kids if she's a mind. But after, not before."

Carosa was about to reply, but his wife had turned around at the sound of their chuckling and beckoned him impatiently. He shrugged elaborate resignation, patted Jake's back and hurried to her side. Jake did not move. From the stoop, he sought his daughter, found her engrossed in conversation with a young man near the band. A smile, then, proud and somewhat sad; so much like her mother in spirit, so little in image—dark auburn hair parted in the center and framing a face rounded, always flushed at the cheeks, sprayed with faint freckles Ellie despaired of ever losing. Her eyes close-set, her thin lips pale . . . the only legacy from her father a nose that just avoided being labeled prominent. When she was older, Jake knew men would call her handsome, as they had her mother before the pneumonia took her.

She laughed suddenly, without parting her lips, and Jake shook his head, remembering the braces she'd worn and how she still wasn't sure she was looking her best, and the day she had confided in him that she wished she had large breasts like Carole Carosa.

A smile again, proud. And sad.

Growing up, he thought with a trace of melancholy; my baby's growing up.

(2)

Ellie saw her father staring at her and turned awkwardly away, wishing he would leave her alone for just one night. She was, after all, practically eighteen, was practically in college and did not need to be chaperoned anymore. Maybe it was about time she had another talk with him, fill him in on what his attentions were doing to her social life. But the thought died when she glanced back over her shoulder and he was gone. Sighing her relief—and acknowledging some guilt —she redirected her attention to Harry Felsom, who was fumbling in the dark for her hands. A tall, lank boy with darker freckles than her own and dulled red hair that never seemed to stay in place, he was not at all like his brothers— both of them working as deputies for her father—but for the time being he was better than anything else she had seen tonight. Besides, the puppy-dog expression and the cleft in his chin that made his jawline rugged contrasted just enough to intrigue her, make her wonder if perhaps he was older than he acted.

"Come on, El," he said, "this is a drag." And an impatient hand slapped over the cowlick bowing forward from his crown.

"I'm not going anywhere with you tonight, Harry Felsom," she said, hiding a smile behind her coy palm. "But I will let you walk me home, if you want." She touched a finger to each temple, scaled them down either side of her face to pull back the dark hair brushed there by the wind. Then she glanced at him sideways, believing her nose was more aristocratic in profile than monstrous head-on.

"El!"

"I said you could take me home, Harry," she told him, softly.

The band swept to a discordant finale, was overwhelmed by applause.

"When?" he asked eagerly.

The smile nearly broke to a laugh. "Now," she said. "Early day tomorrow. Soon as church is over I got that English paper to finish and exams to start working on. 'Course, if you think we should wait on your brothers . . ."

"Ellie," the boy whined; and she wished again he were more like the others, less childish and more romantic, and prayed that the men at the university were considerably more attractive. When he reached for her hand again she pushed him off to the house to fetch her sweater. She was standing by the door when he returned, her father at her side.

"Right home," Jake told her sternly, pinching her back playfully to belie his tone. "You hear me?"

She nodded, grabbed Harry's hand before the boy could say anything and pulled him around the side of the house, onto the drive that took them out to Valley Pike, the town's main street. Without speaking they turned right and walked slowly, almost reluctantly, toward the next corner.

Ellie didn't like the Pike this late at night. The storefronts were all dark—even the neon in Carosa's bar window had flickered to black. There were no cars at the curbing, no pedestrians on the pavement, and the sound of their heels was echoing loud.

I'm a grown woman, she told herself then, though she could not help feeling the night had changed, added an element that she could not fit in.

It was, of course, nothing more than imagination, and a wondering if Harry were as naive as he seemed.

Nevertheless, there were echoes.

And there was no moon.

The few streetlamps were buried in thick shifting foliage, and their six-sided iron posts merged in blackness with neighboring poles. A fold of paper scratched persistently at the gutter; a dead leaf was caught on the rusted bars of a corner storm drain and fluttered weakly for release. In the distance, out in the valley, a dog or a coyote complained at the dark.

The nightbreeze had finally risen to a light wind that carried the faint scent of impending heavy rain. Ellie pulled her sweater tightly around her throat, not bothering to object when Harry, under pretext of assisting, kept his thin arm around her shoulders. Their footfalls muffled abruptly, and the sharp sounds of the party were cut off solidly.

She paused once in full stride, looked back toward the driveway.

"What?" Harry said.

"I don't know. Nothing, I guess."

But there was something—she sensed it. Like the shadow of a small cloud that was here, and was gone.

At the corner of River Road, they turned left and she deliberately slowed the pace as the Pike was left behind. On the right a single small blue light marked the brick firehouse set well back from the street; on the left, a rustic-looking white clapboard that was Windriver's Town Hall. There were no houses at all until they reached the second block; then there were only four, two on either side—all of them dark, and all of them silent.

The shadow-sense again, and for the sake of her nerves she called it a cat, and slipped her arm quickly around Harry's waist.

Two long blocks later they crossed Bank Road, and the pavement narrowed as the street aimed for the ill-repaired bridge over the river. Ellie imagined she could see the cemetery on the water's far side, the creatures that roamed there when the valley was leeched of its sunlight. She shuddered and scolded herself; this was hardly the way for a mature, college-bound woman to behave. Lord, the cemetery was so little used she could barely remember what it looked like.

But there was something not right with the night.

Halfway to the bridge they reached a narrow dirt path punched into a fifty-yard patch of densely bunched trees and underbrush. During the day it was a nuisance to walk; at night it was claustrophobic, and she was grateful when they broke into the open, onto a band of grass and weeds thirty feet wide that ended at the river. Directly ahead was her home, the only structure visible on this side of the water . . . with its back to the town. Why her grandfather had built it that way, and surrounded it with a dozen bloated and grasping willows, she had never been able to understand. But there were times when, as now, the privacy pleased her.

If only she could shake the feeling that something was watching . . .

"Harry?"

"Yeah?"

"Do you . . . you okay?"

"Sure, why not?"

"No reason. Never mind."

They wound single file through the low shrubs and weeds until they were stopped by a man-tall privet with several gaps for gates. On the other side was her front lawn. When she had been much younger she thought the old house and the hedge-wall a fine place for a princess to wait for her prince, or a fortress to be defended by a courageous woman warrior; now she wondered if it had been really so fine to live quite that alone.

"Well," she said then, glad for her voice and turning to face Harry with a smile at her lips, "thanks for the escort, Mister Felsom."

"Yeah. Sure." He looked back once at the blackwall of trees behind them, at the way the hedge blended into the trees behind the house and cut them off from Windriver. "Sure. Not like it was a hundred miles or anything. I don't mind at all. Not at all."

"Well, I appreciate it just the same." She grinned.

"It's okay."

God, she thought, do I have to draw him a map?

He looked around again. "You really like living out here?"

"Harry, it's not like I'm on the moon, you know."

"I know that. But you can't see anything. I mean, the town's gone, you know what I mean?"

She nodded, telling herself to be patient. He was, after all, kind of cute.

"Spooky, y'know?"

She wished he hadn't said that. "Sometimes," she admitted.

"You ever see anything in the river?"

"Fish," she said flatly, tiring of the game.

"Oh."

"Harry, it's getting late." She gave him her prettiest smile. When that didn't work, she moved closer and lifted her face, half-closed her eyes. Waited. Almost laughed. "Well?"

He tried a worldly smile that broke too weakly and took hold of her arms and stroked them gently. He wanted to say something, was about to speak when a finger touched his lips and sealed them. He kissed her quickly, then, before she could change her mind, stepped back a pace without releasing her and searched for her eyes.

"You're beautiful, Ellie," he said in a harsh whisper.

She smiled and ducked her head, hoping but not expecting that he'd be more original. She shifted, and her breasts pressed lightly into his arms. He stiffened for a moment, watching her, waiting, then slid his hands to her waist, up under her arms.

"Ellie—"

She kissed him, hard, her palms cupping the back of his head while her torso twisted to bring his left hand to her breast. She could feel the intake of his breath, the heat of his fingers as they drifted over the flesh she had prayed would grow larger before she left in the fall. A button slipped loose, another, and a third, and she could feel the night air excitingly cool. A fourth, a fifth, and the muscles of her stomach jumped delightedly at his touch.

His knees began to sag, his weight pulling them down.

She pulled reluctantly away from his lips, the dart of his unsure tongue. "Harry," she whispered, closing her eyes against the solid heat of his loins.

"For god's sake, Ellie!"

"No," she said, though she did not discourage the hand creeping under her bra. "Yes, I mean, but not here."

He yanked her shirt from her jeans, ran one hand up her spine.

"The porch, Harry," she insisted, feeling control slipping and not wanting the rock-spiked ground. "Please. The porch." She could sense the struggle and pushed her hips against him, sliding, told him again she would rather have the porch. A nod, short and hard, but his left hand would not release her breast.

Damn, she thought when her own knees buckled.

"God *damn*," she said when suddenly he withdrew, cocked his head and looked around.

"What?" She sounded more sharp than she'd intended, but the ghost of his caresses was still wrapped around her skin.

He shook his head. "Nothing." He looked at her, and licked his lips nervously. "I thought I heard something."

Something not right . . .

"Spooks," she said, her hands fluttering into fists.

"An owl, I guess."

My god, she thought then; my god, he *can't* be a virgin.

"Owl," he repeated, as if convincing himself.

"It's probably my father sneaking after us to make sure you don't attack me," she said sourly.

He turned away from her abruptly and she laughed, yanked on his arm to bring him back to his touching. But his frown became a scowl and he wrenched the arm away. Ellie watched, puzzled and frustrated, as he stared up into the trees behind them, then leaned forward slightly to peer into the darkness under the branches.

"A cat," she said finally. "I've felt it following us a couple of times already. Don't worry, he won't tell."

"I don't know, Ellie," he said. "I would swear on a stack of Bibles that I—"

She didn't hear him finish.

The sensation came again, like the onrush of the wind.

"Harry—" and she closed her shirt over her chest.

First there was the sound, and in the split second before it started she knew she had heard it someplace before. But there was no time to give it a name.

No time at all.

Suddenly, something struck her viciously square across her shoulders, and she was slammed facedown onto the ground, her hands instantly out to catch herself, though not before her forehead glanced off a half-buried rock that stunned her into momentary unconsciousness.

Her cry was a gasp; her breath turned to fire.

Its cry was fire; its breath a rending.

She had no idea how long she lay there dazed, but when she was finally able to pull herself back from the comfortable darkness, she shook herself awake, awash in a tidal agony that began in her head and spread relentlessly down the track of her spine. She pushed herself to her hands and knees, sobbing with fright and anger, trying to force her vision into focus.

It's those damned boys, she thought; they won't leave me alone, they all think they have a claim.

The porch light she had left burning provided less than adequate illumination, but it was sufficient for her to see the blood on her hands, on the rock that she'd struck.

"Harry?"

She swallowed heavily; her throat was dry, her tongue seemed swollen.

"Harry?"

Slowly she rocked back to her heels and lay her palms flat on her thighs. The pain. There was too much pain.

"Harry, please help me. I'm hurt, Harry. I'm . . . god, I'm bleeding. My head . . ."

She closed her eyes tightly, snapped them open and almost grinned when she realized she could see clearly again. The light was a flat yellow, robbing the ground around her of proper dimension; she knew, however, that the river was on her left and the trees on her right. Harry—

She saw him . . . and choked on a scream.

He lay on his back less than five yards from where she knelt, and she could see more clearly than she wanted the glittering flow of dark blood from the gashes on his chest and throat . . . and the thing that was feeding on the flesh of his face.

Feeding . . . and turning . . . and launching itself at her, more silent than the wind.

She screamed and rolled out of its way, scrambled to her feet and held her arms tight about her head as she ran. Weeping. Shrieking. Stumbling once and throwing herself to the right as she sensed a closing, felt it swerve past her with a whispering rush. She landed on her right shoulder and grunted, whimpered, ordered herself to stand and be poised to run again.

The river sighed past her, the trees shimmered in the wind. She swallowed hard and took a step forward, her cheeks streaked with tears and dirt, her hands in weak fists at her sides. Another step, toward the hedge, fighting the shapes the shadows made. Listening. Snapping her eyes closed when she inadvertently looked at Harry, bleeding.

She did not think; all thought was gone. Lips and limbs trembled, and a blade of dead grass dangled from one eyebrow.

She felt it stalking her and moved in a tight circle, turning with every step, eyes wide, mouth open, the blood from her forehead running slowly to her chin.

Stalking, watching, waiting for the moment when her fear was just right.

The hedge loomed, the houselight swayed, and she shook her head once to drive off the fog.

Her whimpering a prayer; her blood the dark offering.

Its cry the acceptance . . . and it came straight at her out of the shadows of the shadowblack trees.

She bolted, not caring now where she was going, seeing nothing but black before her until she was struck again from behind and she felt her flesh tear. She twisted, stumbled backward with arms flailing before losing her balance and pitching without a sound over the edge of the bank, into the Wind River.

Part One
THE RETURN

ONE

(1)

Home again, home again, jiggedy-jig. Jason Clarke smiled at
the child-verse fragment, a brief smile that turned melancholy
before it finally died. Home again. Home. Not precisely the
truth, if truths were to be known. He had lived in Windriver
for only six years, and that was two decades ago when his
family had still been welcome there. Virtually every day of
the final three had been spent in his bed, helpless with a
variant of Addison's disease. Three years of medicines,
therapy, unanswered prayers while his father fought with the
ranch to survive and his mother struggled to keep them
together. Three years before Peter Clarke died in a drunken
crash, and five months more before his widow sold out and
fled to the East.

And now that he was back (home again, home), he was
dismayed that dim memories had been so deceptive.

It was not the size of the mountains, nor the breadth of the
valley's plateau, nor the river that served as a net for
sunbright lances. It was, more than anything, the color of

things that stunned his vision. It was the abrupt disintegration
of a veil he had not known he'd been wearing, beyond which
the spectrum was neither befogged nor begrimed nor pitted
with iron dust.

And the valley was, in every sense of the word, vast; so vast
that he could barely see the far rim's teeth tearing at the
cobalt sky. The longer he traveled the more vast it became as
the carpet of greens and solemn golds and spotted browns
separated into pastureland, into new corn, into fields fallow
and tilled. He tried to make configurations of the homesteads
he could see—there appeared to be only a handful on the
right side of the highway, far more on the left, marking for
him the distinction between large landowners and small,
divided in fact by a broad band of darkwater river whose
banks were high and shrouded in weeds.

For a moment the space overwhelmed him, made him
dizzy, and he had to sit back and regroup, and wonder with a
slight rueful grin how the enclosed avenues of New York and
Boston could ever be thought threatening to anything bigger
than a pigeon.

Names came to mind: Simon MacKenzie, Ted Waters, Doc
Vance, Jake Harmon . . . but he could no longer tell if they
were true memories, or only names which had appeared in
the letters that had finally brought him out here. Stan Kelly,
Steve Felsom . . . had he really played with them before
being stricken, or were they just ghosts of a kid who needed
playmates to remember.

No matter, he thought; I might as well be a complete
stranger for all the relics I left here.

(2)

Jason rode, seated in the first of three rows of cracked leather
benches, in a battered and mud-streaked van that posed as a
bus when the occasion arose. It had left Fort Washakie in the
Wind River Reservation at 10:35 that morning, had followed
the land's river namesake for nearly thirty miles and two
hours before swerving suddenly into a cavern of ponderosa.
The road had become narrow, almost unnervingly so, as it
poked gently through the mountains, scuttling around slopes
like a fragile and apprehensive child around a stolid, stern

grandfather. For another hour it climbed, leveled, skirted several smaller valleys choked with fir before cresting, skimming, then angling into a sharp bend and widening again into a recognizable highway. The peaks backed away, the trees fell huddling to stands and the taciturn driver fought the gearshift to bring it up from low.

Suddenly, from the weedy, down-sloped verge, a small boy on horseback bolted across the road. Instead of veering toward the shoulder, however, the van jerked toward the center line, nearly clipping the horse's hind legs. The driver swore loudly, viciously, not bothering to reduce speed despite the near-collision.

Jason started, almost cried out because his first impression told him the man had deliberately attempted to run horse and rider down. The moment passed; the van straightened; and he laid a trembling hand lightly against his chest to feel the rapid pacing of his heart. The driver muttered another oath, and Jason switched his attention—it was the first sound he had heard from the man since they'd left the reservation. At the time he'd attributed the silence to a natural suspicion of strangers, and didn't blame the man for not talking. After all, if he had not shown up that morning—stale and grumbling from a daylong, nightlong ride from Cheyenne—the driver would probably have spent the day in his rickety office, drinking openly from the bottle he had stashed quickly beneath the insect-stained counter. Apparently, Windriver had very few callers who did not employ their own transportation.

He glanced back at the horse trotting easily across a field, at the dark-skinned boy whose black hair defied the sun. One of the Indians, he thought as he recalled the last letter. And he wondered if that child was a part of the troubles. Wondered if the driver had really made an error in judgment.

Finally, he leaned forward and folded his arms on the thin metal sheeting that blocked off the front seat. "Excuse me," he said, and instantly cleared his throat of the hoarseness that lodged there. The driver—bundled in a thick short jacket lined with sullied white fleece, wearing a cowboy hat stained and wrinkled, and a pair of sunglasses too large for his eyes—only grunted. "The town," Jason said. "How far is it?"

"A while," the man answered without turning his head. "It's in the middle."

"Oh." A glance to his watch; it was nearing one forty-five.

Then he peered at the road ahead, looking for signs, at last seeing the first peaked roofs breaking the horizon. And in grinning satisfaction and relief almost missed the marker for Elkhorn Road. He blinked as the name registered from his right, slid fast over the seat and pressed his forehead to the window, straining to catch a glimpse of the house he could not remember. Or of the tree. His father had been furiously drunk when he'd taken on four men that evening. One against four, and Peter Clarke had nearly killed them.

He closed his eyes briefly and pushed away from the window. There was nothing to see. Not even the tree.

"You're East," the driver said, his eyes still on the deserted road ahead.

Jason nodded, instinct telling him this man wouldn't know. "New Jersey."

"Yeah," the man said. He glanced off to the right, to the left, pushed back in his seat.

An after-image, then, of the search for his house and he returned to the window. In the distance, though nearer than the other slopes marking the valley's north end, was a peak darker, somehow shadowed in spite of the afternoon sun. It did not seem to be any more thickly forested, nor sharper at the edges, nor particularly high; yet it made itself known simply by being. Another memory (part letters, part dreams): Kramer's Mountain, the most visible boundary of the huge MacKenzie ranch. His father had taken him up there one morning when he could still walk, and Jason recalled vividly the chill of its trails. He wondered if the MacKenzies enjoyed seeing it after dark, and wondered why the thought had struck him at all.

The driver coughed. "You got relatives?"

Jason returned to leaning on the barrier, shaking off the mountain's presence with a forced, weak shudder. He was tired, too tired, when something like an ordinary mountain could give him the shivers.

"I say, you got relatives here?"

"Friend." Not a lie; not the whole truth.

The driver grunted.

A mile drifted by. The body of a small brown animal the only break in the blacktop.

"Your friend got a name?"

"Sure."

A pause.

"Look," said the driver, finally turning, Jason flinching at the sight of his own face distorted in the dark lenses, "I can't take you there unless you tell me who. I can't read minds, y'know."

"Sorry," Jason said. "Marsh. Galen Marsh."

"No kiddin?" There was a flash of impressed surprise. "You gonna work for him?"

Jason swallowed a laugh that had almost escaped. From suspicion to curiosity and nothing subtle about it. "No," he said. "Well, yes and no." He laughed at himself and saw the driver shaking his head slowly. "What I mean is, yes I'm going to work for him, but not permanently."

"Oh. A vacation, like."

"Right."

"In April?"

"My boss is very flexible," he said, and nearly jumped out of his seat when a train's airhorn blared. He blinked rapidly and stared as a diesel freight lumbered past them heading west. He hadn't even seen the tracks hidden by tall grass, the occasional barbed wire or fieldstone fencing . . . and the airhorn seemed too intrusive, too harsh—it should have been a locomotive with a red cowcatcher and spiraling embers and a string of boxlike passenger coaches tugging behind them a peeling caboose. It should have been; but the times were wrong, even in this place.

(Lying in his bed, staring at the ceiling, listening to the trains going everywhere but here)

He sighed, rubbed at his eyes, and a few minutes later they bore down on the first of the houses beneath a spreading oasis of freshly green trees.

"You say Marsh?" the driver asked. He pulled back a sleeve to stare at a black-faced digital watch. "Be at the office about now, I expect. I'll drop you off there. He has a car, as I remember."

Though Jason had been prepared and waiting for the sight of the roofs, there was virtually no warning at all for the abrupt transformation from fields to village. The road suddenly sprouted into an intersection ("This here's Valley Ford Road," the driver muttered, a reluctant and sour guide), and they were immediately riding through a community almost too picture-perfect for the most artistic postcard. He gathered from the man's laconic description that the valley was shaped much like a pitchfork with four tines that closed in on each other to become highway again. ("Valley Pike. Folks call it the Pike. Too long otherwise.") All the homes he could see on the elongated blocks—from the western ranch style to a smattering of New Hampshire Colonials and a pair of out-of-place and lonely Victorians—seemed newly painted a universal white; the trees were wide and top-heavy, the lawns and gardens meticulously tended, the sidewalks and gutters remarkably free of any debris. There was no welcoming sign, no city limits with the population proclaimed, no service organization standards with meeting dates duly noted—only the houses, a few women on porches, a handful of dogs mostly tied to revolving stakes, and an occasional toddler chasing birds or ghosts or swinging from tires. Five corners later he estimated eight or nine hundred lived in Windriver, not counting the ranches, but he had yet to see any plants, any subsidiaries, nothing to signal a single major employer.

"What do they do?" he asked, scratching at his sideburns.

"Local stuff, mostly," the driver said; and Jason winced, unaware he had spoken aloud. "Some, they work back down on the reservation there, some in the offices over to Blairs, and a bunch in the candy mill the other side of town."

"The Indians, too?"

"They manage." Granite etched with acid.

Jason shrugged to himself and said nothing more, though he could not shake the feeling that back there on the road the driver would have tried to run that boy down if he'd been alone.

"You get many tourists?"

For the first time since leaving Washakie the driver grinned. "Oh, a few. Hunters, mostly, and a bunch of traveling folks looking for the out-of-the-way-place to spend their money. They got no motels here, but they's a few boardin houses and such. Out to the west there we got a couple of dude ranches. It fair fills in the summer, I guess you could say."

Jason nodded politely as the homes fell away to a business section that appeared to have one of everything, no duplications. And, he noted with a slight lift of an eyebrow, no traffic lights.

They pulled over to park in front of the only shop not faced with either brick, stone or weathering marble—a large, white clapboard grocery. There was nothing else on the block that side of the Pike except a parking lot that had more room for its struggling trees than it did for cars. The brakes squealed, the van shuddered.

Home again, home again, Jason thought, jiggedy-jig.

(3)

Cooling metal ticked and the tires seemed to settle, but before Jason could ask directions to Marsh's office the driver climbed out of his seat, was on the pavement and walking stiffly into the store without a single word or glance for his only passenger. Jason groaned as he stood, more from theatrics that somehow seemed appropriate than from actual discomfort. He rubbed hard at the small of his back, the side of his neck, kicking out each leg in turn to banish the threat of cramps. Then, when he realized he was not going to receive any help, he wrestled his three pieces of luggage to the doorwell and dumped them onto the sidewalk, stepped slowly down after them and squinted into the glare of the afternoon's sun.

"'Theodore Waters, Grocery and Sundries,'" he muttered, reading the gold Gothic lettering on the long, plate-glass window. He glanced to the near corner and saw another sign hanging from chains at the building's edge: "T. Waters, Farm Supplies and Feed Station," with an arrow pointing around to the side. Nice work, T. Waters, he thought, and shivered, wishing now he had worn more than the light sport jacket and trousers. Obviously, Wyoming's climate was going to take some getting used to. He thought it was spring, but here it felt more like late fall, early winter.

He waited, thinking the driver might return to assist him. As he did, he glanced up and down the street, shading his eyes impatiently, pausing only when he saw directly opposite him a brick-fronted trio of alley-split buildings: from left to right, a luncheonette with a bench in front for four stacks of newspapers, a movie house without a marquee, and on the corner the setback office of the *Windriver Banner*. He grinned, checked behind him to make sure the man wasn't coming back, then hoisted his luggage as best he could in his hands and under one arm and strode across the Pike, not bothering to check for oncoming traffic. There wasn't any.

As a matter of fact, he realized as he approached the narrow, frosted-glass office door, aside from the van there wasn't a car parked at any of the curbs.

Beautiful, he thought; the big city at last.

"Are we really *that* bad?"

He turned quickly, clumsily, the suitcase pinned by his left arm tumbling to the sidewalk while the satchel in his right hand swung out in an arc that nearly cost him his balance. As it was, it narrowly missed clipping the legs of a young woman standing behind him. She managed two steps backward to avoid the collision, then put a hand to her mouth to veil a grin.

"Now I know for a fact," she said, "we're not as bad as all that."

She was as tall as he and nearly his age. Her hair was more brown than blonde, cropped short and curled. Behind small, black-rimmed glasses her eyes were large and a startling blue-grey; her nose was stubbed, her chin bore a cleft and her eyebrows were so dark they seemed almost black.

Jason wasn't sure he appreciated the humor, but he smiled nonetheless and allowed her a short laugh. "Sorry. Do I really look that miserable?"

"Like you've been doused in lemon."

He found himself staring at her full, pursed lips. At the push of her breasts against an open-collar plaid shirt. At the slight flare of small hips encased in snug jeans. Against this commonplace background she appeared painfully sensuous, at the same time perfectly ordinary. God, he thought, I must be dead and don't know it.

"You all right?" she asked, her voice soft as air.

He nodded, though he wasn't at all sure. "It must have been the trip," he said, tilting his head at the van across the way. "I feel like I've been moving forever. And no, it isn't that bad here, believe me. As a matter of fact, it's really . . . nice." He laughed again. "Beautiful."

"Much better," she told him, and held out a hand.

It was strong, cool, the tips of her fingers featherlight, close to tickling. But he felt somewhat uneasy at the way she held his gaze.

"Donna Oldfield," she said, and nodded toward a white-framed brick structure on the corner to her right. "That's Doc Vance's clinic, courtesy—like a lot of things around here—of Simon MacKenzie. I work there."

He was determined not to be surprised. "A doctor, huh?"

"Vet. And you?"

"Visiting," and he jabbed a thumb over his shoulder. "Jason Clarke, by the way." He waited; no reaction. "I take it you're the welcoming committee?"

Her smile turned abruptly brittle, the skin at her jawline tightening, relaxing; and when her eyes narrowed slightly before springing wide again in not quite effective innocence, he knew it wasn't due to hostile reserve. Something he had done, something he had said had triggered a moment of remembered anguish and instant defense—a reaction he had seen much too often in his own mirror, his own dreams.

"I'm on my way to lunch down at Kurt Steed's place," she said, recovery complete. The grin returned. "It was your expression, and I was nosey." She stook a step toward the luncheonette, paused and tapped at her chin. "Tell you what. If Galen in there gives me a clean bill of health, why don't—" She stopped, flustered, her face flushed the shade of her red-squared shirt. Her hands immediately plunged into her jeans pockets and she hurried away, not looking back once despite his astonished staring.

"I'll be damned," he whispered as he reached for the satchel. He paused when taken by the sway of her walk, the slim line of her back. And this time he knew it was futile to blame his reaction on the trip—Donna Oldfield had forced him to remember he was human after all, though he couldn't be sure he needed the reminder.

Later, he told himself; I'll worry about that later. And he shouldered open the stiff-hinged door and dragged his luggage quickly inside.

(4)

Galen Marsh was a tree whose gnarled bark had been thoroughly and roughly handled by five decades of winters. There was little about him untouched by a crease, a slight loss of tone, here and there a permanent flush that glowed almost waxen. Asleep, Jason thought, the old man could probably double for a B-movie corpse, which is most likely why the curmudgeon never married. Yet, as he saw him sitting in the small back office, he could only conclude it was womankind's loss, not Galen's. The man had not surrendered a single moment of those fifty-plus years that gave a slope to his narrow shoulders and made him squint even without the sun, had not yielded an ounce of strength in arms deceptively thin, in legs gently bowed. And, as if in defiance, the few strands of hair he had left were a solid and absolute black, combed left to right over a mottled, pink-skinned scalp.

A life that said age had nothing to do with living.

Jason could not help grinning—feeling his cheeks ache with the pleasant effort—could not help a smile as he listened to the editor declaim rather than talk. No offering of honey would temper the acid lurking about his tongue, cloaking his words. Though it was, he knew, the most fallible role to fall into—especially in the West where garrulous, cantankerous old men were a nickel a gross—but Galen had little to be ornery about, and that was his failing and he knew it.

On the other hand, Galen Marsh without something to worry about, however illusory, would not have been Galen.

"So I said to that son of a bitch," the editor scowled, one finger aimed dramatically at the ceiling, "you might as well get that jackass off my property right now, or I'll have its hide for my couch sure as I'm standing here. And blessed if that poor excuse for an equine didn't move. Right through my goddamned fence." He snapped his fingers. "Like it was made of cheapjack matchwood."

Jason nodded, held a glass of whiskey close to his eyes and gazed at it, watching the whorls of pale amber promise him peace. He drank it in a swallow. Coughed. Wiped the glad tears from his eyes and poured himself another. "Other than that, Mrs. Lincoln," he said, "how did you enjoy the play?"

"What?"

Jason shook his head, grinning. "Nothing. Bad joke. You still haven't answered my question, though—how are you, Galen? Really?"

Marsh settled himself by lank folds into a straight-backed chair behind his desk and rested his heels on its edge. His hands were laced loosely behind his head, and he stared at the ceiling. He wore no jacket, his rumpled white shirt with red sleeve garters was open to his breast and the uneven ends of his knit tie were tossed back over one shoulder. Together they watched a fly wend its way over the dull plaster, reach the top of the room's rear window, circle once and dart for the front office. A strip of flypaper dangled from the doorframe; it was empty.

"I'm fine," Marsh said finally, his voice pebbles rasping in the hands of a giant. "Though I suppose that depends on what you mean by fine. Physically, I'm as sound as one can expect these days, not a grey hair to my name; mentally, I'm alert; emotionally, I don't have any hang-ups I can't cure myself, sooner or later, one of these days when I get around to it. I ride now and then. I can still find a choice piece of ass—"

"Galen," he interrupted gently, realizing his cousin would rather ramble an hour before telling him what he really wanted to know, "you've probably noticed by the way I'm dressed and look that I've been on a long trip. And I'm tired. Can you tell me what's up now, or can I find a place to shower, eat, and sleep for the next few days? Preferably weeks."

Marsh's gaze lowered slowly. "How much time do you have, son?"

He shrugged. "As much as you need."

"Must be rich."

"Comfortable. I've been saving for a vacation I haven't taken since . . . a long time ago. When you wrote the first time, I nearly packed then and there."

He waited for the question, had been waiting since he'd first seen the old man . . . and could not remember him except as a face viewed through rippling water. He had been deeply grateful when Galen hadn't told him how much he had changed.

"Your boss must be proud of you," Galen said. "Valuable, and all that."

Jason's smile was something less than mirthful. "No bosses anymore, I'm afraid. I'm on my own again."

Marsh's eyebrows lighted in silent question.

"New Jersey was as close as I could get to New York on a paper," Jason explained. "A good job—the editor had his Pulitzer nominations and a bunch of plaques, but . . ." He shrugged. "What can I say? Maybe I'll stick around and buy you out. Maybe I'll move on, get myself a shack on the Pacific. Who the hell knows?" The last sounded more bitter

than he'd intended, but he only toasted Galen silently and
emptied his glass again.

"I didn't tell anybody you were comin, son," Marsh said
quietly. "Not a word about us bein kin, either."

Jason nodded thoughtfully. "What if they find out?"

"Who's gonna care? Most won't even remember. You
bothered?"

He rubbed the side of his nose. "Not really." He grinned
sheepishly. "Well, sort of. A little nervous, I guess. My father
didn't exactly leave a good impression."

Galen lowered his feet to the floor and pulled his tie around
to his chest. "Well, they sure won't take us for cousins,
m'boy," he said with a smile. "Far as they know, I'm too
bastardy to have any that don't look like scorpions." He
laughed, clasped his hands on the desk and shook his head.
"Forget it," he said then. "You got no problem."

"I know," Jason said. And returned the smile.

Galen sniffed and took a deep breath. "Saw you met
Donna out there."

Jason looked up quickly. "You saw?"

"I'm nosey when the so-called bus comes in."

"That's what she said, too."

"Nice girl."

"She's a vet."

"Don't let it scare you, Jase. She's one of the two level
heads left in this town."

"And you, I take it, are the other."

Galen smiled broadly. "Takes kin to know kin, son." He
stared at Jason, hard and kindly. "Maybe later you'll tell me
the truth about leaving that newspaper."

They both rose, each with a great deal of scraping and
coughing, and moved into the front office. No one was there.
"Got Esther Lynn Vance for help, Doc Vance's daughter,"
Marsh said. "You think about it, you may recall her working
with her dad when he had his office over at his house.
Half-days on Fridays with me now, though. To recoup my
sanity. We're down to twice a week. No sense in anything
more. Huge profits ain't exactly camping on my doorstep."

Jason picked up the two suitcases, Galen the satchel, and
they stepped outside, Jason waiting while the editor locked
the door and slipped the key into his hip pocket. A tug on the
knob and they headed east, past the theater (Weekends Only:

True Grit, Logan's Run), the luncheonette (We Close At Nine, Have Your Supper On Time), crossed the street and paused in front of the grey marble bank where Galen held out a restraining hand.

"You won't remember this, either," he stage-whispered, grinning at Jason's startled, somewhat embarrassed expression. "Wouldn't want you to miss it now."

A man in khaki, wearing a Stetson and an imposingly broad gunbelt, stepped sideways out of the main door, scanning the length of the street before spotting Jason from behind silvered sunglasses; the set of his thin lips told Jason he was glaring. A moment later another man—taller and thinner, dressed in a dark-trimmed grey suit—joined him on the pavement, slipped quickly into the back seat of a tan-and-white patrol car parked at the curb. Instantly the door was shut, the officer took the front seat and the car eased away, making a slow U-turn to speed out of town.

"That," said Marsh, "was our eminent bank president taking his loot into Blairs."

"Doesn't trust it here, huh?"

"Has a bigger bank down there. And a larger police force."

"How nice. I suppose."

"The other one, though . . . that was Jake Harmon. Bill Oaker was doing the driving—his old man owns the garage back there across the street."

"So," Jason said, squinting after the car. "Sheriff Harmon?"

"Yep."

He shook his head and turned back. "He's a blank, too, I'm afraid. And he's not what I pictured him to be, not from your last letter. I thought he was bigger, younger-looking—"

"He was. Once. That's one of the things I got to tell you."

Marsh nudged him and they moved on, past the sheriff's office, past Regan's Drug Store with a wire post office cage stationed near the front, and walked another long block before turning right. Marsh's home was in the center, a neatly kept single-story clapboard made miniature by a flanking brigade of willows whose branches folded themselves on the roof and seemed ready to embrace the three fat-mouthed chimneys. Jason grinned as he waited for the man to unlatch the fence gate and whistle loudly, shrilly. Twice. Immediately, a pair of Irish setters bounded around the corner of the house, tongues lolling, tails back in jetstream flaring. Once they reached the two men they stopped, and sat.

"Mutt and Jeff," Marsh said, kneeling to greet each of them in turn. "Jeff used to be a female, Mutt's a horny gelding. They'll tear out your throat if you touch them," he added quickly when Jason lowered his suitcases and stretched out a hand. He yanked it back and rubbed it self-consciously against his chest, knowing his grin now looked incredibly stupid. Marsh rose, took each of the dogs by the scruff and brought them over, pushing their muzzles against his trousers while he told them who Jason was. It did not take long. Mutt barked once, Jeff echoed, and they were gone.

"Did I pass?" he asked, not entirely in jest.

"I think so," Marsh said. "They'll let you know after they find out you've taken their bed."

"Galen, that's not funny."

"That's all right, I wasn't joking. They usually sleep in the spare room when I don't keep an eye on them. I'll have to change the sheets and things before you bed down."

The inside was far larger than it appeared from the street: the walls were of a rough plaster almost like stucco, and each of the rooms through which he was guided was spare—just enough furniture, just enough prints and primitive oils—but they were not spartan. His own room was in the left rear corner, a shaded window on each outside wall overlooking the boles of the protecting willows. While he hung his clothes in the walk-in closet, Marsh stripped the bed and replaced the linen, fluffed the pillows and made sure the lamp on the oaken nightstand had a working bulb. A moment's awkwardness. A clearing of throats. Marsh squeezed Jason's arm, stepped out of the room and closed the door behind him.

"Thanks," Jason whispered.

A conflict of temptations, then: to stretch out on the bed and rid his eyes of their stinging, or follow the old man into the living room and wait for their business to begin. After he and his mother had moved east to an aunt's (who didn't much like them but had a strong sense of family), Galen had been the only one in town to maintain a correspondence. And when his mother had died, Galen kept in touch—once, sometimes twice a year, but he kept in touch. Then, suddenly, ten years passed without a word and Jason thought he had died. Just as suddenly, a letter two years ago, and another one last spring. Both the latter were constrained, seemed confused, but it was the one he had received only two weeks ago that had jolted him into packing, that had finally brought him back.

Jase, I need you. The town's going to Hell.

He took a step toward the door, his heel cracking loudly on the bare floor, and decided abruptly that one more day wasn't going to make all that much difference. And if an investigation of some sort was what his cousin had in mind, it wouldn't do any good to begin with his head in a fog. So thinking, and grinning knowingly at the rationalization, he dropped his jacket on the nightstand chair, took off his shoes and dropped onto the mattress. The pillow was thick and stuffed with down. The quilt's lacing of air pockets supported him gently. He rubbed a thumb over his forehead lightly, then tented his fingers over his stomach and watched the shadows dance over the swirled ceiling. Trying not to think. Struggling to prevent himself from succumbing to dormant memories.

But there were so few of them: a romping through dust in the schoolyard (there must have been little boys with him), watching cattle, horses, sheep, snowbanks three times his height . . . and a ceiling much like this, a house slightly larger, sixty acres or so that refused to surrender as his father demanded. His mother (just before she died) telling him he used to have visitors (those same little boys?) until his father frightened them all away; his mother telling him (just before she died) about the trains that crept through; his mother despairing but never weeping. And himself in bed . . . always in bed, it seemed . . . never running, never riding . . . in bed . . . always . . .

He shook his head hard, and the images shattered.

Six years here, from four to ten. More years here than he had spent anywhere else. Home again, home again.

He lay back slowly, rolled onto his stomach and grunted when his belt buckle dug in. He shifted to unfasten it, his cheek pressing deeply into the pillow, its cool casing sponging away some of the weariness, some of the fear. Six years lost. Meanwhile there was Galen, and things can't be as bad as he says they are. They can't be. He's exaggerating, as always.

And if he wasn't, it might be the chance he needed to answer one of the questions. Only one. But, he thought, he didn't think he could handle more than one at a time.

TWO

Timmy Sweetwater liked it when the faculties of Windriver's three schools held one of their combined meetings. It meant being freed at noon, no detention, no cafeteria food, and not having to put up with the older white boys who thought it great fun to scare the little Shoshone kids with laughing threats of scalping, torture or a night alone with Ted Waters. Not that they were all that bad—especially the ones like Carole Carosa and Bea Steed—but over the past year something seemed to have gone wrong. Either the whites had put on masks or they had taken them off; whatever the reason, the result was the same, so boys like Hardy Green could push him up against a wall, yank his hair, poke him hard in the stomach, and no one would say anything because they were laughing.

Like this morning. He'd been standing with some of his friends in back of the grade school when Hardy and two others had come through the trees. The other kids had scattered, but Timmy held his ground, tired of being pushed around and too frightened to run. They didn't touch him.

34

They only stared. Then Hardy asked him if it was true he was **a fairy.** At first Timmy didn't understand, and when he did he **blushed** fiercely, making the whites howl, slapping their thighs and shoving at each other until one of the teachers came out and chased them away.

"Are you all right, Timothy?" she'd said, a hand gentle on his shoulder.

He had eased away from her touch as soon as he could so he wouldn't seem rude, and told when she asked what the Green boy had said. Then, suddenly, he'd wanted to know how he'd look as a man.

"Oh, Tim," she'd said, "aren't you a little young to be worrying about that?"

He'd said nothing. But neither did he like to be reminded of his eight years, or the fact that he was what many people called pretty: the planes of his face smooth and unlined, his black hair a perfect frame, his dark eyes wide and his lashes long. There were days when he wanted to give himself a scar (like Michael Wolf had), or poke out an eye, or shred his bow lips . . . anything so the women wouldn't tousle his hair and say *oh, what a pretty child!* Pretty was for babies, and for girls like his sister Dawn.

Who wasn't any help at school, either. All she ever did was strut around and talk about how she was going to Hollywood and be a star. Timmy saw the way the boys (and some of the teachers and the men on the street) looked at her, so he supposed she would probably do what she said. But whenever he asked her to tell the boys to leave him alone (thinking she had some sort of power over them since they always did what she asked), she told him no, was always telling him how silly it was for the Indians to live up here in the valley, and sooner or later they would find out they weren't so special, like Rachel MacKenzie said they were, and they'd leave for the reservation again. Not her, though. She was going to Hollywood, and they could all go to hell. In fact, she'd said that only this morning.

"And Timmy," she'd said then, kneeling in front of him and stroking his face like she did when he had nightmares, "these people are crazy. Whites, Indians, they're all crazy. Rachel is crazy."

"Dawn, don't *say* that!" he'd whispered in a panic.

"Oh, she can't hear me, silly. She's no more special than

anybody else. She thinks we're not like the other Shoshone, but we are. We're people, Timmy. We're not special at all." Then she'd saddened a little. "You are, though. And when I get out of here, I'm going to write you every day. Just you, little fish, just you." She'd kissed him on the forehead then and walked away, and he would have gone after her if he hadn't heard giggling from inside the school.

He frowned and kicked the chestnut's flanks unnecessarily hard. A miserable day, that's what it was. Not, however, that he was in any great hurry to get home, either. At eight (a month to be nine) he was the youngest by eight years of the Sweetwater offspring, and to him fell what he thought were the most odious chores on the ranch: cleaning the boarding stables, hauling feed and water for the horses and bearing the brunt of his father's unpredictable temper.

So he took his time on the scrawny mount, watching with delight the hawks circling the sky, whooping scares into gophers . . . and nearly getting himself killed when the Washakie bus came within a few feet of running him down. He was sure his heart had stopped, was sure he peed his pants. But he refused to let the driver, and the single passenger he'd glimpsed, know how shaken he was. He continued across the rusted steel bridge no one used but him and into the field that adjoined his father's home. His teeth chattered, his vision blurred, but he did not turn around. He was a Sweetwater. He was Shoshone (special, no matter what his dumb sister said). He would not permit his afternoon to be spoiled.

He would tell his father, of course. Not because of the near-accident, but because of the man in the bus. Every Indian who had moved off the reservation and into the valley automatically reported new faces either to his father or to Daniel Tallpines. And Daniel would report to Simon Mac-Kenzie, the largest, richest landowner in what had to be the entire world. Then Simon would tell his wife. After that, Timmy didn't know. And these days he didn't want to know. Ever since Rachel MacKenzie had taken ill last spring the boy sensed a change in the valley, in the land, almost in the air he breathed. Before, when the Sweetwaters had bought their land and Aaron had set up his boarding concern, it was fun here, it was free; then Rachel fell ill, and something about the land, the way it felt and the way it looked . . . he still couldn't put a label to it, but he was scared. Even more scared than the way he was when Ted Waters looked at him as he passed the grocery store, or the way Mister Perkins smiled at him, or the way Mister Regan looked at his sister.

It frightened him. And the worst part about it was, he knew it also frightened his father.

The chestnut whickered, and Timmy looked up, shading his eyes against the midday sun. A dark spot grew against the cobalt, drifting, lowering, and it didn't take him long to recognize one of the eagles that nested on Kramer's Mountain, the northern boundary of the MacKenzie ranch. He grinned and waved at it frantically, saw its golden brown feathers catch the light and turn it to bronze.

He relaxed, then. It was an omen. The day would end well, and his father might even tell him a story.

2:10 P.M.

"So I asks him where he comes from, and he says New *Jersey,* for god's sake."

Ted Waters, surrounded by fifty- and one hundred-pound green sacks of meal and grain, shook his head in slow disbelief. "Ain't nobody from New Jersey gonna come all the way out here just to work for Galen Marsh. He must be from Indian Affairs. It's the only way I can figure it."

The driver shrugged, took off his hat and wiped his forearm over his face. "I don't know about that, Ted. He don't look government to me."

"Hell, you watch too many movies. The only ones that look government are the FBI. The rest are pretty sorry."

"Well, this one ain't all that sorry, Ted, take my word. You can see it in him—he could hold his own if he had to, I think."

Waters climbed over the nearest sack and made his way slowly to the front of the store. He glanced at the glass counter on the far wall where he sold trinkets bought from the reservation and nodded when he noted Lureen, his clerk, had taken off on her break. Then he moved to the display window, his hands on his hips, one booted foot on the low ledge as if he were about to step into the canned goods arrangement. He was wearing a heavy plaid shirt and dusty brown trousers over which was draped an apron stained too often to yield properly to a washing. He snorted. His left hand rose to scratch idly at an angry red birthmark that crawled out of his collar to the base of his jaw—it was nearly four inches wide top to bottom, and made his neck seem thicker, his hawk's face more brutal. He swallowed, grunted again and swiped at a few strands of tired grey that drooped over his forehead. "Well," he said, "he went into Galen's, all right."

"I told you."

"Maybe. Look, I want you to—"

"For god's sake, Ted, I got to be back, okay?"

Waters shrugged, then lifted his hand in an absentminded wave when the driver strode hurriedly out of the store and climbed back into the van. There was a loud grinding, a protesting whine, as Waters watched the vehicle shake its dust and make a sharp U-turn to shimmy back up the street. The telephone rang. He considered ignoring it; he didn't need the aggravation. Then he swore at its persistence before hurrying to the counter to snatch the receiver from its wall cradle and listen for a moment.

"I don't know," he said finally, his gaze still on the front window, at that part of the Pike not yet washed out by the sun's white glare. "Never got a chance to talk. He's with Galen now." He waited, winding the black cord around his wrist, unwinding it and pulling its coils tight. "He's white, and his hair's kind of long, down over the collar. Could be Bureau, or one of them Civil Liberties folks. I don't know. I'll have to get back to you." He waited again, this time his foot tapping impatiently. "I just told you I don't know! What do you think I am around here, a magician? You'll just have to wait until I get a chance to talk to him, all right? All right." He hung up without waiting for a reply, glared at the receiver for a moment before heading for the rear connecting door to his other, far more prosperous business.

Fool people don't have to go all the way to Blairs to shop, he thought glumly as he spotted a layer of grey dust on a row of canned peas. Idiots! He stared into the hazed light of the barnlike structure and watched as the sun drove the shadows toward the rear. The huge double door on the lefthand side had been folded back like an accordian, and in the middle of the open space beyond gleamed a bright yellow tractor nearly twice his size. Puddles of stagnant water shivered around its deep-tread tires. Stan Kelly had ordered it before he'd sold his farm to a Shoshone family; now it stood waiting for someone else to give it a home while Kelly, for some reason not wanting to leave Windriver, spent most of his time in Carosa's bar bragging about the money he'd made and the poaching he was doing on MacKenzie's ranch.

But Stan Kelly was only one part of the problem; there were others, lots of them, and none of the townspeople seemed to realize they were killing the damned town.

A kick of gravel, a muffled laugh, and Waters moved toward the door just as a trio of Indian boys sprang out from behind the tractor, all of them carrying spray cans of black paint. Waters didn't think twice—he grabbed for a claw hammer on a shelf and, with a smile that broke around brown-stained teeth, he threw it. Hard. Catching one of the teenagers high on the shoulder. The boy yelped and stumbled, colliding with the far side of the open storehouse and falling into the shadows. Waters reached to the shelf again and from between a Bowie knife and a machete he pulled an eight-foot length of carefully filed chain.

Before the boy could get to his knees, Waters was straddling him, the chain held expertly, the end catching the sun with a winking silver glare. He sniffed. "How ya doin, boy?"

The Indian rolled painfully to his side, right hand grasping his left elbow tightly to immobilize the arm. His dusty face was sullen, his black eyes narrowed.

"Boy, seems like you ruined a fine piece of property over there." He grinned. "Say, you're Charlie Sweetwater, ain't ya."

Sweetwater nodded, his lips pulled back from his teeth in a long spasm of pain.

Waters crouched, the long end of the chain clanking on the ground. "Let's see that arm," he said. When the boy shook his head, he grabbed the arm, pulled it sharply and held the wrist close to his chest. "Mighta chipped a bone up there, boy. Maybe even broke it." Slowly, without watching Sweetwater's face, he wrapped a length of the chain around the wrist, just below the cuff. "Don't think your old man'd care for what you done, y'know. No need to tell him, right? Just between us men."

Sweetwater stared at him fearfully, a tear slipping from the side of one eye when Water yanked the arm again. He didn't struggle; he was too busy watching the chain tighten coldly around his wrist.

"Sure wouldn't want your daddy to take a belt to you, would we?" Waters whispered, the words coming slowly, like a surgeon describing a delicate operation. "Your friends got names, Charlie?"

Sweetwater shook his head in a panicked convulsion.

The chain tightened again, and a slip of blood ran toward his palm.

"Strangers, huh?"

The boy swallowed.

"You oughta be more careful, Charlie boy. Ain't good for the soul to hang around vermin like that."

Another blood-ribbon, gleaming in the dim light as Waters shifted to block what he was doing from any possible passersby.

"Maybe you oughta say please, huh? Just so we understand what we're doin here, okay?"

Sweetwater's mouth opened, and his eyes rolled away from the blood dripping to the ground.

"I hear you say somethin, boy?"

It was a whisper, a groan: "Please."

"Bet you're sorry you painted that tractor, too, right?"

Sweetwater nodded quickly, bravado vanished, shame full.

"What's that?"

"I . . . I'm sorry."

Waters nodded. "Yeah, I thought you'd be, Charlie. It's a damn shame you ain't human—you might be worth somethin some day."

He stood quickly and gave the chain a practiced twist. The boy muffled a cry and sank back, his gaze searching the dim rafters of the ceiling. He swallowed twice, three times, then jerked to a sitting position and stumbled sideways to his feet. His face was pale beneath the dusk of his skin, and his hair hung raggedly, wetly, over his eyes.

Waters stood in front of him. "Our secret, Charlie," he said, swinging the chain idly to trap the sun in its links.

The boy seemed ready to defy him, but a flash of pain ripped through his shoulder and he gasped, nodded, stumbled outside and disappeared around the corner.

Waters shook his head, laughing silently as he dragged the chain back to its shelf and coiled it again. He didn't bother to chase after the others. They were younger by forty years, would by now be already scrambling over the tracks to some horses or a truck hidden in the field beyond. But little Charlie Sweetwater, he thought, would be scared shitless for a week, especially when he realized the chain had hardly cut him . . . and what it could do if Waters really tried. He retrieved the hammer and tossed it high, caught it and balanced it. Fuckers think a tomahawk has to look like an axe. He laughed aloud and placed it next to the machete, almost hoping the bastard would tell his old man—he would love to take that fat Indian and slice him to bacon.

He considered checking the tractor then, decided he would deal with it later. The way things were going, he would probably have it till it rusted to shit anyway.

He hoped Marsh wasn't going to stir up any trouble. Now that a few of the boys were starting to fight back against the destruction of their valley, the invasion of the damned redskins, he didn't want any fool do-gooders looking to spread oil on nicely churned waters. He grinned. He laughed. Chopped waters. He'd have to remember that one for sure.

And when he returned inside, red-headed, gum-snapping Lureen Baker was at the register, her white uniform tight against wide hips and pointed breasts. Three buttons opened to reveal softly pale cleavage. A broad black belt to accentuate a waist he could encompass without even stretching. His fingers ached. She couldn't add worth a shit, but Christ could she breathe.

"Lureen," he said by way of pleasant greeting, thinking about that Indian and the way his shoulder had cracked, the way his blood took to the gravel. "How's about you and me takin to the hills after work?"

Lureen looked at him wearily. She was in her mid-twenties and seemed a decade older. Rouge on her cheeks, crimson on her lips, her eyebrows plucked and penciled back in sweeping arches. "Fuck off, Ted, huh? I got cramps."

He pressed his stomach against the end of the counter. "My wife don't understand me." He laughed, a cackling.

"Your wife's dead, you jackass."

"See? I told you she don't understand me." He laughed again, and waited. If nothing else, he was patient. He knew what she'd done for a living those three years she'd took off and lived in California. Everybody knew it. And everybody'd

been trying to get into her pants since the day she got back.
The way he heard it, he was the only one in town that got left
behind.

His right hand drifted to trace out his birthmark. "Come
on, Lureen," he said. "Didn't I give you a job?"

She stared out the window, jaw working her gum, her chest
deliberately out-thrust and aiming. "What you give me, Ted,
is a goddamned pain in the ass."

"You mean that?"

"Oh shit, Ted, take a walk. I got no patience for crap
today."

"Really," he said quietly, the birthmark now flaring.
"Well, Little Miss Virgin, I tell you what you got—what you
got is about five seconds to apologize before I fire your ass."

2:10 P.M.

"Young guy," said Deputy Art Felsom, his cheek pressed
hard against the office's front window. "'Bout thirty, I'd say,
a little more, but not much. Nice clothes, but not expensive.
Goin to . . . wait a minute . . . goin to Galen's place, I'll be
damned! God, he must be strong, carrying three suitcases at
once like that. Hate to meet him in a dark alley, believe you
me." He whistled softly. "Oh boy, he nearly dumped Doc
Oldfield. Wonder if he knows her. Nah! No way. She may be
ice, but she's got better taste than that." He grinned at his
reflection—smooth high forehead, smooth brown hair, heavy
nose and chin and a smile of bright white that he practiced
every morning. He turned, then, and lifted his gaze briefly to
the ceiling. "Jake, damnit, have you heard one word I said?"

Jake Harmon sat in the last of three metal desks placed in a
row down the center of the long, narrow room. Behind him
was a steel door through which the three cells could be seen;
the walls were a faint and pleasant green, bookshelves and
framed pictures making it seem less like a jail. And when he
looked up to stare at his youngest officer, Art knew he hadn't
heard a thing, and wasn't seeing, either. Damnit, he thought
in frustration and pity, how long you gonna be like this, Jake?
At least your girl's still alive, man. My poor little brother got
hisself murdered!

He sighed emphatically, received no response and turned back to the window thinking of that night eleven months ago today. Ellie's screams had been heard by his older brother, Steve. It had been too late to save Harry. And by the time things had calmed down, the confusion settled, only two points were clear: something—wolf, coyote, perhaps as one suggested a rabid creature from the mountains—had slaughtered and partially devoured the young boy, and that same something had driven Ellie into the river where Steve discovered her, entangled in bloody reeds near the bridge.

The westering sun on the Pike sent warmth through the plate glass, but Art shivered and hugged himself. He wished the third deputy, Bill Oaker, would get back from patrol so he could talk about women instead of thinking about Ellie.

Ellie. She had been badly cut over her forehead, and across the back of her neck. And . . . and something else. She'd fallen into a comatose state Doc Vance had called traumatic shock. After two months of lying in her bed, seeing nothing, saying nothing, Jake had taken her to a private hospital in Casper where they passed the autumn in painful silence. Art and Steve had visited them several times, as had Simon MacKenzie and the Carosas. Art thought it hopeless, like the shows he watched on the TV when the girl spent the rest of her life hooked up to machines that winked and whirred. Steve, however, demanded a miracle . . . and by Christ, he'd gotten one: on December fifth, a Saturday, Ellie had suddenly come back to life.

On Christmas Day they returned to Windriver.

And on February fourteenth, she and Steve were married.

That should have been that, over and done, God properly thanked and the world moving again. The trouble was . . . it wasn't. Though Ellie was all right, now Jake was acting weird. Maybe Waters was right, though he would cut out his tongue before he would admit it to his face. Maybe Jake should be considering this his last term and bow out gracefully before the elections come fall. It was . . . odd. Ellie's recovery, by all accounts and Doc Vance's insistence, should have brought the old man back to the world of the living. But it hadn't. At first Jake wouldn't believe in the extent of the recovery, had told Art that a million times a day after the Harmons had returned. Then, finally accepting, he soon began insisting

there was still something wrong, something not . . . right;
and when no one else paid him serious attention, when Doc
Vance told him Ellie was only suppressing the details of that
night and no more, he began a steady, inexorable withdrawal
not even the girl could turn around.

Crazy; it was all too damned crazy.

The phone on his desk rang and he jumped, gulping,
feeling as though he'd been caught cheating on a test. He
shook his head, looked to Jake, who wasn't moving at all, and
decided it was probably another farmer complaining about
wolves attacking his livestock. Not that any of the damned
things were ever found—those assholes out there saw ghosts
on the moon, for god's sake. But the animals were dying, no
denying that. Three or four at last count. Stupid. Most likely
a fool Indian looking for a free meal.

The phone kept ringing and Jake didn't move . . . and
when Art looked down at his hand he saw it gripping his
revolver. Jesus Christ, he thought, I was gonna shoot the
crazy old man.

2:30 P.M.

Aaron Sweetwater wore his deep black hair slicked and
combed back over his ears. He was large and meaty, a barrel
stacked on a barrel, and only the grotesque slants and bumps
of his oversized nose hinted at the fights he'd been in. At
times it was enough for him just to stand there and glower—
except with his family, who knew him better and laughed.
Gently; but they laughed. Only Timmy and the horses, he
thought, gave him the respect a man of his age demanded. It
certainly wasn't Charlie, the eldest, who more and more
lately acted like a goddamned city Indian and got himself in
trouble just by walking down the damned street; and it sure
wasn't Dawn, the middle child. Dawn, the beautiful child.
Dawn who, in the old days, would have been a princess, and
who had only two nights ago told him to his face that she
didn't believe in the old ways anymore, and she sure as hell
didn't believe in the crap (her word: crap) that Rachel was
handing out, stuff that wasn't even a part of the normal
Shoshone teaching. Those two, he thought, were a disgrace to

their people. And he knew that Dawn's defection had been a bitter blow to Rachel and Simon. He wasn't sure why they had counted on her so much, but they had. And now she was lost. Like so many of the young people, she was lost to the white world that ate up so many of the legends, so many of the rites, like the nightwolf that took bites from the moon each month until it was filled and regurgitated it again.

Timmy believed, of course, but he was still a child. Empathy for the land and its creatures wouldn't be tested until he was grown and faced with the decision Aaron himself had made—turn your back on the past, or learn to use it. And Timmy, he thought, would take the proper way. Even now the boy seemed to understand there were things a man could do for only so long before the land took its due. He seemed to understand that the belief had nothing to do with pollution and destruction.

Maybe. Maybe. Meanwhile, there was the Teaching.

He stood now in his bedroom, the door closed against his wife—Alice to the whites, Laughing Sky to Aaron. Laughing no more, however. The lung sickness was worse, the blood coughing harsh, and she lay ailing in the connecting room, her curtains drawn and her breathing irregular. Old before her time. It was why he had taken up with the new/old Teaching. The regular gods and the white man's god had done her no good. And Charlie and Dawn were making her worse.

He waited impatiently for the phone to make its connection, wiping a hand nervously under his nose. When he heard the voice finally speak, he sat heavily on the bed, as though his weight were suddenly too much of a burden.

"Daniel, can you talk? Listen, Timmy says the bus brought a man this afternoon. White. No uniform. Son of a bitchin driver nearly ran my boy down, the goddamned bastard! I swear to you, Daniel, I'm goin to get some of my friends back there to visit him one night. I swear it . . ." He closed his eyes, reined his temper. "No, I don't know a thing about the new man. Why don't you stop pumpin gas long enough to see what's . . . all right, all right, I'm sorry. Listen, will you call Simon? Shit no, not me, brother. I talk to him, I got to talk to Rachel and . . . no thanks, you do it. Okay. Okay, let me know what you find out."

He rang off and stared at the rolling land sweeping away

from the ranch house. He had a good business here, better than he'd had in his whole life on the reservation. Lovely horses. Lovely land. A cloudshadow drifted over it, like a black ghost laughing at the sun. And when it was gone, despite his wife's illness, he wished he had never gotten into this mess.

2:35 *P.M.*

Simon MacKenzie instructed Daniel Tallpines to learn what he could. Then he moved toward the door of his wife's room, his palms moist, his forehead laced with perspiration. He knew it was foolish to feel this way about her, his wife and partner of over forty years; nevertheless, the feeling persisted. Since last May when she'd collapsed and during her slow recovery, he had grown increasingly nervous around her. There were things she was not telling him, and there were things he wasn't exactly sure he really wanted to know, in spite of it all.

He did understand the need for the dead animals, and he did believe in the purpose they served. But Rachel was stirring up more than she would admit, something he wondered if she had the strength to control.

It was one thing to have made the blood sacrifice of the boy; it was quite another to realize that was only the beginning.

3:00 *P.M.*

The bedroom window was tall, rounded at the top, and already in hazed shadow as the sun moved over the chimneys to the front of the house. To the left was a king-sized brass bed hauled all the way from Laramie in the pickup; to the right stood a walnut wardrobe scrolled and paneled and seven feet tall. Below the sill was an upholstered vanity bench tipped with brass studs and stretched over with faded blue velvet. Gloria stood on it now, staring down at the barn, the outbuildings, at the lean and muscled man working in the corral with a recalcitrant dapple grey who wouldn't take the harness. She knew the hired man had spotted her several minutes ago and was studiously (and not very successfully) avoiding a glance in her direction.

She grinned, wriggled her bare toes and began unbuttoning her blinding white shirt.

Her hair was as dark as the shadows that backed her, her skin lightly olive and glistening with perspiration. Lips, breasts and hips full and aching. She waited a moment, the grin cold and patient, then rolled back her shoulders to part the shirt like a curtain. She wore no bra and her dark nipples were rigid.

The dapple was skittish; the man lunged for it and missed.

"Look at me, jerk!" she muttered.

A palm trembled over the flat plane of her stomach, pushing the soft flesh this way and that until flesh against flesh was slick and shining. She drew her hand away, licked her fingertips one by one, fumbled with the brass button of her jeans and unfastened it.

How long you gonna hold out this time, lover? she thought. *You ain't got the will, we both know that, don't we?*

She giggled.

The grey eyed the man suspiciously; the man stalked the horse stiff-legged and unsure.

Gloria lifted her eyebrows, and giggled again. She raised her arms and slid her hands under her hair at the nape, piling it slowly atop her head and letting it fall in dark swirls over her face, tickling her shoulders, brushing her breasts until the nipples ached. The man was moving more frantically now, slapping hard at the grey's rump to send it bolting toward the barn door. She watched him kick at his own heel, flail for his balance and grab at the fence before tumbling to the dirt.

Now . . . now he was watching, in spite of himself.

She stuck out her tongue, turned her head and licked her left shoulder.

Come on in, lover, don't be afraid, she willed silently.

She almost frowned, but caught herself in time before it spoiled the game. She had never been able to tempt Riley inside, though she'd been trying since last October when he'd first started working for Billy. He had turned her down cold a number of times, and for a full month she'd seethed at him, thinking maybe he was one of them lavender boys from someplace out East, or from down in New Orleans. It was frustrating. Stan Kelly never came to see her anymore, not since he sold out and banked all his money to spend on his booze; and Steve Felsom hadn't taken her since he'd married that wimp of Jake Harmon's daughter.

She cupped one hand under a breast, thrust the other one down the front of her jeans, her hips beginning a slow rotation.

What was worse, none of them goddamned Shoshone seemed interested at all; and the more men like Tallpines and Michael Wolf resisted, the more exasperated she grew. Were they the same? Did they have secrets no white man could know? Christ knows they got enough kids, so they must know something. And the way they were taking over the valley, it wouldn't be long before she had no one at all but poor Billyboy to use her. And that, god knew, was a hell of a state.

She lifted one bare foot to the sill and wondered if Riley could see her carefully painted toenails. She wondered what it would be like for him to bite her heel. She thrust a hip forward, then put a hand to the windowframe for balance and made a fist of the fingers that were still lodged at her groin. Riley was holding onto the fence. Much like the other hands had done when she'd first shown herself to them; and not one of them had held out as long as this. Her smile grew rigid. The others were simpletons, jackasses, doing whatever she wanted not because they'd fallen in love with her or lusted that much after her, but because she'd threatened each and every one of them with exposure to Billy. And Billy would kill them if he ever found out.

Suddenly, Riley jumped away from the fence as though it had been electrified. He stared at her, at the side of the house, then raced for the barn. It took but a minute for Gloria to understand. She jumped off the bench and kicked it aside, pulled the window shade halfway and had just thrown open the wardrobe doors when Billy came charging into the room. She turned, one hand primly over her half-buttoned shirt, her almond eyes narrowed in surprised outrage.

"Don't you know how to knock?" she said coldly.

Billy was taller than she by a head, full at the shoulders, lean around his chest and waist. His hair was Marine-cut—the result of a lost, drunken bet—and beginning to show signs of premature greying at the temples and ludicrously thick side-burns. She had once thought him handsome, about the best she was going to do in Windriver since she'd also thought she'd never get out; but that was before the first time he beat her.

"I don't have to knock on any doors in my house," he said sullenly, striding to the bed and sitting hard. He sniffed loudly, wiped a sleeve under his nose, then bent over to pull off his boots. "What the hell you doin up here anyway, this time of day?"

"Changing clothes," she said, reaching into the thickly hung dresses and slacks, shirts and blouses.

"Isn't warm enough to work up a sweat." He looked up at her without lifting his head. "Unless you were sweatin for some other reason."

She gave him a disgusted look and turned her back. The white shirt slipped from her shoulders, and she could feel his stare roving along her spine. When she glanced down at her arms she scowled at the gooseflesh breaking out. "You talk to Bob?"

"Yeah. Says he ain't got the firm offer yet, but he expects it any day now."

She turned then, heedless of her partial nudity. "God, I can't wait! All that goddamned money just because some buck wants off his reservation." She laughed, mirthlessly. "I don't see why Simon does it, that's all. He's crazier than they are."

"Simon?" Billy frowned. "What the hell you talkin about, Gloria?"

"Well, for god's sake, Billyboy, where in hell do you think they get their money to pay for this land, from selling blankets to the tourists?" She looked heavenward, then back to her husband. "Billy, sometimes I wonder what you did with the brains God gave you." Then she looked puzzled as he reached under the bed for his good, black boots with the deep green trim. "You going somewhere?"

"Blairs," he said. "Got some papers to bring to a notary there."

"For Green?"

"Well, shit, Gloria, he's not gonna do it himself, y'know. He's a lawyer, not a messenger boy." He stretched, his shirt pulling out of his jeans, his weather-tanned, ridged stomach rippling as he groaned. "Won't be back till late, I guess."

Depends, she thought, on who you get into, doesn't it, Billyboy?

"I'll miss you. You been working so hard I don't hardly see you."

Billy stood and walked to the window, scratching at his side. "Who were you showin to down there?" he asked softly.

"Billy!"

He whirled around and grabbed her shoulders, nails digging hard into her flesh. "Never give up, do you?"

"I don't know what you're talking about."

He grinned. "Riley. Good ole Lamont Riley." He shook his head sadly. "Thought you had better taste than that, darlin." His grin widened, his grip relaxed, but before she could move away his left hand swung up and across her face, the palm cracking over her cheek like a whipbite. She yelped and jumped back, her legs catching the bed and spilling her to the mattress. He stood over her and started unbuckling his belt. "How do you want it, babe?" When she lunged for his crotch he only slapped her hand away. "Ah," he said, as though to a hidden audience, "the lady wants it rough today. I hope, darlin, you ain't plannin on seein anyone soon. You bruise so terrible easy all of a sudden."

Gloria closed her eyes, aware that her thighs were quivering in anticipation, her breasts reaching for the claws she knew would dig into them. But none of it mattered. In the end she would have her release . . . and when Billyboy was catting around Blairs, she would have Bob Green, and the scheme she had worked out to make her a free woman.

3:05 P.M.

Donna Oldfield stepped out of the clinic, saw Galen Marsh and his friend leaving the *Banner* office and ducked back inside. Jason Clarke. When she'd told Doc Vance about the new man's arrival he'd started, almost went pale. But when she pressed him he had denied the reaction and told her to fill out the county forms to alert the authorities of a possible rabies outbreak in the mountains. It was, he had insisted—

and had been insisting since Ellie Harmon's attack last year—the only possible explanation for the mutilations which had broken out since the first of the month. Donna, the veterinarian but the junior member of the team, would not disagree aloud. She would fill out the forms dutifully, send them in and then figure out what the hell was really going on. Not that she totally discounted the rabies theory; but the evidence thus far was much too skimpy for her to be as positive as Vance. She wished she had the creature that was doing it. Get his head, do the dissections and then . . . *then* she would tell Vance he'd been right all along.

"Donna," he'd said when her dissatisfaction clouded her expression, "it's not that I think you're a bad doctor. Far from it. But I've been around these people all my life, know their animals better'n I do them sometimes. I seen more rabies outbreaks than you can count on fingers and toes, and this is what it is, take my word."

She'd smiled, shrugged, taken the forms to her desk and made damned sure her own misgivings were evident in the sections made available for comment. Vance would sigh loudly when he saw them, reach for a plug of tobacco and spend the rest of the day sulking.

That, however, was something she would face when it came. Meanwhile, there was Mister Jason Clarke.

No, she told herself then; you didn't come all the way out here just to get scorched again.

A corner of her mouth lifted in a bitter smile. Scorched was not exactly the way she had put it when it had happened, five years ago. Torched was more like it. Virtually incinerated. And the ironic part, the worst part of it all, was that those she had thought were her friends were the same ones who had, unwittingly or not, set the fire. *She must have led him on, you know how she is* their eyes whispered to each other when they thought she wasn't looking; *he wasn't that big, she must have led him on* were the rumors she began hearing, told to her in innocence, or so she'd thought at the time.

No. This was no time to get interested in anything like that. She had her work. She had her nightmares. Anything else would be a wound-rubbing complication.

But when she stepped outside again, she couldn't help the disappointment at seeing them gone.

3:10 P.M.

Mitch Regan was alone in his drugstore. He was standing on the platform behind the high counter at the back, a position he seldom left to expose his true height. From here, too, you could not see the balding that marched through his red hair, nor look too closely at the slow-forming jowls, the veins breaking in his nose, the Adam's apple that jiggled whenever he grew nervous. From here he seemed the dapper, cheerful and portly druggist who always had a joke, an anecdote, an easy way with credit to soothe his customers away from the larger chains in Blairs. He was, at the moment, working on a prescription for Rachel MacKenzie. A painkiller Vance had ordered. A painkiller Regan knew the old woman would never take. She never took anything he sent her, but he didn't give a damn. As long as he was paid she could give it to the beavers for all he cared.

He paused to wipe a slip of perspiration from his upper lip, made an unconscious move to adjust his plaid bow tie, when the bell over the front door sounded and he looked out, and down. He hoped it wasn't someone for the post office. He hated that silly cage, though the green eyeshade he wore matched his own eyes perfectly.

His eyes narrowed when the lithe cougar-walk became recognizable. He reached for his glasses, but he did not need them.

"Well," he said jovially, rubbing his hands and heading for the steps. "Well, well, well. Another batch of pills for your mother, is it? My word, she sure does need a lot of them things." He waited at the curtained entrance to the back room where he kept a table, a chair, a hot plate and a cot. "Now," he said, the smile leaving his eyes, "how are we going to pay today? With the real money your daddy gave you, or . . ."

The look she gave him drove the words back into his throat. God, she was beautiful! And though he knew exactly what she was doing to him, he banished it from his mind, preferring to think it was his charm and his not inconsiderable prowess that brought her back, again and again. What she did with the money her father gave her for the medicine was her business. Just as lifting her skirt for him in return was, too.

His smile softened as she walked past him, trailing a warm hand along his jaw. He licked at his lips, pulled at his tie. God, he thought, who would believe she'd pick a man like me.

The light in the back room switched off.

He checked the street from the window, then hurried out of sight, his left hand working on his belt, his right reaching for her naked breasts.

"Dawn," he whispered ten minutes later. "Oh god, Dawn!"

4:50 P.M.

The depot was almost exactly as it had been when it was constructed ninety-two years ago. The only changes Mac Felsom had made were the installation of electric lights on the walls and under the eaves of the roof, padding for the five benches that used to be pews, new panes in the arched windows now and then and a secondhand wood stove he had found in Laramie in 1948. He sat there now, ladder-back chair propped back against the wall, a pile of well-thumbed magazines waiting at his side. The warmth was comforting against the late April chill already moving into the corners and threatening to drive him home. But he would not leave. Not yet. Though the Casper Limited had grumbled through only moments before and deposited its handful of dazed and weary commuters, he saw no reason to move on over to his little place on Station Lane just because the Limited was now the day's last train. Nope. No reason at all.

Certainly he wouldn't be leaving to greet and be greeted by the loving arms of his family. Artie would be getting ready to go out catting someplace, Steve had long since moved into Jake's house with Ellie and eleven months ago today Harry had been . . . he grabbed for the bottle on top of the magazines and took a long, gulping pull.

No sense in going home at all.

Unless, by a miracle, Madge had come back. And it would sure as hell take a miracle for that. Gone twenty years, left him for a three-piece suit promising riches on the exotic East Coast. Well rid of her, they told him. Maybe. Maybe. But god there were still times when he missed her like hell.

He grunted, wiped his mouth with an arthritic right hand and pushed himself to his feet. Swayed. Grinned as he walked out onto the platform and stood under the sloping roof, hands in his hip pockets, rocking on his heels. Not drunk, he thought, not at all. A matter of pride. He was scrawnier than Galen, taller than Waters, and could hold his liquor better than anyone in town, including that souse, Stan Kelly.

He belched proudly, covered his mouth quickly when he thought he heard a noise. Not drunk. It was a noise. Damned kids. More'n likely that spooky, white-haired Greg Thornton. For a dumb preacher's brat, the biggest bastard of the lot. He peered along the tracks, saw nothing but decided to wait before going home. It'd be a feather in his cap to catch one of them doing damage to railroad property.

He belched.

The noise again.

He leaned forward, over the four-foot drop to the roadbed, thinking he saw movement on the embankment across the way. His eyes narrowed under black-spiked brows, the deep hollows of his cheeks catching the shadows and holding them. His pocked jaw moved as though he were chewing. He listened. Heard a grunt before spotting a large rock sailing at him out of the dark. He skipped to his left and pressed hard against a squared roofpost. The rocks came as hail, cracking on the platform, the roof, bouncing and tumbling. One flew into the waiting room and took a gouge out of a pew. Another hit the magazines and toppled his bourbon; the bottle shattered, and he watched dismayed as the liquor stained the flooring and drained through its cracks.

And as suddenly as it had started, it was over.

Damn, he thought, puffing his cheeks and blowing. He didn't have to chase them to know they were Shoshone. Had to be. White boys only taunted him, once in a while busted a window. Indians, on the other hand, kept trying to hurt him. It didn't occur to him until much later, halfway through his second bottle, that they could have hit him if they'd wanted, that the first rock had been a warning for him to get the hell out of the way. It didn't make him feel much better. White or red, all kids oughta be shot.

5:10 P.M.

Lamont Riley had worked for Bill Perkins somewhat less than a year, and he'd had enough. It wasn't so much the crazy wife who stood damned near naked in the bedroom window when her old man went into town, and it wasn't that the place did not seem to pick up the overflow of riches from the MacKenzie ranch just north and the Westley ranch across the road—it was the quiet he disliked. Even in the middle of the day there was that eternal, and eternally damning, peacefulness of the land. He was from Kansas, his own family in farming, and he knew he should be used to it. But this place was different. Too high, too many mountains, too much blue sky that burned your eyes when you looked at it too long.

Quiet; he hated it.

And now the twilight had turned to full dusk, bats were in the air and the stupid cattle were still in their pasture.

He swung out of Perkins's army surplus jeep and opened the gate to the west grazing land. The Herefords had clustered beneath a stand of ash, and he scowled at them. Damned Maybelle; a goddamned rock with legs would have more smarts than to wait this long. Didn't know enough to come in out of the rain. He leapt back into the mudsplattered vehicle and gunned the engine, snarling with it as he jounced over the rutted ground, skidding to a halt a shadow's length from the small herd. None of them moved. A few were lying in the cooling grass, chewing. He walked slowly toward them, coiling a length of rope around his forearm while he searched for the old cow and her signal bell. One beast tried to brush against his hip and he slapped its rump hard, raising dust.

He stopped.

A dark shape lay in the tall new growth at the foot of a low rise. He took a deep breath, shook himself and walked toward it. The rope dangled from his hand.

"Damnit, Maybelle!" he called. Stupid name for a cow.

He slowed then, and almost turned to run.

Maybelle lay on her side. Her throat had been torn open so savagely she was almost beheaded, flesh in shreds, muscle exposed, the head shoved back so far her horns grazed her shoulders. What was left of her tongue curled thickly past her lips.

Riley circled her slowly, swallowing at the gorge turning acid in his throat.

One eye was blank, sickly white, speckled with dirt and a few drops of blood; the other was gone, the flesh around the socket ragged and chewed. Flank and rump were slashed. And flies moved in a shimmering black blanket over the dried blood.

He felt Kramer's Mountain pressing hard against his back, and his skin contracted against a midnight-deep chill.

"Aw, shit, Maybelle," he said just for the sound of his voice, and it sounded stronger than he felt so he said it again. Then he looked for tracks, for signs and saw nothing but the blood and the exposed bone and the marks of his own boots as they pressed the damp grass.

By nightfall he knew he would convince himself a wolf had been here, or a family of coyotes. Perhaps, and it wasn't all that unlikely, a bear down from the slopes and hungry after winter. But now, as he forced himself to look at the dead cow again, he could only see monsters stalking the ranch.

He shuddered violently and hurried away, shouting now and whipping the rope to drive the rest of the herd home. He would have to get some of the boys to return with him later to drag off the carcass . . . and he would have to tell Perkins.

Aw shit, he thought. Only three weeks ago, Billyboy's prize Angus bull had been savaged the same way, and somehow Riley had managed to get himself blamed. Aw shit, that jackass will skin me for sure.

And it wouldn't do him a bit of good to let Perkins know that his job did not include guard duty against wolves, or coyotes, or bears . . . or monster.

He glanced back at the cow. Something had disturbed the flies, and they were a shifting, obscenely glittering cloud hovering over their meal.

Riley couldn't stand it; he turned around and ran.

THREE

7:00 *P.M.*

Full dark in Windriver, the valley and the town an ink sketch done in shades of grey, shades of black. The river, swollen from the thaws and the rain, traps the stars and makes them shimmer, traps shadows beneath the bridges and makes them writhe. Streetlamps huddle in the crowns of the trees, and on the Pike the last of the cars from the candy factory's day-shift glare red and white at the gutters, at the curbs. Full dark and chilled, as though a word out of place would climb to a scream.

7:05 *P.M.*

"Daddy, you worry too much. I know it doesn't always seem fair, but I don't mind, really. It's a pain sometimes, but I really don't mind."

Anthony Carosa listened to his daughter with a patient grin as she shrugged into a camel's hair overcoat and scrambled around the living room searching for her schoolbooks. He supposed she was right, that he worried about her too much, knew, too, that it never hurt anything to stay on the MacKenzies' good side. It helped ease him somewhat that he hadn't been exaggerating that night at David's party when he'd told poor old Jake that Carole as much as considered Rachel her grandmother. Especially now that it seemed the poor old squaw was fading fast. Nevertheless, he couldn't stop worrying.

"Rats," Carole said, waiting for him to don his own coat and warm up the car, "I just remembered something."

"What?"

"Oh . . . Hardy's having a party at his house tonight. Not really a party, just some kids getting together, if you know what I mean."

Carosa hesitated. "Maybe I should give Mister MacKenzie a call."

"No, Daddy," she said. "Hardy's a jerk and I promised Rachel." She looked up at him and smiled. "Will you please stop fussing?"

"All right," he said, as though he'd just made a momentous decision. "All right. Then get your butt into the car, young lady, or we're going to be late."

"Mussolini," she muttered as they stepped out onto the back stoop. "You wouldn't talk like that if Gloria Steinem lived here."

"Who's Gloria Steinem?"

She sighed loudly, dramatically. "A feminist, Daddy. She keeps people like you from beating up on people like me."

"Oh, well, in that case . . ." and he opened the car door for her with a sweeping bow. She mocked him a curtsy, and he took a playful swipe at her head.

"Y'know, it's a good thing Rachel likes you," he said a few minutes later, as they drove out of town. And he reached over to jab at an amulet she wore on a silver chain around her neck—a stylized bird hammered from copper.

"Well, that's because no one else in the house will read to her the way I do. God, Daddy, you'd think they were afraid of her or something. I mean, she's an Indian, just like the rest of them."

Carosa said nothing. Beyond the village block there were no lights, and he had to concentrate on the trembling black that extended around his headlamps. He would have suggested his daughter bring Bea Steed out with her if she really felt uncomfortable around the MacKenzie household, but there was something between the two friends he didn't quite understand, though he suspected that a boy had at last risen to contend for their affections; maybe even Hardy Green. He filled his lungs slowly, exhaled loudly, and turned north on Elkhorn Road, bumped over the tracks and aimed for the MacKenzie ranch. Carole turned on the radio, her head inclined toward the dented speaker grille in the dashboard. One of her books slipped to the floor, and she left it there untouched.

A quick sideways glance, and he grinned to himself. She was, unquestionably, a potentially beautiful woman in what Jake used to call the Italian manner. Certainly more exotic than the other girls she knew, most of whose stock was tough-minded Anglo-Saxon. But tonight something veiled that beauty, something his wife had already cautioned him about—the girl was tired, and she needed her rest.

A second book tilted off her lap, and his grin faded. A remarkable girl, he thought; all that work without complaint, and for what? For nothing, unless her scholarship came through. And that, he knew, was as likely as Jake Harmon getting married again. Or David growing two new legs.

Despite the insurance, and the assistance of his friends, the money he'd been saving for Carole's education had been drained by David's medical bills. She insisted she understood, but he couldn't help wondering if the bitterness that frequently clouded her face wasn't in fact aimed directly at him. After all, what had once been a secure, planned future had suddenly exploded, and she was being asked to do more than he knew she was intellectually capable of. She was trying; my god, she was trying! But it wasn't going to work. In spite of all his efforts at building her confidence, they both knew David had been granted all the brains in the family.

"Carole?"

She stirred, glanced at him with a frown before turning down the radio. Then she noticed the books on the floor and groaned as she bent over to retrieve them, slap them on her lap and lay a fist atop them.

"You all right?"

"Sure," she said. "Why shouldn't I be?"

He shrugged, and swerved sharply to avoid a pothole. "No reason. Just asking." A hesitation. "Your mother thinks you're overtired is all."

"Mother always thinks I'm overtired," she said sourly. "Every time I walk out the door it's like she wants to take my pulse."

"Carole, that's not fair."

She opened her mouth, closed it suddenly and tightly.

"You call, hear?"

"Sure, Dad."

"And tell Rachel the family says hello and hopes she's feeling better."

"I will."

"And—"

"All *right*, Daddy," she said, with a slight whine of rebellion. "I know. Gee, you'd think I was still a baby, for god's sake."

7:30 P.M.

It was a dream. Jason knew it was a dream, yet it felt the same as the night it had happened. And the following day. And the days after that.

It was a dream. And nothing changed in it, no matter how hard he willed it.

A motorcraft is strictly for pleasure, the husky voice told him. Midnight, and you drift along the Jersey coast. You sit on a deck chair and sup at quail, sip a tall drink precisely to your taste, watch the boat wake blur to white and back to black again. A nice man in person, your host is a thief, you can prove it, he knows it, and he looks for a compromise that will keep him from jail and salve everyone's conscience. It seems remarkable . . . until the woman climbs slowly up from below, her only sound the gentle whisper of your name. Backlighted, she is ebony, she is shadow, she is intangible. In front of you she waits until your vision adjusts, and the ebony and the shadow fade into soft contours, and what was intangible is now tantalizing and real. She wears nothing and her slender arms are outstretched and her small breasts darktipped a pale marble in the spotlight of the moon. She is tall, she is blonde, she has been touched bronze by the sun, a bronze that gleams heat under the light film of oil that adds a depth to her limbs and a promise to her reach. You look pointedly at her pouting lips outlined in slow motion by the snaking of her tongue, to the shadows of her thighs slightly tilted to greet you. You set your drink down and rise to greet her. Her hands unbutton your shirt (a breath of cool flesh that makes your own tighten) and trail delightfully sharp nails along the sunwarm skin down to the belt and up slowly again (leaning closer, quickly, to nip at an earlobe and breathe a message just short of fire) . . . Down below the belt where a palm cups your groin and up again to your stomach where the muscles begin to quiver. Then up to your shoulders to slip off the shirt to the tune of her rhythmic hissing and down as she leans closer and her pout becomes a grimace as she takes hold of your belt, and before your arms (like lead, like feathers) can lift to her breasts, she takes hold of your belt and kicks a foot behind your ankle . . . and lifts . . . and pushes . . . and you're too damningly surprised to see the grimace become a smile . . .

. . . There are serpents that embroil themselves in your lungs as you strike bottom, cheeks scraped, struggle to the surface, see the running lights distant, see the figure on the stern with hands on her hips, see the shoreline's black wall breached by the lights of an amusement pier in full fury. You are too cold now, too shocked to move, to do more than tread water. You are not that drunk; in spite of everything you were cautious. Amateur, you think of the man, as a skipper and a killer, a summertime sailor who doesn't know there are low tides at night and sandbars and swimming, thinking too much liquor and a heady naked woman will keep a man from rescue. But the ocean rises to give battle, the waves dragging and shoving instead of gathering, and you find yourself sinking, rising, striking out at the air without benefit of strength or will or salvation. And all you can think of . . .

. . . And all you can think of is how stupid this all is because once you get home you will write the story anyway, only this time there will be glorious intimations of brutality to add red spice to the brew. And you do, don't you, Jason? *Yes, damnit, yes.* You find your way home without being seen, without seeing the world. And you write the story with doors and windows locked (in case there are killers) and the air conditioner turned off (in case there is gas) and the food in cupboards and the refrigerator untasted (in case there is poison), and as soon as you are finished you tear all the pages to shreds and burn them in the bottom of your grey metal wastebasket because the woman with the smile and the breasts and the shadow and the tongue is right now watching silently over your shoulder, and the summertime sailor is standing ready on the front porch, (the back porch, the roof, the garage) with a harpoon in his hand, and there are wingéd serpents, Jason, wingéd serpents rising from the moonsilver deathblack sea that are waiting until the last word is typed and the last sentence dotted and the last page pulled before they move with a grin out of the shadows.

Move with a grin, Jason.

Move with a grin . . . with a grin . . . with a

Jason jerked himself up, his arms flailing against the black night that had filled the room without his knowing, his legs thrashing at the air as though water were there to be battled. He gasped and rubbed his hands coarsely over his face and back through his hair, then into his lap where they clasped like serpents writhing. And when his breathing had calmed, he fumbled to switch on the lamp. He blinked rapidly, felt his chest, arms, the top of his head. The shades were up on the two windows, and despite the screen of willows the moonlight slid over his legs, over his jacket, and congealed in a darkgrey puddle on the hardwood floor. There was an aftershock that made him shudder violently before he swung his legs over the side of the bed and gripped his knees hard.

"Not fair," he mumbled to himself, to the room. "Not goddamned fair."

The problem, however, was simple: it was, all of it, true.

The man, the woman, the story . . . and his running. It had happened two years ago last September over Labor Day weekend, and though he had reported to work for the rest of the month he was different. He saw *things* behind the file cabinets, *things* on his threshold, *things* in people's smiles. He had quit when he realized he wasn't doing the newspaper, or himself, any good by walking around like a corpse. And though he never saw the man again, or the woman, or the boat, he saw them everywhere, laughing knowingly and silently, waiting for him to be relegated to the obits. Too scared to stay and too scared to run he stayed in his house and watched the wingéd serpents.

Then Galen had written: *the town's going to Hell.*

Why not, Jason thought; if I can't beat it, I can join it and show it the way.

9:00 P.M.

Daniel Tallpines squatted on the riverbank. Here the trees were gone, long since harvested for the homes of the ranchers, and the settlers in the village. Beside him, Aaron Sweetwater. On his left, Michael Wolf. Behind him, several others. Squatting. Watching the water as it sliced through the dark rich earth toward the rim of the valley. There were no women or children; the men were alone.

"I don't know," Daniel said in answer to a question. In his early thirties, his face was a deep wind-touched brown, with ridged brows and hollow cheeks, a broad-tipped nose and jutting chin. And when he talked it was from the right side of his mouth, as though he'd had a stroke. "He came on the bus this afternoon and he's been with Marsh ever since. No chance to find out. I had a word with Donna Oldfield, but she didn't know anything either. He almost knocked her down, that's all she said."

"Waters," Aaron said bitterly. Just for tonight his hair was like Daniel's—hanging straight and parted down the center. And like the others it did not reflect the afterglow of the moon. "Ted Waters, I bet. He finally got himself some fancy lawyer, some bigshot from New York who's gonna call us brother while he twists the knife."

"Bull," said Michael, tossing aside a handful of plucked grass. He was the only one under thirty, a crescent scar under his left eye and a missing left ear the visible results of a swift knifefight with a friend. The friend was Daniel Tallpines, and Daniel didn't have a scratch. "Bull, damnit. What's a lawyer gonna do with us, huh? We own most of it free and clear, right? There isn't a hundred thousand dollars worth of mortgages left among those who had to borrow." He laughed softly. "That damned bank hasn't a toe on any of our necks."

"I don't know, then," Aaron said, shifting, his boots digging into the soft earth. "Beats me."

"We're worrying about nothing," said Daniel earnestly. "We're making ourselves paranoid."

"Oh Jesus," someone said behind him. "Will you listen to him? Paranoid. That what you get for going to school, Danny?"

Daniel shrugged. He had been to the white man's reservation school, had gone to college on an Anglican Church scholarship, had been in the army for five years after that. He was thirty-four, a master mechanic in Cy Oaker's garage, and had a wife and three children who at least did not have to flinch a smile for the benevolent glare of a tourist's camera. He had never been in trouble with the law, not even after the fight with Michael. Wolf had been drunk, had been armed, had been nineteen. It was a miracle, the others said, that Daniel hadn't killed him. Now they were friends, and kidded about the ear.

They watched the water.

Cigarettes passed among them, flaring, ebbing, the breath of a fire.

It had not been a scheduled meeting, but something in the air, something in the way the wind husked through the trees had brought them from their homes, by horseback and truck. Something, Daniel felt, was trying to communicate with him, and he cursed the loss of his ability to hear.

"I guess I'll try to talk with him," he said finally. "If he's with Marsh, I don't think he could be all that bad."

"Are you sure?" Wolf asked, the voice young, the tone uncertain.

Daniel put a hand to the ground. Something was talking to him down there, whispering, something that had not been living a year ago. He didn't like it. He was worried.

"Dan, are you sure?" Michael Wolf asked again.

"No," he said, "but I don't have much of a choice."

They smoked. They watched the river, tracked the stars, and one by one drifted away to return to their homes. Soon, at a time marked by an owl's soft query, there were only two.

"Daniel," Aaron said, "you have to be patient with them. They think they believe in the Teaching, but they really don't know what they've gotten themselves into. They're scared. After all, it's been nearly seven years and the whites are still here."

"I know." Daniel flicked his cigarette into the water, its

orange track blurring until it hissed into black. "I know." He put his hand back to the ground.

"You feel it," Aaron said.

Daniel nodded. "Feel it, can't hear it."

"It's the world, Daniel. We've been too long in the world. The old ways . . . the whites think there's something mystical about us, but we're still human beings."

"Mystical," Daniel said, grinning. "Don't say that to Michael, he'll think you've been reading again."

"He's a good boy."

"Yes."

Minutes slipped by on the back of the river.

"Daniel? Daniel, I'm worried about her."

"Dawn? Or Laughing Sky?"

"Neither. You know who I mean. She's old, she's sick. What if she dies?"

"Then we have a powwow with Ted Waters and make him our friend."

Sweetwater ignored him. "I don't like it, Daniel, I don't mind telling you that now. The animals are dying and the whites aren't leaving. Simon could kill me for this, but Christ, I don't trust her." He waited. No response. "Did you hear me?"

Daniel would not take his gaze from the river. Nor would he tell his friend that he had had the same doubts. Not in the Teaching and the purpose it gave them, but in the ability of the old woman to see when it was done. And he wondered what she would do when the whites didn't run.

9:10 P.M.

Jason scrubbed at his cheeks harshly to drive away the last of the sleep, rose and moved into the short hall. A bathroom on the left. The corridor ahead to Galen's room and the kitchen. At the archway into the living room was a gun cabinet he did not look at.

Marsh was sitting on a mostly wood couch in front of the fireplace. He was reading, a notepad on his knee already littered with scratchings. He looked up, grinned, waved his hand to a redwood sideboard and a decanter of brandy.

"You, if you'll excuse the expression, look like hell."

"Tired," Jason said, not entirely truthfully. "I hate naps. I always feel worse when they're done. And I always take them on the off chance they'll finally do me some good." He poured himself a snifter and sipped at the liquid, shuddered as he waited for its low fire to reach his nightmare, consume it, and thrust the ashes into the dungeon where they belonged.

Marsh, meanwhile, had taken to a crudely made rocker at the side of the hearth. Jason stood for a moment, drawing serenity from the flames, then sat on the couch and propped his stocking feet on a footstool, drawing it closer so his knees would bend slightly.

He considered telling the editor about his flight, but decided to wait. The old man would find out soon enough.

"Galen," he said instead, "you see before you a man who used to have insatiable curiosity. Once, but not now. That is to say, I have grown patient when I shouldn't be, and impatient whenever I discover the former mistake. I can wait all night if you want, but I frankly don't see what I can do about your trouble. I'm not a lawman or a lawyer. I'm not a private investigator or even retired from the force, as they say on television. To be frank, I don't get it." He grinned. "This is my patient mood."

Marsh reached over his head to the rough-planked mantel and plucked a chipped pipe from a partially filled rack. He rummaged a pouch out of a carpetbag at his side, stuffed the pipe, lit it and grimaced. "This Danish stuff is too damned strong. I don't know why I bother."

"Talk," Jason told him gently.

Galen stretched, and ran the bowl thoughtfully alongside his nose. Jason wasn't sure he liked the penetration of his gaze.

"Jase, this place here, this marvelous piece of western culture we call Windriver, was settled back near the end of the Civil War. It hasn't any oil, or iron, or coal, or such, so it hasn't been in the middle of any booms of late—unless you count the Melancoire candy factory, which I emphatically do not. I doubt the population's been substantially over twelve hundred souls since it all began. You can tell by looking at the land that, according to the geologists, we're smack in the middle of what used to be one hell of a volcano. So we have good farmland, and hunting, some goodly strong timber, things for those who want it and don't want the hassles of living near a large town."

"That you don't have to tell me," Jason said wryly.

Marsh ignored him. "And you would think, aside from the minor gaffs that crop up now and then, we wouldn't have much trouble. But we do, Jase. And we're so gadabout small that it's more serious than it looks."

Jason fingered the hollow of his neck, his gaze drifting back to the fire. "What, a range war? Sheepherders and cattlemen, that sort of thing?"

"God, you *are* from the East, son. No, that's past, nearly a century ago. No, it isn't that, it's the Indians, among other things."

Jason listened carefully, not really believing that the countdown toward the twenty-first century could possibly hold within its ticks the makings of another Indian war. But after the editor had spoken for nearly an hour—with time off to make sandwiches and a salad of homegrown greens—he realized that what was brewing here was a race war, not a land war, though the two in this instance were undeniably entwined.

According to Galen, the entire valley had belonged to the MacKenzies as a result of their traveling cross-country from their home in northern Scotland. Their initial contacts in the territory had been with Chief Washakie of the Shoshone, who had moved his people to the Wind River Reservation—some of the choicest land in the entire state—when it became obvious the Indians were not going to beat the whites in any war, large or small. Washakie was no coward, but his courage was less that of a warrior than it was of a man with foresight who understood the finality of genocide and knew there were other ways of winning besides on the battlefield.

This contact between the MacKenzies and the Shoshone was a mutually profitable one, and most of the Scots males married Indian women as a practical as well as an amorous matter; Simon, apparently, was no different than his forebears.

At the turn of the century, however, and as a matter of economic necessity, the family began to sell off parcels, large ones, for farms and other ranches. Most of this was accomplished beyond the river's southern banks; since then a fair number of families had come and gone, trying their hand, leaving when their hands proved too soft. In the sixties there had been an influx of communal types, who had been tolerated only because they'd brought much-needed dollars to the local merchants. They didn't last, either. Then, seven years ago, Aaron Sweetwater bought his ranch; now, virtually every acre worth mentioning south of the river had been sold by the owners to small families of Indians who were leaving the Wind River Reservation.

"Shoshone," the editor said, "though there's Arapaho down there, too." Then he frowned. "No, wait a minute. There was one, some guy from down south, an Apache, I think. Word travels fast. He came up and bought about four hundred acres. He lasted a month before the Shoshone bought him out. Clannish, I guess."

"Big deal," said Jason, beginning to feel irritated. "You people have lived with them all your lives, right? So why are you getting so nervous just because they buy a few acres of your precious valley? Aren't they entitled, for god's sake? As the saying goes, Galen, they were here first. And besides, not only is it a free country—as they used to tell us—but you yourself pointed out that the MacKenzies are part Indian themselves. You didn't mention them howling like a bunch of redneck crackers."

Marsh, his pipe puffed through furiously, knocked the bowl against the fireplace mouth and set it back on the mantel. "That's not the point, Jase. I don't think anyone around here—well, maybe one or two exceptions—would mind if that was all there was to it. But it isn't. You see, it's not all the Shoshone who are coming up here, just what seems to be a select group. Not troublemakers or anything like that, don't get me wrong, but these are people who are something different from the rest of the tribe. We can't figure it out and they ain't talking. But that isn't so bad, either—it's the other that has us going. Y'see, Jase, they're not doing anything when they get here."

Jason frowned.

"Literally, they are not doing a damned thing with that land. They still keep what jobs they had before, and they're letting all their property go to seed."

"Well, isn't that their right?"

"I sure think so," the editor said, "but you talk to someone like Ted Waters, and he'll tell you different. Every time a farm is sold to an Indian, Waters loses business. He depends on farm products sales, and every time a farm goes off the market . . ."

"That's still their right," Jason said firmly. Then: "Wait a minute. Do you mean you wheedled me all the way out here just to find out why?" When Marsh nodded, reluctantly, Jason snorted. "Come *on*, Galen! You've got two legs, a brain and a tongue—why haven't you asked them yourself?"

"I have."

"So?"

"So they're not talking. At least, they're not talking straight to me. That's why I want you here, son. You're an article-type—and I do have some of them back at the office, so that gives you the right credentials—wait a minute! Don't butt in yet. I've got two or three reasons for wanting to know. I've got a paper that would love the story—and I admit it'd look nice if I could get it on the wire services, too. I've got a damned big dose of cat-killing curiosity. And if someone doesn't come up with a satisfactory explanation soon, there's going to be very big trouble around here, and people are going to get hurt. Bad. We've already had a few ruckuses, little ones, so there's no way anymore any of us locals can talk to them now without blowing each other's stacks."

Jason whistled softly. "Brother, a mess is hardly the word for what you have here, cousin."

Marsh smiled broadly. "I knew if I got you out here you'd come up with an answer."

"Lovely," said Jason. "I come something over two thousand miles so an old fart can turn me into a straight man. Lovely."

A scratching at the door drew Marsh to his feet to let in the setters. When they had curled up on the hearth, Jason pulled at an earlobe.

"You said 'among other things,' Galen. You said in your last letter the town was going to hell. This race thing, it isn't what you meant, is it?"

Marsh ran the flat of a hand over his black hair, ended with it cupping his chin, his little finger over his lips.

"I tend to the dramatic," he said.

"You tend to the bullshit," Jason told him.

"Maybe."

"Galen . . . what is it?"

Marsh pushed out of the rocker and sat beside him. They watched the flames.

"This used to be your home," Galen said quietly, a hand on Jason's leg, patting once and leaving. "Your mom, she told me about your drifting before she died. A job here, a job there, and I don't expect it changed all that much, after." He paused, but Jason knew he wasn't waiting for an answer. "Windriver," the old man said. His face caught the firelight and glittered, shimmered, made shadows across the cheeks and the lines and the hollows of his eyes.

Jason waited. There was nothing but the fire, talking to itself.

"It used t'be . . . when I said this town is going to hell, I pretty much meant it literally, son. It's changed. Not just the folks. Everything. The nights seem longer, the days not so bright as they used to be. Y'take a bunch of mangy, smelly farm animals that got chewed up by something Harmon hasn't got the brains to catch, and a couple of hotheads who think the world owes them grace and fortune as long as it comes in one color, and that poor child, Ellie . . ." He stopped, and sighed.

Jason said nothing. The words had come slowly, laboriously, and were tinged with a sadness and an age that made the man sound defeated.

"Maybe it's because I'm old." Galen smiled briefly. "I've thought of that, y'know. Old. Out of touch. Old." He scowled. "But I've been here too long, Jase, not to notice the change. It's been slow coming, but it's coming. Sometimes . . . sometimes I think the town is turning evil. I don't know if that's possible or not. But there's something out there that doesn't want us here anymore."

Jason shifted uncomfortably, unable to avoid an inexplicable, passing image of Kramer's Mountain. "You mean . . . that is, are we talking about Satan or . . . whatever?"

Galen shook his head. "How should I know? I try to talk to others about it and they won't listen. It's not that they don't believe me—Donna, Carosa, some of them with smarts—but they don't understand. Reverend Thornton, he's got enough troubles with that boy of his, Greg, so he hardly listens to his own sermons these days. I asked him once to say a prayer for the valley and he told me to mind my editorials." He clasped his hands loosely. "No. Not the Devil."

"The Shoshone?"

"Maybe, but I don't think so. They've been here a while, and I see some of them getting edgy these days, too."

Jason shrugged. He really had no idea what the man was talking about, though he was convinced he wasn't simply regretting his age and the coming of the end. He sensed something, and he wanted Jason to sense it, too. Sense it, define it and find some way to cure it.

He almost said he didn't believe in evil. Until, as the words came to his lips, he remembered the boat and the woman and the man who tried to kill him.

Galen shuddered then, and grinned suddenly. "Goose walkin over my grave."

"Wouldn't dare," Jason told him. "Pinfeathers would singe."

"That ain't funny, boy."

"Better than talking about a town going to hell."

The editor opened his mouth, closed it, then slapped his thighs and began to explain how Jason would operate—unless, he said with a mocking grin, he intended to use the commuter special in the morning.

Jason didn't smile back.

10:00 P.M.

Aaron Sweetwater stood on his front porch. Daniel was astride a saddleless roan. Aaron gestured over his shoulder. "That was Doc Oldfield on the phone. Wanted to know how her horse was. It came up lame the other day."

"Is it all right?"

"Sure, just a bruise. She can ride it next week if she wants."

"Good. She's a nice woman."

"She told me I couldn't get through to her before 'cause she was out at Billyboy's place." He rubbed a hand over his face nervously. "Daniel, he lost a full-grown lead cow this afternoon."

Daniel clucked, and the roan turned to head for home.

"Daniel!" Aaron called after him. "It was daylight! It ain't supposed to be able to happen in full daylight. What the hell's goin on? Daniel, damnit, this ain't right!"

Daniel didn't answer him; he was trying to listen to what the black night was telling him, at the same time hoping he wouldn't hear the answer.

But Aaron was right—about the cow . . . about everything. There was something subtly wrong, subtly altering, but he had nothing he could bring to Simon for a confrontation. Nothing but the feel of the air, the sound of the land, the way the stars grew colder and the moon less friendly. Simon, and Rachel, would call him a child.

But for the first time since it had started, he began to wonder if it had all been a mistake.

10:30 P.M.

Set yourself up in my office, Galen had said. *It'll give us some—what shall we call it?—legitimacy. Let's pretend. Hey, do you remember that show, or aren't you old enough yet to remember radio? "Let's Pretend." With Princess Something-Or-Other. Boy, that was a hell of a long time ago. All right, don't laugh. You're much too serious for a young man, you know that, Jase? Much too serious. Whatever it is that's eatin at you, you'd best let it out soon or you're gonna ulcer yourself to death.*

He wore one of Galen's heavily lined jackets; it was tight across his chest, and the arms were comically short. He walked with Jeff at his side until he came to the river, stopped and leaned against a tree whose name he didn't recognize in the dark. He stared at the water for a while, his breath smoking through the soft glare of the moon.

Let's pretend.

He wasn't sure if that had been a joke, but it would serve to help him, for the time being, explain why he had come back, why he had come all this way to solve . . . if not the sins of the world, then perhaps the reason for his own swift damnation.

The setter snuffled at the reeds lining the bank, darting in and out of them as though some nocturnal rodents were teasing her memory of a good day's hunting. He watched her, envious, then shook himself when the evening chill penetrated the coat to seize his shoulders like talons and made his chest feel like perspiration that ran cold in summer. He was tired but not sleepy, and every so often felt the roll of that fool van bus unsettle his legs.

So here you are, he thought as the setter lifted itself on its hind legs to snap at a lightning bug. Here you are.

Again he searched for memories, for faces, and again they slipped from him, fog through his fingers. Nothing there, and no photographs to prod him, no elders to remind him. Yet he knew he had lived here.. He felt it. Here more than anywhere else he had traveled. If it wasn't exactly home, it seemed right now to be far ahead of whatever was in second place.

Then he wondered over what Galen had said about the town. He tried to feel something, pick up the emanations Galen implied were here; but there was nothing but a vague sense of unease which, he told himself quickly, was a result of his traveling to a town he once lived in and a town he never really knew. There was nothing evil in that. Nothing evil at all.

Jeff barked once, sharply, scrambled up from a near fall into the river and trotted to his side. She rubbed up against him. He reached down absently and scratched behind her ears. She gripped his sleeve gently and tugged. He grinned. A babysitter. A Wyoming Irish setter for a babysitter. He yawned, stretched and pushed away from the tree.

"All right, girl," he said. "Take me home and tuck me in. The world starts tomorrow, I guess. Good . . . god!"

And they raced back to the house, Jason almost spilling over the gate when it didn't open at his shove. He grinned, laughed and looked up and down the street. It was dark, silent, houses unlighted and stars unseen. The grin faded. Jeff began to growl, deep in her throat.

"That's telling 'em, girl," he said.

The gate opened, and the setter bounded to the porch, turning as he approached, turning and growling. He stepped inside. The living room was empty. Jeff barked once and followed, making a dash for the hall.

Jason stood for a moment, staring out at the yard, looking for the car or the bird or whatever night creatures a place like this has that would bother a dog. He yawned, nearly choked on a laugh and decided he'd gone travel-crazy for letting it upset him.

Tomorrow would be different; but he made sure he locked the door.

Part Two
THE BLOODING

ONE

(1)

For three days the valley is cursed with midsummer: an extraordinary sudden heat untempered by wind and undiminished by sunset. But on the fourth day clouds rise in black mountain formation, with gusts that command bowing and a cold that settles like shadows in the blood. There are cannonades of thunder and striking blind lightning, the river that churns froth into hillocks on its banks. Yet the sun on the sixth day brings no sense of cleansing. An expectation instead. And a confusion—a standing in the doorway without knowing why you're waiting.

(2)

When Jason woke, the windows in his bedroom were indistinct grey squares in the surrounding gentle darkness. Groaning softly and stretching, he rolled languidly onto his stomach and tucked his arms under the pillow that bunched to a feather mound and cradled his cheek. Beside the bed an easy breathing, a dog's faint whimpering, the breathing again. He grinned; if nothing else, Wyoming and Windriver were working wonders on his system. Friday had come around again, and in spite of the heat and the storm he'd had more sleep, more rest, more welcome energy than he'd had since college . . . no, high school. He ate a large breakfast where before the very smell of food in the morning had made him gag; he took showers that invigorated rather than enervated; and when he crossed the river to the fields he was much less intimidated by the space, the size, the sheer power of the land.

He did not miss the traffic, nor the pedestrians. His natural nervousness at meeting new people had been partially abetted by the weather, which had prevented most encounters save those Galen had nudged: Kurt Steed at the luncheonette, Bob Green, the lawyer, and his son, Hardy, Earl Carson, the haberdasher and part-time mayor, part-time judge, and a few others whose names had not yet chosen to stick.

He heard the gossip, too. Of Gloria Perkins and her escapades with men married or not, of Harmon's rescue of David Carosa, of Carole Carosa and the stir she'd caused just two summers ago. Apparently, she had been caught in the stationhouse half-naked with Charlie Sweetwater and, unfortunately, the man who had found them was Ted Waters. Ordinarily, Galen had said, such matters would have been kept in the family, but Waters had decided to use the incident in his self-appointed holy war against the Indians. He made sure everyone in town knew about it and had managed to blow it so out of proportion that even Reverend Thornton had made references to it from the pulpit of his church. Despite the fact that most of her friends thought it a lark, and people like Galen thought it none of their business, it was halfway through winter before Carole was able to face the community again without bursting into tears.

The one person he had not seen again was Donna Oldfield, and more than once over the past week he'd found himself standing at the office window, not really thinking about anything in particular until he realized he was hoping she would walk by. He grunted in disgust, and in just a bit of self-pity. As forward as she seemed the day he had arrived, he sensed the next step would have to be his, a step he would have to watch because involvement in Windriver, here where he had grown, and almost stopped growing—involvement might mean something more than coupling, even if coupling were as far as it reached.

Jeff yelped once in her sleep.

"Go to it, girl," he murmured into the pillow, and decided that sleeping late for a change would not destroy his image. Most of his daylight hours had been spent in the house or in Galen's office, reading and rereading the accounts and rumors of vandalism, animal mutilations and foolhardy speculations that had swept the valley over the past twelve months. The picture was clear enough.

And with the occasional help of Galen's secretary, Esther Lynn, he was beginning to build portraits of the community's leaders, the followers, the camps, the neutrals.

It had been Galen's idea to keep him secluded for so long a time. He wanted things stirred up just enough to provoke slips and, as he'd put it without the grace of a wince, passions be aroused. And though Jason wasn't sure Marsh knew what he was doing, he went along until he felt confident the town wouldn't drown him.

In a week's short time this had become vitally important to him; important because he wanted Windriver saved. Without clearly understanding why yet, he knew this place had to be protected. It had to be around when he finished with his job.

And that, he reminded himself, would begin in earnest today.

Galen had arranged a meeting between him and the MacKenzies.

"It isn't as if they don't know you're here already," the old man had said, paring his nails with a dull Boy Scout knife. "There's folks here would tell them when you shit if they wanted it. But Simon hasn't said word one about anything that's going on. He just sits out there like a hermit, Jase, like there's nothing going on. None of us can budge him."

"So what makes you think I can?"

He shrugged. "I don't. Maybe you will, maybe you won't. But you got to know him sooner or later and it might as well be sooner."

If that's what it takes, Jason thought; if that's what it takes to give me a place to come back to.

He took a slow deep breath, held it and released it as he drifted gratefully away from the dawn.

He had no dreams; the wingéd serpents were gone.

(3)

Esther Lynn Vance was a fifty-one-year-old spinster who was determined to end that condition as soon as she possibly could, and end it by marrying Galen Marsh. After all, the eight years' difference in their ages at this stage was hardly a difference at all. Which is why she worked so hard for him for the wages he paid. Her Bible-toting sister, Rose, scolded her constantly about the provocative way she dressed and the shameless way she threw herself at the *Banner*'s editor, even when he wasn't looking. But she didn't care. Marsh would be hers if she had to kidnap him to do it.

She admitted to other reasons for staying with the paper. It had been the perfect excuse to get out of the family's house on Deerfield Street, away from all those sick people who, before the clinic had been built, tramped through the parlor office day after day, seemingly without end. Unlike Rose, she'd never been able to steel herself against blood and disease. And by renting her own place on Laurel Street, she had determined her own freedom, even if she'd not yet been able to trap Galen in her bedroom, her sitting room or the front porch on a summer's cool evening. That was only a minor setback.

She was also, by virtue of lineage and position, in the most admirable position to know most of what went on in Windriver. Her "People And Personalities" column, and her excellent bridge game, assured her entrance into virtually every home.

Esther Lynn *knew;* and Esther Lynn loved to talk.

Now, however, she wasn't sure she knew anything. Not since that young Easterner had come into the office. He'd been introduced quickly and closeted in Galen's office for the better part of a week. He was there when she arrived, there when she left, but he seldom came out to ask anything of her.

In truth, she would have been hard put to give a good description of him . . . though there was something about him, something that tantalized without coming to full fruit. And once it was clear she wasn't going to be let in on whatever was going on, she decided to play the "top secret" role as well as she could until she had something—anything! —to tell the girls, who were dropping by her desk with increasing, and alarming, frequency.

"Esther Lynn, have you died and forgotten to tell me about it?"

To stifle a yelp she clamped a hand over a small mouth prim even in laughter, looked up from her typewriter (with a blank paper on its platen) and essayed a wan smile. Marsh, with his white suit jacket hooked over one shoulder, stood grinning in front of her desk.

"I've been trying to talk to you for five minutes, woman."

"I'm sorry, Galen. Mister Marsh," she said, wrestling with the stammer that betrayed her whenever she grew nervous, "I was thinking about . . ." Her powder-white hands fluttered over the keys and dropped lamely into her lap when he laid his hand on the carriage. Then she saw Jason Clarke waiting just behind him. His expression was solemn, but there was no mistaking the glint of faint bemusement in his dark green eyes.

I don't care what he says, she thought suddenly and rebelliously; there's family there or I'm a coyote.

"Just so you don't go runnin for Jake, I wanted you to know Jase here is takin my rust heap out for a drive," Marsh told her slowly. "And seein as how it's too close to noon to call, we will be headin for lunch first down to Steed's. If," he added dryly, "that's all right with you."

She touched a lace handkerchief to her sharp-edged nose and sniffed. "Long as you don't forget to bring the paper into Blairs."

Marsh looked to Jason, back to her and scowled. "Now how in hell am I gonna forget somethin like that, Esther Lynn?"

She glanced pointedly at his hands, then lifted to her face a pair of rhinestone glasses that were strung from her neck by a length of silver ribbon. "You won't forget it," she said, her voice a decade younger, a decade softer, and somehow twice as stern. "But you'll spend so much time gabbing with Kurt, or anyone who walks in, that you'll be late and we won't get the Saturday edition until Sunday."

He scoffed. "Never happen."

"Twice in March."

"Lucky break for the damned printer."

"Twice in April."

He stood back from the desk and bumped into Jason, but he refused to take a step toward his office. "Don't suppose you'd do me the favor."

She smiled, more at Jason than Marsh. "I always do, don't I?"

Galen stormed outside, muttering, and Jason paused with one foot at the threshold. "Miss Vance, I'm going out to the MacKenzie ranch this afternoon, so I doubt I'll be back before you leave."

"I'll lock up, then," she said, feeling ridiculous for the blush that came after his smile.

"Thanks," he said. "Have a good weekend."

As the door closed behind him—more gently than Galen had ever closed it in his life—her hands went immediately to fuss with the blue-grey fluff of her hair, stopped when she realized what she was doing. She waited until Marsh's blue and white Studebaker sailed past the window.

Marsh. Clarke. Not quite like mirrors, but *damn*, there was something . . .

She tried to hold the thought, but it faded when she recalled Jason's destination. The MacKenzies? She knew Galen had been out there several times since winter broke, and each time he'd returned in a dark, foul-mouthed mood. Not that she blamed him; as much as she sympathized with the Shoshone attempts to make independent livings for themselves, she couldn't help wishing they were a little more friendly. She was afraid that the silence of the Indians and the belligerence of Ted Waters and his crew were drawing a line down the center of the valley, a line that one of these days could be fatal to cross.

And then, she thought sadly, the *Banner* definitely would have something else to print besides market prices and the weather.

The MacKenzies. She shrugged, and reached for the

telephone. What she had wasn't much, she knew as she dialed the first number, but it was certainly better than nothing. Now, if she could only figure out who Jason Clarke *really* was.

(4)

Bea Steed, her pale blonde hair twisted into hasty braids that slapped against her back, tossed her books angrily into her locker, slammed the door and glared at the air vents as if attempting to close them by the sheer force of her rage. Then she turned abruptly to Carole, whose snug plaid shirt and equally snug jeans were more than enough to distract most from noting she was not quite as beautiful as her figure implied.

"He didn't really," Bea said.

Carole nodded solemnly. "I swear to God."

"No," she said, refusing to believe it. "He wouldn't say anything like that. God! I mean—" She stopped herself when she saw Carole's lips twitch. "You're making it up."

Carole's eyes widened in feigned shock. "Who? Me? Do something like that to my best friend?" She crossed her hands over her chest. "Never. I'd die first."

"Carosa . . ."

Carole considered continuing the joke, and changed her mind when she realized it wasn't worth the effort. Once Bea herself got herself started on a rampage, only a full blow-out would settle her, and she wasn't in the mood for a tantrum just now.

"All right," she said wearily, "all right. So he didn't say you got laid last night."

Bea sagged against the locker, one hand grasping the back of her neck. "It wasn't funny, Carole."

"Your trouble is, Steed, you don't have a sense of humor."

"Oh yeah? And suppose someone overheard you, huh? Then . . . then I'd be the one under Reverend Thornton's whip, just like you were." She stopped suddenly and put a hand to her mouth. "Oh. Hey Carole—"

"Don't worry about it, okay? It's history, right? No harm done."

"But Carole, I didn't mean—"

Carole chopped the air with the flat of her hand, and Bea

quieted instantly. They both headed for the school's rear exit, to the treed yard where they could have their lunch and gossip. But as they walked Carole's irritation deepened, and though she knew she was bringing it on herself, she didn't know how to stop. She realized she was getting as bad as Ellie Felsom, finding every little thing wrong with this town—the people in it, her friends—and if she wasn't careful, she wouldn't have any friends, period.

But what difference did it make, she wondered. Once they all graduate, they'll be gone and I'll be stuck here. Playing nursemaid to a big brother and clocking in every night with a chronically worried mother. At the door, she slammed a fist lightly at the frame, ignored Bea's stare and stepped out to the grass.

"I don't see Hardy," she said.

"He's sulking."

"Ah, you wouldn't give him any, huh?"

Bea turned to her, scowling. "Damnit, Carole!"

"Hey, lighten up, all right? God, you'd think the way you talked you had a reputation or something."

As soon as she said it Carole knew she shouldn't have. But there was no taking it back. Bea stalked off to find a table for herself, and Carole leaned against the outside wall, her lunchbag between her feet, unwatched and forgotten.

Shit, she thought sourly; damn, it just isn't fair.

(5)

The top of the railroad embankment was still somewhat soggy after the week's storm. Yet it was the most peaceful place to be in the middle of a schoolday, when all the kids took to the yard for lunch, and the little brats from the grade school wandered over to stare. Not that Hardy minded being stared at; he was used to it, especially from the boys who looked up at his solid bulk and gaped. He knew they were imagining him in his football uniform, and, though it made him feel uncomfortable more often than not, sometimes he couldn't help puffing his chest and putting his hands on his slim hips as though thinking of the next play. Some of the other guys did it, too, and they played the hero for all it was worth.

He finished the roast beef sandwich and drained a quart

carton of milk. Belched. Ran a tired hand through long
brown hair that was combed straight back from his forehead.
He was handsome in a way that older women called rugged,
though his large mouth often seemed too soft, and his black
eyes held none of the sorrow of life that would one day mark
them as his own.

He looked up and saw a hawk circling on the high currents,
and wondered if MacKenzie would ever give him permission
to hike up Kramer's Mountain to see the golden eagles
nesting there. He'd promised Bea he would ask this weekend,
but the nerve wasn't there. He knew he'd been pretty hard on
the Shoshone kids lately, and sure as shit the old man
probably heard about it and would scalp him. And it bothered
him, because while he was doing it it felt fine, it felt harmless;
but when the others bragged about it later he couldn't
remember why he'd done it.

He heard a footfall behind him, and he waited, hoping it
was Bea so they could talk some, or do some making out.

He frowned, deep furrows suddenly creasing his brow. He
didn't understand how she could be so friendly with those
people, or understand what you talk to them about. They
weren't stupid or anything, but god, they were *Indians;* they
might as well come from Russia or something.

A twig snapped, and he half turned, the bright sun partially
blinding him.

"Bea?" He listened. "Hey, Bea, that you?"

They stood in a row just above him, black against the
brilliant blue backdrop. Five, and he recognized the middle
one: a pudgy-faced kid, built thin and lithe with one shoulder
slightly raised. Broad flat nose, high cheeks, high forehead;
his face, unlike Hardy's, was lined, like an old man's.

The milk curdled in his stomach.

Charlie. Oh, shit, Charlie Sweetwater.

He rose slowly, one hand out to give him balance on the
slope. The five Shoshone didn't move or speak, only stared.

"Guys," he said, smiling a greeting that he cursed for being
nervous.

"You like to play with little boys," Charlie said. His left
arm was held away from his body at an odd angle, and Hardy
could see a thick bandage bulging beneath his shirt just above
the wrist.

"What're you talkin about?" he said, and cursed his voice

again. Oh shit; oh . . . shit. He glanced around without moving his head, searching for a weapon.

The two boys on the end began to slip down the slope to flank him.

"Hey," he said, looking only at Charlie, "hey, I'm sorry about your brother, okay? It was . . . I was only . . . hell, you know how it is. We were only teasin, for god's sake." He took a step up. A stone rolled from beneath his boot, and he had to hold his breath to keep from running.

Charlie shook his head in slow, sad disgust. "He's only eight, you stupid hero."

"Hey, man."

"You're a hero, ain't ya? Carry that ball, hit that horse-hide? You got broads up the ass, don't ya? Why'd you wanna pick on a little kid for?"

Another step up, one step to go. Low weeds brushed against his jeans, and his throat suddenly felt painfully dry. The urge to cough was overwhelming. He swallowed instead.

"Your father's a bigshot lawyer, man," Charlie said, backing away to give him suspicious room. "Matter of fact, he's my old man's lawyer." He grinned—his teeth were almost too white, too perfect. "Drew up the papers, hero, so's we could move in, y'know?"

Hardy listened to the tone, searching for a soft spot. He nodded quickly, though the hairs at his nape were beginning to rise. "Yeah, yeah, I remember now." He smiled and reached the top of the embankment. "Yeah, sure. Your father boards horses and stuff like that."

"You shouldn't hurt little kids, Hardy," Charlie said softly.

"What hurt? What the hell you—"

Something—a fist, a branch—clubbed him in the middle of his back, snapping his head up and throwing him forward. A knee clipped his jaw, but he rolled with it to his right, slamming out his hand to the ground—three-point stance, Hardy, charge!—and lunged at the nearest pair of legs, enveloping them and carrying the boy down with him. His head butted into the rib cage, and he was off and up just as two more took him from the left.

"Not the face!" Charlie called out, aloof and watching coldly.

Fuck you, Hardy thought, and lashed out, grunting when

his knuckles split open against teeth, groaning when a
boot-toe caught the top of his thigh. His leg shuddered and
buckled, and a push tipped him over. An explosion in his
buttocks, a blur of red across his eyes. Hands, he thought
desperately, when there was time to think at all; and he
covered his head with crossed arms and drew his knees to his
chest. He felt a lance near his spine and another by his neck, a
rock gouging his chin, a heel crushing his side.

There was no laughter, no instructions, just grunts and
scuffles.

He suspected it was over in less than a minute, but a year
must have passed before he uncovered his head and felt the
tears on his cheeks. He muffled a sharp cry by biting hard on
his lips. Gradually, his legs began to stretch; slowly, he
maneuvered himself onto his knees. Vomited. Spat. Saw the
blood on the weeds, on the cuffs of his shirt. Felt the dirt in
his hair, and the sweat on his face. He was alone. Kneeling in
the dust and wondering how the hell he was going to explain
this to his father.

And: if the Indians enjoyed five-to-one odds, he was
awfully damned sure he could do better than that.

(6)

Jason sat behind the wheel, and Galen leaned toward the
window.

"You look a little nervous, son."

"The Lone Ranger always was, I hear."

"Bullshit."

"I heard that, too."

The fingers of his right hand were drumming on the seat
beside him.

"You know how to get there now?"

"You've only told me six times."

"All right, then."

He looked straight ahead. David Carosa was crossing the
street on his crutches, the sun with every pace freeing a glint
of aluminum at his ankles. A young blonde was waiting for
him at the opposite curb. Jason grinned.

"That Esther Lynn?" he said.

Galen stepped back and squinted into the sun.

"She's not a bad-looking woman, you know."

"Sure."

"I think she likes you."

"How the hell do you know that?"

"I have the eye."

"Then close it. I'm not in the market."

Jason laughed, poked his head out the window to say a quick goodbye and saw a dark shadow sweeping over the town. "Hey, is that a hawk up there?"

Marsh followed his pointing finger. "Eagle."

"Well, I'll be damned."

"Take it easy, son, your city is showing."

Jason started the car, and winced at the grinding before he'd even touched the gearshift. "Onward," he said. "I'll meet you back home. Assuming, of course, that I escape with my life to bring the message back to the fort." He hesitated. "Shouldn't I call ahead or something, Galen? I mean, suppose he doesn't want to see me? It's possible, you know. I'd look like a damned fool."

"Don't worry about a thing, son. By the time you hit MacKenzie land they'll know you're there. They'll probably have lunch cooked and ready to serve before you can find the house. Simon's no ogre. And the only reason he hasn't come to you before this is because he wants to find out what the others think of you first."

"You mean—"

"I told you, didn't I? He knows about you, all right. All you have to do is act natural."

"I hope that wasn't meant to be comforting."

"Oh, it wasn't, Jase, it wasn't."

"You . . . are a bastard."

"Just tell Simon I said hello."

"Will he run me off for it?"

"Try it and see."

Galen touched his elbow. "Good luck."

Jason grinned, and felt the strain. "Ace reporter, remember?"

"Damned good at stallin."

"Yeah . . . well . . ." And he released the hand brake before he started trembling.

(7)

The pinto was small, nimble, the grace of its lines and the brown and white of its markings marred only by a dim blotch of inexplicable red that began beneath its chin and snaked down its throat to the center of its chest. It barely needed more direction than a slight pressure of its rider's knees; and that, thought Greg Thornton, was worth its price in spades. They were partners. They knew the valley, the inner slopes and the drops on the outer rim where the world fell away more than a thousand feet below, better than anyone living; they knew the caves, the nesting places, the aeries, the winter paths almost as well as the birds and animals themselves. They had to. They were poachers, and had been since Greg was fifteen and a tourist on one of the dude ranches had offered him fifty dollars for a hawk's egg. Fifty goddamn dollars for one lousy egg.

Four years he had been defying the law and Simon Mac-Kenzie, and in those four years had been caught only once. His father had paid the fine, and they'd barely spoken since.

Just as well, he thought as they made their way up Kramer's Mountain; being the son of a preacher was bad enough without having to listen to sermons all the time. It wasn't that he didn't love his father, but he felt about the Reverend the way he felt about Windriver—he simply didn't care.

He clucked, and the pinto halted. The trees here were mostly pine, the branches high overhead and the footing centuries cushioned. The light was dim and golden, sometimes tinted with bronze, and he wanted to listen before he broke into the open. His tongue brushed his thick lips, perspiration dropped from the sideburns that swung down along his jaw almost to his chin. He knew they made his face seem more cadaverous than it was, but without them and the mustache they might see the scars. His face was pimply enough without those damned talon scars.

He took off his hat and wiped his brow with a sleeve, blew out a breath and realized he was nervous. And why not? Just three months ago he'd bolted from school and had ridden into Blairs where he'd joined the army on a delayed contract deal.

Then he'd told that fruit of a principal, and the fruit'd been so damned glad he'd just about promised all Greg had to do was show up at graduation and the diploma was his. Anything to get rid of the preacher's shitty kid.

His grin was wide, and held no mirth. Again, he didn't care. He didn't care if the Indians bought up every foot of land, and he didn't care if Ted Waters and his stupid Ranchers' Association burned all the Shoshone out. None of them mattered because he was leaving this burg and everyone in it to go out and be a general.

He laughed, and the pinto shied.

A general. Why the hell not?—

And for his so-long-and-go-to-hell present he was going to take the one thing from Simon MacKenzie that the old half-breed loved more than his wife—the golden eagles that nested midway above the treeline. There were a lot of hunters he knew who would pay over a thousand dollars for one of them birds, a full grand just to say they'd shot it themselves. They were jerks, too.

Again the pinto shied, and Greg frowned, his left hand slowly sliding back over his thigh to touch the butt of his rifle. He never had liked this place. The forest was too thick, the birds too quiet, and the storms that moved over the valley seemed to park here and renew their thunder and lightning for hours. He knew the Indians thought it was special, but he'd never learned why. But he sure as hell agreed it wasn't like the others.

An hour later the trees fell away, and Greg slipped from the saddle to have himself some lunch. The pinto moved off to graze. A wind was soughing in the upper branches, and the animal's ears were pricked high. Greg watched as he ate one of the sandwiches he'd brought, his free hand scratching behind one jugged ear. Ahead and above him the land was treeless, spotted with shrubs and low grass, pocked with large clusters of boulders as the mountain twisted itself into crags and drops, all of it in greys and browns like a capstone of dried mud. He looked away, down to his hands leathered by the sun.

He knew what his problem was: he'd listened too often to the stories about the mountain, the hunters who had gotten lost here, died here, with only their bones found gleaming the next morning. It was dumb thinking about that now; he'd been along these slopes a full dozen times and nothing had ever happened to him. But the browns and the greys and the blinding blue sky seemed somehow *different* from the world he was used to. Dangerous.

A grunt, a spitting; he ordered himself to think about the eagles. Golden eagles. A deep golden brown, never more than ten or fifteen pounds, made huge and vicious only by folks' imaginations. A finger to his jaw. He'd tried to rustle an aerie once, three years ago when he was sixteen, and the female had come at him talons first, screaming. He'd been lucky he'd rolled away or she would have gouged out his eyes. As it was, she had caught his jaw and torn it all to hell. Small. Ten, fifteen pounds tops. Wingspread so wide and powerful it could bat your head off.

He shuddered. That wasn't making him feel much better.

"Hell," he said to his shadow on the ground. "Hell," he said louder. And when he rose to stretch, to get it over with and get the hell out (and the hell with graduation), he saw that the pinto had worked itself back into the trees.

"Hell," he said; and this time it was a whisper.

(8)

Jason held on grimly as the Studebaker's front wheels tried to maneuver their way over patches of winter-raised blacktop, apparently determined to bury themselves in potholes that seemed large enough to hold a cow. He cursed loudly at one shuddering thump, louder when he lifted his foot from the accelerator and ground the gears downshifting. It had been years since he'd last used a manual transmission; since then it had been merely plunking the thing into "Drive" and aiming. He hoped as he shifted again that Cy Oaker or one of his mechanics would know how to repair this beast, because he was as sure as his nerves were fraying that Galen's car would never be the same.

Relax, he told himself then; relax and enjoy the day. If you don't think about it so much, it'll all come back to you and you'll do fine.

The sky through the dust-streaked windshield was filled with a soft golden warmth he usually associated only with New England; the blue was gentle, the peaks less forboding, the breeze carried scents his nostrils ached to discover. He took a deep breath and smiled. On a day like today all things could be conquered.

Galen had said little to him in the office that morning, only mentioned that if he took Middle Valley he'd arrive at the MacKenzie Ranch much later. On the other hand, if he went farther east and used Elkhorn Road—a less traveled route— he would find himself passing the Perkins place.

A pothole snapped at the left front wheel and he bounced, his head thumping against the roof.

Less traveled route, he thought sourly; the last time anybody came by here was in a covered wagon, for god's sake.

He slowed abruptly, his tongue darting to his lips, when the stone fencing on the right gave way to cockeyed railing and a long, fragile-looking counterbalanced gate. Beyond it, on a low rise, was a three-story frame house surrounded by roof-tall trees whose trunks were far too thick to put arms around. The front porch faced the road, and he could just see the corner of another at the rear. A sparkling white barn-and-silo and several outbuildings poked over the rise's back. But his gaze remained on the house, on the tall windows curtained in white, on the chimneys above the roofpeak, on the ill-kept lawn and the ragged garden at the side.

He almost stopped.

And he would have if some ghostly memory had pricked him, some surging of his unconscious had warped the planks he'd laid over the past. But there was nothing. Not a hint, not a whisper, and he nearly wept because somehow he hadn't wanted it this way. It wasn't fair, he told himself with a light slap at the wheel; it wasn't fair to forget a place where one had spent close to six years. It was a part of him, and he should know it. It didn't matter that half the time had been wasted in a bed in a room he could not remember; it didn't matter that he'd overcome the disease that had nearly crippled him. He should at least be able to remember the damned ceiling!

But there wasn't even that; not even the ceiling.

The car sputtered, and he realized he was staring at a dim figure veiled by the front screen door. Must be Gloria Perkins, he decided, and looked away before he could be accused of spying.

Spying on his own house. Oh yeah, I think I remember now, playing with some of the kids in the backyard, walking along the road toward the river, barefoot, hot, watching the grasshoppers buzz at the sun. Oh yeah. Oh yeah. Just like in the movies—everything a shimmering ghostly white, faces blurred, dust lifting, harmonicas playing something in the background. Oh yeah. Oh yeah.

Oh . . . yeah.

Not even the ceiling.

As the house drifted by he wondered if Gloria knew, wondered if she were any kin to the men his father had attacked. And wondered as he looked back to the road if the tree that had taken his father's life was still standing. Not that it mattered. There would be no plaques raised or gun salutes, not for Peter Clarke and the drinking he'd done.

"He was lost, Jason," his mother had told him from the pillows that supported the back she could no longer use. It was a year before she died, the first time she'd spoken of Peter's death to him.

"He left the army thinking he was still back when God was kind and a man could carve himself an empire from the wilderness. He'd been writing to cousin Galen for years, bought that place without asking me. I didn't mind. It was what he wanted. He wanted it so badly he'd sit in the kitchen all night, drawing maps of the land, where he'd build this, where he'd raise that. I saw the letters. Galen tried to tell him the land didn't much care if you were a general or a sergeant, it does what it wants and you have to work with it. Your father, though, he tried to beat it. He couldn't stand not being in control. That's why the army was good for him—he had his place and he controlled it. All those recruits they didn't know any better, and he controlled them.

"Then there was you, Jase. There you were, running around and chasing butterflies and gophers, going with him up the slopes and scared to death of horses. Do you remember that, Jase? You were scared to death of horses. Then you got sick, not walking, something he couldn't control at all, not even the doctors.

"And the land. All those years and he wouldn't admit it, wouldn't take advice and get out. He just kept on trying, his hair going white, thinking if he made it you would walk again, just like that. And he . . . it didn't work. And he started looking for pride in the bottle, I guess. Lots of people kept away, then, and he hated them for it because they pitied you, pitied him. It wasn't their fault. They tried to help out, god knows!

"Then, that last spring, he couldn't take it anymore, I guess. Got himself so drunk . . . took on four hands from MacKenzie's ranch and bloodied them all over the street. He broke two legs, an arm, three wrists, some ribs, nearly poked out an eye and pushed one of them through a window. He didn't have a weapon, Jason, only his fists and his hate. Sheriff Harmon said he took out three yard fences driving out of town, so it wasn't so hard to imagine him hitting that . . . that *damned* tree."

He shuddered, trying to blink away the image of the once-robust woman sinking in front of him. She'd remained in Windriver as long as she could, but though his father was dead the voices, the whispers, the glances wouldn't stop, and she'd run to the East Coast where Galen's letters had kept her from screaming. But when she died the letters slowed. Galen had visited him three times over the next ten years, and Jason found it disturbingly easy to fashion him into a surrogate parent. Too easy, and more than once he'd tried to break away and stand on his own.

And in standing on his own, discovered he was lonely.

He shook his head violently; the present returned. This sure as hell wasn't the right way to get in the mood for what he was going to do. Later, he told himself; feel sorry for yourself later.

Fifteen minutes, and he spotted a large herd of cattle on the left. On the right, a field newly plowed and dark. He squirmed in his seat, anticipating, his attention momentarily caught by Kramer's Mountain. He was four miles closer than when he'd first seen it, and it still bothered him for no discernible reason. And the mood it cast reminded him that the family he was visiting were people who might have stopped all the trouble with a single word, a single warning. He was approaching power, and that power hadn't been used.

He squinted and dropped his gaze to what looked like the mouth of a tunnel rising abruptly above the roadway. He rubbed a knuckle over one eye, leaned forward and saw it was a massive stone-and-wood archway anchored to each shoulder by ten-foot fieldstone pillars. Into the top had been carved the name MACKENZIE. Not too shabby, Simon, he thought, grinning as he realized he'd half expected some sort of fortified gatehouse manned by armed and vicious cowboys whose sole purpose in life was to string up from the nearest cottonwood nosey strangers who might disturb their master.

Not too shabby at all. The man definitely had a honed sense of the dramatic.

The road cleared, potholes and chasms gone. The richly crowned trees lining the narrow verge were too stately and perfect to have grown there entirely naturally. The branches —winter-bent and twisted—laced overhead, and the temperature dropped perceptibly in the foliage tunnel. He wished the air drifting into a green-hazed twilight wasn't quite so filled with wind-writhing shadows.

A gopher scuttled in front of the car, rotund and daring.

A raven perched on a grey-black rock and eyed him, its beak open, its wings partially fluffed.

He looked suddenly in the rearview mirror, saw nothing but the road, and the shadows, and the distance closing the tunnel.

"You're spooking yourself, pal," he muttered without smiling.

Another ten minutes and the road divided—the left branch was solidly blocked by a tall gate entwined with barbed wire and chains, the right open and leading in a gentle sweeping curve to a large house he saw squatting in the open almost a mile away. Behind it was the bulk of Kramer's Mountain, paradoxically lending the house size instead of diminution. He slowed, breathing easier, savoring the luxurious profusion of wildflowers and shrubs that added stark, raw color to the landscape. The resulting impression was admirable: he was coming to the home of a man who had considerable wealth and who did not permit himself to use it in rearranging nature. It was at once blatant and subtle, and he found himself admiring the family for resisting the temptations their bank account must have offered. There could, in fact, have been a castle back here, or a misplaced chateau, or any one of a dozen variant mansions that proclaimed rather than stated.

Though he would not call it a reporter's instinct for a story, he couldn't help a wry grin at the electric sweep of anticipation through his chest.

It was then he realized he hadn't seen a single vehicle on the road since leaving the Pike. Not that there should have been; from what Galen had told him, the MacKenzies were the only ones at this end of the valley—the dude ranches kept to themselves on the far western rim. Still, the back of his neck began to tingle.

"Ah well, into the breach, old son," he said for the sound of his voice. "Be charming, be innocent, and keep your foot out of your mouth."

The road narrowed gradually and became a drive that crept up to and away from the house, doubling back on itself to form a black river around an island of bright spring flowers centered by a single white birch. There were no other cars that he could see.

He stopped.

Kramer's Mountain was gone; there was only the house.

It was low, long, evidently rather deep. Stone and slate were smoothed to dull gleaming by the weather's polish, broken only by a profusion of rounded windows crouched under the porch's broad roof. Low evergreen shrubs hugged the foundation, and a meticulously trimmed lawn carpeted at least three acres. A few dark birds nestled comfortably between the brick chimneys rising above the roof's peak. When he turned off the engine the echo of its grumbling was swallowed whole, without a whisper.

Slowly, he wiped his hands against his trousers, and opened the car door. He climbed out, stared at the porch and sensed he was being watched. He tugged at the edges of his suit jacket, straightened the tips of his open collar and walked calmly around the car's hood, one hand grazing the warm metal while the other dove for the protection of his pocket.

He was almost at the steps when the front door opened and Simon MacKenzie walked out.

(9)

Greg stretched out with a rock at his back. He had seen the eagles moving away on the hunt, so there was plenty of time to take a nap. He checked for intruders, for MacKenzie's men, then sloped his hat down over his eyes and folded his arms across his chest. His rifle lay close at hand, ready for firing in case someone jumped him, or if he was stalked by whatever was killing the animals. That bothered him. He'd never seen anything like it before, and though no one had asked him he was positive it was some kind of winter-maddened bear. The trouble there was, the feeding that was done wasn't extensive enough.

He hugged himself snugly and thought instead of the money he'd be getting for the eagles. He snorted aloud. After all these years he'd be getting back at them damned birds for what they'd done to his face. That, he decided, would be worth doing for free.

(10)

The room, like the exterior, had been designed to appear much larger than it was. The ceiling was vaulted and criss-crossed with thick oak beams from which hung mobiles. Jason was startled to discover they were constructed of animal bones and feathers sculpted into stylized semblances of the original creatures. A major portion of the broad-plank floor-ing was dropped to form a pit in front of the huge stone fireplace, and the furniture scattered throughout was dark ponderosa pine and heavily upholstered. Wall hangings de-picted buffalo hunts, dawns, sunsets, storms and a few deep-shaded scenes he didn't understand. Over the black marble mantel was a large elkhide shield in the center of which were arranged four eagle's legs, talons extended as though they were grasping.

There was an abundance of light from the windows and floor lamps; nevertheless, there were shadows, areas of shifting darklight, especially around the ceiling where the mobiles hovered and waited.

Simon MacKenzie sat in a high-backed chair in front of the hearth. He wasn't as tall as Jason imagined him to be and was thick-waisted and round-shouldered, the breadth of his arms the only unaffected signs left of a once powerful and physical-ly intimidating man. His light-skinned face was walnut-lined, his hair dark and straight, and the sharp nose and prominent cheekbones were the most visible and recognizable legacy of his Shoshone mother. When he smiled—which Jason was pleased to see was often—his incredibly blue eyes vanished into rippling folds, and when he laughed he held his hands over his paunch as if to prevent the flesh there from burying his silver buckle.

He had greeted Jason warmly and effusively, demanding politely to know why he hadn't come out earlier, paying absolutely no attention at all to Jason's sheepish, fumbling excuses. He took hold of his arm and brought him inside where the old man bellowed for coffee and biscuits, which were served by a plain young woman in a deerskin dress and spangled headband.

She said nothing, not even when Jason thanked her.

"This is Palemoon," MacKenzie told him as she poured his coffee. "You probably know we don't have any children, so—" He frowned briefly, and the girl left. "I'm trying to think of a more polite term than servant. Assistant?" He laughed. "No matter. She's Rachel's favorite, and they're all women around here. Making up for what I can't produce, I guess."

He picked up a mug of rich dark coffee and toasted Jason silently. "Rachel doesn't mind, of course. The young people these days, especially among our own kind, have what you call your modern notions, even on the reservation. They don't respect age, they think only of money and how it'll get them into the cities. They're too young to understand what they have, and too impatient to learn."

Jason nodded politely, though he couldn't help feeling that he'd missed something there, something he hadn't been intended to know.

"I suppose you're not married, Mister Clarke?"

"No. I've never had the chance, been on the move too much."

MacKenzie nodded. "Yes. Yes, I can see that in you. I can see it." He smiled, and the eyes vanished. "But you'll do all right," he said quietly. "I think you'll do all right."

Jason brought his cup to his lips, sipped and nearly gagged on the coffee's strength. He did not know what to say, and could not force his gaze away from the pleasant stare Mac-Kenzie leveled at him. Not impolite, but querying; not demanding, but patient. It was evident the man was filling time, preparing for an entrance that would mark his wife's arrival. And it was just as evident he had a few things of his own on his mind.

Jason waited, wondering which would come first.

"Mister Clarke," MacKenzie said then, leaning forward with his hands grasping his knees, "why are you here? I don't mean at the house. Why did you come to Windriver?"

A door at the far side of the huge room opened before Jason could swallow and fashion an answer. He smiled weakly at the man's fleeting scowl, set the cup on the table beside him and rose.

Rachel was a full head taller than her husband, far more slender, her ghostly white hair braided thickly and hanging down over her chest. She wore a simple dress of deep earthen brown, short-sleeved and fringed at the hem. Her feet were bare and she wore no jewelry. She walked heavily, leaning her left hand hard on the top of an ivory-headed cane. At a distance she was aged; by the time she reached the two steps leading into the pit he could see that her face belonged to a woman one-third her age—the planes soft, the mouth softer, the eyes brown and youthful, only a slightly wrinkled neck betraying her years.

She was beautiful.

She smiled and held out a hand. "Mister Clarke," she said, and more years dropped from her.

Her fingers were smooth, her touch somewhat warm, and the dark eyes that examined his face brimmed with amusement at his confusion.

"Rachel," MacKenzie said, his voice coated with concern; but she waved him silent without glancing once in his direction and settled herself on a couch midway between them.

"He worries about me," she said to Jason. Her hand brushed lightly over her chest as he sat. "I've been plagued with infarctions and infractions and who knows all what else." She smiled again. "He worries."

No need, he thought. From the moment she'd entered the room it had been obvious which of them wielded the power in this place.

"Simon," she said then, "there's a poacher on the mountain."

Jason glanced quickly at the far door, back to see Simon

rising from his chair. The walnut creases of his face had hardened, and the blue of his eyes had shaded to flint. Then, as though someone had touched him, he dropped back and crossed his legs.

"Excuse me," Jason said, remembering something Galen had told him, "but don't you have eagles up there?"

"Goldens," Rachel said, her smile this time inner-directed.

"But aren't you worried that this poacher, whoever it is, will—"

"He'll be taken care of," Simon told him.

"Yes," said Rachel. "We'll send someone after him."

Jason waited, but neither of them moved.

Between them was a coffee table hewn whole out of redwood, and MacKenzie reached into a humidor placed on it for a thin, long cigar. He looked to his wife, then lighted it and tossed the match over his shoulder into the fireplace. The smoke eased between his lips. He watched it, followed it to the ceiling, settled back and said, "Galen sent for you, didn't he."

The abrupt change of topic startled him, and he caught himself before he bridled, understanding he'd not been asked in malice. "Galen was . . . worried," he said.

"He has reason to," MacKenzie said solemnly.

"He thought perhaps someone from the outside, without any deep attachments here, could get a better grasp of things. An uninvolved observer, something like that."

"And what if that happens, Mister Clarke," Rachel asked him softly. "What do you plan to do about your . . . observations?"

"Easy enough," he answered earnestly. "Talk."

"Lots of that around here," MacKenzie muttered.

"So I've heard," Jason said. "But it's been a good deal of the wrong kind, don't you think? Now, I'm no expert in these matters, but if I keep my nose clean and stay honest with people, there's a good chance somebody will listen to me better than to someone else. I'm not known to be on one side or the other, so I'll just try to talk as much as I can. To you, for example."

MacKenzie seemed startled; Rachel not at all.

"Look," said Jason eagerly, "if half of what Galen tells me is true, and if half of what I hear and see I'm interpreting correctly, you're about the most influential man within fifty miles, Mister MacKenzie. Now I . . . I don't mean to be rude, but I have to be blunt—why haven't you done anything to calm things down? Why haven't you gotten those Indians and whites together and really talked out what's going on around here? It's your valley too, right?"

"I do what I can," MacKenzie said after a moment's hesitation. "But talking with someone like Ted Waters is like talking to a brick wall. And it should be clear I'm in a rather awkward position myself."

Jason looked to Rachel, but her eyes were closed. Listening. Absorbing. Her hands were carefully folded in her lap. "How so?"

MacKenzie's smile was rueful. "I'm not exactly the whitest Scot you've ever seen, Mister Clarke. I may have power when it comes to finance, but I'm still an Indian—worse, I'm a half-breed to Waters and his kind. Anything I say to favor the Shoshone wouldn't be listened to because I'd be accused of having a personal interest. A racial one. And if I argue the other side, I'm a traitor." He spread his hands in a gesture of helplessness. "I've decided, reluctantly, that the best I can do now is stay out of it until I can come up with a way to initiate a compromise."

"And what about the killings?"

Rachel's eyes flicked open, but she said nothing.

"I know nothing about them," the rancher snapped. "They're dreadful, obscene, tragic, whatever you want to call them. But when Harmon catches whoever is involved, we'll—"

"Whoever? I thought it was some predator doing it."

MacKenzie laughed silently, shaking his head. "Jason, if you listen very carefully to the people who say that you'll learn it's only a smoke screen. Nobody, and I mean nobody, believes there's a ravenous wolf lurking around here just waiting to pull down a ton-and-a-half bull in its prime. They're talking animals, and they mean people. The only thing is, nobody wants to be the one to make the first accusation."

Jason hadn't come to argue, only to discover where this family's sympathies lay; yet he found something in the man's manner that was curiously bothersome—almost as if he did not want the power which automatically came with his position. And when faced with it, he denied he could control it. It didn't make sense; not for a man who had ruled a virtual empire for over half a century.

"Accusations," MacKenzie repeated. "And that means Indians, pure and simple. Don't let anyone kid you, m'boy, they're talking about Indians." He paused and shifted. "Jealous, of course. They're jealous of all the money, made and offered. Jealousy, mark my words. But damnit, if men like Daniel Tallpines have the means to get off the reservation and back to the land that belonged to their ancestors, why not? Why the hell not? It isn't a crime, is it? It's their land, isn't it? Who says they have to do what the previous owners did? You know, Jason, it's bad enough they're laughed at by their own people—Daniel and his friends—for what they believe in, so where is it written that they have to do—"

"Simon," Rachel said quietly.

MacKenzie held his breath, sucked in his cheeks, released the air in a slow, silent whistle as he sat back and shrugged.

Barely concealing an apprehensive frown, Jason looked to the woman and wondered at the power she possessed that could shut off a man by the simple mention of his name. But when she glanced in his direction he looked quickly back to Simon, replaying silently the fervent speech with undisguised fascination, seeing his own attitude and hearing his own voice arguing those identical points with Galen. Further, he realized the rancher was too emotionally involved despite his protestations. He warned himself to end it, now, before he said something inadvertently, something to snap the thin leash Rachel held on the man's temper.

He couldn't.

"Nevertheless, sir, you have to realize that what they're doing is causing trouble. And I find it hard to credit that they don't know it. And even if, as you say, you can't talk to Waters, couldn't you at least have a word with Tallpines, to kind of nudge him into taking some steps to calm some fears? Isn't it fair—"

"What," said Rachel, "is fair, Jason? To Mister Waters, fair is being able to sell his products as he always has, to no matter who holds the land. To the Shoshone, fair is paying very good money for the land to do with what they wish." She smiled sadly. "You're not totally young, Jason. You should have learned by now there is *no* universal fair." The smile suddenly grew mischievous. "And isn't this, after all, what the white man wanted of the Indian? To learn capitalism? To learn to survive in the white man's world? And in that world, Jason, don't you admire the survivors, the initiators, the forward-seeking?"

He almost lost his temper in the struggle to tell her this was hardly a classic circumstance, but in the glow of her expression he could only sputter until he was laughing, his palms up to concede the point and end the subject for now.

"Besides," MacKenzie said, "we're not complete ogres to everyone, you know. Lots of young people come out here to talk to my wife, isn't that right, Rachel?"

She nodded, shyly.

"Why . . ." The man gestured grandly. "Why, there's that little Carole Carosa, the barber's daughter? She likes to sit and read to my wife just about every week, and has done so since my wife's illness last year."

"Now, Simon . . ."

He snapped his fingers. "And don't forget that skinny one, Bea Steed. Seems like every time you turn around she's doing another term paper on folklore and things like that. And then . . . then there was Ellie."

Jason sat up.

MacKenzie sighed. "Before her troubles, that is. She was like Carole, she was, and Bea. Almost like a daughter." His face darkened, "Of course, her husband—Ellie's, that is—he doesn't much care for us, you know. After she came back from the hospital . . ." He shrugged philosophically. "Only see her in town now and then."

"A lovely girl," Rachel remarked gently. "They're all lovely girls."

"And they put our Indian girls to shame," Simon muttered. "Like that little tramp, Dawn Sweetwater."

"Simon."

"God, Jason, you'd think Rachel's own people, *our* young people, would want to help out the way those other girls have. But no, they're too interested in boys, white boys, and in forgetting where the hell they came from, where the hell—"

"Simon." Spoken easily, stopping his tirade like a gag.

Jason held a polite smile, believing MacKenzie grew incensed over what was probably an imagined snub, or simply an example of the clichéd generation gap.

"They're children," Rachel said by way of excusing. "Just children, Jason. No different from any other."

But you, he thought admiringly, are a remarkable woman. And he lost himself deliberately in her trilling voice while she told stories of how she'd met Simon, how she'd fared those first months away from the reservation, how Simon and she had taught the children—Indian and white—the history of the Shoshone in hopes of diluting what they saw on televison and in films. Her hands sketched tapestries in the air between them, erased and recreated them. Her young woman's face aged slightly, and rightly, and he saw in her a matriarch neither haughty nor vainglorious, not self-pitying or stalking martyrdom. She was, simply, a self-assured woman who treasured her family, reason . . . and her people above all else.

She was the calming.

MacKenzie, on the other hand, managed to imply a threat in a simple grunt, a sideways glance, a shifting in his chair when Rachel enthused too greatly.

Jason absorbed it all; the sorting would have to come later, when he was free of her delightful influence, and MacKenzie's glaring.

And before he knew it he was back behind the wheel, the MacKenzies leaning over to bid him farewell.

"It's to Galen's credit that he's trying," she told him, one hand covering his. "But it will end as it will end, Jason. Some people will be hurt and others untouched. It's change. To stand before it is like trying to dam the Wind River without having its banks overflow."

"Maybe," he said, hoping to match the gentleness of her tone, "but it wouldn't hurt to put up some sandbags along the banks, would it? Just in case."

She laughed lightly and nodded, though her eyes were serious. Simon invited him back, any time, for a feast he claimed would put meat on his bones for the coming winter.

"And Jason," he said as Rachel made her way back to the house, "would it surprise me to find you're Peter Clarke's son?"

"No," he said, suddenly wary.

"I didn't think so." He straightened, surveyed the garden, the lawn, then thumped the car's fender. "Welcome home."

Jason drove away quickly, too many conflicting emotions

and thoughts vying for his attention. It wasn't until he was well into the foliage tunnel that he realized the sun was already beginning to edge over the horizon. The air chilled, and he turned on the heater; the sky darkened hazily to twilight, and he didn't look at the raven still perched on its boulder. He hummed tunelessly. He kept his eyes on the road. He told himself he should be pleased with the meeting's outcome, but he couldn't help feeling something had been missing. A vital part of their communication had been fogged over and nearly forgotten. Which part, however, he couldn't say yet.

He slowed at the archway and twisted around for a glance at the lower slopes of Kramer's Mountain. He wondered if Simon would pursue the trespasser himself, wondered how Rachel had known about it . . . and could not help feeling that the poacher, whoever it was, had picked the wrong woman to defy by threatening her eagles.

The car jounced out of a pothole. The twilight thickened. Jason couldn't help wishing he were comfortably (safely) home.

TWO

(1)

The Teaching began with a woman they called Dark Moon *(Father Wind I am ready, Mother Night I am waiting);* and it began again with the words that brought the dying *(bring me power bring me strength).* The pain had been there when the words were first said, the pain that was lessened to a prick upon the soul.

And when the words had been spoken *(let my spirit be my brother's, let my spirit be my brother's),* had been chanted *(Father Wind, Mother Night),* had been sung *(set me free)* . . . when the Teaching and the words *(let me) (hunt)* had faded with the pain *(let me hunt)* . . . *it moved into the evening with a cry to mark its freedom. A cry that was different from those which came before. A cry that told the darkness it needed nothing but itself. Itself, and the words that brought a prick upon the soul.*

Instructions had been given, and it sped toward the woodland, toward the Mountain. Swift. Silent. No longer accepting instruction for command. It was free, and those instructions were taken only for direction. It moved toward the woodland because it wanted food.

(2)

The door at the end of the long corridor was six inches thick and solid unadorned oak. Its black iron studs and bands were edged with brass unpolished and fading. No sound bled through the wood, no light crept past the threshold, and when it was closed as it was tonight, not even Simon was permitted to enter.

The corridor was dark; the room nearly so.

Two candlesticks four feet tall had been placed in the center of the floor an arm's length apart. Their bases were clawed (the talons of an eagle), their posts carved and unpainted in a hideous design that only vaguely resembled a grizzly, an otter, an elk and a wolf. At the top of each was a sharply hooked beak to hold a thick candle. The candles were lit, but the light did not touch the walls of the room, or the ceiling, or the floor except to form a shimmering golden circle within which Rachel knelt.

(Father Wind, Mother Night)

Her hair was unbraided now and fell rippling to her waist, its edges forming a cloak of sparkling fog. In her left hand she held a small, fragile bone to which a brown feather had been tied; in her right hand a leather bag that held dead grass and earth, pine needles and cones, the dried heart of a cougar, the waxen eyes of a snake, small beads formed from flower seeds and blood and a sinew-bound parchment upon which the Words had been written.

(Let me hunt)

Her eyes were closed, and her lips quivered with strain, and the mask of youth she had worn for the young man's visit had been stripped away by her effort. Now she was old. Ancient. Vitality and purpose eroded with pain; her skin turned sallow, flaking, as though the husk of a wind would strip her to the bone. Her back was straight, her spine rigid, and she ignored as best she could the knives circling her thighs. She could not move; she dared not move; she kept her face lifted to the light of the candles, her arms slightly outstretched and her fingers gripping the relics.

And she would stay there if she had to until the next dawn.

In the beginning it had been so simple she should have known there would be trouble. All the complications that had been envisioned she had reasoned away with this argument and that prayer, this holy dream and that telling nightmare. And when the reasoning was done and the preparations made, she knew she had set in motion the formation of the perfect circle that, once completed, would prove to the doubters that the Teaching had not been in vain.

She had planned for three stages, three segments in one month for the circle to be drawn.

She would first send a message to all those who might oppose her, perhaps kill her . . . a message intended to invoke fear and running, and the message at the start would be transmitted through Simon. Once the fears had been implanted and the running begun, then would follow the Words of the Teaching, the Words that would be the midwife to the birth of the True Messenger, adding to the fear of confusion the very real fear of death. And this Messenger born of midnights and bloodings, of screams and anguish, this Messenger would at last close the circle with the bright shout of triumph, of completion . . . of a singular conquest that would, in itself, mark the beginning of yet another circle, a larger one, that would reach out from this valley to encompass the sky.

From message to conquest in the life of a moon.

The muscles in her legs began to tremble, and she sagged. She struggled but could not bring herself upright for more than a few seconds at a time.

In the beginning she had been fortunate. Simon had his money and the sharing of her dream. The smaller dream. The first circle. She herself had had decades of careful studying and painful practice, and only the treachery of her own body had prevented her from working the full Teaching last year. Now, however, she had overcome. She had spurned the diagnoses of the white doctors, defied the pummeling of winter, and with Simon's unstinting help was ready for spring.

Her buttocks reached her heels, but she kept her arms high.

Faintly, through the French doors that broke the north wall
of her room, she heard a horse pounding over the grass
toward the mountain. It would be Simon, a distant part of her
part acknowledged, riding to the place of the feeding in case a
burial was needed. She almost smiled. She almost wondered
how a man could love a woman so much that he would bury
himself as Simon had in the pursuit of a conquest that would
surely mean his dying.

She almost thought, she almost wondered, but a renewed
surge of concentration kept her thinking safely penned. She
could not break away now. As it was (and she couldn't help it,
the sensation was too strong), she was afraid she had already
lost it. The idea tormented her and robbed her of sleep—that
somehow her body's treachery had returned, and the control
she had was gone. It was the only thing she feared, the only
thing she dreaded; as much as she had tried, she could not
trust the Teaching to complete the circle without her. Not
now. Not when she had so much to do. Not when it was
time for her people to know what it meant to have true
power.

And true power meant the control of men's lives; and the
control of men's lives meant the control of their dying.

The boy had been the sacrifice to give life to the Teaching.

The animals were only food, and used for mere practice—
but now they were spared.

It was men who would run, and men who would bleed, and
men who would know soon that she was their breathing.

Two more weeks, she thought. Two weeks of dying and the
circle would be done.

Her arms weakened. She sobbed.

I control you, she commanded; you are mine, you are
mine. . . . *It plunged into the shadows, its cry very much like
laughter.*

(3)

Jason decided he was going to stop trying to estimate people
by outside appearances; facades, it seemed, were determined
to get him. He grinned wryly and belched behind a loose fist.
He reached for the tall glass of beer that had been placed
generously in front of him, then changed his mind about

finishing it. It was tempting, but enough was enough, at least for the time being.

After he had returned from the MacKenzie ranch and, at Galen's suggestion, changed his clothes at the house, he and Galen had had their supper in the luncheonette, where Jason had extolled Peg Steed's cooking at Galen's morose expense. Then the editor had concluded it was high time the new boy stopped playing the hermit (as if it had been Jason's idea, not his) and dragged him over to Carosa's bar, where curiosities could be sated and Jason stuffed with ale.

He was, almost guiltily, impressed.

The place was far larger than he'd imagined from the small window and narrow red door outside, replete with a fair number of small round tables and blue-and-white-checkered cloths centered with red-and-gold faceted lamps with fat-bellied candles. There were oils on the walnut-paneled walls depicting the valley at varying turns of the seasons and, as far as he could tell, not a speck of dirt to be seen. Mary Carosa (a shorter, red-cheeked, flat-bosomed version of her husband) cheerfully and noisily waited tables; Tony and David—on a special platform which made allowances for the wheelchair— were settled behind the mahogany bar. Sandwiches could be had if Mary weren't busy, and at the prices Carosa charged for liquor Jason wondered aloud how he managed to stay in business.

"Volume," the grinning Italian said, his hairy left hand scratching vigorously through his curls. "Ain't no place else to go. I got the monopoly."

In the back corner were several pinball machines, a dart-board, billiards and a shuffleboard table; the complete home-away-from-home entertainment center, Jason thought. And thank god it didn't have the maddening pings and buzzes of those electronic games.

It was obvious to Jason from the start that Windriver considered the place its major attraction. Virtually every age was represented, every home, and the only one who didn't seem to be enjoying himself was grizzled Stan Kelly, who had staked out a lone stool at the bar's far end and was keeping himself in the shadows, drinking slowly but steadily. In a quick aside between drinks, Marsh told him that Kelly's ranch, just west of MacKenzie, had been sold a year ago, and the man (unlike the others who'd given up their land) insisted on sticking around to drink up his profits.

"Not to mention wandering around and muttering about Custer and Sitting Bull. You can find him during the day over at the graveyard, sweatin' out the booze from the night before." Galen had grinned. "He sees more ghosts than an old maid. You just smile and walk away."

It was not difficult to note, however, that by nine-thirty not one of the Indians had come in. Nor had Ted Waters. Jason didn't have to ask, nor did he need telling that it had not always been this way.

Someone in passing nudged his back with an elbow and he turned, curious, trying to make out the face in the gloom. There had been so many, and so many new names, but he thought he had filed most of them and would have no trouble bringing them out when the occasion arose. In addition, many of the locals—from Mac Felsom to Doc Vance—had spent a good deal of time at the table his cousin had chosen. It was, he thought somewhat uncomfortably, rather like holding court; but courtesies had been observed, and his acceptance was far more swift than he would have imagined in such a small community.

He was grateful, and relieved, and the disquiet he'd felt after leaving the MacKenzies was smothered for a time. So he beat Earl Carson and Carosa in a long game of darts and was beaten soundly in return. He exhibited a certain prideful prowess to some of the older high school students at the pinball machine (wondering as he did if Hardy Green was always so stiff); argued heatedly and marvelously with Mac and his son, Artie (off-duty and prowling), over the nebulous future of the western railroads, OPEC notwithstanding; and spent a lot of time—more time than he thought—hoping Donna Oldfield would come in to join him.

Finally, he told Galen he had to step outside for some fresh air before he keeled over. Marsh only nodded, caught as he was by Esther Lynn and Bertha Castlewitz (the business half of the team that owned the theater) in a crossfire of rumors he couldn't pass up.

At the door Jason heard someone call his name. He was tempted to ignore it but looked back over his shoulder and saw David Carosa at the end of the bar. He had heard several

times of Harmon's life-saving rescue, had seen the young man
earlier forsake the wheelchair for his crutches. Later, the
crutches had vanished as David tested his legs' prosthetic
balance. It wouldn't be long, he'd thought, before the
crutches would be gone and the wheelchair collecting dust
and the only sign of the accident would be Carosa's peculiar
awkward gait.

"Jason," David said, beckoning him close. His hair was like
his father's, his face like his mother's. A twenty-five-year-old
cherub with permanent anguish marked about his eyes.

"You leavin?"

Jason grinned. "Need air, Dave. Got to walk off some of
the drinking."

Carosa nodded. "Yeah. Well, listen, if you should run into
Steve Felsom, would you do me a favor?"

"Sure."

Carosa looked away to his father's back, but not before
Jason had seen his jaw tighten. "I, uh, have this book, see,
that Ellie's been wantin. If you see Steve, ask him if Ellie's
better, if I can bring it over to the house."

"Why don't you ask him yourself? He doesn't bite, does
he?"

Carosa's expression turned sour. "No. He and I, we don't
always see eye to eye on things, is all." He shrugged. "Just
thought I'd ask."

"If I see him, I'll tell him."

Carosa grinned. "Thanks, Jase. Appreciate it."

Jason waved vaguely and left, slipping a note into his
mental file to ask Galen what, if anything, had gone on
between Dave and the sheriff's daughter. If there was something, it apparently ended with the young man's accident.
And Ellie's surprise marriage.

Gossip, he scolded himself; no, he replied, only grist for
the mill.

The air was paper crisp. He leaned back against the bar
window, shoved his hands into his pockets, lowered his head
and waited for the mustiness to pass. He was grinning, he
knew, but did not care. The people of Windriver had assessed
him, and, for the most part, favorably, he thought. Not one
of them had asked if he'd ever been here before, and most of
those who might remember hadn't shown up at all. His grin

widened. It was a comfortable feeling; not yet a sense of belonging because he knew, even in his daydreams, it was far too soon; and he wasn't even positive he was really looking for that. Not yet. He was, he reminded himself as he began to walk down the street, in the West, not New England. Here it was not the years that brought the belonging, but the proof of ability.

Maybe, he thought and not entirely casually, maybe I'll take a walk over to Donna's place. His grin broke into a short barking laugh. A memory: in love and in high school, accidentally-on-purpose walking past a house in which his lover was waiting—not for him, but for her date, because she didn't know he was alive. But he wanted, he needed just to see her through the window. A shadow. A glimpse. And perhaps she would look out, see him strolling and beckon.

It never happened. But neither had it stopped him from taking that walk.

He looked up and saw a woman standing on the corner, fumbling in her purse. A woolen cap was pulled down over her hair, a heavy beige cardigan covering her to the middle of her thighs. She wore jeans and boots. He smiled automatically as he passed, stepped down off the curb, then stopped.

"Jason?" she said with uncertainty, and a touch of amusement.

(the shade snapped up; the girl/woman beckoned)

"Oh. Hi!" He returned to the sidewalk, reminding himself of his age while he looked everywhere in town but at her face. "How are you, Miss Oldfield?"

"Donna."

"Sure."

He rolled a pebble with the toe of his boot, hands still in his pockets and pressed hard against his legs, as he prayed fiercely and suddenly not to be too drunk.

"It's funny," Donna said, indicating with a nod his Stetson and leather coat, "but you don't look like a cowboy."

He grimaced. "If you must know, it was Galen's idea. I feel like an idiot."

"Actually," she said, stepping back and appraising, "you don't look too bad. Not great, mind, but not bad."

He grinned inanely. "Were you, ah . . ." and he gestured blindly toward the bar.

"Yes, sooner or later. I was on my way to see a friend first."

"Oh. Well, that's . . . good."

A silence expanded as a car pulled to the curb, snapped off its lights, and several young people clambered out on the street, crossed it and darted into the movie house.

The patrol car ghosted by.

"Is there such a thing as loitering in this town?" he said, watching the sedan brake at the next intersection.

Donna laughed quietly, into her hand. He looked to her sharply, suddenly tense, suddenly warm, until her gaze lowered to his fractured shadow on the pavement.

"This friend of yours," he said, sniffed once, cleared his throat. "Would he mind if a stranger bought you a drink?"

"How do you know it's a he?"

A dozen coyly gallant phrases leapt to mind and were discarded. "It's Friday night," he said lamely.

"It's a boxer," she said.

"Huh?"

She laughed again and took hold of his arm, turning him and leading him back to the bar. "A boxer. A pregnant boxer. I'm a vet, remember? Cy Oaker has a pregnant boxer and I was going to stop by to see how she was doing. Due any day now, and Cy's worse than a father."

His smile was dutiful, his reactions confused, and he felt the blush swarming up from his neck when she opened the door for him and waved him inside.

Jason, he told himself, you are getting into trouble.

(4)

Greg stood in the center of a large clearing and glared defiantly at the cold stars above him. His hat was tilted far back on his head, and the short leather coat he'd slipped on an hour ago was zipped to the neck. Damn, he thought, somehow those frigging stars had been a part of all this. They sure as hell weren't giving him any help now.

He had awakened from his nap long after dark, shivering, his teeth chattering like a scolding squirrel. The pinto was calling to him nervously. The tops of the trees below were beginning to bend to the rise of a slow wind. He had filled the air with his curses, alternately damning himself and the sunset for not waking him in time. Now he would have to take on both eagles at once, and he definitely wasn't looking forward to the way he knew they would work in perfect tandem. It was, in fact, only a glimmer of a reminder of the money he would make that sent him scrambling up the slope, slipping, sliding once ten feet down an incline slippery as mud, wondering when in hell the stupid moon was going to give him some light.

And when it came it was grey, adding shadows to the boulders to give them height, creating cave mouths in the hillside where none existed. He used the rifle for a staff, moving in a low crouch so he could avoid spills of rock that would betray his approach. For a while he was confident. He had made fairly good time, and even in the dark knew where the aerie was—on a projection of rock overlooking the valley. From below it was inaccessible, but there was a broad ledge that approached it from the south. If he could make his way around a protruding finger of granite he would have a clear field of fire. Two shots, on the wing or in the nest. Two shots, and he would be two thousand dollars richer.

But the moon had tricked him.

It showed him a path he hadn't realized was there, seemingly a quicker way to the ledge than the trail he was following. The trouble was, it brought him to a precipice a hundred yards below the aerie. And now he was stuck. He could just about make out the nest directly above him, but he wasn't sure he would be able to retrace his steps and get up to the ledge without making a sound. He had to be close to have a proper chance.

Silently he tapped the rifle against his leg, trying to think while the cold tightened the pocked skin that climbed from his beard. He couldn't go straight up; that would be suicide even in daylight. He had no choice. What he had to do was wait for a while until his disgust and temper calmed and his instinct took over. They had never failed him before, and they wouldn't fail him now.

Luck. What he needed was a little bit of luck. He had been given the bad streak, now he waited for the good.

Meanwhile, he gazed out over the valley, at the starpoints of houselights winking through the foliage lining all the streets, at the blacker slash of the river that rejected all reflection, at the distant rim where the Pike suddenly leapt over and down and made its way to Blairs where his future was waiting.

He was staring so hard he almost missed the windsound.

(5)

Stan Kelly's tractor had been driven into the warehouse for the night, and a light dangled above it, casting too many shadows for Waters to be comfortable. The others, however, didn't seem to mind, and they grumbled as they perched on packing crates and sacks, or leaned against the posts that supported the peaked roof. There were a dozen of them, and they were angry. At Billyboy Perkins.

"It's wrong," said Waters, recapturing his spokesman's role after a flurry of muffled shouting. "I don't care how much you're gonna make, Billy, it's wrong and you know it. They're up to something. I don't know what, but I'll bet my life on it. And now you come here bald-faced like that and sell us all out."

Perkins shook his head sorrowfully as the others echoed Waters's rage.

None of the men assembled in the feed-store warehouse had more than a subsistence stake in the valley; but subsistence was what most of them knew, and they worked hard for it. And seeing Perkins ready to cut loose just when it appeared Stan Kelly had been the last of the desertions intensified their anger and frustrated disappointment.

"Now, wait a minute," Perkins said harshly, his Marine-cut hair like a black skullcap under the dim bulb, perspiration staining his shirtfront and under his arms. "There's nothin better I'd like to do than stick around here, and you all know that for a fact. But damnit, a man's got a right to live, and if he gets a chance to live big he's gotta take it. And you know that, too. Do you think . . ." He took a deep breath to hold back his fury. "Do you guys think I'm really gonna pass up one hundred and fifty thousand bucks just because you're afraid of a few drunken Indians who don't do nothin all day but sit on their asses? Do you really think I'm gonna pass all that up?"

He spat dryly and turned his back on the group for a

moment, looked over his shoulder and saw them glaring at him. Not because he was wrong, he thought, but because they knew he was right. Because if they were in his shoes and an offer of that much money was made for their land, they'd grab it in a minute and the hell with Ted Waters and his god-damned Ranchers' Association.

"Besides," he added sullenly, "Gloria was in to see Bob Green the other day"—someone snickered, but he held his temper—"and he says the offer ain't been made final yet. I ain't leavin on the mornin train, if that's what you're so all-fired worried about."

"You lost your lead cow, your best bull, damnit," someone said from the shadows. "Christ, don't that make you mad?"

"Of course it makes me mad, what the hell you think I am? But what the hell am I gonna do about it, huh? Doc Oldfield goes out there and walks around a lot and mumbles to herself and then she tells me what the hell I already know—the fucker's dead. Well, I don't see anybody doin anything about that, do you? I want someone to tell me what it is that's doin it, and Oldfield, she don't know. I mean, she's a damnsight better'n Doc Vance ever was and you guys know it, but when she don't even know what's goin on, what am I supposed to do?" He waited for a response, received none and relaxed slightly. For the time being he'd managed to deflect their anger elsewhere. "Then," he continued, "I went to Harmon and told him about it, and he said what he always damn says about it—some hunters'll be out in the mornin to do some trackin. Did anything turn up? Shit, no. Just like always. I swear to Christ the man's goin senile!"

There was a silence then that made him swallow heavily. He had forgotten Steve Felsom was in the room, there when he was supposed to be out on patrol. He wanted to apologize, but the words wouldn't come. Even when the deputy moved to the center of the floor, Perkins said nothing.

Felsom was a short man, wiry and ill looking, his sleek brown hair cut short over his ears and high above his collar. All of it accentuated the weasel look of his sharp-ridged face, and made more deathly a perpetual smile that glowed without a shred of mirth behind it. Officially, he should be reporting —if only to his brother—what was happening here tonight.

They all knew he would not. He had his own axe to grind, and he ground it well.

"Bill," he said, his voice thin and shrill, "we're talking about more than money here. There's people involved, and I know that better'n anyone."

"Steve, there ain't been anyone killed—" The words were cut off as though someone had wrapped an arm around Perkins's throat.

"I know that, I know that," he said. "Bulls, calves, ewes . . . not since Harry, okay? I know that. But there's something else here, gentlemen, that had better be understood—just because it stopped with my little brother doesn't mean it isn't going to happen again. Whoever's slaughtering your stock isn't necessarily going to stop there. There are people behind this, Billyboy, not some idiot wolf or somethin. People, and I ain't gonna let them get away with it."

"Who?" The demand was anonymous.

Steve's smile stretched to a death's head. "One little, two little, three little . . ." he sang softly. "Just think about this, folks—not that you haven't already. But everything was fine around here until Dan Tallpines bought that first piece of property south of the river. Then Sweetwater comes along, then a bunch of others. Then . . . then Harry and Ellie and . . . my daddy may be a has-been who works for a has-been railroad, but it makes a lotta sense when he tells me there isn't any such creature as coincidence, not when we're talking about something like this. There's cause and effect, cause and effect, and I'm here to tell you that if we don't cause something soon, we're not gonna like the effects one damned bit."

"Talk," Titus Arnold said into the ensuing smattering of applause. His hands were tucked into the bib of his denim overalls, his carpenter tools poking out at odd angles from the pockets like the sandy spikes that passed for hair on his head. "Talk. We been talkin and bitchin and moanin and cryin, and meanwhile, case you ain't heard, Bob Green's kid got hisself thumped by some fuckin redbellies just cause he teased one of their little bastards in the schoolyard. I heard a dozen of 'em jumped Hardy. And all you bastards do is stand around and talk. Talk only makes the wind blow. Think of somethin, damnit, and let me go home to bed."

"He's right," Felsom said sharply. "The man is absolutely, one hundred percent right."

"So?" Arnold said, challenging.

"So," Felsom said, grinning, "you all listen very carefully and I'll tell you all something to think about."

(6)

Donna took off her black-rimmed glasses and lightly pinched the bridge of her nose.

"Tired?" Jason asked.

She looked at him steadily. What did his question belie? Relief? Regret? They had been talking about nothings, he telling her about one or two of his assignments, she some stories about the town and its people, as if she'd lived here all of her life. It unnerved her to think that it mattered what he was thinking.

Galen was gone, the bar had emptied. It would fill again once the movie was over, but for now there was a relative silence. Movements became studied, self-conscious, and when Carosa came over to the table and set a mug of beer in front of each of them, she started because she hadn't heard him coming.

"This," the man said, "is the last on the house, Jason. From now on you gotta pay, just like everybody else."

She grinned at the smile on his face. Anthony, she thought, couldn't have said anything more perfect.

"Hey," Jason said then, leaning his arms on the table and staring at her over the sputtering candle, "you got a minute?"

She looked at him sideways, over the top of her glasses. "Why?"

"I think I'm going to tell you my life story."

"In only a minute?"

He shrugged. "Reporters have to be concise."

"Live a little," she said, lifting her glass to her lips. "Take two and bore me."

(7)

It was the *hush* of something moving swiftly toward him, something large, something deadly. Windsound, growing.

Yet despite the moonlight Greg could see nothing except the grey of the slope, the grey of the boulders and the faraway black of the first line of trees. No stones rattled, no dried weeds or twigs snapped. There was only the windsound, and the catch of his breathing through tightly clenched teeth.

The aerie was forgotten. He had been foolhardy, thinking he would be able to do his hunting at night; and he cursed his greed as he slipped away from the edge of the precipice, away from the eagles. Still in a crouch he began to hurry toward the path that would take him down. His rifle lowered once and clanked against a rock. He froze, then listened and brought the weapon to port arms and made sure there was a round in the etched-silver chamber. His lips were dry and he licked at them nervously. His eyes narrowed as he scanned the way ahead, every so often glancing at star-bright sky, where he looked for clouds that might give him some cover.

The hunter in him insisted there was nothing out of place, that he had simply stayed too long in a dangerous position, and the beauty of the valley below was luring him with a euphoria that had made him wonder what it would be like if only he could fly. He had felt it before. A surging of the blood, a slight leaning forward, a sudden and complete belief that dropping over the edge would cause no harm, would produce a miracle. But tonight's urge had been the strongest yet, and twice he had to jerk himself away from the fall.

This time, however, he knew the hunter was wrong. Out there in the greydark there was something—bear, wolf, something with a name—something that produced a sound like the dying of the wind. Moving toward him. Invisibly, for now. Though he had never heard of a ghost that haunted like a—

He whirled around and dropped to one knee, rifle to his shoulder, cheek resting against the stock. A shadow had darted just beyond his vision. Using the Winchester as a pointer (and ignoring its slight trembling), he swiveled his torso in slow degrees from right to left across the face of the slope above him and back. His ears began to ache from straining for a sound, and when he swallowed it was as though a burr had lodged in his throat.

It was cold. And he was sweating.

Though he could not see what was there, he decided at last it had stopped moving and was waiting. Was watching. He rose and inched backward, his left hand now sweeping clumsily around him to intercept obstacles before they tripped him. He looked for light, a glimmering reflection of the moon in an eye or a claw or on a barely exposed fang. He tried to separate each rock and boulder from its neighbor, and from the shadows that insisted on dancing around them. He knew that during the dark hours he should never look directly at anything he was seeking, that the brain and its eyes would create illusions of movement and illusions of substance. But he couldn't help it. It was *there*, damnit, and he suddenly knew two things about it he had not known before: it wasn't a man, and it was forcing him away from the golden eagles in their aerie.

Jesus, oh Jesus.

Forcing him away as though he were disdained.

He stopped. The fear that had been scuttling through his chest like a slow-prowling rat was momentarily supplanted by a rage that made him blind, made him quiver, made his mouth fill with fire. Herded. Goddamnit, he was being herded! Just like he was some kind of stupidass sheep or empty-headed cow. Herded. Like he had no brains at all. He pulled himself up to his full height defiantly, glowering, the rifle clasped to his waist, his finger teasing the trigger. He could feel at his back the pressure of the open space leading down to the trees, the curious vacuum above as the night swept up to the sky. For a moment it made him dizzy, and he swayed. And in that moment the rage was lost and the fear returned.

Jesus, oh Jesus . . .

All right, all right, damnit, he thought; if we're gonna do this, let's get it the hell done, okay? Come on . . . come on . . . let's do it and found out what the hell's goin on.

His left foot began tapping nervously on the ground. He swallowed again. He considered firing off a single round just to hear something besides the sound of his rasping breathing. And maybe, if he were lucky, it might flush out whatever it

was that was watching him from up there. He sniffed, and his
head jerked up in spasm. Then he closed his eyes tight against
the writhing of the boulders and decided the hell with it, there
was no sense trying to keep quiet anymore. He immediately
turned on his heel and hurried farther down the slope, not
caring what he kicked now, not bothering to fret that he was
beginning to sound like a one-man avalanche.

The more he hurried the greater was his fear. It goaded
him, tripped him, had him running as fast as he dared within a
few yards. It stopped him abruptly when he heard the
windsound again.

"Oh . . . god . . ." he said, part prayer, part scream, and
moaned when he saw it coming toward him.

*Lazily, gently, riding the black shadows rippling out from
the moon. It was hungry . . . but it wasn't ready.*

"Jesus God," Greg whispered, and threw himself to the
ground, forgetting the rifle as he curled himself into a ball and
waited for the end. Then he lifted one elbow when he realized
he was still alive and pushed himself unsteadily to one knee
and looked around him wildly. The rifle's embossed stock
glittered at him, and he grabbed it frantically, hugging it to his
chest while he continued to move downward, scraping on his
knees.

A gnarled dead shrub caught at his heels, spilling him in a
flurry of stone and grey dust. At the same moment, the stars
wheeled through his vision, and he saw it gliding toward him
just a few feet off of the earth as though coasting on its
shadow. He took no time to think; he snapped the rifle to his
shoulder and squeezed off three shots. It banked to expose its
massive breast and disappeared back into the dark.

He had hit it. He *knew* he had hit it, and it had not even
faltered. Arrogantly, it had tempted him, dared him to fire
again; and that arrogance created a sullen rage Greg could
not control with any common sense. It had taunted him,
herded him, and he would be goddamned and gone to hell if
he was going to be pushed around by some bastard kind of
freak.

His knuckles had whitened where they folded around the
rifle, and it took him several seconds to loosen his grip and
reload the breech. Then he turned slowly and began to make
his way down toward the pinto. He admitted his fear to
himself now, but would not allow any speculation on the size

of the thing nor would he dwell on the mocking red eyes that had pinned him to the ground. He needed to be the hunter again, no matter what the creature was. If he failed in that, he would never make it to the trees, to the pinto, to the safety of the forest.

His shoulders hunched. He felt it coming. He spun and dropped, rifle up, and aimed four careful shots, this time directly at its head. There was no mistaking the impact—the creature was so big even a blind man could have downed it with one arm tied behind his back.

But it swept past him with a soft gurgling laughter, and instead of raging he was stunned. His head swiveled to follow it, and he looked up at the stars blotted out by its passing. His mouth gaped. His eyes blinked disbelievingly and he almost fell backward in his attempt to give it measure.

. . . *sweeping through the air of its domain, barely feeling the contact when its wing struck* . . .

. . . his shoulder, toppling him as if he had been clubbed with a bole. His outthrust hands were torn open when he hit the ground, and though he attempted to roll with the fall his forehead and jaw slammed the earth hard. Spangles of light and a deep numbing pain blanketed his mind. His shirt was torn from shoulder to waist. Blood rose in small bubbling pellets to stream down his spine. He knew he was running, but he couldn't see where he was going . . . dodging the slightest sound, shaking his head fiercely to clear it and calling out with the pain.

A boulder rose ahead, directly in his path, and he embraced it, huddling at its base, hugging the stone like a child at its mother's skirts. Drooling, mewling, whimpering. The hunter was dead, and the nineteen-year-old boy was praying for his father.

A minute passed. His breathing grew less ragged, the pain where he had been struck felt like white fire. It took several minutes more before he could open his eyes without feeling he had to shriek, another two or three before he understood he was alone.

The slope was silent. The wind had died. He looked over his shoulder to the hundred yards that would take him into the sanctuary of the trees. He could not see the pinto, and was not surprised; it had probably bolted as soon as it had sensed the other creature's presence.

But that didn't matter. He could walk forever if he had to, as long as he knew that the sky was clear. He began to think of what he would tell his father and decided to say nothing at all. The best thing would be to call that recruiter in Blairs and tell him he was ready now and to hell with graduation.

He choked back a sob.

There was a faint scratching.

"No," he whispered.

(when he was five his father took him into the mountains and showed him how he could stand flat against a high rock and look up at the clouds moving in his direction, look up and suffer the illusion the rock was falling on him)

Don't look up, he thought, and the sky won't fall.

Scratching.

He backed away from the boulder on hands and knees, and saw it perched above him, red eyes watching.

He screamed and jumped to his feet, his arms pinwheeling helplessly, and his legs out of control, paying no attention to the trail he'd been following. He knew only to head for the trees.

Lifting from the boulder, climbing, furling its wings. It was still hungry . . . and now it was ready.

He reached out for the first tree, and saw his arm torn apart. A scream exploded from him while he flailed for balance, intensified when he felt the talons grip his thin neck, and died when the weight that had landed on his back shoved him facedown to the grass. He thrashed, not believing it was his back being shredded; he was flipped over, and his eyes nearly burst from their sockets when he saw the red only inches above him, felt the puncture that slipped a talon under his ribs, felt the tearing at his throat and the blood in his mouth.

And . . . nothing. No pain, no sound, no feeling of weight.

The stars, and the red don't look up the sky is falling.

It heard something and raised its head quickly. A horse. Slow-moving. It tested the air, the soundwaves, the scents. No danger. No hurry.

It dipped its beak down and pulled another strip of flesh.

THREE

The corner luncheonette was filling rapidly to capacity; all the high-backed wooden booths along the side wall and most of the red-topped stools at the counter were taken by teenagers, here and there infiltrated by adults determined not to be uneasy. The noise level was high: spontaneous choruses of songs bordering on the ribald, cheers and shouted instructions as one group left to be replaced by another. Laughter blossomed, and silences lasted less than the blink of an eye.

Jason looked at the Sierra Club calendar over the magazine rack several times to check the season, to be sure he hadn't slept through to the middle of an autumn football rally. What it was, he'd discovered from Peg Steed and her husband shortly after entering, was the weekly May gathering that amounted to a Wyoming safari: assemble the pickups, the battered and painstakingly polished sedans, and whatever else moved on wheels, load them with a horde of shrill voices and trek them west through dude country, down the far side of the plateau wall into Blairs. The trophy today was the district baseball championship; the enemy, and a perennial one, apparently, was Blairs' only, but far larger, secondary school.

The excitement was infectious.

Carosa stood outside his barbershop in animated, sometimes heated conversation with a quartet of older men in baseball caps and worn Dodger windbreakers; Doc Vance, who also served as the school system's team physician, rabbited around his clinic trying to remember if he had forgotten anything, his liver-spotted hands pulling at the white puffs of hair behind his ears in increasing frustration; Artie Felsom pulled up alongside the depot and screamed at his father to get the hell off his butt or they'd miss the first pitch; a small yellow school bus waited in front of the school, an hour early, for the boarding of the players, the driver immersed in a dog-eared comic book; even Ted Waters paced anxiously in front of the grocery, not yet convinced he could safely leave Lureen in charge of the cash register.

The handful of young Indians who stood in a loose group opposite the school went virtually unnoticed.

Also unnoticed was Reverend Thornton standing on the rectory porch next to the church, checking his watch frequently and nervously while listening to the clamor drifting down from the Pike.

It was a blue and green and goldwarm day.

But Jason could not help feeling increasingly restless. He had considered a number of invitations for rides to the game and had rejected them politely without explaining he thought baseball was boring and how he thought it was a pity that a small town like this needed a game like that to spark Saturday fire.

Nevertheless, he chided himself for being too cynical and grinned at the flirtations some of the girls sent his way. He nodded seriously as Hardy Green divulged an ambition to play pro ball in the East, laughed quietly at the practical jokes and wished he hadn't drunk so much the night before.

He and Donna had stayed at Carosa's until closing, talking quietly, Donna listening attentively to his judiciously edited life story. He was pleased she hadn't appeared surprised when he told her about his father (not realizing he had done so until the story had come out), and had startled himself at the temptation to tell her about the man and the woman and the boat. He hadn't, but the urge had grown. By the same token, he suspected she had held back on him as well. She'd mentioned her birth (they were the same age), her education, her generally unexciting life in western Connecticut, a few trips abroad to keep her sanity in trim, but she had not told him her reasons for fleeing to Windriver. And flight it had been. He knew it. He could see it in the pinched creases at the corners of her eyes, the way her hands gripped her glass whenever she skirted something unpleasant . . . and in the pavane that had risen to entrap them, sending them into courtly, self-conscious patterns of engagement and avoidance.

It hadn't been uncomfortable to the point of discouragement, but it had warned him about wounds still to be tended, to be patient, to give it time.

He had walked her home, to a small single-story home. A split-rail fence. A battalion of black oak and a solitary glowering elm.

"If you say 'I'll call you,'" she'd told him at the gate, "I'll scratch your eyes out."

They stood in gentle shadow. His hands drifted windsoft to her shoulders and he kissed her cheek lightly. "I will, though."

She grinned, but did not move closer. "Okay. But not tomorrow." Her smile at his disappointment was sympathetic and kind. "I have to bring some tissue and blood samples to Casper. The mauled animals. Doc'll be with the team in Blairs, and I don't trust the mails. I'll be back Tuesday at the latest. I think."

"What's up?"

"Doc claims it's rabies. I'm not so sure."

"How can you tell without the infected whatever?"

She'd patted his cheek, once. "You stick to reporting, Kent, and telephone booths. I'll play the vet."

"My mother always told me I'd never learn anything unless I asked questions."

"Sure." She kissed him, touched his chest and was gone.

He had walked home in a light-footed daze, telling himself it was the liquor, not the woman, standing on the porch and grinning until the cold drove him to bed.

He had awakened late, suddenly, sitting up and realizing the silence of the house was what had snapped him from

sleep. Galen should have been grumbling loudly in the
kitchen, the setters barking for their breakfast. But there was
nothing. He'd showered hard (punishment for the fog that
encased his brain), dressed quickly, poked his head into
Galen's bedroom and frowned when he saw Marsh still
huddled under the covers. The man, even in the dim light,
seemed unnaturally wan, his flesh waxen, drawn snugly over
his skull. Jason had begun to head for the telephone to
summon Doc Vance when Galen groaned and sat up, smiling
and nodding, his eyes opened wide. He was still asleep and
responding to ghosts who stalked his morning dreams. He
looked like a corpse risen from its casket. The air in the room
smelled slightly sour. Sinking again into the two stacked
pillows, he folded his claw-hands over his stomach. The
blanket and sheet now bunched around his waist as he sighed
and snored slightly. The eyes fluttered closed, and Jason
backed out, trembling.

Now, as Kurt Steed poured him another cup of coffee, he
wondered if he should have pressed harder with Donna and
also if he should have awakened Galen immediately and
brought him right over to the clinic. Two *should-haves,*
and nothing done. It was no puzzle, he thought as he watched
steam curl over the brown surface; he was still somewhat
leery about making the business of the people of Windriver
his business. Donna had her problems and would tell him
eventually; Galen was clearly ill, and would tell him in time.
Eventually. In time. But he didn't like knowing that he could
have acted instead of observing, didn't like the feeling he was
wavering again and looking for glimpses of the wingéd
serpents at his door.

A squeal sliced to silence in midclimb; then laughter. He
turned and saw Hardy Green red-faced and ducking a
roundhouse swing from Carole Carosa. Outside, a horn
blared and another answered, and someone played a cavalry
charge from the back of a slat-sided produce truck that was
draped with faded bunting.

Not exactly, he thought then, like a town on the verge.

Not exactly at all.

As the luncheonette crowd ebbed and renewed and eddied
around him, his restlessness eased, and the wingéd serpents
vanished. He would find out from Doc Vance where Donna
was staying and call her tonight; he would corner Galen and

demand his rights to a gentle intrusion. It wasn't much, but it was a start. So were the voices that continued to urge him to the game, the exchange of tolerant glances with Kurt Steed at the teenagers' pranks, the hands that slapped his back on the way out and on the way in . . . he blinked rapidly and held his cup at his mouth, remembering suddenly the day he had first left his sickbed. Remission, the doctors had called it. And an invitation back to the spin of the world. One step at a time, but no one can take it for you.

He sipped without tasting, wondered if he were making too much of it, but decided that was better than ignoring it altogether.

And with the town in such a mood, he might even find it profitable to speak to Daniel Tallpines. Sometime today; but after, he grinned, all the pretty girls were gone.

11:25 A.M.

Cy Oaker's garage was on Valley Pike, directly west of Ted Waters's grocery. With two islands of three pumps each, four wide working bays and the office building, the establishment occupied most of the main street's frontage between Suncrest and Elm. The block immediately to its right (and the last block in town) held the three-school complex; opposite was Starling's Funeral Home and three small shops that catered primarily to tourists. Because of the surroundings, Oaker considered it vital to keep his business clean, quiet and as friendly as possible without seeming bumpkin.

Daniel Tallpines agreed, because he recognized the potential for unbearable arrogance. As the only garage in the valley, Oaker's serviced nearly all the population. Ted Waters had proven what sort of contempt a monopoly like that could breed—even before the Indians, Waters had swaggered instead of strolled. Oaker, on the other hand, was more interested in the possibility of his son moving up from deputy to sheriff than he was in anything else. Consequently, much of the daily work and administration away from the pumps was left to Daniel. And Daniel didn't mind. Not only did he like Cy, he also made more money than a mechanic usually did, had three young men working under him and could pretty much take every weekend off.

Then why, he wondered sourly, was he here instead of home? He could be playing with his girls, walking across his land, luxuriating in the day instead of standing glumly in the office. He knew his presence was bothering the two young boys pumping gas, and he tried not to stare at them. The alternative, however, was pacing through the bays, picking up tools and setting them down, swiping a rag at a fender, straightening workbenches that had been straightened twice already. At home he had felt caged, but it was no better here; at home the sky had been too vast, but here he could barely see it at all; and at home his wife, Sharon, would ask him about his problem.

He had almost left the garage an hour before, when he had seen Jason Clarke go into the luncheonette. Though he'd had no contact with Galen since the new man had arrived, he knew that Marsh was moving quietly along his own path. Sooner or later, then, that path would cross his. It had already reached the MacKenzies; it was bound to reach him soon.

Today, then. Talk to the new man today and find out if he was different.

But each time his hand reached for the door, it stalled.

Waters was out there, gabbing with his cronies. Charlie and his friends were in front of the empty lot across the street, and they would glare at him, knowing he was part of what had brought their families to this unhealthy place. There were too many cars at the islands, and the boys needed his help. He didn't know Clarke yet, wouldn't know what to say.

He caught his reflection in the plate glass, couldn't hold it and turned away.

Later, he decided; maybe later.

11:50 A.M.

Kurt Steed leaned gratefully back against the canted controls of the griddle and folded his arms over his thick chest. His apron, spattered with grease no washing could erase, bulged over a stomach that threatened to spill over his belt. There was a faint sheen of perspiration at his hairline, but he didn't feel it; nor did he feel the missing weight of his right leg. Unlike David Carosa's modern replacements, his was by contrast almost archaic—a strap and padded peg leg he had worn when the original had been shattered in a lumbering accident fifteen years ago in Idaho. Despite Peg's quiet pleading and his doctors' combined pressure, he hadn't wanted anything that reminded him of a real one, and found the oddity enough of a conversation piece that it had become a staple in Windriver. Some called him Long John, others called him Ahab, but as long as they were smiling he didn't give a damn. It was a miracle he was still living, a miracle he had a wife and lovely daughter, a miracle he had been able to make a success of the luncheonette—three miracles in one lifetime was enough for any man. He didn't need a fourth; he didn't need cosmetics to remind him of what he had had.

With a call, Hardy Green began to lead his teammates single file out the door. Kurt watched as they filtered out of the booths, watched as Jason Clarke sipped at cold coffee and smiled faintly at the wall. He didn't notice his blonde wife until she'd snaked an arm around his thick waist and hugged him, wearily.

"Bea's complaining again," she said, her voice light and not complaining at all.

Kurt snorted. "What's she want this time, a million dollars?"

"She doesn't want to have to come home right after the game. She says she and some of the others want to stay in town and see a movie."

"What the hell's wrong with what we got here?" His voice had risen, and Jason looked at him without turning. He smiled, half turned and glowered more fiercely than he felt when Bea came through the swinging door from the kitchen. Slight and more blonde than her mother, her walk was a glide over ice despite high boots and snug jeans. Her pinstriped blue shirt had been pulled out of her waistband, the ends tied in a broad knot beneath her breasts.

Jesus, he thought, she's gonna get raped on the spot.

"Hi, Daddy." She smiled, her large mouth showing him all her perfect teeth. A soft smile. One that said, *I'll get what I want anyway so why argue and raise your blood pressure.* A long-fingered hand touched at her short hair, but instead of bringing her case straight to court she began helping her mother clean off the counter, clean out the booths. Kurt knew he was being outflanked, knew the sensation well, and he pressed harder against the grille and grumbled deep in his throat.

She passed in front of him, smiling at Jason and giving him a new napkin. "Excuse me, Daddy." When she bent over the hair at her nape rose, exposing three small scars faint and not long: one centered directly over her spine, the others reaching outward from it at a gentle angle. He had once heard Bea tell her mother Hardy Green thought them sexy, and he'd almost thundered the house down. Sexy. This was his daughter, damnit, and she sure as hell wasn't sexy! Carole Carosa with her big tits and dark skin was sexy. Bea was an angel, and they never screwed at all.

"Who'll you be with?" he muttered as she squeezed past him a second time.

"Oh, Carole, Hardy . . . you know." A slight shrug.

She worked her way to the end of the counter, dropped the damp rag into a bin and sat on the last stool. Spinning. Humming. Her mother taking refuge in straightening the magazine rack by the door.

"You be home at a decent hour," Kurt said.

"Daddy!" A protest.

He knew he could trust her, but he felt he had to go through the motions just to be sure. Hardy Green may be a star and his father a lawyer, but he was a boy, goddamnit, who thought his daughter was sexy.

"Decent," he repeated.

She grinned, slipped off the stool and came over to him, leaning over the counter so he could kiss her forehead. "I know, I know," she said, putting a hand to the sandy sweep of his hair. And kissed his cheek soundly.

"Yeah, well . . . you have a good time, hear? Hope you win."

She grimaced. "We won't. We never do. This stupid place can't even win a stupid baseball game." She backed off and raced for the door. "Hi, Mister Clarke," and was gone before Jason could swallow and answer.

"Beautiful girl," Jason said.

Kurt accepted the compliment with a nod.

"I take it she doesn't like the town, though."

"What can I tell ya." He shook his head at the silence of the place. "She ain't never satisfied, Jase. Always askin questions, always runnin here and there. I don't know. Some days she comes in here and works like a demon. Other days she spends so much time with them Indians I think she wants to be one."

"She thinks they're interesting," Peg said, taking the stool beside Jason. "And they like her, too."

"The MacKenzies?" Jason liked Peg Steed, liked the spray of freckles that swept over her cheeks to vanish in her hair.

"Yeah," Kurt said, shifting. "Used t'be she'd go out with Carole to the old lady. Not anymore, though. Likes boys now." He grunted.

"She's growing up, dear," Peg said with a wink to Jason. "Seems to me I was her age when I met you in Boise."

Jason grinned, and Kurt spun around to clean the griddle already gleaming. Mothers, he thought angrily, slapping a spatula hard on the hot surface; what the hell do they know about fathers, anyway? Shit, she could get raped right under the stands! He looked up at the metal backplate, at his distorted reflection. Been a long time since I've seen a ball game. But before he could reach for the ties of his apron, Mitch Regan came in and ordered a sandwich.

12:15 P.M.

Doc Vance stared blindly at the Audubon prints on the wall of the clinic's waiting room.

"Exhausted is what she sounds like to me, Simon," he said, anxiously shifting the receiver from one ear to the other. "You just gotta keep her in bed, damnit! Tell you what. I'll come out after the game, all right? I'd do it now, but Donna's in Casper with those samples. You just keep Rachel quiet and warm, try to get her to take some broth, if you can." He listened, laughed. "Chicken soup, turkey soup, whatever. If there's an emergency, get hold of Esther Lynn at her house. She never goes anywhere, the old biddy. She can get hold of me at the game on my CB." He listened again, walking around the desk as if MacKenzie could see him and understand his urgency. "All right, all right, I'll tell Jake, too, just in case the volunteers need rousin. Look, I have to go now, Simon. But if you do as I say, she'll be all right. She just has to learn . . . look, when she wakes up, give her a little hell. Tell her it's my prescription until I see her."

12:25 P.M.

Jason's smile was genial but forced as he dropped a bill over his check and slid off the stool. He wanted to say that here in Wyoming's grand high country, where appetites were stimulated as a matter of course and even the air tasted fine, Kurt Steed's thick hamburgers were the best he'd ever had. But he could only manage a halfhearted wave as he walked quickly outside with one hand rubbing consolation at his stomach. He grinned wryly. Like concrete, he thought, or superbly disguised rubber. Mitch Regan, however, seemed to love them, ate four while Jason watched in unabashed awe. But when the rakish little man had ordered another pair, Jason had had enough, thinking that the druggist couldn't possibly be human and still stay on his feet.

He burped and massaged his stomach again, and stood back against the narrow brick wall that separated the luncheonette from the movie theater. He adjusted his Stetson lower over his eyes and jammed his hands into his pockets, thumbs hanging out, crossed his feet at the ankles and wavered until his shoulders found comfort in the brick and balance in his stance. Then he let himself feel the warm May sun, and the vibrations that shimmered from the activity in the town's streets.

Groups of men still talking, though now moving westward; schools of youngsters and guardian adults walking, calling, seemingly wandering. A string of horses carrying early dudes from one of the ranches made its way out of a side street, hooves clopping against the blacktop, riders grinning self-consciously at the greetings they were given. There was a minor rear-end collision between a station wagon and a pickup, and Jason saw Jake Harmon come out of his office and stand at the curb, hands on his hips, eyes hidden behind silver glasses as an anthill of teens swarmed over the two vehicles, shouting instructions and eventually freeing the bumpers. As soon as they were gone, the sheriff vanished again.

Beautiful, he thought. Madness, and it was beautiful. And within the hour it would be over. Those going to the game would be already on their way, those thinking of entertainment outside the valley would be readying themselves at home. It would be quiet. A peace as comfortable as napping.

Unless something happened to spark the tension again.

He scowled at his pessimism and kicked away from the wall. His eye had been caught by a car refueling at the gas station, and he reminded himself of his promise to see Tallpines. But when he was about to step off the curb someone thumped into him and nearly spilled him to the street. He turned quickly, almost angry, then grinned when Timmy Sweetwater disappeared behind his father's back.

"It's all right," he said, as much to the father as the son. "Just startled, that's all."

Sweetwater nodded brusquely, tapped the boy on the head and went into Steed's place. Timmy made to follow, then changed his mind and turned around. "You're the reporter."

Jason nodded. "You think I'm Clark Kent?"

Timmy's face twisted in disgust. "No, silly!" He glanced back over his shoulder, then stood beside Jason at the curb as the pedestrians filed by. No one paid them heed.

"You like workin for Mister Marsh?"

"It's a living."

"You like it here?"

"I think it's great."

The boy looked up at him suddenly. "You mean that?"

"Sure," Jason said, one shoulder lifting. "It sure beats where I come from."

"New Jersey." And a nod.

Jason wasn't surprised; Galen had warned him. "Too many people," he said, lowering his voice in a solemn conspiracy. "They're not stacked up like New York, but there's too many people anyway. This, now, is nice. A couple of blocks in any direction and you're out in the open." He touched the boy's shoulder. "You like it here?"

"It's all right," Timmy answered, matching Jason's tone. "I don't like school, though."

"Who does?" Jason said sourly. And grinned when the boy gave him an astonished look of respect. "I mean, it's all right when you think about what you have to do in the future, but with all this stuff going on and the sun out like this . . . who needs it?"

"You ever see an Indian before?"

"Only in the movies." And he was proud his response came as quickly as it had.

"I'm an Indian, you know."

"I sort of guessed."

"Shoshone."

"I guessed that, too."

Timmy covered his mouth and laughed silently. "You guess a lot," he said, his palm muffling the words. "That makes you a reporter?"

Jason nodded. "But it makes me wrong a lot, too."

The boy laughed again. "You're funny." An older couple walked by, the woman telling her husband what a pretty boy that was. Timmy scowled and lowered his head, his hands dropping to his sides.

"You get a lot of that, huh?" Jason said softly. When the boy nodded, he touched his shoulder once. "Me, too."

Timmy stared at him, blinked once, slowly, until he saw the grin ghosting Jason's lips. "But you're not pretty!"

"No, but I'm short."

Timmy puzzled that for a moment, was about to ask another question when his father rejoined them, a large brown paper sack in his hand.

"He botherin you?"

When both of them shook their heads and looked at each other and laughed, Aaron's expression marked both doubt and relief. Then he extended his free hand and Jason took it, held it, released it with silent thanks the Indian hadn't been testing for strength. From the looks of him, he thought, he could bend iron bars without losing a drop of sweat.

"He's a reporter and he works for Galen Marsh and he's short," Timmy said in a stumbling rush. He quieted when Aaron stared, but kept the smile on his face.

"True to all three," Jason said. "I was about to—"

A shout cut him off, and he turned quickly to his right. Two blocks up, across from the school, he could see the fringe of a small group of teens. Dust floated in churning clouds over their heads, and from their agitated gestures he guessed a fight was going on. Timmy started toward it, but stopped at a grunted word from his father. Jason looked to the man, nodded his understanding and began to walk away. Others were following, a few rushing across the street. Three boys in baseball uniforms had climbed to the hood of the school bus and were shouting, and when Jason reached the corner he heard Hardy Green's name.

Without completely knowing why he broke into a trot, his momentum carried him through the line of boys before anyone thought to try to stop him. He halted when he saw the two boys wrestling fiercely on the ground.

Hardy Green and Charlie Sweetwater. Hardy was on top (still not in uniform) and doing his best to smash Charlie's head through the ground. They rolled and Charlie tried to put a knee through Hardy's stomach. Their faces were red from exertion and grey from the dust, their shirts torn at the elbows, their jeans gaping at the knees. Jason heard fist meeting bone, boots pummeling the earth; all of it to the accompaniment of a strained and sudden silence.

The circle was wide, now. The girls who had been watching had turned away in disgust, and not a few of the boys averted their faces when Jason scanned them intently, demanding intervention.

Not your fight, he thought as Hardy kicked Charlie in the ribs; don't get involved.

Something flared up from the struggle. Red. It was blood.

The hell with it, Jason thought, and pushed his hat back from his forehead. He shouted once, but the boys wouldn't part. Someone behind him ventured weak-hearted encouragement, but the call died swiftly when it was lifted alone.

Jason spat and approached them, reached down without thinking and dodged the fists and the legs to find two fistfuls of hair. He pulled gently, speaking urgently and softly and ignoring the blows that landed blindly on his legs. Finally he shouted their names once and yanked their hair. Hard. He ignored the sudden startled and enraged screams as they broke apart and rose, scrambling to their feet and grabbing at his wrists.

"Shit, man!"

"Goddamnit, who the hell—"

"Shut up," Jason said, his voice low and hissing. His hands switched quickly to their collars, and he dragged them off to one side, away from the crowd, still keeping them off balance though he was shorter than both. He shook them once and released them, noting grimly the astonished fear in their faces as they sidled away, one to either hand. He could see they wanted to rub at their aches, but they kept their hands at their sides and stared sullenly at the ground.

"You guys want to kill each other?" He kept his voice quiet. The crowd had stayed near the pavement, but most of it was already breaking away. "You really want to kill each other?"

"He started it," Charlie said bitterly.

"Big man," Hardy sneered. "Who jumped who the other day, with a whole goddamn tribe?"

"Who picks on little kids, huh? Who calls them fairy, huh?"

They took a step toward each other and stopped abruptly when Jason shifted without nearing. His gaze flicked from one face to the other; both boys were close to tears, but his sympathy for them had died. "You'll be late for the game," was all he told them and turned and walked away. His arms were trembling and his chest felt tight, his clenched teeth making his jaw ache. There was no one left on the sidewalk by the time he reached it, and a man in coach's jacket was screaming at Hardy from the middle of the street. Jason looked over to the gas station, decided he wasn't in the mood and headed back down the Pike stiff-legged and raging.

Idiots, he thought, and was afraid to think further.

Idiot, he called himself; if they had turned on you, you'd be dead.

He was lucky and he knew it. But he knew the fight had lasted far too long. Too many faces, too many grim smiles.

He almost knocked Timmy Sweetwater to the ground.

"Now we're even," the boy said, faked a punch and ran away. His father turned from staring blankly at the bank window.

"It was Charlie," Jason said, brushing at his shirt.

Sweetwater grunted, nodded once. "I'm not surprised. He's been standin there all morning."

"You knew he was fighting and you didn't . . . ." He blinked rapidly, unable to find the logic.

The man glanced after the little boy. "I wade in there, who knows what happens. Charlie can take care of himself. He don't need me to fight his battles for him."

Jason heard the bitterness, the echo of authority grown slowly impotent.

"Thanks for helping." Sweetwater made a helpless gesture, then shrugged and followed his son down the street.

Jason watched them walking, the giant and the mite, and he scowled at the tears of frustration that momentarily blinded. There was no sense in sticking around now, he decided; his mood had been shattered, the dreamlike peace over. Maybe, he thought, he would take a long ride in Galen's car. It didn't matter where. As long as he was moving.

1:50 P.M.

Carole sat at the top of the half-filled stands and watched the teams warming up on the dusty field. She knew it was going to be a slaughter; Blairs hadn't lost to Windriver in over a million years, it seemed, and she saw no reason—even with Hardy Green—why that should change now. But she didn't let on to Bea that she couldn't care less. The important thing about the afternoon was that she was free. Free of her parents' constant nagging about her grades; free of the people on the streets staring at her and remembering (despite the fact her father told her it wasn't so); free of her stupid, lovesick brother, who spent more time mooning over Ellie Felsom than he did with his physical therapy on the Universal Gym her father had bought with her money. Her money. College money. Her freedom money!

She started then, and looked around guiltily, as if those sitting near her had been able to read her mind. One afternoon early last winter Galen Marsh had found her sitting by the river and crying, screaming at the skies like those Greeks she read about in English. He'd known her despair. Old men always seemed to be able to sense things like that. And he had talked with her until the sun had gone down, holding her hand and staring at the water, and at the early ice in the reeds. You get knocked down, you get up, he'd said. You get knocked down again, you get up again. In this whole damned world there isn't any such thing as fair, so you're doing nothing more than wasting time blubbering about it out here where pneumonia is just waiting to grab you. You get knocked down, you get up and you get a little wiser about ducking next time. What the hell, he'd said; is it really worth the effort to be so all-fired mad?

She had loved him, then, because he wasn't afraid to tell her she was screwing up her head walking around in a rage, and because after their talk she was able to walk the streets again and not care what folks might be thinking about her, whether it be pity, sorrow or shame.

But he hadn't been able to take the anger from her dreams, and she resented him for that.

For the first time she really understood why Ellie and Bea couldn't wait to get out.

She looked down to the field and saw Bea standing by Hardy. She smiled and waved, and lifted her face to the sun.

Free. She was free. At least for the day.

1:55 P.M.

Bea was well aware that Carole disapproved of public displays of affection, but she kissed Hardy anyway just before his team took the field. Then she traced a gentle finger around the bruise that was spreading along the side of his jaw.

"What you did was stupid, you know," she said mildly.

He looked sheepish. "Yeah, I know. But—"

"No, you didn't have to do it," she told him. "All you have to do is give him half a chance. He isn't as bad as you think he is."

"I suppose."

She kissed him again, giggling at the catcalls erupting from the bench. "Play well," she whispered, and ran back to the stands.

2:40 P.M.

They sat on the top of the embankment across from the depot. The others made no mention of the street fight, but their silence and their glances told Charlie his timing had been lousy. But they also gave him their pity, knowing he had to face his father when he went home.

They sat for nearly an hour before scrambling down the weedy slope and crossing the tracks to Fieldview. Walking slowly, listening to the sound of the town in near desertion, their own footsteps unpleasantly loud.

Ten feet from the corner Charlie stopped them. Across the Pike they could see the side of Regan's Drugs. The narrow door was open, and through the high shrubs that masked the gap between building and pavement he could see a girl standing at the threshold. She was pushing her hair fiercely back from her eyes, wiping her face with the back of one hand. It was Dawn, and Charlie's breath congealed in his lungs. One of his friends muttered something, and he silenced him with a gesture. He stared, unbelieving, convinced that somehow Dawn was in trouble.

She turned suddenly and pushed her way through the shrubbery to the street and headed quickly down toward the river. Her head was low, her legs stiff, and she kept one hand pressed to her stomach. Even from where he stood, Charlie could see her dress was wrinkled.

"You busy tonight?" he asked the air. When there was no dissent he nodded. "He closes around nine. I know where he lives. Meet me this side of the Middle Valley bridge."

He said nothing more. He only wanted to vomit.

4:00 P.M.

Daniel flicked a willow switch idly at a bee droning up from a flower. He missed, grunted and kept on walking. The house was already several hundred yards behind him, dwindling to a dark blot that would blend with distance into the horizon of slopes and shadowed peaks. Sharon was cooking supper and, probably, on the phone with Little Star, Michael Wolf's wife, talking about Michael's birthday coming up in three weeks. They were planning a party to throw for him. A surprise party, if everyone kept his mouth shut. He smiled and shook his head. It wouldn't happen. Every year they tried it, and every year someone blabbed. And every year Michael would walk into the room, scratch at the scar of his ear and pretend he hadn't known.

Normal. It was all so damned normal.

He found a narrow stream and stepped over it, then turned and sat. His knees were drawn up, his hands clasping his shins. The switch lay bowed across his lap.

Sharon had not asked him where he was going when he'd left, or why he'd changed his mind about staying at work. She was like that. If he had something to tell her she would wait until he was ready. Her patience astounded him, her strength supported him, that she loved him more marvelous still. Despite her obvious apprehensions all those years ago, she hadn't argued when he'd explained the Teaching to her—as much, that is, as Rachel had told him—and had showed her the land he'd bought with Simon's help. And though she read the new magazines and books, and dressed as often as she could in the new puzzling styles and chided him gently about his old-fashioned chauvinism, somehow she had managed to retain a respect for something no white could ever really grasp. He wasn't sure she actually believed in what Rachel was doing, but as long as he did she called herself content. There was food on the table, a nice home to work with, the children growing and happy and learning much at their school. For the time being it was enough.

And that was the catch—for the time being.

Last night, after his daughters had flurried off to bed, he and Sharon had taken their chairs on the porch and watched the stars dust over the black. They didn't speak. Their presence was sufficient for comfort, for ease, a communication complete and envied by others.

Then: "Dan?"

He turned and could not see her. The lamps were out in the front room and she was little more than a star-edged silhouette. His hand moved absently to his breast pocket before he remembered he'd quit smoking when winter broke.

"You know," she said, her voice like chimes in the wind, "when we first came out here I felt funny. Strange funny. A lot of my friends didn't believe in Rachel, they said all my college should have taught me better. They didn't believe for a minute there were others of the People who used to live up here. They all followed Washakie, they told me. Nobody stayed behind. Nobody made this place sacred." She paused, but he'd known it wasn't the time for his response. "The children," she said. Another pause. "I know there are a lot of things that aren't in the history books, that come down through the telling. I understand that." He heard her take a breath. "Dan, that map you showed me. The one Rachel drew of the places here. We have it all now." Pause. "I just wanted you to understand I know that."

She had said nothing more, and he had not responded. Now he watched the westering sun, felt the heat, saw a sliver of silver dart through the shallow water toward the cut of the Wind River. Something made him want to chase it, and something kept him still on the ground.

Beyond the house, beyond the river, beyond the highway . . . the MacKenzies. He squinted north and could almost see the house with all the outbuildings behind it. Could almost see the old woman walking over the grass with her lips moving silently and her eyes focused on places he had never seen. Her power. That was what had moved him, had stirred him. His time in college, his years in the army, nothing before had reached him as she had. And he suspected she knew that much of what she claimed in that web-spinning voice he simply could not believe. But there was no mistaking the appeal—to regain what had been lost, to develop a place that belonged to the Shoshone without having it trampled by tourists and scholars. A private place. A place of relics long since ground to dust and joined with the earth.

That moved him. Nothing else.

Sharon was right. They had it now, all of it. And Rachel must know it. After all, it was her idea, her plan; she must know it, and yet she said nothing to him, nothing to the others about stopping. And in her silence he felt suddenly blind. After all this time of being able to sit with her and listen to her stories, of being in on the planning, of going down to the reservation and finding those who would come with him for the right and proper reasons . . . after so long he was cut off, he was deaf, he was blind.

He didn't like it. And he wasn't sure there was anything he could do about it now.

He spat in the water in self-disgust—or weakness—and pushed himself to his feet. Jason Clarke. Suddenly, he was flooded with shame at having run that morning. He had seen the man talking with Aaron and Timmy, had seen him wade into the fight between Green and Aaron's son. He should have waited. They could have talked. He had no idea what would have been said, but at least they could have talked.

Maybe they could have talked.

No, Rachel had said at such a question early last year. We tell no one, or they will laugh. Worse, they will not sell. They have their church and they have their god, but we have the Teaching and it tells us the way. We can do nothing else, Daniel. After. After it is done, we will let them all know. Only after. When it is too late for it to be taken from us.

"Hell." He sighed.

He had even, not more than an hour ago, seen Marsh's Studebaker riding the back roads this side of the river. He had been positive it was Jason Clarke driving. He could have caught up.

"Hell."

It would be so easy to tell someone—just to let it all out and stop this foolishness, in spite of Rachel. Stop the fighting on the streets, the angry glances, the gestures. It would be so damned easy to shrug the burden from his shoulders.

But if he did, he would have to face Rachel, and Simon, and despite the fact that he liked to believe he was afraid of no one, neither did he want to provoke MacKenzie wrath. He didn't believe all the old woman claimed, but he sure as hell didn't want to test it. He had seen Perkins's bull, had seen some of the sheep and the calves. He hadn't been in the white man's world that long that he'd forgotten what could be done with the right words, the right spells. It was foolish, perhaps, but it was also safe.

He stepped back over the stream and walked slowly toward the house.

Films and novels always stressed the mystic quality of his people.

But no, he decided. There was nothing mystical about himself or his people. What they had, rather, was a finely tuned appreciation of the land and what went with it. What went with the land, and its potential. No mysticism there; just generations of gentle teachings.

"All right, then," he whispered to the rippling grass, the stirring air. He would say nothing about the Teaching to anyone. But he would talk to Jason anyway, because Galen had taken the trouble, and because he needed another voice.

Tonight. It would happen tonight.

5:15 P.M.

Carole commiserated with Hardy on the loss of the game. Not a slaughter, but a loss just the same. Then she turned to Bea and said, "You know, if I had my way I'd flatten this whole damned state out with a single bolt of lightning."

"Tell me when you're ready," Bea said. "I'll give you a hand."

7:05 P.M.

Simon took his chair in front of the fireplace and snatched a fresh cigar from the humidor. He had smoked it almost halfway through before Doc Vance waddled into the living room and slumped onto the couch.

"Well?"

"I told you," Vance said, lacing his fingers over his paunch, his concerned frown wrinkling an already deeply mapped face. "I told you she was exhausted. I swear to Christ, Simon, I don't know what you let her do around here, but whatever it is, it's too much. She's got to stop, or it's going to kill her." He didn't care if he was being too blunt; he was tired of giving advice and having nobody listen. Esther Lynn, his wife, even Donna Oldfield. Nobody listened to an old man anymore. He pulled off his wire-rims and stuffed them into his pocket. "You talked to Jason Clarke yet?"

Simon nodded. "Came out last week, one afternoon."

"Figures. I finally figured out who the hell he is."

"Peter Clarke's boy."

Vance hid his surprise. Damnit, nobody tells me anything, he thought; I might as well be dead.

"Why do you figure he's back?"

Simon waved his cigar; the ash fell to his lap. "Galen asked him, why else?"

"Because of what we did to his mother."

"What," Simon said slowly, "did we do to his mother?"

Vance squirmed, but didn't back down. "We ran her out is what we did, and you know it, Simon. We blamed her for what that drunken bum did and we ran her out. With a crippled kid, we ran her out. I don't expect he's forgiven us that."

Simon smiled. "Doc, I had a nice long talk with him. If you're worried about revenge, I think you can forget it."

Vance was doubtful. "I don't know."

"I do."

"Galen's just ornery enough to enjoy it."

Simon laughed, shook his head. And when he had sobered he looked toward Rachel's door.

Vance didn't bother to turn around. He knew what the man was thinking, he had done the same: what would it be like? What would it be like to live without your wife?

9:10 P.M.

A cramp knotted the underside of Jason's left thigh, and he rubbed at the muscle hard, cynically amazed he hadn't been stricken before. Now that he was driving into town the pain seemed somewhat anticlimactic, an afterthought of the gods just to remind him they were still around.

He had been on the move virtually all day, and for the first few hours hadn't realized where he was going. He only knew he had taken the first spur off the Pike and had thumped and glided over the plateau until the road had narrowed to a path, the path to a trail. That's when he made his initial stop, climbing out of the car and walking toward a large pond traced across with placid geese and ducks, erupting here and there with the leap of a fish. Cattails browned the banks; wildflowers mostly gold and white hummed with the bees that crawled over them; a slithering in the grass warned him of snakes. He'd sat on a rotted log and watched the water, and the sky.

Then he'd risen and taken to the car again, backtracking to another spur and winding with it past several small farmhouses, a large flock of sheep, through stands of trees he did not recognize, until he'd reached the Pike at the eastern ridge where it plunged to the downward slopes. He'd stopped the car in the middle of the road and stared over his hands. Thinking how supremely simple it would be to depress the accelerator just enough to nudge him over the edge and glide him under the belly of the pine forest to the outskirts of Ft. Washakie.

It wasn't worth it, he'd told himself wearily. Two boys ready to tear each other apart. People just standing there— thumbs up for the Indian, thumbs up for the white—make up your minds, you simpleminded bastards. Their blood dark on the ground.

He'd turned around and hadn't stopped again until he was parked in front of the house on Elkhorn Road. Standing at the gate, he waited for his father's ghost to appear. *You remember me, son, don't you?* Thinking maybe he really ought to find that tree. So he could touch the scars the automobile had made, perhaps find a shadow of the blood where the man's head had struck the bark after smashing the windshield. Just to touch. Just to know. *It's a bitch of a life, kid, as long as you don't weaken.* Seeing himself at four running all around the maples and knowing full well he didn't see himself at all.

Then, riding on toward the MacKenzies, riding on and turning back.

Pulling over to the side of the highway just as the sun dropped below the mountains and resting his head on the steering wheel.

For an hour, or more.

He pulled into Galen's driveway and killed the engine, listening to the tick of the cooling metal before sliding out and stretching. The houselights were out, and deep shadows lay in bars across the street. The wind had worked itself into a chill that slipped through his clothes and raised gooseflesh on his arms. He walked down the gravel to the pavement and faced the river, wondering if the sensation of home was real or only pleading, and if his annoyance was a reaction to an inability, his inability to locate the panacea that would solve Windriver's problem with a hell of a single genius stroke.

It was possible.

It was also possible he didn't want to find the answer. And if he did, he wasn't at all sure he would have the courage to use it.

He grunted. That was it.

He had failed once before and there was no reason why he shouldn't fail again. It just wasn't in him to be a Cid or King

Richard. The idea that he was the Unknown Stranger riding into the dusty little town and putting things right was ludicrous. After all, the Stranger always rode out again . . . and he had no intention of leaving.

But was he home or hiding?

He followed the progress of the wind as it pushed fragmentary shadows through the sprays of white from the streetlamps, his gaze arrested when one of the shadows approached him.

"Mister Clarke?"

Jason's hands fisted and his breath lodged painfully at the back of his mouth. An Indian stood by the gate. Tall and lithe, his face cut sharply by the shadows and the light. His hair was held away from his eyes by an unadorned leather headband, his clothes from short jacket to trousers were denim untrimmed.

"Mister Tallpines?" He was glad that his voice hadn't broken into falsetto, but he glanced from side to side, staring, listening, and frowned when he heard the man laughing at him softly.

"It's not an ambush," said Tallpines, "if that's what you're thinking." He extended his hand; it was hard and dry, feeling slightly of grease and the harsh soap used to cleanse it. "I have some friends who are interested in you."

A small leaf blew across Jason's cheek, but he did not flinch, thinking that somehow it would be wrong if he did. "Apparently, a lot of people are," he said dryly. "You and your friends would be about the last I've met."

Tallpines, seemingly oblivious to the wind and the spring cold, slid his hands into his pockets and leaned a hip against the gate. He studied Jason for several moments, his eyes narrowed. "It's very simple, Mister Clarke," he said flatly. "We know you're here with Galen. We just want to know what side you're on."

"Just like that?"

"You're not stupid, Mister Clarke—"

"Jason, please," he said, ignoring the comment.

"All right. Jason. But Galen must have told you what's going on, and you've had, uh, a taste of it yourself this morning. It was a nice thing you did for Charlie Sweetwater."

"I did it for both of them," he said quickly, angrily. "Nobody else seemed to care."

Tallpines looked at him, examining, searching. "There will be more fights, I'm afraid."

"I suppose."

"We get hurt, Jason."

"I don't doubt it."

"It isn't our fault."

Jason pursed his lips. Took a deep breath. "I'll tell you something, Daniel, and I don't mean to offend you or your people. But I'm inclined to doubt that. I don't think you're doing it deliberately, but the fault is there nevertheless. The fault is definitely there."

Tallpines pushed away from the gate with his rump and stood defiantly in the center of the sidewalk. "You listen to Waters, then."

Jason shook his head. "No. I listen to you and to Waters, and I know you're aware I spent most of a day listening to Simon MacKenzie." His smile was without humor. "I'm not stupid, Daniel. I don't read minds, but I'm not stupid." He looked at his hands, then up again and shook his head slowly. "MacKenzie thinks he's helpless. You say it's not your fault. Waters and the others say it's not theirs. You all say it to people like me, but have you tried to say it to each other? You're in a hell of a mess, Daniel. Why?"

Tallpines held out his arm. "See the color?"

"No, I won't buy that. If you and that so-called Association had already given it a try, then maybe I'd agree. But as far as I can tell, you haven't. Just like you haven't bothered to tell them why you're not using the land. Sitting on it, and not using it." He lowered his voice, suddenly aware he'd been close to shouting. "You've frightened them, Daniel. You know that, don't you. You've scared them so much they're not thinking straight."

"They should understand."

Jason thought he'd heard a hesitation, but dismissed it as anger flushed color to his cheeks. "Understand what?" he demanded. "What the hell is there to understand when no one bothers to explain anything? You know, I've been here over two weeks already, and everybody I talk to blames someone else. It's not your fault the place is falling apart, it's not the Association's, it's not anyone's. Of course not. It's the color of your skin. It's entropy. It's Fate. It's a crock of shit, Daniel. It's all a crock of goddamned shit."

He wanted to spit, to strike out, and only looked away in disgust, at the moment not much caring if they all drove themselves to hell. He'd hoped to find foundation to Galen's hope there were reasonable men to be found on both sides, but all he'd uncovered were children talking back at the dark.

"I understand you're married, you have children, Dan," he said suddenly. "How have you explained this to your family?"

The slow smile took him by surprise, as did Tallpines's slow turn toward the river. "They understand perfectly, Jason."

He put a thoughtful hand to his chin, watching the carefully staged exit in grim admiration. Then he called the man's name and Tallpines stopped but did not look around.

"One more thing," he said. "You live here like the rest of us—aren't you worried about this town?"

A moment for the wind.

"No," Tallpines answered, so quietly Jason wasn't sure he had heard it at all. Then the Indian walked on, crossing the street and fading by degrees into the shadows.

Though the urge was there, Jason did not try to follow. He doubted the man could be coerced into saying anything else, or that anything he could say would penetrate Tallpines's apparent blindness. But he was positive of one thing, for no real reason save an unsettling instinct—that Daniel Tallpines was lying through his teeth. And he was frightened. Damned frightened, and no amount of clichéd Indian stoicism had been able to hide it. He was frightened, and he'd almost told Jason why.

9:40 P.M.

Mitch Regan knew it was Saturday night, but he was tired and had to have a good hot shower and a change before he headed on over to Carosa's. Earlier, through a stroke of luck he didn't dare question, he had managed to talk Lureen into meeting him there for a friendly drink. She'd also mentioned she was running out of the expensive cosmetics Mitch had ordered for her a couple of months ago, and when he swept out the massive order book, grinning and bowing and telling her not to worry, the gleam in her eye had dried out his throat and tightened his trousers.

Ah Lureen, he thought, Nirvana comes tonight.

He nudged open his latchless gate with one knee and strutted up the flagstone walk. The river was at his back and he could hear it whispering, urging him to hurry before she lost her ardor. He grinned and stopped, fumbling in his pockets for his key ring and muttering because he'd forgotten to set the timer that turned on the porch light.

He heard a rustling, and he glanced up into the trees. Owl, he thought.

Then, a shuffling, and he realized he'd looked in the wrong direction. He turned slightly to his right, just in time to see the fist coming out of the dark. It caught him above his left eye, jarring him back several paces. Before he could cry out another buried itself in his paunch, whooshing the air from his lungs and sinking him to his knees. A blow across the back of his head smashed his nose against the flagstone. A boot hit his kidney, another his thigh. He tried to push himself back to his feet and something—fist, knee, boot, elbow—slammed into his larynx. He gasped and grabbed for his throat, rolled onto his back and tasted the salty sweet flow of his tears, and his blood.

Part Three
THE HUNT

ONE

(1)

"Yep," said Mac Felsom, gesturing grandly toward the embankment opposite the depot. "Right over there they had them big lights and things. Must've been a hundred people runnin around here. At least a hundred."

Jason nodded agreeably, but he was finding it difficult following the grizzled man's narration. He was too busy peering down the tracks, waiting for the 9:35, a twice-a-week passenger train that stopped at Windriver only when there were passengers to discharge. It was Tuesday. Donna was coming home.

Felsom spat over the edge of the platform and hitched his belt up. "Damnedest thing you ever saw, Clarke. Funny little man in a silly hat orderin these big guys around like they was kids. He didn't have much t'say t'me. He said, 'Mister Felsom, you just stand here like you always do and flag the train down. Got it? When I say action, you flag the train down.' Naturally, I don't tell him I don't flag no trains down. Not even back then. Nineteen forty-three, it was. M'boys

155

weren't even a gleam in my old eye then." He hawked and spat again. "You hear anything about Red?"

Jason took off his hat and slapped it impatiently against his leg. From the tracks to the storehouse and from the waiting pens to the land sweeping away from the embankment to the distant peaks, his gaze would not rest on anything for more than a few moments at a time. He was beginning to feel ridiculous, standing here waiting for a train, for a woman. As if he were the hero in an old English film, huddled against the cold in Victoria Station while the heroine sat anxiously in her compartment, her cheek pressed hard against the window so she could see him as soon as possible and blow him a kiss. Ridiculous. If he were lucky, she would be pleasantly surprised; if he were not, she would be unbearably polite.

"Hey, Clarke, you still with me?"

He forced a smile. "Sorry, Mac, daydreaming."

"Asked if you knew anything bout Red."

"Red?" He frowned his puzzlement, then nodded quickly. "Oh. Regan. Yes. As a matter of fact I was down to Blairs yesterday."

"What I heard is true?"

"What's that?"

"He lost an eye?"

"No." Jason peered down the tracks again. "No. A couple of ribs broken and his right leg, lost a lot of blood. His face was pretty cut up from what I could see, which wasn't much because of all the bandages. He has one hell of a concussion. He's still unconscious."

"He gonna live?"

"His doctors think so."

Felsom stomped the length of the platform, poking his head into the waiting room as though there were customers there who needed to be checked. "Bastards oughta be strung up."

Jason made no comment. It was a common sentiment in town, and had been since word had spread of the attack on the druggist. The problem was, there were no hard suspects, no viable clues. Doc Vance had returned from tending Rachel and had heard faint groans from the house next door. He had almost ignored them, thinking Regan had probably drunk too much and hadn't made it to his door. Then he'd seen Lureen high-heeling it down the street, muttering loudly about being stood up by a sawed-off, goddamned poor excuse for a man.

The two of them had found Regan sprawled on his steps, his clothes drenched in the dark of his own blood.

Lureen was now a minor celebrity; and Mitch Regan was in Blairs, fighting for his life.

"Oughta be strung up," Felsom repeated, slapping one of the posts.

"Who?"

The stationmaster sputtered and could not meet Jason's sudden, rage-weary gaze. He shook a fist in ambiguous accusation and retreated to his office.

Jason wasn't surprised. He had seen the same reaction most of Sunday and all day yesterday—men and women gathering in small groups around the sheriff's office, waiting for word of capture and trial, for old-fashioned rope justice. It wasn't so much that Regan was beloved as it was the cowardice of the act: at night, the odds against the middle-aged man, no apparent chance given him to defend himself. Then, worse, leaving him there to die without even an anonymous phone call to alert the authorities.

Late Sunday afternoon Galen had asked Jason to cover the story for him.

"Why me?"

"Because you're a reporter and you're drivin me nuts sitting around here moonin like a lovesick calf."

"I am not mooning."

"The hell you're not. And she isn't gonna be back until Tuesday and don't you think it's about time you earned your keep around here?"

He had almost argued but changed his mind when he saw the faint trembling of his cousin's arm, the tension at his neck where the muscles stood out like cords. He'd sat in the rocker by the hearth practically all day. Jason had been amazed to learn that Esther Lynn had offered to come by to prepare them dinner, and that the offer had been accepted. Still, he had said nothing. Galen would tell him what was wrong in his own good time. Meanwhile, the old man was right. His walking around, talking, listening and theorizing had done him no good at all. Nothing had changed, and nothing was likely to change, at least not for a while.

The town divided itself into three main camps in assessing the blame. The first was positive Mitch had found himself a married woman, possibly Gloria, and the husband had meted out the oldest justice in the books; the second suspected that Mitch's frequent evening journeys into Blairs had somehow, rather mysteriously, gotten him involved with some of that town's more unsavory personalities; and the third pinned the blame directly on the Indians. The fact that no one could develop a reasonable theory why the Shoshone should pick on him did not deter them. Ted Waters, among others, was convinced Jake Harmon was supremely derelict in his duty by not arresting every damned Indian in the valley.

By the time Jason had returned to the house, his notepad was filled with his own personal brand of shorthand and he was bone-weary and irritable. But two hours later, after he had transcribed his notes into a legible ordering, he was also feeling marvelously spurred. His mind was working on something other than Windriver, the fingers of his left hand falling into a soundless snapping—a habit he'd developed to goad his thinking. When he'd looked up from the couch just before eleven, Galen was standing in the hall doorway, smiling.

"Feels good, huh."

Jason tried a frown, couldn't help a smile. "Therapy, I guess."

Another hour and the notes were reorganized, and Galen promised that Esther Lynn would type them up in time for inclusion.

"Inclusion? In what?"

"You ever hear of the *Banner*, son? It's a newspaper. You work for it, remember? If Esther works her ass off, it'll be out in Tuesday's edition." He'd saddened, then. "Nuts. A day late and a dollar sorry." Then he'd brightened. "But we got the story and that's what counts, right? She can also call it to Blairs. They got a rag there, a daily, that isn't worth wipin your ass with. Still, what the hell."

"What the hell," Jason agreed, and poured them both a brandy.

"I called Daniel before you got back."

"Really? Why?"

"Use your head, boy. He's got to keep his people from comin in town for a day or so. We don't need Waters more aggravated than he already is. If he talks loud enough, there might be more like we had on Saturday."

Jason wasn't sure he agreed. He'd thought now might be the perfect time for the whites and Indians to get together, pool their resources and find the assailants on a cooperative basis. But he had been tired, had not argued. Then yesterday, when he'd returned from visiting the unconscious Regan in Blairs, there'd been a message for him from Donna, telling him which train she would be taking back to Windriver.

"Did she say she wanted me to meet her?" he'd asked Galen in his office. "I mean, did she specifically ask me to meet her?"

"No," Galen said, unable to conceal a smirk behind his hand. "She gave me the information, I took it down, and I thought you weren't mooning."

(2)

The land in shades of green, shades of gold, shades of brown swept away from the embankment uninterrupted save for the occasional blur of a shady pine stand. Grass and weeds were naturally low, and Jason started when a streak of dark plunged out of the sky. He grabbed the nearest post and watched in amazement as it swooped into the bottom of a curve and vanished for a moment into the field, returning almost as rapidly to climb back toward the blue.

"Damned fast, ain't it," Felsom remarked behind him. "Them things, I tell ya, they ain't nothin in this world what can get outa their way." He belched long and low, and Jason smelled the sour liquor on his breath. "Them birds they live like kings, o'course, since old MacKenzie posted all his land right to the top of the mountain. They come down from Kramer's, take what they want, leave again and got no worries in the world. Recall a man—back in nineteen and fifty-seven it was—he tried to bag the female. MacKenzie— he was a bit younger then—he caught the fool halfway up the slope. Beat the living hell out of him. The living hell. Eagle, see, that's the family totem. Kind of like a pet, y'see, only more so."

"Incredible," Jason whispered, watching the golden brown bird soar effortlessly with its dangling burden toward the distant mountain.

Then, without warning, he was jolted by a memory. Not from a photograph, not from his mother's ramblings; but a real memory, and he was off the platform before Felsom could stop him. He skipped over the eastbound tracks and knelt on the graveled bed of those heading west. He looked up squinting as he laid a hand on the warming rust-colored steel.

"Clarke, you crazy?"

He waited, holding his breath. *Put a penny on the rail, the train'll jump the tracks. Use a nickel, it'll blow up. Use a quarter and you'll die.* His lips twitched into a smile. He could feel it, and as the memory surged through him, he laughed aloud. By god, he could feel it! The rail was vibrating; the train was coming.

"Clarke, you wanna get yourself killed?"

He stood and dusted his knees, took off his hat and slapped it to his thighs as he headed back for the platform. He felt great. He had remembered, and though it wasn't the house and it wasn't his father before the change had twisted him, it was a real memory.

"I swear to god you Easterners are all alike, I swear to god."

"No," Jason told him, punching his arm playfully. "There isn't one of them like me."

(3)

The train pulled away only five minutes late and she was crossing the tracks awkwardly, a sample case in one hand, a suitcase in the other. When she saw him waiting on the steps her blue-grey eyes widened in surprise, then narrowed in mock suspicion when Jason put two fingers to the Stetson's brim and reached for her luggage.

"Are you the welcome wagon?" she said as they walked slowly away from the stationhouse.

"Yep."

"You must have gotten up awfully early this morning."

"Yep."

"Don't tell me." She stepped ahead of him and began walking backward, a finger to her chin, the other aimed at his chest. "Jimmy Cagney, right? Or is that 'You dirty rat'?"

"Yep."

She laughed and grabbed his arm, hugging it briefly, while he astonished himself by recalling so much about her. The pale band beneath her glasses where the sun hadn't tanned as darkly; the way her short hair curled out and away from the collar of her shirt; the way her hip brushed against his, the way her left hand drew portraits in the air whenever she talked. It had only been a few days, but he realized now how long it had seemed, and hoped she wouldn't leave again.

At the Pike they turned left. Two blocks straight ahead and another left brought them to her home. This time he didn't stop at the gate but followed her to the front door, waiting silently as she unlocked the door and gestured him inside.

It was a spare room, no frills. The wallpaper was faded floral, the throw rugs hooked and color-banded. There was a dining area to the right and a couch and armchairs to the left, arranged in deference to the fieldstone fireplace. Draperies covered the windows and watercolor portraits in ornate oval frames hung on the walls. A scent, her scent, pervaded the mustiness that had grown during her absence.

He stood awkwardly in the center of the large room while she bustled through the chores of opening the windows and dumping her luggage in a room whose door was in the corner at the right. She returned to push him into a quilted armchair and stood in front of him with her hands on her hips. He set his hat on the floor beside the chair and crossed his legs at the knees, only to uncross them and fold his hands in his lap. Then he grabbed the ends of the armrests and kneaded them hard.

"You must be tired," he said finally.

"Not really." She pulled a similar chair over the floor and sat down in front of him, their knees almost touching. "I slept most of the way back. It's really pretty comfortable."

"You, uh, find anything exciting?"

"Nothing, and I really didn't expect to. I did it mainly to show Doc what a jerk he can be sometimes." She brushed an invisible strand of hair off her forehead. "But it was good to get away. You want some coffee?"

"You had breakfast?"

"Nope." And she was gone, calling out to him from the kitchen enough description of her trip to inform him she'd been bored. Vindicated but bored. And when she returned with a laden tray in her hands, he shoved her chair to one side and set a low pine coffee table between them. He hadn't realized how hungry he was, and smiled to himself when he realized he'd forgotten about eating in his rush to meet her train.

"And you," she said when they were done and nursing their tea. "What have you been doing?"

He could see no way to summarize it gracefully, so he began with the sandlot fight on Saturday afternoon, the attack that night on Mitch Regan, reactions of the people and what Harmon was doing to keep the lid on the town. "Which is," he said, "just about nothing. Oh, he's kept Waters from forming a lynching party and I suppose that's something. But other than that, you'd think he was working on a traffic accident."

She grinned, holding her cup like a veil to her face. "He won't rush around, if that's what's bothering you. This isn't the East, remember. No sirens, no indignant politicians, no TV cameras. Jake's been around here for a million years, and he has his boys trained well. Believe me, he knows what he's doing."

"I hope so."

Her gaze softened. "You care, don't you."

He nodded without hesitating. "Yeah. Yeah, I think I do, Donna. A lot."

He sat with his legs outstretched and crossed at the ankles, his hands loose on his stomach, and what felt like a permanent quiet smile at his lips. He could see she was more tired than she would admit, and thought several times of protesting her idea of going to the clinic once she'd showered and changed. It wouldn't do him any good, however. He knew she had patients waiting anxiously for her return, could see in her manner a restlessness that another day off would only inflame.

She placed her cup on its saucer and leaned forward, hands clasped over her knees. "In spite of inflation," she said, "I'll give you a penny for your thoughts."

He stared until her smile wavered. "You want me to be honest?"

She sat back immediately, uneasily. "I don't know. I'm not sure."

"I was admiring your dedication to duty. And I was wondering why you were out here."

Why are you here, Mister Clarke, MacKenzie said; I mean here in Windriver.

"I . . . I could ask you the same."

"Yes."

She lowered herself to the floor and began stacking the dishes onto the tray. Distress made her movements awkward, clumsy, and she kept pushing her glasses back even though they weren't slipping.

"Donna . . ."

"No, it's a fair question."

"It's none of my business." But he was startled by the look that said *I want it to be.* "Listen, we can talk about it later. You're tired, I'm tense, and it just wasn't fair." He reached out to take her wrist, found his hand gripped tightly instead.

"There's always a later," she said bitterly, and brushed her hair back from her eyes. Then she pulled gently on his arm until he was kneeling beside her. "Have you ever been to Connecticut?"

He nodded. "Once or twice."

"I lived there," she said. "Once my studies were done I worked with this really nice guy in a small town west of Hartford. Very swank, very nice. Couldn't ask for a better place to start. He taught me a lot, let me make my own mistakes—one of the best teachers I ever had. He really loved animals, and it was easy to see he wasn't out there to latch onto some of that money those people throw around. It was really nice, Jason. He did everything for me but buy me my own place." She gulped for air, then. "I was coming back from a movie one night. A Friday. It's a funny thing, but I can't even remember what the movie was called. It was probably a comedy, something to ease me into the weekend, if you know what I mean. But I still don't know what it was called, and . . . anyway, I lived in this little apartment building. No guards or anything like that because this wasn't the big city and everybody was proud that we didn't need any guards. There was this man, a big man, he . . ." A tear slipped to her cheek, was followed by another. Jason reached for it, but she stopped him by jerking her head away. "He had a razor, and it's easy to watch all those news programs and documentaries that tell you you have to scream and kick him in the balls and spray him with Mace. But he had a razor. And I was so terrified I couldn't even breathe. I remember that. Not being able to breathe. And he had this goddamned fucking big razor and he cut my shirt down the front and cut my bra in half and punched me in the gut and . . . I couldn't even breathe. Even while he was doing it I don't know how I was breathing.''

Jason sat back on his heels. His hand was aching from her grip, but he only gave her the other and she took that, too.

"I saw him. I mean, it was like he didn't give a damn, so he didn't try to hide his face. And when it was over I went to my apartment and I threw up. For hours. Then I did the proper thing and I called the police and they caught him two days later. I answered a lot of questions and looked at a lot of pictures and they caught him in Hartford. He had taken the train out. He was a nobody. A guy. He still had the razor and he still had my shirt in his apartment. There was a trial, and he . . . he wasn't convicted, and a month later no one was bringing their precious pets to me anymore because it was my fault, don't you know, my fault because I didn't scream and I didn't kick him in his balls. I liked it, you see. I'm a woman. I'm supposed to have all these fantasies of liking it. One plus one, and so I must have liked it.

"I had girl friends—a few, and none of them very close— and they couldn't look me in the eye anymore. They wanted to ask me about it and they didn't dare, so they couldn't look me in the eye anymore. The guy I worked with, he was very nice about it and very liberal in his understanding, but he said he had a family to support and I was losing him a lot of business because the people in this really wonderful town, this little goddamned pissant town, they either pitied the hell out of me or they . . . they couldn't understand how I could allow someone to do that to me.''

She rocked on her knees. Slowly. Seeing nothing. Seeing it all.

"It wasn't an assault, you know. It says that in the records some goddamned place, but it wasn't an assault. It was a fucking violation. There's a difference. It was *me* he raped, not just any woman. *Me,* and everything that *is* me.

"And then . . . I used to come out here every year or so on vacations. Get away from the East, all the people. A make-believe cowgirl. Doc knew me and would call on me once in a while if he got stuck. Since it was the only other place I knew I took all my money and came out here again. I started spending more and more time with Doc because he'd taken ill for a while and . . . I just never left. I just . . . never left.''

He could feel the heat of her hands, the heat from her cheeks, and watched her tears and felt like weeping himself. Finally, she raised her head and gave him a smile that was bitter and wondering. He pulled out of her grip gently and lightly took hold of her shoulders.

"Don't you dare," she told him. "Don't you dare feel sorry for me."

Still kneeling, he let his hands slide slowly to her back, not pulling, not insisting, until she was in his embrace with her head on his shoulder. His fingers traced her spine, trailed across her waist, returned to her shoulders and slipped into her hair. He could feel her tears drenching his shirt, felt one hand curled tightly into an impotent fist. She stirred and pushed away without breaking the embrace, and stared at him, searching, a frown marking her puzzlement.

"I'm sorry," he said quietly. "I just . . . I just got so angry for you."

She laughed then—a halting, relieved sound—and kissed him. Held him, then eased him away and asked him to tell Doc she would be in after lunch.

He didn't mind the dismissal; there was little he could say. He was tempted to tell her of his own flight; but the moment was wrong for another exposure of a scarred soul—it might seem as though he were playing a topping game that wasn't a game at all. So he kept his silence, kissed her again and left the house wondering if he could find for her what she'd lost.

(4)

It wasn't until midafternoon that Jason was able to drive Donna's image from his mind, her eyes swelling red and her hands stumbling over the dishes on the tray. He had eaten a tasteless lunch at home with Galen, then began wandering through the streets in an effort to find a new approach to Windriver's problem.

"You might talk to Kelly, y'know," Galen had remarked while eating. "Word is he wasn't at the bar Saturday night, and that's unusual. He sure as hell hasn't run out of money."

So he headed for River Road, to the worn wooden bridge that stretched sixty yards across the river. Though he was another hundred yards away from the low spike-iron fence that surrounded the graveyard, he could see Stan Kelly seated on a stone bench to one side of the wide gates. There was a crumpled brown paper sack on the ground beside him, a sandwich in his hand. He looked up when Jason approached, his eyes falling deeply into dark-rimmed sockets, making his face look more cadaverous than the bodies he interred.

Jason stood in front of the open gates, scanning the array of new and old tombstones, noting there were none of the angel-and-saint carvings so common in the East. Grey slabs, white slabs, weathered and brown slabs in orderly rows over almost fifteen acres. An elm in each corner and one in the center. There were some withered flowers and a wreath, and just inside the gates a lawn mower, a rake, a scythe and a bundle of plastic garbage bags.

"You thinkin of buyin?" Kelly rasped a laugh and wiped his mouth with the back of his hand.

"Not for a while," Jason said, turning to him and smiling.

"No," Kelly said then, twisting around on the bench to pull up one leg and take hold of the knee. His shirt was off and his chest and arms were extraordinarily thin, sundark and corded. He wore a wide-brimmed hat to shade his eyes, and a stained red bandana tied loosely around his neck. "No," he said again.

"No what?"

Kelly smiled; he was missing four front teeth and his tongue poked out from between blackened gums. "No, I didn't see nothin that night. I was huntin Injuns."

"No kidding?"

"Wouldn't shit ya, reporter. Damned redskins aimin to surround us like we was a wagon train, scalp us in our beds and take all our women. Nope. Had my duty that night, and I did it."

"And you didn't see a thing."

"If I had I would've gutted the bastards."

Jason nodded, silently cursing Galen, and shoved his hands deep into his hip pockets, squinting at the sun. "Quiet out here."

"It serves, reporter."

"The name's Clarke."

"Yeah. So I heard."

He stiffened, waiting, then swiveled slowly in place and

spotted the Harmon residence on the other side of the water. Someone was sitting on the front porch. Ellie, he supposed; Steve would be in bed, resting for the night shift.

Kelly set his boots firmly on the ground, groaned loudly and rose. "Gotta work. Keep the place right for the dead, y'know."

"It looks good."

"Sure does. Folks think I can't work no more. Then they come out here and they see what I done for their people." He laughed hoarsely. "Best thing about the job, ain't no Injuns to bury. They gots their own place down to the reservation." He spat over the fence. "Sons of bitches."

Jason looked at him sideways. "The way I hear it, you sold out to them for a fair piece of change."

Kelly picked up the rake and held it across his chest. "I did. But just because I took their money don't mean I gotta like em. Christ, a man's gotta live, y'know."

Jason nodded and walked away, ducking under a low branch from the corner elm. Injuns, he thought with a grim smile; he didn't think people really said that outside the movies. And as he recrossed the bridge, he wondered if Jake Harmon had talked to the man. It didn't seem likely that he'd heard nothing at all that night, not if he were wandering around town like he said.

He shook his head slowly, and found himself heading toward the Pike up Suncrest, passing the rectory just as Bea Steed and Carole Carosa came out the front door. They were struggling with David's wheelchair, thumping it down the steps in a hurry while David used his crutches to follow. Reverend Thornton stood on the threshold, nodding his white-maned head and rubbing his hands dryly. When he saw Jason he smiled a quick greeting and vanished inside.

Jason had gone a few steps past the trio, but stopped when Bea called to him. He turned and waited, comparing the two girls quickly and surprising himself by not being able to pick a clear winner—Bea's frail blonde looks were too much a contrast to Carole's almost sultry brunette Italian. "Hey," he said, "aren't you supposed to be in school or something?"

"Half day," Carole said, pushing David's chair with no apparent effort. "Seniors have their exams this week. Ours are next week." She made a face and Bea laughed.

Jason fell in beside them. "I take it you wish you two were seniors?"

"Are you kidding?" Bea said. "If we were it would mean a whole year closer to college." Her tone was much clearer: *a whole year less we'd have to spend in this town.*

He jerked a thumb over his shoulder, toward the rectory. "You getting some religious guidance?"

David looked at him sharply. "We were asking about Greg."

Jason frowned. "Greg?"

"Greg Thornton," Bea said, trying to sound bored. "He's the preacher's kid. He's a senior."

"Only because of his father," Carole said. "If he were anybody else he would have been kicked out years ago. What a creep!"

"Carole!"

"Well, he is, Bea."

At the Pike they hesitated, the girls obviously in a hurry to get someplace else. When Jason offered to wheel David over to the bar, they were almost embarrassing in their thanks, effusive in their fussing over David and lightning quick in their escape. Jason looked after them, not knowing what to say.

"Don't worry about it," David said then. "I'm punishment."

Jason couldn't think of a response and contented himself with an unintelligible mumbling before taking the young man across the street to the bar's red door. It was locked. David lifted a hand in exasperation and asked Jason if he would mind taking him around back. His father was in the barbershop, and David hated going in there. "If they're not joking about me carryin around my own chair, they joke about me and the girls." He grimaced. "I can't take it."

Once in the backyard David wheeled himself beneath one of the trees, gesturing for Jason to join him and have a seat on the grass. It was cool, quiet, and Jason abruptly realized how much walking he had done. He sat and leaned his back against the trunk, combing his fingers through his hair and massaging the back of his neck.

David stared at the house. "It's true what I said, y'know."

"What is?" Lazily, not really listening.

"About punishment. I can walk, you've seen me, but Dad's decided Carole's gettin too big for her britches. They had a hell of a fight last night and he slapped her."

Jason's eyes had been closing, snapped open in astonishment.

"Yep. Right across the kisser. Wants to get herself a place of her own, she says. Says she's almost eighteen and she can do what she wants, so she wants to move out. God, what a kid."

"She doesn't sound any different from any other kid I know," Jason muttered. "Sooner or later they all want to get out. She's probably not the only one her age who's champing at the bit."

"Yeah, well . . . of course, Bea doesn't help at all, y'know," David continued without looking up, as if he hadn't heard. "All that one does is bitch about how great it'll be when they can get out of Windriver. You've heard that one before, right? They can't wait. Kids. You can't figure them, Jason. So she tells Dad she wants to leave after Christmas and he tells her not on her life. She calls him a dumb wop and he slugs her." He grinned. "She needs it, though. She really can be insufferable."

"Like you said, she's a kid," Jason said, with a shrug of resignation.

"She's a bitch. She can't see the trouble the folks have because the money's gone on account of the hospital, and she can't see me in the goddamned chair. It's her, and it's Bea, and they think they're the hottest things to hit this town since the day Gloria Perkins rode in on the train. Would you believe Dad thinks she's still a virgin?" The laugh was loud, and framed in acid.

Good god, Jason thought, I do not want to hear this.

David shook his head, now in reluctant admiration. He pointed to a narrow window just over the back door. "That's her room. She and Bea sneak out at night, probably go drinking with Hardy Green and his friends. She made me promise not to tell."

"You worried about her?"

"Who? Me?"

Jason nodded to himself. David was only twenty-five and already feeling old. He was stuck in a wheelchair, or on legs that weren't his, and wished he could turn back the clock and be a teenager again. Whole again. Like his sister and her friends.

"You talk to Ellie Felsom?" David asked casually. "About Mitch, I mean."

"Why? Should I?"

"She never goes out. She might've heard somethin, seen somethin. You never know."

Jason hitched himself closer to the tree and stared at him. He'd only spoken with David a few times, and each time he somehow managed to bring Ellie into the conversation. A lost love? Was the kid carrying a torch, for god's sake?

"No, I haven't," he said carefully. He plucked at the grass, tossing the blades high and watching them ride the soft breeze. "What's this about Greg Thornton?"

"You ain't heard? Man, he's been gone for four, five days. And graduation's comin up damned soon. If he doesn't get his butt back here he's gonna miss out. Idiot."

Jason stared at him, trying to make the connection between the preacher's son, Ellie and David's sister. When he failed, he rose unsteadily and managed an excuse to get him out of the yard. Once on the Pike he stared over at Harmon's office, a finger rubbing at his chin while his left hand made a quiet snapping sound.

(5)

It wasn't until Wednesday afternoon that Jason was able to corner the sheriff in his office. When he'd tried the day before he only trapped himself in a long monologue from Art Felsom, complaining about the changes in the town, in Harmon, and how the place was too good to let itself get run down the way it had. Jason hadn't argued and escaped during a phone call and ran into Galen on the sidewalk. From there it was a sidetrack into the luncheonette where the editor held court until nine and Jason once again marveled at the old man's repertoire of half-baked stories, top-of-the-lungs grumblings, and how it was received with affection and good humor by everyone. On the way home he had hugged his cousin impulsively, and Galen told him angrily he was upsetting his stomach.

"Bad enough I got to take some foul red stuff Vance gives me for m'ailments. Now you got to screw it all up. Just like you, Jase. It's just like you."

Jason had laughed, had slept well and late and found Jake sitting in a wicker chair outside his office just after lunch.

"Nothin much to it," Harmon told him a second time, pushing until the chair thumped back against the window. From the inside came the clatter of Ellie's typewriter and the static of the dispatch radio. "We've been out the past two nights, ever since that fool Reverend got round to tellin us Greg was gone. And we haven't found a thing. No horse, no clothes . . . no bones."

"I gather that's unusual," Jason said, leaning against the doorframe, his arms folded over his chest and his hat pulled low over his eyes. He could see Ellie working, but she had not looked up to acknowledge him.

The sheriff shrugged, his gaze seldom pausing as the two of them scanned the street, the houses, the dull storm-warning blue of the overcast sky. "If the boy was hurt by a fall or whatever, yes, I'd say it was. That pinto of his, the one with the red neck, it knows its way back to stables and should've shown up by now. If he's run off, though . . ." and he shrugged again.

"I take it you're not worried."

Harmon tipped back his hat, scrubbed his upper lip. "Son, I worry all the time. But if you're askin me am I gonna call out the whole town and cover them slopes inch by inch—no, I ain't gonna do that."

"Why do you say the slopes?"

"Christ, boy, ain't you learned nothin yet? That kid's the state's goddamnedest best poacher! It's the first place to look. But this ain't the first time Greg's pulled a stunt like this. Last time—let's see—back in March, I think it was—he took off, had us fussin around for damned near a week. Then he come back from Cheyenne by way of Blairs all joined up with the army and sayin how sorry he was everybody got their dander up. Bullshit. Once or twice a year he takes off, just like this."

"But what if—"

"He's not where he should be or might be," Harmon said, shifting with impatience. "Simon has some of his own men checkin around. And Lamont Riley, the hand over to Perkins's place—he's got a few boys lookin. If he's still out there,

and thank god the weather's been good, he'll be found, one
way or the other. If he's not, there isn't anything else we can
do, Mister Clarke."

"The State Police—"

"—have been duly notified. They got a Greg file, too."

Jason straightened. It was hopeless. He was crazy for
thinking there was a connection here, and he chided himself
for not asking Galen about Thornton first. Badgering the law
about what was obviously nothing wasn't going to do his
standing much good.

"All right, Sheriff," he said. "Sorry to bother you." He put
a finger to his hatbrim, smiled and walked off.

"Galen must be hard up."

Jason stopped, frowned and turned in place.

"I mean about the story," Harmon said genially. "Thornton up and leaving ain't exactly news around here, like I
said."

Jason considered a moment while tucking his fingertips into
his waistband. "It's possible, just possible someone hurt
him."

"Oh?" Harmon nodded as if he hadn't considered it
before. "Nope. Not if you're talkin about all that hot air
comin from Waters's emporium over there." He laughed
quietly, kindly, when Jason wasn't quick enough to conceal
his guilt. "Listen, Mister Clarke, Ted makes a lotta noise, and
god knows I've been listenin to it for nearly fifty years, but
Greg isn't one he wants to hurt."

"You mean because the boy's white."

"I mean," the sheriff said harshly, "because Ted's not the
hurtin kind." He squinted. "You ain't thinkin he maybe had
somethin to do with old Mitch, are you?"

Jason shook his head.

"Good." Harmon dropped his chair back on its four legs
and rose, slowly, one hand to an armrest to aid his balance.

Jason nodded his farewell again and continued on toward
the *Banner* office, wishing there was a hole nearby he could
drop into.

"You're Peter's son, aren't you."

He stopped at the curb.

"You should've changed your name, son. Old farts like me
got memories, y'know."

He sifted through the words for a threat, but found none

and grinned. When he took the opposite curb he paused and glanced back over his shoulder, but Harmon was gone, the chair stark in the bright hazed sun, etched into the still air without a shadow for definition. Then he walked past the luncheonette and theater and had his hand out for the newspaper office's door when he heard a muffled cry from around the corner. He cocked his head, listening, and let his curiosity take him to the edge of the building. A woman was leaning against the brick wall, reaching down and rubbing her right ankle gingerly. She sensed him and glanced up, her lips taut in pain suddenly loosening and smiling.

"You all right?" Jason said, coming up beside her.

She pointed to a rise in the concrete. "I wasn't watching where I was going, which is pretty usual for me. Thought I twisted my ankle for sure, but I'm more embarrassed than hurt, I think."

Her white shirt deepened her olive complexion, and it opened to let him see the push and rise of her breasts. She turned and leaned a shoulder against the brick. "You're Jason Clarke. I'm Gloria Perkins. We haven't been formally introduced." She held out a hand and he took it, surprised by the strength of the grip, and the play of her long fingers across his wrist. "Seems to me I heard you used to live in my house."

My house. He searched for mockery or scorn and found none, but wasn't completely sure. She released his hand, letting one finger drift over his palm, then crossed her arms under her breasts and smiled at him sideways.

"I did," he admitted. "It was a long time ago."

"You drove by once or twice," she said, mildly accusing, pouting disappointment. "I would have let you see the old homestead if you'd asked."

"Thanks," he said, lifting his chin, looking at the street—anyplace so long as he wouldn't have to look in her eyes. "I, uh, don't think—"

"It's okay, Jason. I *can* call you Jason, can't I? Really, it's okay. Anytime you want to drop in, do. You don't even have to call."

He looked down to her feet. Bare, in sandals, the toenails painted a deep solemn red. He imagined her legs beneath the snug jeans which hugged the hips and waist so tightly the material outlined her groin.

"You married, Jason?"

He blinked. "No. No, I'm not."

"You lookin?"

He smiled. "Not really." And immediately chided himself for having said it.

Her smile became almost feral. "Well, I'm sure my husband would be glad to meet you, Jason. He's always talkin about going East for a vacation. One of these days." Her arms shifted higher, and the shirt opened wider. "He talks a lot, Billyboy does, but nothin much gets done." Suddenly she straightened and put a hand on his arm. "Got to be goin. But you do come out, Jason. We may not be rich, but we do have hospitality."

She touched a finger to the point of his chin as she walked by, and though he knew it was what she wanted he turned to watch the tidal roll of her hips as she strode deliberately away. At the corner she turned, gave him a laughing wink and walked on.

He laughed aloud. He felt like a helpless adolescent, and kicked at the ground as he considered her reputation, and the temptation. When he dropped into the chair in front of Galen's desk and told him about it the editor threw a pencil at him.

"Damnedest woman I ever saw," Galen muttered. "Christ, right out on the street!"

"I'm flattered," Jason said, grinning.

"Don't be." He swiveled his chair around in a complete circle, mimed a shot at two flies circling low under the ceiling and caught the pencil Jason threw back without even looking. "The manhunt continues," he said then, "am I right? No clues to Regan's attackers yet? Nope," he answered himself. "As for Greg Thornton, all agencies have been informed of the kid's last known whereabouts and description, Reverend Thornton is praying for his safety and nobody has the faintest idea in hell where he's gone if he hasn't bolted the place for his pretty uniform."

Jason glared at him. "If you know so damned much, why did you make me go out there?"

"I didn't make you do anything. I only suggested it at breakfast."

"You're splitting hairs."

"You're getting restless."

Jason tossed his hat on the floor in disgust. "Yeah, I guess." He sniffed. "Galen, Harmon knows who I am now, too."

He saw Galen pick up a pen, drop it, push away from the desk. "It was bound to happen, son."

"I suppose."

"You're not bothered, are you?"

Jason shook his head slowly. "It's just unnerving. I mean, it wasn't like he did more than go on a drunken tear—"

"That's right," Galen said. "And people around here—" He stopped and chuckled. "I was going to say they don't hold a grudge, but I just thought of one."

"I'll be damned. Who?"

"Ted Waters. Seems he was havin a hard time back then for a while and took himself a weekend job here and there. For a few months he even worked for Simon."

Jason stared, a slow grin growing to match Galen's. "You're kidding."

"Nope. Your dad broke an arm and a rib."

"Good lord, should I watch my back?"

Galen laughed. "Son, when it comes to Ted Waters, everyone in this town watches his back." He sobered, then. "Poor old bastard. Been takin on the world ever since his wife died of cancer fifteen years ago. Course, he wasn't all that sweet and wonderful before, either, but the woman held the reins then. So . . . nope, you don't have to watch your back, but don't be surprised if he remembers with something less than affection."

"Marvelous," Jason said. "You really know how to make a guy feel welcome."

(6)

He walked that night, long after dark. Avoiding where he could the lights of Valley Pike, skating, it seemed, from one streetlamp's tiny white island to another until he found himself in front of Donna's. He had been trying to piece together what it was about him that made the people of Windriver apparently level with him—talk to him without restraint. Perhaps they sensed a kinsman, or perhaps there was something in the clouds of his eyes that hinted he was very much like them, in no way privileged to wear the good guy's white.

It bothered him, and it pleased him, and he almost didn't see the flare of a cigarette rising slowly from behind a carefully cupped hand.

"I thought it was you," she said, a dark figure on the stoop.

He sat beside her without invitation. "It's a beautiful night."

"It's going to rain. There aren't any stars."

He rested his forearms on his thighs and clasped his hands between his knees. He hesitated. He wanted to ask if she were all right, if she had recovered from the morning before, but all he could do was stare at the gouges the shadows made on the sidewalk.

"Jason?"

There was a rumbling in the distance, like the sound of mountains sliding painfully into the sea. A glow of blue-white that lasted less than a second.

"I don't know you yet."

He understood what she meant and closed his eyes against it. They opened when he felt the press of her lips cool against his cheek.

"How patient are you?" she wanted to know.

He shrugged with a tilt of his head. "As patient as I have to be, I guess."

"Do you mean that?"

"You ask a lot of questions."

"You haven't given me any answers."

Blue-white. Rumbling.

He told himself it was tension reaching out from the distant storm, but something new had been added, an extra ingredient to a dark brew already simmering. He recognized it as the reaction he'd had to his first sight of Kramer's Mountain, and was about to dismiss it when he heard a husking through the foliage. He looked up, and stared out into the dark. There was no breeze; the husking continued.

Donna's hand covered his wrist.

There was no breeze.

He was glad there was no porch light, or light seeping from the windows. But he wished the nearest streetlamp were about fifteen yards closer.

Donna's hand shifted. "I know," she said, her head bowed, her voice whispering. "I've felt it all night."

He was relieved that he wasn't crazy, that he wasn't alone, but it still didn't explain why the leaves moved without a breeze.

"My father," she said then, cleared her throat and said it again. "He used to say it meant the ghosts were out walking. It has something to do with the way the air up here reacts to a storm."

He thought of Stan Kelly sitting in the graveyard chewing on his sandwich like a cow on her cud; no ghost would dare, he decided. When the breeze finally reached him it was cold . . . too cold, and he slipped an arm around Donna's shoulders without asking permission. The storm and the town, he thought: two sources of electricity bound for collision. The hairs on his arms suddenly tingled like spiders scuttling toward his hands, and he shuddered and Donna hugged him. He turned and she kissed him; but he didn't like the way the leaves moved against the wind.

TWO

(1)

The heavy curtains on the French doors were brown tinged with gold, and they darkened the room to a light born of caves. The pervading scent was that of age and earth, the intermittent sound that of ragged, desperate breathing. The bed had been moved to the center of the floor, the totem candlesticks placed behind the headboard. At the foot of the bed the coverlet was neatly folded, revealing sheets the same shade as the curtains. Two long down pillows spanned the mattress.

(Father Wind, Mother Night)

Rachel stirred but kept her eyes closed. Her arms lay at her sides, her left hand clawing weakly at the sheet, her right tightly closed around a wand of crackling parchment. There was no youth left at all in her face. Flesh sagged and skin became waxen. She took a deep breath that sounded like drowning.

(Father)

Moisture gathered in the purple sockets of her eyes, and as soon as she felt it she blinked it angrily away. This was no time for weeping. It was done, and there was nothing in her powers that would alter the fact. Any sense of betrayal was reserved for her nightmares; any sense of her failure was twisted by the pain. Brief pain. White pain. Building in her chest, her shoulders, encircling her throat and dissipating when she parted cracked lips for a soundless scream.

A fragment of the white man's prayer: . . . *left undone those things which ought to have been done.*

Her lips quivered into a sighquick smile. Undone, perhaps, but no longer unfinished. The deterioration of her body she understood as punishment for assuming power not rightfully hers. She had used the Teaching and personally killed the boy Harry for the blood sacrifice when she should have found herself a nestling, as the Teaching had warned. And now she was paying for her vanity (though the nestling had been found), and she accepted the extraction as the price for her preening, and the price for her success.

It had been darkly glorious, that one evening of soaring, that one night of death; despite the price, she still remembered the blood with a satisfied smile. And though ever since then it had been the nestling on the wing, the nestling working the Teaching, she liked to pretend she was there by its side, there as the creature dove in for the kill.

She coughed, and her throat felt laced with lingering sparks.

Undone, but no longer finished.

(Mother)

The price, and the memory, and nothing left now but the hope. She knew if she surrendered that hope to despair she would not be able to die in the way that she wanted. The hope was what held her, gave air to her weakening lungs and a rhythm to her stubborn heart; the hope was what hurt her far more than the pain, waking her at midnight to utter a prayer. She was convinced that her loss of control was meant to be. That nuances in the Teaching had foreshadowed it, and she had missed them. That the Circle would be closed, and would be started again, despite the fact the nestling was now beyond her.

It was possible.

It had to be possible.

She stirred again, her head palsied until her eyes snapped open and she stared blindly at the ceiling. Slowly, her right hand lifted from the sheet and she listened as the parchment's autumn voice filled the dark room.

She smiled.

A moment later the door opened. The corridor was dark; no light disturbed the progress of the dying. A figure slight and apprehensive crossed the bare floor to the bed, touched Rachel's arm and remained there, waiting.

"Palemoon."

A voice filled with the command of age, the resignation of ending, the fervor of belief . . . the venom of hatred.

The hand that held the parchment whipped at the air.

"The one who was marked."

Palemoon nodded, reached across the woman and took the parchment from her. Before she could pull away, however, her forearm was snared, skin pinched hard between bone and withered bone.

"You understand," Rachel said. Swallowed. "The one who was marked."

Palemoon nodded again; the hand fell away to thump on the mattress.

Rachel closed her eyes for a moment, weary and fearful. It was the first time she had allowed the Teaching out of her possession since Dark Moon had come to her in a vision years ago. But there was nothing she could do, unless she wanted the Teaching dead. She was forced to trust the child-woman who had served her for twenty years. Fitting, she thought then; an old woman dying, and a young woman once primed to take the role of the nestling. Until it was discovered she had no will of her own. Palemoon. A holy child. Eager and loving, with the mind of a babe.

"Palemoon," she said, "what day is this now?"

The girl trembled; the room scared her.

"Palemoon, what day?"

"Friday," she said. It was the third time that morning she had told Rachel that.

"The storm?"

Again the third time. "Yesterday."

Rachel sighed, the exhalation a rattling. Time lost and not known. It was ending. It was over.

"Palemoon?"

(Father . . . Mother)

"Tell Simon . . . nothing."

"I won't."

Rachel's eyes opened, and Palemoon stumbled backward. A dim light there, and fading, and flecked with angry crimson.

"He will try to stop the Teaching if he knows that you have it. He understands little, and knows little else. Tell him nothing. Do not see him. For your life, Palemoon. For your life."

Unfinished, but not over.

(let me hunt!)

Rachel smiled.

(2)

The law office, set directly across from Harmon's jail, was paneled in deep walnut, its windows sealed with the air conditioner already running though the afternoon's temperature had not quite reached eighty. The receptionist was dressed in mint green and white lace, and she made no comment when she opened the door to Bob Green's inner sanctum and ushered Gloria Perkins in.

"Bitch," said Gloria tonelessly when the door closed behind her. "I'll give you my right arm she's a virgin."

Green, an older and more scrubbed version of his son, shrugged off his camel's hair jacket and yanked his brown silk tie down. "She does her work, she keeps her mouth shut."

"I suppose."

Green watched as she took the green leather chair that cornered his desk. Then he took his own seat and folded his hands on the blotter. "You took a chance coming here today."

"Billy went to Blairs." She grinned. "Wants to see what he can buy with that hundred-fifty thousand he thinks he's getting. He even drove me in and told me to say hi."

"Hi."

She leaned forward, hands on her knees, her gaze drifting over the desktop though she could see him glancing at the shadows where her white shirt had crinkled open. She held her arms closer to her sides, pushing up her breasts. "So, has the old man made an offer yet?"

Green took a moment to answer. "No, not yet. You have to

admit, Gloria, the asking price is awfully high, even for this valley."

"Bull," she said. "It's prime land, and with MacKenzie north and Wheatley across the road, how can it miss, huh? Hey, look, just because Billy doesn't know his ass from . . ." She shook her head impatiently and stood, moved to the small side window facing the brick wall of the real estate office across the narrow alley. She lay her hands on the sill. "I'm getting worried, Bob. Do you really think we can get away with it?"

"I see no problems at all. The money all comes through me, as agreed. Billy'll never know."

She sighed. "I don't think I can wait much longer."

Green shoved back his chair and hurried to stand behind her, one hand snaking around her waist to pull at the cord that lowered the blinds. "Don't fret," he said into the warm scent of her hair. "Don't ask me how, but they always manage to come up with the loot." His hand shifted to her stomach, pressed flat against it and rotated slowly. "Don't worry. It'll happen. Soon, I promise you."

"A quarter of a million," she whispered, leaning back to rest her head on his chest, shivering as his fingers slipped up to brush the underside of her breasts. "Two hundred and . . . honest, Bob, can we do it?"

"You've trusted me this far."

She spun around in the circle of his arms, grinning as she ducked closer to flick her tongue at his chin. "You busy?"

"Always."

"Yeah." She gnawed at the inside of her cheek while her palm rubbed hard over his crotch. "Yeah, you bet your ass you are."

(3)

The choir was scattered over the church's back steps, practicing for Sunday and enjoying the sun. The *a cappella* four-part harmony floated languidly over the trees and the river, reminding Steve Felsom of deep summer nights and the soft rush of the water. But now, in the middle of spring, it matched the perfection of the afternoon and accompanied Ellie as she sat in the rocker, watching the Wind River glare back the sun while she worked on the quilt she wanted done by first snow. He glanced critically over the hedge and decided it could do with a trimming. Jake sure as hell didn't do it anymore, nor took a hand with the lawn, the gutters or hauling down the storm windows and hosing off the screens for the first spurt of warm weather. Jake seldom did anything these days but sit in the front room reading on his days off, every so often glancing up at his daughter. It was stupid. Ellie was bright and laughing and so what if once in a while she fell into a silence that was bothersome, so what if she woke up in the middle of the night and came down to the porch because she had nightmares.

So what?

What did the old bastard expect anyway—that she might suddenly remember what had happened to her and Harry that night? Sometimes he wished Harmon would just retire and disappear to a warmer climate.

"Love?"

He looked down at his wife, feeling the love, wanting to touch her. "Huh?"

"You gonna grow roots or something?"

He grinned and shook his head. "Tryin to talk myself out of working, that's all."

"The clippers are under the porch."

He laughed and took a playful swipe at her shoulder, then jumped over the railing and pulled the shears from their place on the suspended shelf under the flooring. Snapping them viciously, he walked over to the hedge. It was kept higher on the right so that Ellie, from her favorite spot on the porch, wouldn't be able to see the place where . . . he snapped at a branch. Then another, and imagined each leaf, each twig was a small bloody part of Daniel Tallpines's head. By the time he had finished he was grinning without mirth, scarcely able to wait for his shift to begin.

"Darling?" Ellie called. "You want something to drink?"

"It's already four," he said with a glance at his watch. "Got to go on in a couple of hours. I'm takin some of Oaker's time so's he can chase his stupid women or something. He do love his Fridays, and he do love his drinkin."

She giggled with one hand coyly over her mouth. "I meant coffee, silly."

He waved his agreement. "Coffee'll do fine, love. Easy on

the sugar, though, okay? Read the other day that stuff'll kill you."

"Everything does," she said.

He glanced at her sharply. Damn. Hell. It's comin again.

"Darling . . ." She frowned, brushing a light hand over the scars the assault had left on her neck. "Darling?"

"Yes, dear," he said, trying not to sound weary.

"You sure would look awfully nice in a state police uniform, you know? You'd sure look good."

"Yes, Ellie, I know."

Her voice softened, dreamlike and gliding. "Lots of places to live when you belong to the state police."

"Ellie, please."

"Big city, lots of streets and lots of cars. The shops, Steve, and the movies!" She sighed, loudly. "Lots of things we don't have here."

Like no nightmares, he thought as he felt guilt beginning to stir, rallying against his selfishness. And no useless old men and no fuckin Indians.

"I know," he said. "Maybe someday, when we have a nest egg big enough. You know we have to have that, Ellie. You know we gotta keep savin, love."

"I know," she said sadly. "It's just that I like to think about it sometimes, that's all." She stared at him suddenly. "You don't mind, do you? My thinking about it sometimes?"

"No, Ellie." She didn't hear him. He raised his voice. "No, you know I don't."

She set aside the quilting and walked to the front door while he wiped the shears clean on the grass. "Steve?"

"Yeah?"

"That music. The church music."

He looked up, his brow slightly furrowed.

"It was very pretty, wasn't it."

It was, he thought; and it had been over for two hours.

(4)

Jason pulled up in front of the clinic and sounded the horn. His smile was gentle as he watched the traffic build on the Pike, and lifted one hand in an indolent wave when Esther Lynn came out of the *Banner* office. Galen, he knew, would be working late tonight, finishing an editorial commending the town for its restraint and its good sense. The alleviation of tension was by no means complete, but the fierce storm that had swept through the valley the day before had been enough, it seemed, to keep tempers below boiling.

He whistled several notes of a titleless melody and honked the horn again, glancing at his watch now and wondering about Donna. She had called him only ten minutes before, asking for a lift out to the MacKenzie ranch. Trouble, she'd said, with Simon's palomino. Nothing serious, but her own car was at the garage and she wouldn't mind the company. Neither would he. He had left her home late Wednesday night, and though they had not made love they had just the same, with a touch, a kiss, a whisper and a dialogue that required no speaking. Then they separated while both struggled with their fears.

At home he'd taken Jeff for a walk and hoped he knew what he was doing.

The door opened and startled him, but he was grinning foolishly as Donna tossed her gladstone to the back seat and slid in beside him. She patted his hand, kissed his cheek and pointed at the road.

"I thought you weren't in a hurry," he said as he pulled into traffic.

"I know this car," she told him. "The sooner we're out there, the sooner we're back and I can cancel my flight insurance."

"Galen'll kill you."

She slouched and pressed her knees against the dashboard. "You have a good day?"

"So-so. Thornton's still missing, Regan's doing better and I almost got up enough nerve to have a word with Ted Waters."

"Nerve?" She looked at him, uncertain.

"A long story," he said, leaving the houses behind. "Galen also told me he's trying to get up support for a town meeting next week." He shook his head in amazed disbelief. "Y'know, if I live here a million years I'll never understand why they haven't done that before. I mean, it would be so simple! You get all the parties together and you let them bash it out, and sooner or later something comes they can live with."

"That's theory," she said. "And this is Windriver. Things

are supposed to work themselves out. It's like . . ." She took off her glasses and polished them on her shirtfront. "It's kind of like evolution. The settlers came out here and only the strongest survived, the ones with the most courage, the most common sense. You don't go crying to your neighbors until there's nothing left to try. And even then you don't cry. You admit you need help, one way or another, and you get it. Respect. Pride. Am I making any sense at all?"

He swung onto Elkhorn Road.

"I think so. I don't know, I guess it explains why they haven't done it yet."

"Timing," she said, five minutes later.

"What?"

"Timing, Jase. You're still used to working thirty hours a day, ninety minutes an hour. It's the East Coast Syndrome." She twirled the glasses by one temple. "Very simple, really. You'll notice there are no clocks on the street, not on the bank or anywhere. None in many of the stores, either. A few, but not many. Things get done when they have to be done, not before and not after."

"Now that," he said, "I'm not sure is right. This whole mess could've been cleared up with . . . ah, the hell with it. Let's talk about something else."

"The weather?"

He curled his lips into an exaggerated sneer. She laughed, and slapped his leg and asked if he'd heard anything more about Rachel. He hadn't. He knew she was ill, but if anyone knew anything they weren't talking.

"Neither will Doc," she said sourly. "It's like an appointment to the queen, y'know? And every time I say something he looks at me like I'm trying to steal state secrets."

"She's a hell of a woman," he said, and told her about his meeting. "I expect in the old days she would have led the whole tribe."

Donna kept her eyes straight ahead. "I don't like her."

"What?"

"I don't like her. Oh, she's strong enough, and she certainly knows how to hold an audience with those stories of hers, but . . . I can't put my finger on it, but there's something about her I don't trust." She laughed abruptly. "Maybe it's because she's so much older, knows so damned much. I mean, when she looks at you, you feel like there's nothing left inside. She's got all your secrets, you know what I mean?" She hugged herself. "What it all boils down to, I guess, is that—and this is only a scientist's opinion, you understand— she's spooky."

They passed under the MacKenzie arch before Jason realized he'd missed taking a glimpse at the Perkins ranch, and at the house. And when it didn't bother him as much as he thought it might have, he glanced quickly at Donna, as if the answer were in her sun-touched profile.

"What are you looking at?" she said.

"Nothing," he said, and nearly drove the car off the road when she punched his right arm. He laughed and rubbed it gingerly as the tree-tunnel engulfed them and swept shadows over the hood. A sudden silence. A silence laced with static when he saw the raven on the boulder, saw the house leap from the base of Kramer's Mountain. Cloud-shadows rippled across the lawn as he parked by the steps, and when he looked up as he slid out he saw two dark shapes weaving through the currents.

"Beautiful, aren't they," Donna said, hoisting her bag from the back seat.

The eagles, Jason thought, and reminded himself to ask Simon if the poacher had been caught.

He watched, enthralled, and didn't hear MacKenzie's approach until the man had greeted Donna. Then they were brought swiftly, almost rudely, to the stables in the back, Donna listening carefully as Simon explained his palomino's symptoms. Jason felt excluded and hung off to one side watching several chestnuts and a dapple cavorting in a corral. They seemed young, and he leaned against the plank fence to stare. But as soon as they sensed him, the horses clustered in a far corner, eyeing him and pawing, finally trotting around in a tight group that finally made him nervous.

The stable was a long, low white building, and he rested a shoulder against the open doorframe, taking in the scents of hay, manure, sweat and leather tackle. It was dim inside. The stalls were along the back. One of them, at the far end, was closed roof to floor and he walked toward it slowly, listening to Donna's whispering, to the palomino's snorting. He smiled at the sounds, knowing the animal trusted her, thinking, as he stared blindly at the rope-tied latch, of the expressions he'd seen when others talked about her: confidence, respect, no question at all about the matter of her sex. She was skilled, she was proven, and if the valley had its way she'd be here until she died.

It surprised him to realize he felt a little jealous.

"Crazy."

He slapped a hand to his chest and turned, blinking as Simon grinned and took his arm, leading him outside.

"That animal in there," MacKenzie said, gesturing back toward the closed stall. "A brood mare late in foaling. It's made her a little crazy and we have to keep her away from the others."

Jason nodded as though he understood, and MacKenzie took him to the corral and named each of the horses that came up to him, nuzzling his hand and chest until he brought small lumps of sugar from his trouser pockets.

"Dumbest animals in the world," MacKenzie said. "They'll run till they drop. No sense, but goddamned loyal."

"They're beautiful," Jason said.

"Absolutely. That dapple there, now, she used to be Rachel's." He slapped at a muzzle to push it away. "When she could ride, that is."

"How is your wife, Simon?"

MacKenzie turned around to lean his back against the fence, sticking his hands in his pockets. "I was going to invite you both to dinner since you came out here so late, but . . ." He shook his head sadly. "She's not doing very well, Jason. One of her bad days."

Jason mimicked his stance, and they both stared at the back of the house. "I have a message for you," he said, glancing at the stable. "From Galen."

"I know."

"It's late in coming, but I think you ought to be there."

MacKenzie sucked at his teeth and spat. "I don't know, Jase. I'd like to, believe that, but now it all depends on Rachel. Her bad days, they're coming closer together. I don't want to leave her alone."

"I understand," Jason said, trying to sound more sincere than he felt, "but if you don't show up the others might not, either. Daniel, I mean. You could take this town a long way, Simon, just by showing up."

"I'll call you," Simon said, ending it by turning to ask Donna what was wrong with his stallion.

Their conversation kept Jason on the sidelines. He listened for a moment to instructions about dosages and exercise, diet and riding and finally strolled aimlessly toward the drive. He wished he had had more time with MacKenzie to somehow force the man to understand his influence, which he so offhandedly dismissed. It was frustrating and maddening, and only Donna's smile kept his temper from doing much more than making him sullen.

Like beating your head against the wall, he thought as he climbed back into the car; it feels so good when you stop. Only this time, stopping might mean the collapse of the wall.

"You philosophizing?" she asked him as they headed back toward the Pike.

He grunted.

"Oh. Pouting."

"I'm not pouting."

"You do a good imitation."

"I'm not pouting, I'm grumpy."

She smiled at him, and he almost managed to hold his own smile back.

"You like venison?"

"That sounds barbaric."

"Good," she said. "But I do have some honest to god real cow-type steaks. If you don't mind missing Galen's cooking for a change, how about dinner at my place?"

He ran his palm over the steering wheel. "I have to deliver Simon's answer to Galen."

"I have a telephone."

"He may want to—"

"Jason," she said, "if you don't want to come, just say so."

"I do," he told her. "I mean, I really do."

"I won't bite, I promise."

There was no pleading, no promises. He put a hand on the seat beside him and she covered it with her own.

"I still need company," she said.

"Okay. Yeah." He took a deep breath. "So do I."

(5)

Valley Pike was deserted. Bea walked with her head down, her eyes watching her shoes snap in and out of sight. She tried not to listen to her heels cracking against the pavement, nor to the soughing of the light wind through the trees above her. She was tired, and her imagination could very easily go wild if she let it. Yet, despite the fact that she knew she'd probably be a nervous wreck by the time she reached home, she didn't want Carole walking with her. They'd talked themselves out once their work was done and she wanted . . . needed a little time to herself, away from the polite and vaguely insistent questions her father and mother would produce.

After the last book had been closed and the sample exam questions answered, Carole had jumped down from her bed and begun exercising: toe-touches, windmills, a giggling running in place. Bea, stretching her arms over her head to relieve the tension in her back, had been astounded. "Good god, I could sleep for a week. I don't know how you do it."

"Vitamins, this crap every night, and my father's firm guiding hand," Carole had said, puffing, then slapping her buttocks hard.

"You're crazy. It's after nine, for crying out loud."

"I like to stay in shape."

Bea looked to the ceiling. "Christ, you're like me, you eat like a damned bird. How the hell can you not stay in shape?"

She watched for a few minutes, her gaze caught by the copper bird flapping against Carole's chest, by the brightness in the girl's eyes. "You're just trying to make me feel flabby."

Carole had laughed and collapsed to the floor. "If you didn't have that phone glued to your ear every night, you too could be in the Windriver olympics."

Bea shook her head and gathered her books into her arms. "I still think you're crazy."

"Helps you sleep, too," Carole said, stretching out to begin a series of rapid sit-ups.

"Helps you be dead."

"Creep."

"Bitch."

They laughed.

Bea leaned against the door, listening to the faint sounds of the television downstairs. "How come you're not at Rachel's?" She wanted it to sound innocent; it came out almost sneering.

"She's sick. Besides, exams start on Monday, right?"

"I suppose." She watched the frantic workout for a few moments more. "You heard anything about Greg?"

"Nope, and I don't care. That creep can rot."

"I think he kinda liked you."

Carole grimaced, red-faced and panting. "Slime. He's slime."

"He's not that bad."

"Don't you let Hardy hear you say that, he'll break your neck."

"I don't belong to Hardy Green," Bea said huffily.

Carole stopped, her hands splayed across her stomach. "You all right?" She kept staring at the ceiling.

"Yeah." A pause. "Had a fight last night. My father, not Hardy. I wanted to stay out later, he told me my ass was his until I graduated."

"Yeah," Carole said softly. "Yeah, I know."

Bea waited a full minute, then lifted her hand in a burdened farewell and left.

Now, as she reached the corner, she wondered if Carole had plans for fall sports she'd not said anything about. Not that she'd be surprised; the two of them had recently discovered chinks in their relationship that had never been there before, not since they'd started school together back in kindergarten. Her father had told her once that high school friendships, sad as it may seem, were virtually fated to evaporate as adolescents struggled into adulthood and discovered their own lives. She didn't want to believe it. She didn't want to believe that Carole found boys more interesting than her, that she'd rather be babysitting an old Indian squaw than going to the movies here or in Blairs. It made no difference that Bea understood the need to save money for college; it just wasn't fair she was missing out on so much fun.

She stopped beneath a streetlamp, shaking her head. The air had cooled, the sky once again filling with clouds she could not see. As her skin tingled to the lowering of the temperature she was tempted to take a short walk before going home. But she'd promised her mother no diversions tonight, straight home and no complaints. Damn! Here she was, practically a senior, for god's sake, and she was still being treated like a stupid child. Her fingers scratched across the back of her neck. Damn. She was hungry.

She heard footsteps and she tensed, looked to her right and saw a short, slender young man striding toward her, in and out of shadows. She saw black hair and dark skin. By the time he reached her she was smiling politely. Ordinarily, she would have been pleased to see him, especially after all the help he and his wife had given her with the research for her papers. It had been Rachel's idea, and a good one—for the time. Now, however, she was still seething over the MacKenzies' appropriation of Carole, and she was in no mood to take away the bite of her greeting.

"I thought you were going to lay off the firewater," she said, nodding back toward the bar.

Michael Wolf started, recognized her and grinned. "I was in the barbershop. A sneak visit to see how David's doing."

They're taking over the whole family, she thought.

"How's Little Star?" A formality.

"Fine." He frowned as though uncertain what he'd done to incur her hostility. "Fine as you can be with your mother hanging around all the time. I think she likes being off the reservation." He laughed and she grinned, finding no way to part without being rude. "You're out pretty late," he said then.

"Studying with Carole. Finals start Monday."

"Carosa?"

She nodded. "Don't see you around much." It was deliberate.

"A little tense," he said, staring at the tip of an unlighted cigarette. "You know how it is."

She softened. "Yeah, I know. Your kids okay?"

He smiled and reached for her arm, a grateful gesture that lingered almost too long. "Just fine. They feel it, too, but they're all right."

The touch of his hand had startled her, and brought the sourness back to her mood. "Well, why don't you and your friends stand up for your rights or something?"

He looked down at her, snapping the cigarette in half and tossing it into the gutter. "Oh, we are, Bea. Don't you worry about that. We are."

She couldn't stand the smile about his eyes, the self-assured cock of his hip as he waited for her response. "Got to go," she said abruptly. "See you." And she strode hurriedly away, head down again, ears pricked for a laugh or a sigh. But there was nothing but the sound of the wind and the sound of her angry steps.

(6)

Ted Waters stood in the shadow of the grocery's doorway. His left hand gripped the stiff flesh of his birthmark and twisted and pulled at it, while he watched Michael Wolf talking soft and low to Bea Steed. He couldn't hear what they were saying, but he almost groaned aloud when he took hold of her arm for a brief moment. Bad enough the land's going, he thought; now the red bastards are planning to take off with the women.

Behind him, in the store, he heard shuffling. The Association was trying to decide what should be done about Mitch Regan since it was obvious the fool sheriff wasn't about to do his job properly. He glared until Wolf vanished into darkness and Bea crossed the street; then he kicked open the door and walked in, glowering. He'd had enough. No more, damnit, no more. He didn't give a shit what Steve Felsom would say, he wasn't going to let one more damned day go by without them high-and-mighty redskins learning where their place was. It was going to have to be just like the old days—you had to teach them their place, show them who's boss, give them a little whack alongside their thick little heads to make sure they was listening.

The dumb bastards.

They'd gone too far this time. Fighting was one thing; little Bea was something else.

(7)

Carole lay on her bed, a towel wrapped loosely around her, her hair wet and cool. Static-laced music played softly from a radio rising from the untidy forest of bottles and tissue boxes on top of the dresser. She wasn't listening. She was trying to

decide if she were really jealous of Bea for Hardy Green, or if
she was just feeling sorry for herself again. From the funnel of
the stairwell she could hear her mother talking, her brother
grunting his answers. And a clatter when a crutch toppled to
the floor.

She smiled without mirth.

She may not be the smartest kid in the world, but she knew
a con when she heard it, and she was getting awfully tired of
David trying to con her into the friendship they'd had before
his accident. Like he really cared. Then her hand drifted to
her cheek, and she winced, still feeling her father's slap, and
the burning that had followed.

They'll be sorry, she thought then; when I'm gone they'll
be sorry, and then it'll be too damned late.

(8)

"Palemoon, the day."

"Saturday."

Another day gone. Another day.

She slept without wanting to, and opened her eyes hours
later as if she had been struck. Perspiration broke along her
forehead and ran down her temples onto the pillow. The
casing was stained, and there was a sour smell to the room.
She licked futilely at her lips, and her eyelids fluttered. She
tried to call for Simon, but her throat was too dry, her tongue
felt too swollen. Her hands scrabbled at the sheet as she
stared at the French doors, open now to give her the benefit
of the night air. Her deep breath wavered like the light of the
candles, jumped like the shadows that cowered near the floor.

Had she asked Palemoon if the parchment had been
delivered? She couldn't remember.

Had Simon been with her at all today? Had he held her
hands and bathed her face and spoken to her in the old
tongue about the land and the Teaching? She couldn't
remember.

Suddenly she stiffened, a reaction against the dozen white
fires that broke out in her chest, at her elbows, at her knees,
along the small of her back. White fire. Licking. Subsiding
when a gust swept in from the yard. She sighed and closed her
eyes, then forced them open again to avoid dropping into the

dreams. She didn't want to dream now, she didn't want to sleep. Awake, even in her condition, she would be able to tell if her darkchild was prowling.

And an hour later she knew it was. It was out there. With no concern at all for her or the Teaching . . . it was out there. And it was hunting. And for the first time since it started, Rachel didn't know the quarry.

(9)

Lamont Riley knew he was in awfully big trouble, and it didn't make him feel better knowing it wasn't all his fault. He'd just been unable to contain himself one moment longer. Jesus Christ, he was only human, and a man can take only so much.

It was bad enough she stood naked in the window while he worked around the barn, and offered him coffee, cakes, a small tot of liquor when the weather grew cold. Bad enough Perkins the jerk had finally told him he was near ready to close the selling of the place and Riley would have to find new work. It was bad enough his car had broken down and he couldn't get into Blairs to raise a little hell . . . but now that fool Billyboy had gone off somewhere and had left her alone. Alone, for Christ's sake! And then she'd come out to his shed back of the barn and she'd told him it was too cool tonight and she couldn't get the furnace started. A lie. He knew it. He'd followed her anyway and climbed down through the trap in the kitchen floor with flashlight in hand, looking back up at her standing beneath the bulb hanging from the ceiling, at her dark figure shimmering like anxious shadows under her white print dress. Looking up, licking his lips and thinking, you're in trouble, Monty; Christ, you're in bad trouble, while he fussed with the furnace Perkins had been too cheap to replace ten years ago. Finally he'd hit it with the heel of his hand until the switch clicked on and the flames whooshed and the heat made him sweat even though he was cold.

He'd been fool enough to accept her offer of some fresh hot coffee and homemade devil's food cake—a sign, you ass, it's a sign—but he had also not pulled away from her when her long hot fingers trailed over the back of his hand. He'd shuddered slightly when she stood behind him and idly massaged his shoulders while she chatted on about how much money they were going to have once the place was sold and wouldn't it be nice, Monty, to get the hell out of this hole and live in real civilization for a change.

He couldn't comprehend the figures she was throwing at him. He didn't know how much he'd made during his lifetime, but for sure it wasn't even one-tenth of what she was telling him. All that money just waiting to be spent. All that goddamned Indian money.

Trouble.

Bad trouble.

When she somehow managed to slide around him and into his lap, nibbling at his ear, her tongue soft and demanding, her buttocks wriggling over his groin, he did nothing but sit there, petrified—he's coming back, you jackass, he's coming back *now!*—until she slipped a cool hand inside his shirt and circled his nipples with her nails and he groaned and lifted her like he was some kind of muscleman and carried her into the living room.

They never made it to the couch.

His legs gave out and he sagged slowly, with her underneath him tugging frantically at his buckle and zipper as he pulled apart the front of her dress and saw he was right—she wasn't wearing a goddamned thing but that light-soft flesh that rippled when he touched it with his hands and his mouth.

Trouble. Because she was too much for him, and he knew he couldn't last.

(10)

In addition to the road that formed the valley's axis, there were other ones, smaller and more often than not demanding four-wheel drive for passage and a strong back to keep necks from snapping. They were used primarily by the postman in his army surplus jeep, and by produce trucks that seemed permanently encased in swirling dust clouds. None had been constructed for speed and, after Thursday's heavy rains, most were barely passable.

Clouds thin and flat covered the stars, covered the moon, and the only moving lights came from the mud-dulled headlamps of a pickup that jounced and slid across the gouged ruts south of the river. Barbed wire fences became stone walls. Fog eddied about the tires, closing swiftly behind the vehicle as though it hadn't been. The windshield wipers slapped loudly, scraping into a shriek where one small section of rubber had worn away near the base. The heater was on, the grinding blower keeping feet overly warm while pinched, solemn faces tightened in the chill.

In the back, five men huddled under a tarpaulin.

The truck stopped in front of a low frame house set a hundred yards back from the road. Behind it loomed the black bulk of a barn, in front a colorful spread of garden closed down for the night. A ewe bleated mournfully somewhere to the left. The scent of rain was still strong, and the mud-and-grass had a gleaming hard look about it. The driver's door opened and briefly illuminated the inside of the cab. Four men were packed inside, and the five in back had already flung aside the tarpaulin and were hurrying, crouched and anxious, toward the front. No one spoke. Ghostbreath slipped from between taut lips. Gloved hands clenched until gestures were made and packages were passed gingerly back and forth, the only sounds the stamping of a nervous boot, or the hiss of a warning.

At last, eight of them clambered over the waist-high fieldstone wall and made their way to the right. They slipped past the silent, darkened house. The mud sucked at their heels and clung to their cuffs, and one man slipped hard to his knees, grunting, freezing, then struggling to his feet again to rejoin the others.

No dogs barked.

Two men, without really knowing why, noted with amazement how well kept the house was. It seemed freshly painted, newly strong, without any of the dilapidation that marked so many of the smaller places these days, places like old man Whitcomb's further down toward the ass-end of the valley. They noted, but they said nothing to each other. It didn't make a difference to them if the house were kept like the goddamned Taj Mahal. They knew who owned it, and that was all that mattered.

The clouds began to shred.

The men slipped through the dark, eyes squinting against a slow-rising wind, picking out the stumps, the water bucket lying on its side by the well, the trough, the hoe, the fence of the corral that fronted the barn. They separated to surround, three of them climbing the fence and landing softly in piles of mud-smeared hay. The packages were placed along the foundation. The doors were barred. A thin man fumbled with a length of fuse.

From within the house a dog began barking, high-pitched and furious.

Eight men froze, heads cocked toward the sound.

A light flared in a back room, softened by a curtain. A shadow split it, then vanished. A light appeared in front, followed by the rusted, grating squeal of the back door's hinges.

There was anxious hissing and vehement swearing, and matches cracked into flames held to the packages, and the packages *whoomped* into a blaze that crawled high up the walls before the men had a chance to run clear of its flickering light. Fleeing, they became gaps in the retreating darkness, outlined in red and gold, their heads down and sprinting for the road.

A woman raced out of the back and leaped off the stoop with a broom in her hand. She shouted. A man swerved, his fist clubbing the side of her neck. Her feet slipped on the mud and she fell, hard, the broom snapping in half, her cry smothered by mud before falling unconscious.

The front door opened as the truck's engine coughed.

"Damnit," a man cried out. A silhouette with a long stick in his hand, he vaulted the porch railing despite the screaming of a large woman on the threshold and called out again when a horse screamed, a handful of sheep sounded, a dog howled. He landed square and the stick in his hand exploded blue fire.

"Oh shit!" one of the men muttered, grabbing for his thigh as a handful of pellets embedded themselves in the muscle. He took the wall in a single ungainly dive, rolled across the verge and jumped for the tailgate as the truck slewed around in the mud and bucked toward the highway. Hands grabbed his wrists and pulled him aboard, but not before he'd been dragged for nearly ten yards.

The man from the house fired again, seeing the pickup slowly gaining speed, sprouting shadows from its sides that kicked frantically at the air. He cracked open the shotgun, plucked out the empty cartridges and slammed one more in the chamber. He had locked it and aimed it when a stout branch crashed down on his shoulder. He staggered forward, his arms outflung, when he was struck again. As he landed on the ground the weapon bolted from his hands and fired into the grass.

The barn torched the corral, which in turn torched a workshed.

Sparks sifted from the roof, fell on the prone woman and within moments the cloth on her blouse began to smolder.

The sheep were silent; the horse had stopped its screaming.

There was only the large woman shrieking on the threshold, the sound of the pickup and the crackling of the flames as they fed upon themselves.

(11)

Jason was at the gate and whistling for Mutt and Jeff when the siren on the River Road firehouse began a two-tone wailing. He almost ignored it, thinking instead of the evening spent with Donna, when the alarm intensified and he raced back toward the Pike. The bar and the luncheonette were spilling customers into the street, most of the men charging for their cars, the others sprinting for the firehouse and the two pieces of equipment donated by MacKenzie. Swallowing hard and panting, Jason searched the sky, half expecting to locate the blaze within walking distance of the corner. He could find nothing, however, then yelped and spun around when Galen grabbed his arm and tugged him back toward the house.

"Ranch!" the editor shouted as they scrambled into the car, the ignition firing before Jason had settled.

"Whose?"

"No idea. South. Could be Whitcomb, Tallpines, Wolf, anybody."

"You know anything else?"

"I'm not God, Jason. Gimme a break."

He grabbed the dashboard as Galen wrenched the Studebaker into a U-turn and barreled out to the Pike, worming his way into the writhing snake-dance of automobiles that were trailing the fire engines.

And once out of town he saw it—a small virulent sunrise, topped by a boiling cap of white and black smoke.

"Jesus," he whispered.

"Yeah," Galen said, and nearly spilled Jason into his lap when he skidded into a righthand turn, pelting onto an access road barely wide enough for the fenders.

Nothing passed them in the other direction.

(12)

"Come *on*," Gloria panted. She lay spreadeagled in the middle of the living room floor, her hands desperately massaging the sagging lumps of her breasts. "Come on, come on, come *on!*"

"Give up, lady," Riley said in disgust. He'd been right. Trouble. Too many goddamn beers or something, and she moved so friggin fast and he . . . well, he'd had it. A man is capable of just so much, no matter what the damned books say, and he wasn't about to stick around long enough to explain to Billyboy why his wife was freakin out in the middle of the floor without any goddamned clothes on. No way. No way in hell.

"Bastard," she said, glaring at him now.

Riley turned his back as he zipped up. She wasn't beautiful any longer, nor was she desirable. She reminded him of a film he'd seen in Denver one weekend, the hooker in the dim light lying there like some kind of stone animal waiting to be serviced. Stone; no emotions, no caring, no fucking anything. Less than an animal. Even in rutting season there's a reason for the rutting.

"You bastard," she said again, pushing herself upright and grabbing for her dress. "Queer."

"I done it, didn't I?" he said sourly, buttoning his shirt, then heading into the kitchen to hunt up his jacket.

"Done it?" she shrieked after him. "What the hell do you mean, done it? You call that . . . you call that sex? Huh? You listenin, stupid? You call that sex?"

Riley consigned her to hell in as many ways as he could think of and left by the back door, going straight to his shack to pack his bags. Enough was enough. He'd given into temptation and he didn't want any more of it. He'd find a way into Blairs, and the first thing in the morning get the hell out of the state. Long as he was this far he might as well head all the way to the coast. Oregon. Why the hell not. If he were lucky he'd die there without seeing another goddamned cow.

"I hate you!" Gloria screamed after him. "You're not even a man! Goddamned queer!" She drew a shuddering breath. "You think my husband's gonna pay you, Riley? You think that? You can go straight to hell, Mister Lamont Riley, because my husband's not gonna give you one goddamned red cent. Not a fucking penny!"

She slammed the door and leaned heavily against it, her eyes closed to blot out the anger, gulping at the suddenly close air. Furious, because that simpering queer Riley had excited her too much without giving her anything in return. She strode weak-kneed into the front room and stared at the telephone. Artie, maybe. If not, there was always Stan Kelly. They knew what she liked, and they knew how to do it so there wasn't anything showing when it was done. Tenderness she could get from Bob Green on his desk; tonight she needed something more.

"Shit!"

She slapped at the wall, flung open the front door and stepped out onto the porch. She stood there with hands on her hips, her breasts rising and falling as she sought to calm herself. She dropped the dress back inside. She didn't want it on. The air felt cool, like hands, lots of hands spider-walking over her skin; and she was nearly herself again when she spotted Riley scurrying across the lawn toward the road, a duffel bag slung over his shoulder. She almost called out to him as he passed out of the light creeping from the house.

Idiot. Bastard. So dumb he couldn't keep their best live-stock from getting killed off, even though everyone knew it was those creepy Indians doing it, trying to scare them away so they could have the land for themselves. The hell with them. The hell with them all.

She moved to stand at the top step and tilted her head when she saw the pulsing faint glow rising beyond the river. Fire? she wondered. Then she grinned. Billy was part of the volunteer fire department. Even if the fire was a small one, even after the rain, he'd be there most of the night seeing to it that not a single precious ember escaped to catch the grass when the sun came up.

It was beautiful—absolutely perfect.

When she heard the rustling beyond the maples, she laughed. Riley was coming back to her fast, coming back smoking to finish what he'd started.

She hurried down the steps onto the lawn, one hand tucked into her hair, the other stroking her breasts to bring up the nipples. "Hey," she said, lips in a smile. "Hey, I'm sorry, Monty. I'm really sorry. I just get . . . well, you know what I mean. I can't help myself, is all."

The grass was cool beneath her bare feet, and she shivered. Christ, she thought, it's gonna happen before he even gets here.

She looked back at the house then, at the shimmering stage the lights prepared for her, and she grinned. "Hey," she whispered, peering down the road. "Hey. Hey, what about here, Monty? Right here, okay?" Her shadow on the lawn was dim, was grey, and she liked the way it gave mystery to her figure. "What about it, Monty? Fat-assed MacKenzie could ride by and wouldn't even know what was goin on. C'mon, Monty. You wanna take me right here?"

She turned slowly, spreading her arms to take him in, her eyes half closed, her knees already buckling.

It moved so swiftly into the light Gloria only had time to see the mocking red of its eyes before she felt the tearing at her chest, the ripping at her neck, felt the ground suddenly slam like a club into her back. Her scream died bubbling through the blood that spewed from her throat. There was little time for fear; only an astonished disappointment. Her heels kicked once in the grass, her left hand reaching for the moon behind the clouds.

Her left eye was punctured.

Her dark lips were shredded.

Her fingers spasmed as though the hands were still alive.

(13)

There was cold, and dying heat.

There was muttering, and angered silence.

The thick grey hose was streaked and clotted with mud and torn grass as it stretched from the well, through the pump and into the hands of the men directing its flow onto the barn. But the barn was little more than a skeleton, blackened bones that groaned toward the nightsky under the weight of the water. And finally, without warning, it collapsed inward with a slow shrieking that raised not sparks but gouts of black soot.

Jason kept his hands in his pockets to keep them from trembling.

It was the light, he told himself, more than just the fire. The clicking circle of red lights on the fire trucks, the swirling blue band atop Steve Felsom's patrol car, the flashlights moving too quickly, too erratically, from one place to another and the deceptively warm glow from every window in the house.

It was the light. It had turned the valley into a hideous portrait of Galen's hell.

He stood on the porch and watched faces catch red, blue, purple, white, red. Saw the mud and the grass bleached of their natural tints, saw boots stomping from the ruins of the barn to the patrol car where Jake Harmon sat, examining unrecognizable things others passed into his hands. Plastic-lined canvas sacks reeked of kerosene. The stench was everywhere. Only shards were left, and each time one was handed to the sheriff his shoulders sagged a little more.

Behind him in the house, he could hear Doc Vance muttering to Michael Wolf's mother-in-law; and a few minutes later Little Star was borne out on a stretcher, her face pocked with burns. Behind her, on another stretcher, was Michael, his face pale and wiped clean. A bandage had been set around his forehead and his shoulder was heavily taped. His shirt had been cut off to expose a thin, muscular chest laced with welts and small cuts daubed in iodine. The old woman, ponderously fat in a shapeless green dress, stayed behind with the children, and every few minutes her harsh cracked voice would lift in a keening that finally drove Jason away. The ambulance, an old Cadillac that looked more like a hearse, accepted the double burden. Vance climbed in and the doors closed. The siren screamed out once before muffling itself and the flaring red light quickly became a pinpoint soon swallowed by the night.

"God *damn*," Galen said when Jason joined him. The editor was perched on the Studebaker's hood, craning his neck, calling out once in a while to ask a question of the workers. He had taken off his jacket and draped it round his shoulders. Jason saw the flush on his cheeks and the severe set of his lips. He said nothing.

He heard the fat woman's keening again; saw the sudden flare of ugly grey smoke when water struck a patch still burning beneath the debris; heard a man coughing, another slapping his back.

"Clumsy bit of arson, don't you think?" Jason said.

"Clumsy isn't the word for it, son." He muttered something at the ground, looked up and shook his head. "This business here was touched off, you know. It didn't just happen. A couple of the fellas didn't just suddenly decide to fry a few Indians."

Jason shrugged his ignorance. "Could be. Jake know who did it?"

"Little Star—my god, did you see her face?—she says there were ten, maybe fifteen of them. She doesn't know, it was too confusing and she was hit too soon. Michael got off three shots. The old woman there doesn't know if anyone was hit. They came and went in a truck."

Jason rubbed at his jaw. "Why isn't someone after them?"

Marsh put his hand on Jason's shoulder as if he expected him to leap on the nearest horse and be his own posse. "You've been snooping around. You asked questions. Do you doubt they were local?"

"No."

"Then they're not goin anywhere. Jake'll sniff 'em out."

Jason wondered. Harmon hadn't been all that successful—hell, he hadn't been successful at all in finding out who or what had mutilated those animals, or attacked his own daughter, or jumped Mitch Regan. And despite the clear-cut evidence he was accumulating, that didn't mean he'd be able to find the right truck in a valley filled with trucks, or the right dozen or so men in a town that seemed to be filled with them once the sun went down. Of course, if Michael had hit one or two the job would be easier, or if he'd been lucky enough to catch a glimpse of one . . . but the Wolfs were on their way to Blairs General. Little Star was knocked out with drugs and Michael was unconscious with a possible concussion and internal injuries that could keep him out of the picture for several days.

He decided, finally, to say nothing to Galen. Not because

of the potential for argument, but because of the man's expression—one of professional eagerness but something else, too . . . his occasional glance toward the smoldering barn seemed a great deal like fear.

The sheriff walked by without looking up, crossed the trampled garden and stepped into the house. Five minutes later he left, zipping his jacket to his chin and yanking his hat down hard over his head.

The keening had stopped.

Another hour passed before Galen sighed loudly. "Let's go, son. There isn't much left to do here, and I'm freezing my ass off."

The police and more than half the fire fighters had already left. A few men stood under a scorched elm smoking and talking, keeping a desultory watch over the grave of the barn. It was quiet now, and cold. The lights in the house were still burning, but they might as well have been out for all the comfort they gave.

An owl ghosted by, but no one looked up.

With eyes aching and lungs working in spasms to flush out the stench of burnt wood and animals, Jason slumped in the passenger seat and confined his responses to Galen's bitter comments to a few meaningless grunts. He was tired and drained, although relieved that no one had been killed. He wanted nothing more than to crawl into his bed and dream about New England in the fall, or the Jersey hills in spring. He fumbled a handkerchief out of his hip pocket and blew his nose. He yawned. He considered running for mayor so someone would pave this goddamned road.

By the time they reached the village, however, he surprised himself by snaring a second wind. When Galen parked in front of the house, Jason told him to go on ahead. "I thought I saw a light in Harmon's office. Think I'll wander over and be nosey."

Galen grinned at him over the roof of the car. "Wander over, huh? You sure you don't mean mosey?"

Jason threw a pulled punch at his head and walked away. Wander. He laughed silently. Back East, wander was something you did when you were lost. Gallop was something you did when you thought the cops had something for your next story, you knew it, and the other guy didn't. Mosey was something Ken Maynard or Bob Steele or Tim McCoy did when they headed for the barn.

Back East. Somehow the phrase sounded not bad at all.

The Pike was deserted, its blackness untouched save for a spill of grey-white from the sheriff's office. A curiously two-dimensional effect, Jason thought, except for the sounds of the leaves and a peculiar push to the wind that seemed not wind at all. He couldn't help glancing around and he hurried into the office without knocking, almost slamming the door in his haste to feel safe.

Harmon was bent over some papers on his desk while a strapping, top-heavy Bill Oaker stood to one side, yawning widely without bothering to cover his mouth. He nodded to Jason, then poked the sheriff's shoulder.

"Up late," Harmon said, stretching his arms over the desktop. His hair was unkempt, his collar open, and dark sweat stains crossed his chest and streaked down his sides.

Jason smiled; it had no effect. "I've got an assignment."

Oaker laughed and stroked his thick sandy mustache. Jason was pleased to find no malice there, but rather a genuine appreciation of the irony in the jest.

The sheriff, however, scowled, tapping a pencil impatiently against his chin. "Well, if you must know, Steve and Artie are checkin up on that truck. Things happened too fast, apparently. Found some fuse wire, so they probably had to drop matches and run like hell. Couldn't have gotten too far."

"Nice to know you're so confident."

"I have t'be."

"You don't think they'll leave the valley, then?"

Harmon said nothing.

Oaker yawned again, loudly.

"Jesus H., Bill—"

"Aw, c'mon, Jake, huh? Have a heart, why not. God, it's already past three. I was two hours in bed when Steve called. Man, at least give me a chance to open my eyes."

"You got days startin tomorrow, y'know."

"No shit. Me and Steve." He grinned at Jason. "Jeff Chandler and Audie Murphy, the B-movie heroes. We strike fear into the hearts of the human race, by god."

Jason lifted an eyebrow, but Harmon cut off any comment with a slap of his hand, hard on his desk. "Bill," he warned.

"Okay, okay. Look, why don't I take a look around." He rocked his hat into position, touched Jason's arm on the way out. "See you around, Kent."

"I'll wear my *S* so you'll know me."

He did not turn to watch the husky deputy leave; it was enough of an astonishment to hear, in a place like Windriver, the younger man talk like that without having him make a point of it. As it was, he was trying not to let his irritation get the best of him, an irritation born of an unpleasant stare the sheriff leveled at him. He shifted his weight to one foot, stuck a hand in his hip pocket and used the other to gesture vaguely around the office. "You don't have much call for arson around here, I take it," he said when it was evident Harmon wasn't about to volunteer anything.

"Why do you say arson?"

Oh god, he thought, not this game here. He pointed at the sack of debris lying on the floor by the desk.

Harmon glanced down, and shrugged. "No," he admitted. "Not much call at all."

"You heard from Doc Vance yet?"

"Nope. Hasn't called in. Tests like he has to do take time, y'know." He pushed away from the desk a few inches. "Where were you tonight?"

"With Donna Oldfield," he said before he realized the implication. And when it struck him he swallowed hard. "For dinner. We talked a bit and I walked home. I was going in the door when I heard the siren and Galen grabbed me."

Harmon nodded. "Your mother still alive?"

"What? No. No, she isn't."

"Rough stuff, leavin here the way you did. Damned shame. Real damned shame. Time passes, though, y'know. Heals all wounds, and all that. Though I got to admit there're some things that just keep on eatin away at a man, if you know what I mean."

"Yeah," said Jason. His chest tightened, and the hand in his pocket curled to a fist.

"But," the sheriff said, making the word a sigh, "I can take it, I suppose, you had no call to have a grievance or somethin like that with Michael Wolf. Am I right?"

"I never even met the man." Though the tone said: *for Christ's sake, do you mind, Sheriff?*

Harmon nodded and leaned back, hooking his feet around

the legs of his chair. His gaze rested for a moment on a covered typewriter on a small, wheeled metal table pushed against the wall. Jason saw his expression go blank, then return with a start. "Damn." He rubbed at his face fiercely, leaving behind an angry blush over his forehead and cheeks. "Damn, Clarke, this is gonna be hell."

Jason would have said something, but the weariness that weighted the man's voice stopped him. Weariness, and the same skittish fear he'd seen in Galen earlier.

"I'll drop by in the morning, Sheriff, if you don't mind."

"Nope." Harmon looked up, then, and smiled suddenly. "You ain't nothin like your daddy, y'know."

Jason touched a finger to his brow, nodded and left. He had no idea what he'd done to deserve the compliment, but somehow he'd managed to endure and pass some sort of test. And while that pleased him, it was also infuriatingly frustrating. For every person he met in Windriver there was another test. Are you really and truly worthy, Jason Clarke, or are you just passing through like the rest of the world?

Two blocks up, speared by a fragment of streetlight, he saw Bill Oaker hunkered down behind a red pickup, his hand pushing at something under the frame. He considered walking over, and just as quickly changed his mind. It would only be another test—though he suspected Oaker had already graded him, and graded him high.

It didn't matter now, anyway. What mattered was sleep. His mind would mull the information, the impressions he'd received, and perhaps give him some clues by the time he'd awakened. Tomorrow would be soon enough to find out who had decided Michael Wolf needed a lesson in knowing his place. And it gave him no satisfaction at all to know that the names most likely to pop up wouldn't astonish him one damned bit.

(14)

Perkins leapt off the truck and scrambled over the railroad tracks. Hidden in the tall weeds was a barely serviceable bicycle he kept there for other occasions, usually to get back to the house while Gloria was still sleeping so there wouldn't be an engine noise to wake her and let her know what time it was.

He could hear the firehouse siren in the distance as he grunted onto the seat. He wasn't worried about a chase; they would be too interested in trying to save the Indian's buildings. The Law would come later. Much later. And he would be safely in bed, sound asleep, his arms around his wife as if they'd been grafted there.

He pedaled stiffly, gasping, the pains in his left leg like the stroke of a white-hot blade. He'd have to take care of himself tonight, no doctors, and find a way to fashion himself an accident so there wouldn't be any questions. Especially from Gloria. If she thought he was messing around again she'd never let him hear the end of it. Then he'd just have to slap her around some until she begged him to stop. But then the jokes in town would start all over when she went in to shop and he would have to find some painkiller in Carosa's . . . and then . . . ah, shit. A minute from now wouldn't be soon enough for that pansy Green to settle the selling and give him his money.

Not soon enough for damn sure.

Thirty minutes later he lurched against the yard gate and tossed the bike aside, wincing at the metallic clatter. There was blood in his shoes, and his fool leg had gone almost numb. Stupid. They should have known the red-bellied bastard wouldn't let them go without a fight. Someone should've thought to bring a gun. Dumb. And it was a damned sure bet the others had gotten off without a scratch. Damn.

He shivered against the cold, against the ground fog that turned the grass a fish-belly grey, and stumbled twenty yards up the gravel drive before realizing most of the lamps in the house were still on. And someone had dropped something out there on the lawn, just at the edge of the lights' reach.

Goddamnit, if that's another one of . . . if Riley ain't been doin what he's bein paid good hard money to do . . . if he's gone . . .

He stopped. The exhilaration of the night's raid faded in a rush that made his sway, made him forget the fire in his injured leg. He blinked and looked away, looked back and blinked again, once and slowly.

It was blood that he saw, and bone; it was the practically fleshless face of his wife staring blindly into the night while the fog eased around her like a long grey rat sniffing for food.

The only color he saw was red. As though she had dressed in it.

Like the aftermath of a slap in the face he spun around and fell to his knees, jaw aching and eyes burning until, finally, he vomited. Crying, he asked himself stupidly why she was naked, and wiped his face with a sleeve. He spat, took a deep breath and rose, awkwardly, stumbling backward as he sought the courage to face her again . . . and failed.

With a strangled cry of disgust and supplication he bolted for the house, taking the porch steps in a single leap and racing through the open door. He fell against the foyer wall, his face drenched in perspiration, eyes closed and mouth open slackly.

Silent. The house was silent. Bright, and silent.

He snatched a coat from the hall rack and left again, holding it in front of him like a shield until he could see her feet—red, slashed, gleaming—and dropped it over her as if it had suddenly caught fire.

It was the lambskin spring topcoat he'd given her on her last birthday.

His shadow fell over her body.

"Gloria," he said, the tears coming again, crying now because he knew the horror would come later. "Gloria?"

A second shadow, fleeting.

He heard the airsound, the *rush* that was soft and gliding, and he dropped automatically into a crouch, his hands splayed to either side, fingers flexing. His head turned like a radar dish, listening, scowling, fear weakening his bowels. The pain was gone and his throat was sandpaper dry. He listened, his back to Gloria while he peered at the edges of the house, the undersides of the leaves, the muted white radiance of the light in the windows.

They knew. Somehow they knew and they'd come for him, found Gloria and were waiting out there for him to crack.

A quiet noise, and he frowned. It sounded like a woman; a woman, giggling.

He shook his head once, violently.

Shadowfast.

The impact was like an uppercut to his chin; he was flung

up and back, sprawling over Gloria's body, his eyes wide and his hands up in feeble protection. They grabbed something and pulled, but it wasn't enough to stop the eyes from staring (almost smiling) into his, or the slashing that drew glittering red ribbons over his cheeks and forehead. He screamed, but the weight on his chest refused to allow him to roll off the corpse, and he could feel it shifting softly beneath him. He grunted when something punctured the flesh just below his sternum and gasped when two of his fingers were snapped off as they reached out in a panic to gouge at those eyes.

Arms flailed and legs thrashed, but the slashing continued calm and swift—nose split, chin split, temple pierced, in and out like a manic needle; thumb gone, palm halved, the fog was scattered by the blood that was lost.

He turned his head away, his scream now a whimpering, and stared straight in at Gloria's orbless left eye.

He sighed, a long and low exhalation that stilled him before he even knew it was done.

And when it was done, the shadow remained, oblivious to the sirens, the distant flaring lights and the growl of engines that faded to the south.

It settled itself on what was left of Billyboy's chest and shook itself and preened. Perhaps later it would investigate all that other noise. Perhaps. But not likely. The flesh here was still warm and its stomach wanted filling.

And it was enough to know at last what its true quarry would be.

THREE

Dawn

Sunday began with an exorcism of shadows, a laying on of the light. The night-clouds had vanished, leaving no trace behind but a thin white webbing that unsettled the pale blue. The slopes greened, the fields tinted and the livestock moved sluggishly beneath the balm of the sun.

The temperature climbed toward eighty long before noon, threatening the brief hold of spring with a summer sun's heat.

Only the river remained cold, holding close to its bed patches of dark, swirls of night . . . like the sweep of a slow wing that slices through a star.

7:20 A.M.

Simon grunted when his arm snapped back and struck the corridor wall. He sat up rubbing the bone, the thin blanket that had covered him falling to his waist. His hair was tangled, his eyes shot with red, and along his left side was a dull

212

throbbing from the floor. He grunted again and glanced at his wife's door. And remembered how he had approached the room late the night before only to be stopped by Palemoon's frown. When he asked her as gently as he could what was wrong, she told him Rachel was sleeping, was praying, she couldn't make up her mind which. He didn't pursue it. Had Rachel wanted to see him she would have left word; as it was he had dismissed the girl with a light kiss to her cheek and a solemn promise he would stay here until one of them was needed. But as she'd headed sorrowfully for her own room, he had stopped her with a question: *Did you ride the dapple today, child? Did you leave the ranch, go out on your own?* She had nodded guiltily, and he'd smiled. The girl was in love with her mistress's horse, and though she rode well enough she often got lost when there was no one to ride with her. He'd waved her away and stared at the door, listening, hoping and finally taking a blanket from his room against the chill. He'd sat with his back to the wall, slumping, then, at last, sleeping (and dreaming of shrill sirens in the night).

He opened the door, his nose wrinkling against the smell of must and sure dying. She was still in her bed, her hands folded on her stomach, and he pulled a chair to her side and took it, laying a hand on her arm. She stirred, muttered, her eyelids flickering without revealing her eyes. Her skin was dry, and her pulse when he found it was erratic and weak.

Palemoon returned with a cup of steaming coffee.

"She's . . ." He couldn't say it, and was surprised when the girl simply nodded and left. He stared after her, wondering, then looked at his wife. "Rachel," he whispered. The room was growing warmer, but he could not shake the cold. "Rachel, what's going on?"

10:50 A.M.

Carosa looked with faint disgust at the crowd of men waiting on the lawn outside the church, gossiping while their wives planned the day's passing. About the fire, and the Shoshone, of course. From the way they were talking any minute now he could expect to see a thundering herd of ravenous, crazed, liquor-powered, war-painted Indians riding down the Pike, torching the houses, raping the women, stealing all the children. They weren't talking trouble, they were talking fear, and whatever hope there might have been for Galen's Town Meeting later in the week was gone. Blown away because some stupid ass couldn't hold his temper. He was getting damned sick of it all. Sick of what was happening, and of the way his daughter was defying him. Only this morning, she'd told him straight out, without permission, she was going into Blairs with some of her friends and if he didn't like it he could stick it. Just like that—stick it. He'd almost belted her, the way he had when she'd called him a wop. He even had his hand raised until Mary took hold and calmed him. It was just a stage, that's all, and he would have to be patient. Wasn't Kurt going through the same with Bea? Just a stage. What with Rachel being so sick and exams starting tomorrow he would just have to be patient. Crap. What she needed was a damned good thrashing to remind her whose house she lived in. Then Earl Carson told him with a laugh that the look on his face didn't belong in front of a church. Carosa told him to stick it.

11:00 A.M.

Esther Lynn opened the *Banner*'s door with something of a flourish. She didn't care if it was Sunday; after last night she had a feeling there'd be work today, and she wanted Galen to be impressed with her devotion.

11:05 A.M.

Reverend Thornton made his way slowly down the center aisle, replacing the hymnals the congregation left in the pews instead of in the racks. He told himself his sermon pleading for moderation after the evening's tragedy had reached every townsman's heart. He had seen it in their faces, even when he asked for a prayer for the Wolf family. They were stirred. His best sermon in years. He wished with a scowl he could stir himself to worry more about Greg. Then he looked up to the altar. The Prodigal Son be damned—Greg was nothing more than a pain in the ass.

11:30 A.M.

After letting the dogs out, Jason mugged at himself in the bathroom mirror, hunting without much enthusiasm for the proper expression, something that would make him look at least half human after so little sleep. Despite a long shower he could still smell the fire's acrid smoke on his skin and in his hair, and he could still see Wolf's mother-in-law through the living room window, crooning to herself while she held the Wolf children.

Finally he gave it up and hurried into the bedroom to dress. But when he dropped the same boot four times running he admitted at last that he was excited. In spite of it all, he was definitely excited. There was movement now in Windriver's valley, a surging confluence of forces that would not be stopped until equilibrium had been reached. There were questions that had to be asked, answers that had to be given . . . a threat to be defused. And there was no way in hell anyone was going to shut him out.

He grinned and chuckled, and when images of the boat and the woman and his running rose to remind him, he batted them away with a graveyard clearing whistle.

But the smile faded to perplexity when he strolled into the kitchen and didn't see Galen. Gone to church? There were no cups or bowls on the counter or table, the chairs were neatly arranged and the fresh bottle of milk in the refrigerator was still unopened. He looked at the clock, then rushed to the old man's room. The door was ajar, and he pushed in without knocking.

Galen was still in bed, sheets and thin blankets shoved down to his lap. The cream shades were still drawn, adding a sepia tint to the age of the flesh that he saw—thin arms and staved chest no longer camouflaged by the oversized white shirt, pouches and jowls menacing without the sun, the lips trembling, the left hand arrested as it reached for a plastic bottle on the nightstand.

Jason picked it up and read the label. The instructions had been typed in black—Mitch Regan used a red ribbon. "Gas, huh?" he said, thumbing open the lid and spilling the dosage into the editor's palm. "Foul red stuff?" He sat on the edge of the bed while Galen swallowed the clear capsule without benefit of water. "Nitro for your heart, right?"

"Shake me," said Galen, "and I'll probably blow up."

"You okay?"

"Fair. Ain't immortal."

"No shit."

Galen blinked, slowly.

"You stayed up after I went to bed," Jason accused gently.

"I wanted to be sure I got everything down. Can't trust the memory, y'know."

"Old Wyoming saying?"

Galen shrugged.

Jason lifted a sheaf of legal-pad papers from the floor and rifled through them. Then he folded them in half and pushed them into his hip pocket. "I'll have Esther Lynn type these tomorrow."

Galen looked at him, not trying to rise.

"Oh, for god's sake, it's all right," Jason told him with a half-smile. "I'm not out to steal your rag. You conned me out here to do a job, so I'm going to do it for a change instead of sneaking around like someone was trying to bite off my butt." He lay a hand on the old man's forearm. The flesh was cold. "You're not twenty anymore, cousin. Why don't you take a few more winks?"

Galen examined the rills of the ceiling. "I suppose I could. Bein Sunday and all."

Jason grinned. "Day of rest, the way I heard it."

"Yeah. Me, too."

A pause.

"All right," he said briskly, rising and brushing at his shirt. "I'll get back to you soon as I learn something. You think of anything yourself, jot it down for when I get back. Meanwhile, sleep!"

Galen's eyes were already closed, and Jason backed out as quietly as he could, closed the door softly and stared at it a moment before turning sharply on his heel and hurrying outside. He touched the pen jammed into his breast pocket, and the small notepad he'd picked up from a living room table. He almost felt as though it were old times, when the heat in the air was matched by the fever of the job.

It was a good feeling.

And suddenly it was frightening.

No, he cautioned angrily; don't kill it before it starts.

But he touched the pen again—a talisman. He reached the Pike's corner in time to see Daniel Tallpines and two other Indians he did not recognize climb out of a blinding white Continental and walk into Harmon's office. He quickened his pace, noting the unusual number of people walking the streets. Church was long over, and the luncheonette would be closed soon, yet people still moved under the flat white of the sun. He was relieved that they did not appear to be hostile, but they moved hastily, as though escaping the brunt of a rainstorm, eddying here and there to speak softly with a friend, a neighbor, to gawk at the Continental and glance fearfully at the office. Dressed in their Sunday best they all looked as if they were going to a funeral.

A few lifted a hand in greeting, and more than once he thought he was going to be stopped and questioned—after all, if a reporter didn't know what was going on, who did? Across the street he saw Bob Green, in a mint sport jacket and matching slacks, huddling nervously with three men who were working hard not to appear as if they were keeping an eye on the sheriff's doorway. Jason wondered if Green normally worked on a Sunday.

After an absent glance at Regan's drugstore he turned determinedly into Harmon's place.

The sheriff was behind his desk, the Indians standing around him. Ellie's place was empty and none of the deputies were in sight. Jason gave Harmon a casual salute that was returned (he thought) with rather a relieved smile, and leaned against the doorframe, arms folded loosely over his chest. A deliberate attitude that bordered on disinterest but invisible, he was tolerated; conspicuous and he might be out on his butt.

The Indians ignored him.

"I'm surprised to find you here, Jake," Tallpines said after a flurry of murmured greetings.

"I'm not," Harmon retorted, pushing away from the desk but not leaving his chair. "I can't be in ten places at once, y'know."

A large, white-haired man in a tailored, three-piece cream suit settled his thumbs into his waistcoat pockets. "I would have thought, Sheriff," he said in a cultivated courtroom voice, "that you'd at least be looking around some."

"Walter, Walter," Harmon said, exaggerating his patience, "at this very moment, my son-in-law is gettin some much needed sleep after workin until after dawn tryin to find a certain pickup. Bill Oaker is takin up where Steve left off, and Artie—you remember Artie—he's on his way to Blairs to take a statement from Michael. Mister Wolf has regained consciousness, accordin to a call I received not fifteen minutes ago, and he claims to be able to identify at least one of the men who allegedly destroyed his property last night and maimed his wife." His smile was little more than a stretching of his lips. "But I'm sure you know that already."

"Why?" Tallpines asked quickly.

Harmon glared at him. "Because I ain't senile yet, you goddamned pup! You think I don't know you had people with the Wolfs all night? Jesus, give me some credit for—"

Walter Gregory lifted a placating hand. "Now, Jake, there's no need for that tone of voice. We're all friends here."

Harmon looked at the well-fed Indian with ill-disguised dislike. "Then I'll thank you, Walter, to state your business and let me be about mine."

"We just want to make sure things are being done," Tallpines said bitterly.

"Oh, really?" The sheriff rose slowly, eyes narrowing to a belligerent squint, his palms flat on the desktop. "And just what makes you think they might not be, Mister Tallpines?"

"Daniel," the lawyer warned. Then he looked to the third man, younger but just as heavy, just as carefully dressed. "Franklin, I think it might be best if Daniel didn't say anything else."

Tallpines scowled, but he backed away when Franklin Gregory moved to stand beside him. It was obvious to Jason his composure was precariously maintained, and just as obvious that the lawyer's brother wasn't going to allow him another word if he had to take him out bodily.

Gregory waited a moment for the air to drain before continuing. "Now, Jake, if we can—"

"Bullshit," Harmon snapped. "There ain't nothin here you can get your teeth into and you know it, Walt. I'm doin all I can, under the circumstances. Right now, what I'm hopin is that Mike can positively identify the man he says he can."

Gregory perched on the edge of the desk and lifted his gaze to the ceiling. "He'll say it was that carpenter, Titus Arnold."

"I know."

Jason stiffened, but resisted the urge to take out his pen.

"Then why aren't you over at his shop, Jake?"

"Because if it was Titus—and I ain't sayin for sure it was, mind—but if it was I ain't goin there alone. I ain't no fool. And I'd rather have a sworn statement to hand before I do anything I might regret later."

Tallpines stirred, glared at Jason, but said nothing.

"Because he's one of yours?" Gregory asked offhandedly.

"Bullshit."

"Then because he might get violent."

Harmon nodded without hesitation. "Listen, Walt, you know Earl Carson, for cryin out loud. It's what comes of havin a part-time judge who sells rack clothes. The man will want no loose ends before he issues a warrant, and I sure as hell don't blame him. This is no time for gettin caught on technicalities."

Gregory nodded. "Can't argue with that, Jake."

"Good." Then, suddenly, he turned to Jason. "Jase, you keep your mouth shut about this, hear?" When Jason mimed pulling a zipper over his lips, none of them smiled. "And you tell Galen for me to keep his hands off that damned typewriter till we get all this worked out, you understand?"

"Sure," he said, pushing himself upright. "But would you mind telling me why you don't have someone watching Arnold?"

"Because for one thing he don't know Wolf saw him. And for another, even if he did know he wouldn't go nowhere. He's a hothead, but he ain't stupid."

"But won't he tell the others?"

"What for?" Gregory said. "An alibi? They already have one lined up, you can bet on it."

"Then it doesn't sound to me like he's going to be in jail for very long, not if he has a good lawyer, Mister . . ."

"Gregory. Walter Gregory."

"Pleased to meet you. Jason Clarke. And no offense."

"None taken, Mister Clarke. It's true. He'll be out as quick as Carson sets bail. I expect Green will represent him. I'd say five minutes after Arnold is brought in here, Green will have all the right papers on the judge's desk."

A muttering outside made Jason turn, and he saw a half dozen men standing at the curb, talking to a short, incredibly thin old man who was patting the outside of his pinstriped serge jacket. His grin was toothless and the others looked grim.

"Oh Lord," Gregory said when he saw the group.

"What?" Harmon said.

Gregory looked to Daniel, who shrugged as if to say one more problem didn't matter at this point.

"What?" Harmon demanded.

"Well," the lawyer said reluctantly, "we made a previous stop, Jake. Over at Green's, as a matter of fact."

Harmon peered through the window, dropped back into his chair. "Great. Whitcomb sold out."

"Yes."

"Lousy timin, Walt. You should have put it off a few days."

"I had no choice, believe me, Jake. Whitcomb said it would be today or he wasn't signing anything. My clients agreed, in spite of the . . . unpleasantness. Jake, I didn't do it deliberately."

"Sure." Harmon sighed. "Well, it's done I suppose. Shit."

"Mister Gregory," Jason said then, "would you mind another question?" He avoided the sheriff's warning glare and kept his gaze on the lawyer. "You'll have to forgive my ignorance, but back East—where I'm from—the concensus is that Indians who live on reservations barely have enough money to keep their heads above water. How, all of a sudden, do they come up with payments for such large parcels of land?"

"This was only a few untilled acres, Mister Clarke."

"Daniel here has more than a few untilled acres, Mister Gregory. And no offense again, Daniel, but a mechanic hardly qualifies for the *Fortune* Five Hundred club."

He knew he wasn't going to get an answer, but it didn't matter. He had already reached a conclusion and all it would take to verify would be a little digging and perhaps a phone call or two. Then, with the obvious confirmed, all he had to do was ask Simon why. And that, he told himself glumly, would probably get his head wrapped around a tree.

"Jason," the sheriff said quietly, "are you through?"

The request was clear and he nodded, smiled at the others

and stepped back outside. Whitcomb and his audience were gone, but he doubted there'd be many angry reactions once the word spread. It was the Shoshone who had the proper grievance now, and if Daniel's attitude was any indication, lawyer Gregory was going to have his hands full keeping some of the younger men from retaliating. In fact, he thought as he headed toward the newspaper office, it was amazing nothing had been done yet.

Unless, of course, they were waiting for dark, as the whites had done.

His free hand groped in his pockets for the keys until he realized the door was unlocked. He stared, looked around, then pushed in and saw Esther sitting at her desk. Amazing, he thought, and closed the door behind him. Esther Lynn looked up anxiously and he smiled at the disappointment keen in her eyes.

"I made him sleep in," he explained, dropping Galen's notes on her blotter. "He'd like you to make these scrawls legible. We were at the fire most of the night."

She snatched up the papers and scanned them swiftly, put her ribboned glasses in place and made a quick correction with a worn pencil. "How is he?" she said without looking up.

Jason paused on his way to the back office. "Tired."

She flipped to the second page. "Is he taking his medicine?"

"For his stomach?"

She snorted disbelief, and disappointment he should think her so dim.

"Yes," he said.

She swiveled her chair around. "I did learn something all those years I lived home, y'know. You just make sure he don't get too excited. I'll manage things here."

"Why, Esther," he said, grinning, "I didn't think you cared."

She scowled. "You don't know me well enough to talk to me like that, Jason Clarke."

He laughed, blew her a kiss and ducked inside, waiting behind Galen's desk until he heard her start working. Then he put his hands to his face and massaged it softly, his excitement spiraling into a dim apprehension. It was possible people might believe the arson-assault would finally put the lid on the tensions in town. But they would be wrong. He knew as sure as he breathed that much, much worse could happen, and the resulting devastation would be far worse than just physical. What he needed now, he decided, was a sane voice to calm him. But Donna didn't answer the telephone. He chewed on his lip, then called Doc Vance, grunting when he was told she was out at a dude ranch, tending to some horses.

"Horses. More than one? What happened?"

"Don't know. Fella called, said his stock was spooked all night."

"Sasquatch," Jason said, grinning at the far wall.

"Don't sasquatch me, young man," the doctor said peevishly. "I got enough troubles around here without you starting fool rumors."

Don't we all, Jason thought as he rang off, don't we all.

He shifted the chair until he faced the typewriter and stared at it a moment before switching it on. The humming of the machine and the clatter of the element against ribbon and paper made a combination of dreamlike sounds that channeled his thoughts into a series of impressions of last night's horror. It wasn't a story. No one would read it but him. Yet it served to clarify the event in two distinct columns—one of fact, one of emotion. Nearly thirty minutes later he realized with a start there was someone in the doorway. He turned. It was Esther Lynn, and she was holding her glasses nervously against her chest.

"I'm sorry, Jason."

"It's all right," he said, forcing himself back from the world of his writing. "What's the matter?"

"There's someone . . ." She stepped aside and Daniel Tallpines walked in.

Jason smiled reassurance until she retreated, then reached over the desk and shook the Indian's hand. Tallpines was markedly less arrogant than their last, nighttime meeting. His face was drawn into deep-etched lines, and his headband was skewed unnoticed over his forehead. He sat in the chair as though he were ancient.

"You look natural back there," he said with half a smile.

Jason scanned the desk, and could not help a brief feeling of satisfaction. "I suppose. Actually, it feels kind of strange."

He tilted the chair back against the windowsill behind him and folded his hands over his waist. "What's up?"

"An apology," Daniel said. "I was . . . back there in Harmon's office I was frustrated." His smile was sardonic, more so since he used only the right side of his mouth just as he did when he spoke.

"I can imagine," Jason said. "But in spite of everything, I think Jake knows what he's doing."

"That's not what I meant."

Esther Lynn began typing furiously. A bottlefly slammed repeatedly against a pane. The typewriter was still on and its hum became a growling. Then a horn sounded and a voice shouted and the not-quite-rhythmic passage of a number of horses could be heard.

"Jason," Daniel said, "I know you don't understand what it's like to be . . . like me, like my people. But if you don't mind me saying so, I think you understand the situation."

Jason kept his expression neutral, although he felt an irrational fear sweep through him.

"I have to talk to you."

"I'm listening."

"Not now. There's too much out there now." Daniel tented his fingers and placed them against his lips. "It isn't easy, but we've got to talk. You, me, maybe Galen." He blew a sigh between his palms. "I'll tell you one thing—Anglos have no monopoly on being downright stupid. Tonight, if you don't mind."

"Your place?"

Daniel shook his head emphatically. "No. Yours. As soon as Gregory stops playing his Clarence Darrow. And knowing Walt, that won't be until sometime after supper." He looked up questioningly and Jason nodded. "All right, then."

Before Jason could move he was up and gone. And before he could even begin to think, the telephone rang. It was Ted Waters asking for a moment of his time.

"Just a little bit," the grocer said. "I think we need to talk."

1:15 P.M.

Jake Harmon bunched a fist in exasperation. "Well, here, damnit, talk to Artie yourself!"

He slapped the receiver into Earl Carson's pudgy hand and waited impatiently while the judge listened to the deputy, then listened to the Blairs cop who had been Felsom's witness, and listened to Artie again and asked him several questions. Then he hung up and looked slowly around the haberdashery's cluttered storeroom as though he were seeing it for the last time.

"Hell, Jake," he said.

"Yeah, no shit. So let's get it over with."

"I'll have to go to the Hall. Got all the forms and stuff there."

"I don't care," Harmon said, pushing him toward the door. "Just do it, Earl, all right? Titus ain't gonna wait forever, y'know."

Carson reached for his suit jacket, changed his mind and sighed. Harmon patted his shoulder in commiseration, but kept his hand there in case the judge got cold feet.

1:30 P.M.

Jason hesitated at the curb, not at all positive he really wanted to make the crossing. He waited, a thumb under his belt, for several cars to pass him heading west, realizing as he did so that the sidewalks were almost deserted. The apprehensive small gatherings had either disintegrated or relocated, but it seemed as if their wakes, like shimmering heat, left specters of tension to blur his vision. The Continental was gone, too, and there was no sign of Tallpines when he looked over to the garage.

Well, pardner, he thought, and hurried across the street, making his way around the side of Waters's building to the farm supply area in back. A large yellow tractor baked in the sun, head-tall wheels massive and clean, paint polished, with a laboriously handprinted *For Sale* sign hanging from the snow-removal blade in front. He walked around the vehicle slowly, touching it, checking the steering wheel and complexity of gearshifts, wondering what kind of genius you had to be to keep from ramming it into a tree. He thought of Galen's Studebaker immediately, and his laugh was quick and sharp.

When he came back to the blade he stopped, one hand in his hip pocket. To his left, he could see Oaker's garage facing the Pike and behind that an expanse of motley trees and small pens he assumed belonged to the blacksmith's shop, itself a weather-weary jumble of barnlike openings and tiny office that faced the tracks. On the right the storehouse doors had been accordianed open. He moved, and the gravel beneath his feet was inordinately loud. He looked back to the tractor.

"Shoulda been Kelly's," Waters said.

He tried not to flinch, but his shoulders wouldn't listen.

"Sold out, the fool," Waters continued. "Now I'm stuck with it, and Kelly's a miserable drunk." He was standing in the doorway just beyond the reach of the light. His hands were buried in the high pockets of worn denim coveralls, expertly patched, and sagging at the knees. His birthmark had deepened almost to black. "Don't like drunks much. A sign of bad character, my daddy used t'say."

Jason understood the bait but refused it and caught movement in the aisles between the sacks and crates and odd-angled shapes of farming equipment. He didn't know how many there were—four, perhaps five—but he made it a point to ignore them. "You wanted to see me?" he said, as calmly as he could.

"Heard about that meetin. Words'll be said against me."

"You were invited. You'll have your chance for a say."

Waters shifted his weight, one foot to the other. "Lot of talk, that's all."

"Doesn't hurt."

"Don't do no good, neither."

Jason leaned against the tractor's near front wheel as he told Waters he understood about the loss of his business, but there didn't seem to be much anyone could do about it. "How can you force someone to buy what they obviously don't need? Or want?"

"They don't buy their food from me, neither."

"The way I heard it, neither do a lot of other people," he said as neutrally as possible. "Look, I got your problem, but I don't know what you want me to do about it."

"You could write," Waters said. "You could tell folks one of their own is goin under, somethin like that. You could say that instead of crap about Indian rights."

Jason smiled to underscore his helplessness. "It's not my paper, Mister Waters. Galen makes the decisions, not me." He paused. "And since I'm new around here, who would listen?"

Waters spat loudly, and the stirring behind him took shape, slowly.

"Word is you care about this place, Clarke. That ain't wrong, is it? I didn't hear wrong, did I?"

"No."

"But you ain't gonna do nothin to help it."

Jason checked the sky, amazed he hadn't lost his temper. In spite of his obvious fear of going under, Waters was still baiting him, the ghost of Peter Clarke putting a faint sneer to his words. "I'm trying," he said finally. "In my way I'm trying."

"Trying, huh? You still don't do no writin about it!"

"I don't burn down barns, either, Waters, or kill harmless animals, or attack people from the back, or nearly burn a woman to death." He held his breath suddenly, thinking he'd overstepped it when the man stiffened as though struck. He waited. Then: "Look, why don't you just come to the meeting next week—if you haven't ruined it already—and see what happens? Good lord, Waters, what the hell have you got to lose?"

"Sonofabitch," someone said from the shadows. "I knew it, Ted. Damnit, I knew it."

"Knew what," Jason said coldly.

Titus Arnold strode into the light. His hair was wild, his eyes red-rimmed and half his right eyebrow had been scorched off. "Knew you'd be just like your old man, that's what."

From behind a large keg of nails a smothered cough.

"Well damnit, look at him!" Arnold said, whirling around. "Christ, can't you see the deer in his eyes? Same like his old man. Same goddamned pukin sheep. Liquor him up, though, I'll bet he's a real badassed tiger."

Jason took three calculated steps forward, swift and silent. When Arnold turned around, sneering, Jason smiled at him, and buried his fist in the man's stomach. Arnold gaped and sat down, hard, rapidly blinking his astonishment. Jason leaned down. "Fuck you, Arnold," he whispered, "and the horse you rode in on." Before the carpenter could react he was back against the tractor, his trembling fists hidden in his pockets. He waited and noted that Waters looked almost embarrassed.

"Ted," someone else said, someone still in the shadows, "this here's a waste of time."

"I think the man's right," Jason said, ignoring the carpenter struggling to his feet. "But I'll tell you right now I don't see a bit of difference between you and the Shoshone when it comes to being stupid and downright pigheaded." He looked to Arnold, who stared at the ground and scowled. "And even if I am like my father, at least neither of us went around sneaking through the dark and scaring old women and children half to death."

"Hell, we never touched the old squaw," Arnold protested.

"Jesus," Waters muttered and punched at the nearest sack.

There was a scuffling, and four men darted out of the storehouse and disappeared around the back corner. Jason did not recognize any of them, nor did he move when Arnold hurried to stand by his friend.

"Christ, Ted, what did I say, huh? I didn't say nothin. I just did what—"

"Oh, shut up, Titus," Waters said wearily.

"But I just did what I was told, man! That's all I did."

"For Christ's sake, Titus, will you button up?"

Jason permitted himself a sour grin at the exchange which widened when the four others came back to the graveled yard. They didn't have their hands in the air, but their attitude was the same. Behind them Jake Harmon and Bill Oaker, who was carrying a shotgun and smiling. The sheriff, with a glance at the storehouse, walked over to Waters and pushed back his hat. He was wearing his gunbelt, and the revolver he carried was clearly loose enough for drawing.

Waters shrugged.

Harmon turned to the carpenter. "Titus," he said, "you really are one sorry idiot."

Arnold sputtered, threw up his hands in disgust and stalked

angrily into the open. Oaker nodded to him and followed him
and the quartet out toward the street. Waters jammed his
hands deeper into his pockets and vanished into the store.

"Nice," Jason said when Harmon joined him.

"Neat, but not nice," the sheriff said. "I've known Titus all
his life, but I didn't know him as well as I thought." He
moved away, and Jason fell into step behind him, reaching
the Pike just as Oaker walked into the office and closed the
door behind him. A small crowd had gathered on the
sidewalk and did not move away, even after the blinds had
been dropped over the window.

"Beautiful," Harmon muttered.

"Sharon claims there were more than that."

Harmon whirled on him, backing up a pace. "I know that,"
he said tightly. "You think I don't know that? Maybe four
more. And you know what I think?" Fury raged across
Harmon's face until his shoulders were quaking. Then, as
though a switch had been thrown, it was gone. "Hell, it don't
matter what I think, does it. I got a job, right? You got a job.
We got them on the outside of the pass, and that's all that
counts. Should've gotten them sooner. Hell." He started to
walk away, changed his mind and turned. "Jase, I'd like for
you t'do me a favor."

"Whatever I can, Sheriff."

"When you write this up and all, do me a favor and don't
mention the fact we still ain't got Mitch's stompers. Folks like
Waters, they're gonna put two and two t'gether soon enough
without you helpin them out. Tit for tat. Sonofabitch."

Jason lifted a hand in farewell, but the old man was already
crossing the street, shaking his head and muttering to himself
while his right palm slid across the butt of his revolver. Great,
Jason thought; the bust of the century and I feel like hell. He
considered trying Donna again, then returned to Galen's
office and began to write his story. Twice he found himself
editorializing and struck it all out viciously. He looked up
once, sniffing, a curious sense of dislocation swamping him
until he remembered where he was.

When he was done he glared at what he'd written and
shredded it into the wastebasket. He started again, and this
time kept the implications at bay.

3:00 P.M.

Rachel could hear Simon whispering to her, but she could not understand the words. All she understood was the urgency, the fear, and there was a moment when she nearly told him what she'd done.

The moment, however, passed, and she sighed.

And prayed to herself that the nestling would spare him.

3:30 P.M.

Jason took the finished sheets in to Esther and placed them carefully on her desk. He knew that first thing Monday morning she would run the final copy into the printer's in Blairs, and he was reluctant to ask her if she wouldn't mind proofreading story before she left today. "I don't know what he likes," he said. "You're the Galen expert around here."

She preened without lifting a hand.

"And . . . would you do me another favor?" he asked, almost timidly. "I've left blanks where those other names should go, the men Harmon picked up this afternoon. There's also the matter of Green maybe getting them out on bail. At least that's what that lawyer, Gregory, said would happen. I . . . I've got something to do now. I probably won't be back today."

Esther Lynn pulled off her glasses. "You mean you want *me* to go down there?"

He smiled his uncertainty. "Sure."

"But Galen *never* let me do anything like that."

"Ah," he said, seeing she wasn't really objecting. "But Galen is under the weather, right? And you yourself told me he shouldn't get excited, right? If I called him now and told him what was going on, what do you think'd he'd do?"

She considered as one hand toyed with the ruffles of her blouse.

Jason waited.

"Well," she said finally, "it isn't like I don't know anything besides doin my column."

"That's right."

"And he is a good teacher, y'know."

"The best."

"You don't think he'll be mad?"

He grinned. "Sure he'll be mad. He'll probably yell his fool head off."

He was startled when she grinned back at him and nodded sharply, once. "All right. You go ahead with . . . whatever. I'll take care of everything, don't worry."

"Esther Lynn," he said, refraining from kissing her, "you are a marvel." He backed out of the office quickly, closing the door softly and turning to face the street. The crowd had left Harmon's, but the Indian lawyer's car had returned. Green, too, was probably inside, and he told himself it would be a simple thing to walk down there, poke his head in and ask for the names himself. It's what he should do. Most definitely. But the look on Esther Lynn's face when he'd ask her to handle it was well worth the screaming Galen would do.

He had one foot off the curb when someone touched his shoulder from behind. He froze, his stomach suddenly taut in expectation of a blow.

"Hey, cowboy."

She was wearing a tan windbreaker over a loose plaid skirt, her dusty grey hat hanging from its chinstrap down her back. Her smile was strained when she saw his expression, and it took several seconds for it to switch to pleasure.

"You okay, Jase?" She looked to the sheriff's office and grimaced. "Oh. I heard, y'know. Listen, if you'd rather I—"

He took her arm and hurried her across the street. "What I would rather," he said, "is get some fresh air. And don't ask. Just lead."

"Where?"

He shrugged. "Don't know." A vague gesture. "Anywhere."

"You been riding yet?"

"You mean, on a horse?"

"No, on a cow. Yes, I mean a horse. Have you been riding since you came out here?"

When he shook his head she took hold of his elbow and guided him quickly toward the blacksmith's shop. Twenty minutes later he was on the back of a small chestnut mare that was, as she'd promised, docile enough to handle a baby. Her own mount was a stormcloud grey, high-stepping and oddly skittish. They had picked their way over the tracks—waving to Mac Felsom lounging on the station platform—and plunged eastward into a field of low grass and isolated groves of thickly crowned trees. There was a breeze here that soothed the burn of the white sun, a droning and rustling orchestrated to submerge all memories of trucks, of shotguns, of radios and automatic washers. He expected to see a stagecoach lunging over the horizon at any moment and had to look back over his shoulder at the town's roofs to reassure himself he hadn't been swept into a vortex of jumbled time.

He said little at first. He preferred to concentrate on the mare's monotonous swaying, trying to follow Donna's instructions so the saddle wouldn't keep thumping into his butt. Within minutes it worked, much to his silent astonishment, and he finally relaxed enough to enjoy his escape.

Every few dozen yards the mare would toss her head sharply or slap with her tail to discourage the gnats that billowed from hidden thickets and the flies that banked solo over their heads. A bird called out in a peculiar whistling rise. A gopher sat up on a flatheaded rock and watched them pass, his nose twitching, his forepaws dangling. In the middle distance the land was spotted with cattle.

For a moment, he found himself draped in unwelcome melancholy. In the East he'd thought of himself as a misshapen cog a hair out of sync with the rest of the machinery; here he'd hoped he would mesh with his surroundings, but he found the grandeur, the dimensions, the *space* still incomprehensible, despite the fact he had accepted it, embraced it. But accepting and embracing were not the same as understanding, and he wasn't sure of the scheme in which mountains and hawks and men were a part. He wasn't at all sure he would ever understand. It was unnerving. Like Peter Clarke before him, he saw the threat of annihilation as all too real. And with a rueful smile he finally knew what his mother had meant when she'd told him it was the land that had eroded his father, not the town, and not the old-fashioned pioneer dreams.

"Jase, are you sure you're all right?"

He nodded without thinking.

"It was a nasty business, I guess."

It took a second to realize what she was referring to. He told her what he'd seen last night, what he'd heard this

morning, trying to shake his memory of the elder Clarke, a
retired sergeant who, like a disjointed Kipling hero, would be
king if he could.

. They stopped at a shallow stream and sat on the bank while
the horses drank and snapped at the tall grass.

"What else is it, Jason?"

And he knew it was his turn. It came in spurts and in
stutters, as he yanked fistfuls of grass from the ground and
tossed them in the water. The sweat polished his face and
made him wish he'd worn his hat. It came in undulating
shadows like mantas over the field, in faded visions of his
mother dying when he was twenty.

He told her of the naked women and wingéd serpents, and
of the house he had turned into a self-condemned cell.

Donna held his hand, and as he touched her cheek she
kissed his palm. When he kissed her he felt her tension; as he
undressed her he saw the trembling. He lay out their shirts to
give them a bed and lay down beside her. Her eyes were
loosely closed. He wanted her, but waited, thinking of the
man who had raped her and of the fear that had crippled him
and had stolen his soul. He felt like weeping and then she
snaked an arm around his neck and pulled him to her. He
whispered, and she nodded, although the trembling didn't
stop.

On elbows and knees, his hands cupped behind her head,
she waited while he kissed her from hairline to chin, using his
nose to dislodge her glasses and making her grin.

Their loving wasn't perfect but it served.

And in serving, stopped the trembling.

They rode slowly, easily, silence slipping in to calm them.
The sun was beginning to wester, just enough to cast a
shadowveil over her face, to set her profile in relief against
the purpling backdrop. When she caught him looking, he
scratched his head and turned away. The stream meandered
in a series of switchbacks, and the sounds of their crossing
were swallowed quickly by their passing. She asked him about
his illness, though she kept her gaze ahead.

"It doesn't let you grow much," he said, staring over the
mare's head, seeing nothing but Kramer's Mountain. "It
doesn't let your muscles do what they're supposed to. There
were as many doctors as my father could afford, and the best

they could do with what I had was wait. See if I would stick to the norm and ride it out, or become a statistic. I rode it out." He held out an arm. "Both my folks were quite a bit taller than me, so I guess that's why I lifted weights and things. If I couldn't be big, at least I could be strong."

"Are you?"

He laughed. "I never let myself get into a fight to find out. I'm hell with a shadow, though."

"I think," she said, and paused. "I think I always wanted to be a vet. Were you always going to be Clark Kent?"

"Yeah," he said, not having to think. "I watched a lot of old movies. I wanted to be Cary Grant ordering Rosalind Russell around and scooping the rest of the world. That remake of *The Front Page,* y'know?" He wiped a sleeve over his face. "You ever go back East?"

"No." Her cheeks puffed. "Not yet, anyway."

Another hundred yards and he reined to a halt, standing in the stirrups to see the land better. "Good lord," he said, "I think we've found the end of the world."

"We haven't gone that far."

"I think my butt disagrees."

She laughed so loudly their mounts broke into a canter they maintained until they reached Elkhorn Road. A break in the fencing brought them to the blacktop, and it wasn't until they were abreast of the Perkins ranch that Jason realized just how far they had come. He was about to comment when he noticed the gate was open, and noticed a gathering of agitated birds far up on the lawn. Donna said something to him, but he didn't hear her; instead, he urged the mare through the opening and up the drive, riding fifty yards before the animal began to balk, tossing her head, her eyes showing white. A breeze carried an odor that made him want to gag.

"Jason?"

Donna rode up beside him and he told her to wait. He slipped from the saddle and hesitated, shaking his head violently to rid his nostrils of the stench. The birds were large, glistening grey and black, and shoving each other off a mound partially covered by someone's coat. Crows instantly wheeled protesting into the air as he approached, the buzzards waiting until he yelled and windmilled his arms before lifting clumsily away from him to land a few yards distant, watching, fluffing, a few of them strutting.

What they'd been scavenging was clear now, and he turned suddenly, swallowing the bile that lurched in his throat. "Donna." It was more like choking. "Go into the house. Call Harmon and Vance."

She frowned at him and tried looking over his shoulder. What she saw apparently convinced her not to argue, and her mount raced to the porch and barely stopped before she'd leapt to the ground and was up the stairs.

The buzzards settled and the crows scolded from the trees.

He tried to tell himself that people were not meat, that when they died they didn't look as if they'd been slashed with countless razors until nothing remained but raw, browning flesh. Bone. Matted hair. He put his hands on his hips and stared at the sky until his eyes watered. He did not hear Donna until she took his elbow gently and tugged him away. At the gate they embraced. They had nothing to say.

7:50 P.M.

Palemoon stood alone on the porch and watched the slow-fattening moon coast among the stars. She wore no coat, and her hair had come unbraided, slipping in dark tangles over her shoulders to her chest. There was no sound inside; Simon was still with Rachel, as he had been since dawn. She tried to be sad, but all she could think of was the important thing she had done that day. Riding all by herself into town along the river, tethering the dapple and walking the rest of the way to the house. No one was home. She had been scared that someone would see her. And when there was no one home she didn't know what to do. She had thought hard, and left the Teaching inside. The door was open, and she found the room that belonged to the one who was marked without any trouble at all. Then she had run away. Proud of herself, and scared, and grinning like an idiot all the way home. It was very important, what she had done. She knew that. She didn't know exactly why, but then she didn't really understand anything of what Rachel told her. She only knew that Rachel was like a mother and had to be obeyed, and Simon was like a father and had to be loved. And protected. Just like Rachel said, he had to be protected. Fathers didn't always understand what mothers did sometimes.

Palemoon didn't understand either, but she could pretend that she did. Then she would be like Rachel and take care of Simon. And take care of the place. The place where the Old Ones had lived and the Old Ones had died. All the bad people would go away, and she would help Simon take care of it.

The wind blew and she shivered. She looked up to the moon and saw a shadow drift past it. She frowned, bewildered. Rachel was still in her bed, so the shadow couldn't be. But she had seen it. She stiffened when she saw it again, saw it moving closer. Hovering. Gliding. Black on black, like the ghost of a dead star.

Whispersoft. Shadowfast.

She backed toward the door, one hand stretched behind her to grope for the latch. Rachel had told her it wouldn't hurt her. You are very special, Rachel had told her some very long time ago; and Simon and I will take care of you better than anybody else. That was true, the taking care part. But she couldn't help feeling that if she were standing on the lawn, the shadow would come down and do something bad. It was the first time she had felt that way, and she didn't like it at all. It wasn't supposed to happen like this. She was a very special Shoshone, and nothing was supposed to happen to hurt the New People. But it would do something bad. She knew it. And it wasn't supposed to be this way. She wondered then if Rachel knew it. If Rachel knew that the shadow in the sky could hurt anyone it wanted to, even those who loved it.

Shadowfast. Whispersoft.

She thought: I have to tell Rachel.

Whisper . . .

I have to tell Rachel.

. . . fast.

9:35 P.M.

The river swept between its banks in a single silent march. The stars were blurred and greyed, frozen beneath its surface, and the moon distorted to a smear of deathly white. There were no rocks to break its surface, no snags for interruption. The latticed supports of the bridge had long since blossomed slime.

The railing was only waist-high, and Jason was nearly bent double over it as he stared at the dark water, at the occasional brief froth that eddied about the surface. He had tried to sleep but failed, and had taken the setters out for a walk after Galen complained he was turning the house into a morgue. An apt comparison. Even now he couldn't recall leaving the ranch on Elkhorn Road; there'd been cars, the ambulance, Doc Vance and Harmon asking silent questions. Someone volunteering to take the horses back to stable. A ride into town, a funeral procession without benefit of a hearse, and another, swifter ride to Blairs General where the police surgeon there, one Martin Trumble, had assisted Vance with the autopsies. They both had returned to the coroner's office in full-blown argument.

Vance insisted, at times almost hysterically, that Billy and Gloria had been viciously murdered, and the damage done to their bodies was easily accounted for by the presence of the scavengers. Trumble, however, had called in Donna after the preliminaries had been completed and made it quite clear he agreed with her somewhat more expert impressions—that something far larger had come down from the slopes. Those birds, he'd added in an almost patronizing way, hadn't been there long enough to do what Vance claimed. And though he disclaimed a hunter's experience, he discounted cougars because they would have dragged the bodies off, and wolves were too small. When Harmon, who had kept silent through the tirade, pressed him, Trumble demurred to Donna, who suggested the only possibility left: a bear. Winter-starved, crazed, she really didn't know.

"But it wasn't a human being who did it," Trumble said with a glare at Vance. "That you can take as fact."

"What the hell do the two of you want, then?" Vance had yelled. "A goddamn giant chicken?"

Trumble stomped off without bothering to reply; Vance followed him a moment later, to get a breath of fresh air.

After Donna had completed her part in the examination, she and Jason had given Harmon their statement. When Vance left, Donna rubbed a fist over puffed eyes and watched the sheriff pacing before she stopped him with his name.

Harmon had turned to her, and from the expression on his

face Jason knew the man was wondering if the same thing had
happened to Gregory Thornton.

"Jake, Doc's wrong. He's wrong, and you've got to understand that."

"You ain't no hunter either," he'd said softly.

"No, but I am still the vet around here. I do know
something about animals, in case you'd forgotten. And Jake,
bears . . . it's not impossible for them to become rabid."

The room had gone cold; Jason felt her shivering.

Harmon frowned as he thought, then shook his head
slowly. "Donna, this has been goin on for nearly a month.
Are you saying this is what did in the livestock, too?"

"It answers a lot of questions, Jake."

"But a month, Donna! It would've been dead by now."

Her gaze lowered, then lifted again, stubborn. "It could
infect others."

"You believe that?"

She clasped her hands knuckle-white in her lap. "I'd sooner
believe that than believe a . . . a person did this. Jake, Doc is
a fine man, I love him, but he doesn't know animals the way I
do."

"Jesus, Donna, you know what you're sayin?"

She waved one hand wearily, a partial disclaimer, but until
Vance returned and announced he was ready to leave,
Harmon paced the room and muttered to himself. What
Donna had said made sense, it was an answer, but she'd said
little else since they'd left the ranch and Jason was worried
their discovery had driven her close to shock. Vance agreed
as soon as he saw her, the fight with Trumble and his feeling
she'd somehow betrayed him dismissed. He made her take a
dose of phenobarbitol and sat with her in the back of the
patrol car while she mumbled and dozed. In front, Jason
stared ahead at the road and fought off red dreams.

"You okay?" Harmon asked when they reached the plateau.

"Nope. But I will be." Then a name slipped by and he
almost missed it. He frowned, and muttered, "Riley."

"What?"

"Riley," Jason said. "There was a man who worked there,
the one you told me about. Riley. Maybe he—"

Harmon shook his head emphatically, and the car swerved
gently to the right. "No."

"But Jake—"

"I know what you're thinkin, son, but forget it. You're reaching."

"He wasn't there," Jason said. "He should have been, but he wasn't."

"Yep, but I've already checked. While we were out there. His clothes are gone. He's gone. My best guess is, he either had a run-in with Billy, or he found the bodies and couldn't take it. Nope, Doc Oldfield is right—ain't no person did what we saw, Jase. I'll get word out to find out what the guy knows, but I ain't chasin him." Then he reached into his shirt pocket and pulled out a clear plastic bag. "Those birds you saw."

"Buzzards," Jason told him, for what sounded like the hundredth time. "Crows or ravens. Jesus, Sheriff—" He stopped when Harmon pressed the bag into his hand. He held it close to the dashboard and peered at the contents. "Looks like part of a feather."

"I think it is. A big one."

"Brown, right?"

"Yep." The sheriff cleared his throat and gave a glance to the rearview mirror. "I found it in Billy's hand. Don't belong to what you say you saw."

Jason stirred and handed the bag back. "Well, if you're asking me what it is, don't. I'm lucky I know a robin when I see one. Besides, he could have had it there when he was attacked. He must have, if it doesn't belong, like you said."

"Yeah," the sheriff said. "I was afraid you'd say that."

Donna was taken home and put to bed with another sedative. Galen had been waiting with Esther Lynn at the sheriff's office. Esther immediately scolded the man for leaving Donna alone and went off to sit with her with the announcement that she shouldn't have to wake up alone. Then Galen launched into a red-faced tirade about not being kept informed of things that were happening right in his town, practically on his own damned doorstep, and was still at it when Jason succumbed to a headache that drove him outside.

Bears, he thought, still staring at the river. Mountain lions. Giant chickens. Wolves. A bunch of dead cattle and two dead people. Good lord, it was enough to drive a man back to the city where at least you knew what the hell a mugger was. And where you survived the mugging at least recognizable.

A bat skewed across the water out of the trees by Harmon's unlighted house. He tried to follow its erratic silent hunting and lost it in the shadows near the embankment on the right. He waited (a warning, perhaps a memory: *keep your head covered at night so the bats won't get tangled*), but saw nothing more. It had been swallowed. It was gone. He shrugged, straightened and half turned to call the setters to his side, hoping they hadn't run out of hearing while he'd been thinking. But the words never slipped past the sudden clenching of his teeth, the sudden constriction of his throat.

He wasn't alone.

He kept his eyes on the water, on the shadows, on the place where he had last seen the bat.

A feeling he wasn't alone, and the skin tightened over the back of his hands, across the back of his neck.

A feeling. A tingling at the tips of his fingers, and he was painfully aware of the slow cold breath passing through his nostrils.

Someone laughed softly: the sound of a young girl in a dark corner, a shy woman in a bar.

He wasn't alone and he could not turn. The stretch of the black river held him in an illusion: he was on a raft and he was traveling backwards, into the gaping mouth of a Lorelei demented. He was floating. He was watching the bloodrun of a Gorgon slain behind him.

He knew it was illusion; the cold was in the air, not his heart; it must be delayed reaction to the murders and the fire.

But someone was laughing, he wasn't alone, and he slowly closed his eyes when he heard a quiet thumping. The laughing stopped, and the thumping stopped, and something jabbed him in the middle of the back.

"It's peaceful," someone said. Jason felt his lungs collapsing as he sprawled against the railing, spinning around, half ready to leap over. Then: "Hey, Jason, I'm sorry. Jesus, I'm sorry."

David Carosa wheeled his chair (thumping over the irregular planks on the bridge) to Jason's side, peering at him anxiously. He held a cane in one hand, aimed down now at the water.

"David," Jason said harshly, "you do that again and I'll break both your—" He stopped and blinked, and David broke into a quick laugh. He took a deep breath, and shook his head sharply to free the lock in his neck. "Hey, now it's my turn to apologize."

"No problem," the younger man said. He rose after locking the chair and used the cane to hobble to the railing. Jason returned to his staring, watching a shadow cross the ripple of the moon, one hand still at his chest as if massaging it would resurrect the habit of easy breathing.

There was a distant barking, coming nearer. The canine cavalry, Jason thought, charging to the rescue, five minutes too late.

"You come out here often?" he asked then, knowing he sounded stupid, though he could think of nothing else to say.

Surprisingly, David nodded. "Yeah. It's nice." He spat into the river. "I just come out to think, that's all."

And to watch Ellie's house, Jason guessed, though he kept it to himself.

"Lately, though, I don't think I like it."

"Don't blame you," Jason said. "The problems this place has don't stop after dark."

David shook his head and rapped the cane against the railing. "No, that's not it. It's different, some nights. I know this river here like the back of my hand, especially at night. These days, though . . . I don't know. It still looks the same, but it isn't. Does that make sense?"

"If it does to you, then it does."

David laughed, and Jason realized there was nothing girlish about it. "Y'know, you sound like the shrink who was helping me while I had physical therapy. But it does make sense to me. Damn, I should've worn a jacket."

Jason nodded but said nothing. He had ignored the chill as long as he could, but now that Carosa had mentioned it he felt it crawling through his hair and over his arms, brushing like a feather down the sweep of his jaw. He rubbed his throat lightly and scratched at his chest, and the two setters suddenly broke onto the bridge. They swarmed around him, snuffling, demanding attention, and Jason shrugged with a grin when Jeff took gentle hold of his wrist and pulled.

"Home," he said in apology.

"Better dogs than a nagging wife, huh?"

"I suppose. You going to stick around?"

David kept his gaze on the river. "Yeah. For a while."

"Okay. Take care." He followed the dogs off the bridge, glad to be gone. It wasn't, he told himself with more than a trace of guilt, that he didn't like Tony's son; but the way he was talking tonight, combined with what had happened . . . it wouldn't have been long before they were both seeing ghosts.

Within ten minutes he was at the gate. The porch light was on, the rest of the house dark. He stumbled up the walk with the animals playfully trying to trip him, laughing and almost forgetting the scare Carosa had given him when Mutt turned abruptly and stared at the car parked in the drive. Jeff froze.

There was a silence.

"What?" Jason whispered. "What is it, fella?"

Despite himself he listened for the laughter, hearing nothing but the rainhiss of a car speeding out of town.

"What, Mutt?"

The dog's growl was deep and sustained. His teeth were bared and his hackles risen. While Mutt took several stiff-legged paces onto the lawn, Jeff moved to stand in front of Jason, her tail switching hard against his legs until he backed away.

He tried a whistle and failed. Mutt's haunches lowered slightly in preparation for a leap, but Jason forestalled him by clapping his hands sharply and making both dogs jump. Again he clapped, and they snapped at the air, snarled, while he told them to forget it and get in the house. They refused to move. He hurried to the porch and shoved open the door, ordering them a fourth time and nearly losing his temper when they only backed to the steps and stayed there, their growls slipping into querulous whines.

"Damnit, you coming or not?" he demanded angrily.

Jeff lay down, muzzle between her forepaws. Mutt sat, incisors a dead white.

The hell with them, let 'em stay outside, Jason decided; dead people he could deal with, but not crazy dogs.

11:40 P.M.

Rachel heard Simon talking, urgently and low. *Get some water, child, hurry.* But she could not smile to tell him it was already too late. She had already seen the shadow of Dark

Moon standing on the mountain, staring at her, smiling. It
was time, then. It was time. She had done all she could, and
now it was time. Simon, I do love you. And I tried. I tried to
hold on until the first circle closed, but there was too much
power. Too much of the spirit. *Rachel Rachel can you hear me
Rachel* Simon, I'm afraid. *rachel* I did what was written,
Simon. I almost did it all. Simon. Watch. Please watch. If it
goes wrong *rachel* you must kill her. No. Yes, kill no Simon
it's dark. I can't think. Must think. Simon *rachel* it's very
dark, Simon. Dark. Moon. Wrong. All wrong. Simon,
it's . . .

11:45 P.M.

Palemoon rushed back into the room with a pitcher of cold
water, but stopped when Simon rose from the bedside and
placed a gentle kiss on Rachel's forehead. When he turned,
there were tears in his eyes.

"She didn't hear me," he said helplessly. "I tried to tell her
about Whitcomb. I tried to tell her Perkins would sell by the
end of next week. If she had only lasted one more week!" He
stopped, the tears now icing his cheeks. "It's over. We will
prepare her, then have Vance come to make good the Anglos'
laws." He sighed. "It's over, Palemoon. When Vance is gone
we'll call the others and tell them we'll have to be content
with what we have. Don't cry, little one. At least now it's
over."

11:45 P.M.

Jason stirred, half dozing, trying to decide if the soft
laughter he heard was in a dream or from something that was
standing outside his window.

FOUR

(1)

With the barbershop closed on Mondays and the bar not scheduled to open until three, Anthony Carosa had taken his time getting out of bed. It was a reluctant laziness, however; he just was determined not to visit the Pike until he was good and ready, determined not to join the others he knew would be there. Talking. Wondering. Gossiping as they had done after church yesterday morning. Not, he thought as he poured himself a third cup of coffee, that they didn't have anything to talk about. There was the Perkinses' dying (and being quickly buried that afternoon), Rachel dying (a phone call just after dawn that Mary had taken) and talk of a hunt to flush out the animal that had ravaged people now instead of livestock. A hell of a lot of talk, a damned lot of hot air. He stood at the back door and sipped the hot brew carefully, staring at the trees and the lawn, telling himself it was right he hadn't told Carole about Rachel. She had an English exam this morning (he glanced at the clock; nearly twelve, the test almost over) and in spite of her rebellion he wanted her grades to be as good as they could.

It was a beautiful day. Low seventies, he guessed, and a few fair-weather clouds. A beautiful day, yet he could not help feeling it should have been raining.

Mary came up behind him, tidying the folds of her simple black dress, fussing her hair into place. He turned and smiled at her.

"You sure you won't go?" she said. Even in black she was still plump, still gay.

"Gotta open up."

She kissed him quickly on the cheek and left, hurrying up the drive to the Pike, where she stood hesitantly on the sidewalk. A cool breeze ruffled her hair, and she sighed, wondering why she bothered to brush it at all. Then she crossed to the luncheonette, deliberately avoiding a glance at the collection of campers, jeeps and pickups in front of the sheriff's office. It was the hunting party, as many men as could be spared from their jobs milling about with rifles and shotguns, voices low, faces solemn. An army, she thought . . . and shuddered as she walked inside. Peg was already waiting at the counter's end stool.

"Did you tell Bea?" she asked as she took the seat beside her.

Peg shook her head. "The exam," she said. "I'll tell her later."

"That's what Anthony says."

"You don't approve?" There was no reproach, only sadness.

"I don't know." She stopped as a series of grumblings shattered into a roar. "They're off."

"I hope they get it. God, Mary, what a thing to happen!" Kurt limped out of the kitchen then, and she glanced at him, concerned. "You sure you can handle this okay?" she said, waving a hand toward the filled, quiet booths.

Kurt nodded sharply, once, and Peg hid a smile behind a feigned yawn. With a nudge to Mary and a blown kiss to her husband she slid off the stool and made for the door. She had been hoping Bea would return before she left, partly so she could find out how the examination had gone, partly so the girl could be harnessed to help her father. She almost said something to Mary about it, but changed her mind when she remembered that her friend was having enough problems with her own daughter. Funny, she thought as they headed slowly for the church, when they're born you can't wait for them to walk and talk, and when they walk and talk you wish they'd get back into their cribs and shut up . . . or grow up. And when they grow up you wish they'd either hurry up and find themselves, or get back in diapers, the bad times forgotten.

She smiled to herself, then, and shook her head slowly. Such thoughts on such a beautiful day! But when she looked to Mary she knew the unease was not hers alone. And it wasn't the funeral or the death of Rachel MacKenzie—it was something else that belied the sun. The foul blue exhaust that clung to the air, perhaps, from the hunting party's departure; or Bea's needling of her father; or—

She grunted, surprised, when she collided with someone and backed away sputtering apologies while Mary laughed quietly and Ellie Felsom assured her it was quite all right, no harm done.

In fact, Ellie thought as she watched the two women hurry off, it was a fortuitous collision. She hadn't been feeling well for days, had tried once again to work until five at the office and, once again, found herself saddled with a headache that felt as though her head were in a vise. Bill Oaker, left to mind the office, had muttered to himself when she'd told him she was leaving, but she didn't care. She had to get out for a while. Walk, maybe, along the river. Feel the sun on her face, the wind against her cheeks. She had wept when Steve had brought her word about Rachel's dying in her sleep, but the tears hadn't lasted very long. It had been months, over a year since she'd seen the old woman and talked with her and laughed with her. And she had this damned headache! In the middle of the most perfect day of the year she had this infernal headache!

When she had collided with Peg Steed she had been walking in the wrong direction!

A dusty station wagon with its top peeled off was still in front of her father's office when she passed. Jake was standing up in back, sunglasses on, hat pulled low, a freshly oiled rifle held loosely in his left hand. She waved to him vaguely and ducked around the corner, a finger lightly rubbing at her temple, and an oppression weighting her shoulders until they were rounded.

Jake was about to call out to her when Artie, squirming

impatiently behind the steering wheel, demanded to know when they were leaving.

"In a minute," Harmon snapped. "Hold your horses." He watched his daughter walking toward the river, and was suddenly tempted to leap out of the vehicle, chase after her and demand to know what was wrong, why she couldn't finish a simple day's work anymore. Last night around midnight he had awakened to her screaming and leapt from his bed and found her on the front porch, naked and shivering against the cold. When he'd touched her shoulder she'd screamed again until he'd held her, thinking it was about time he took Steve off the night shift so the man could comfort her the way he was supposed to.

When she'd quieted into a silent weeping, she insisted she remembered nothing, she must have been sleepwalking. Harmon had accepted it, though she'd never done anything like that since the night her mother died.

When he learned about Rachel—

"Hey, Jake!"

"All right," he said. "All right, all right."

He climbed over the back of the seat and took his place behind Artie. The vehicle, loaded with weapons, bear traps, netting and clubs, pulled away from the curb. A walkie-talkie on the seat between them crackled static.

"Still think you should've picked up Ted," Artie grumbled suddenly, a theme he'd been airing since Green had posted bond for Titus Arnold and the others.

"No proof," Harmon said without taking his eyes from the road. "No one implicated him, what can I do?"

"Lawyers," Artie muttered sourly. "Oughta be shot."

"Tell me about it, boy, tell me about it."

"Maybe we should've waited until after the funeral," Artie said. "I mean, what with Billy and Gloria not havin any folks and all. It isn't gonna be very crowded."

"I'll pay my respects later, after we get that damned bear."

"You really believe that?"

Harmon slumped, and glared. He didn't know what to believe, but was convinced Doc Oldfield knew what she was talking about. He would be derelict if he didn't mount this massive hunt, and keep at it until something turned up. He didn't bother to mention they might also find Greg Thornton.

A car sped past them in the opposite direction, and Harmon grinned when he saw Artie's arms stiffen, then relax. Reflexes, he thought; a good cop has to have good reflexes. Artie may not have the brains, but he damned sure has the reflexes. Then he turned in the seat and frowned, wondering why Galen would be out this way, instead of banging at his typewriter, an extra million words for the next day's edition.

Jason glanced in the rearview mirror, thought he saw the sheriff staring after him and lifted a hand in a vague wave. There was no response and he eased his foot off the accelerator, slowing to the speed limit as he reached the first group of houses in town.

He yawned, and decided that in his next life he would be something like a cow. Not very exciting, but at least he would get some decent sleep once in a while.

After deciding last night the laughter he'd heard was only his imagination catching up with the scare David had given him on the bridge, he had tried to sleep. But when he did . . . his water dream had returned. He'd struggled back to consciousness, but every time he closed his eyes there was something waiting to take him.

It was ten o'clock when he'd finally pushed himself heavily out of bed and cold-showered to goad his blood. He entered the kitchen and Galen told him Rachel had died, then pushed a slip of paper into his hand.

"What's this?"

"People to talk to in Blairs," Galen said. "I don't know them personally, but they're friends of friends of friends . . ." He grinned. "They might tell you something about MacKenzie."

"Yeah," Jason said. "A hell of a day to do it."

"She's dead. You're not."

Jason looked at him sharply, almost angrily, and saw dark pouches under his eyes, and the same fear he'd seen the night Michael Wolf had been attacked. He'd wanted to ask then if Galen had heard the laughing, but picked up a coffee cup instead and said, "Is it raining yet?"

There was no answer. He looked to the window and saw the bright sunlight. Galen picked up a pencil and drummed it on the table until the point broke. Then Jason folded the paper into his breast pocket.

"I'll probably be gone most of the day."

Galen had nodded.

"I want to talk to Daniel first, though, before I leave town. He was supposed to come here last night, he had something to tell us."

"What?"

"I don't know, but he never made it. It must have been because of Rachel. If he calls, tell him I'm on my way, tell him to stay put until I get there."

"Why?" Galen said. "They have their grief, and Jake's got his hunting party about ready to move out."

Jason stopped at the doorway. "Because none of this is going to go away just because someone shoots a bear, cousin. There's still going to be Ted Waters and the others who are losing business. If they find what killed . . . what did the killing, that's only going to be part of it. Only part of it."

He had reached the front door before Galen came after him.

"Jase, you recall what I said when you first got here? What I said about the town?"

He did, and he nodded.

"The sun's out," Galen said, "and I feel it worse than ever."

Jason hesitated and smiled tightly. "Be careful, Galen. Don't work too hard."

"Do I ever?"

He waved and left, took his time driving out to Tallpines's home and cursed his dallying when he discovered the family wasn't home. Neither were they at Sweetwater's, and Michael Wolf's ranch was deserted, disturbingly bleak under the noonday sun. He assumed, then, they had all gone to MacKenzie's for some Indian ritual or other, paying their respects to an ancient, powerful woman.

By the time he had passed Harmon he realized he'd wasted too much time. It would be after one before he reached Blairs, and if he were lucky it would be near dark before he returned home. Damn, he thought with a punch to the wheel, why the hell didn't I use the phone?

(2)

The newest of the three-building education complex was the high school, brick and polarized glass that provided a hard contrast to the grade school and nursery. Each of the three faced a different street so that the trees and grass in the center of the block provided an equal play-and-rest area for all the students. The afternoon examination (Secretarial Practices) was already in progress, but a few students still lingered in the shade, waiting for friends or just not bothering to head home to waiting chores.

Carole and Bea sat silently at a redwood picnic table, both red-eyed, and every so often sighed loudly and stared through the foliage to the unfairly bright sky. A number of their classmates had joined them on the benchseats a few minutes at a time, some weeping with them if bonds were close, others fumbling for words they did not truly feel. Most of them thought the old woman was all right in her way, but her dying wasn't anything to get hysterical over. It was the bear they were excited about, a savage, ripping creature that had been stalking the town for weeks without anyone knowing it. Most of them had been certain the Shoshone had been behind the deaths of the animals, and in a way that too had been laced with excitement. But a bear! A bear foaming at the mouth and tearing Gloria Perkins apart limb by limb and leaving her brains all over the grass . . . god! They shivered when they thought about it and sat closer to their friends, and tried as best they could to keep Carole and Bea from breaking into fresh tears.

Timmy Sweetwater saw them during a moment when they were alone. In his left hand he clutched a piece of composition paper, in his right an envelope that bulged with money. He had been chosen to go to Steed's for the faculty's lunches, and though he knew it was a job any kid would kill for, he didn't want to go. At least, not alone. There would be men there, and women, and they would stare at him and maybe one of them would ask him about Rachel and if that happened he knew he was going to cry. He just knew it. From the minute his father had staggered into the bedroom and told him what had happened, he had fought against the tears.

It wasn't right. His father wasn't crying, so he mustn't, either.

He had been angry, though. When Charlie heard about it he said, "Well, that sure shits us, don't it." And Dawn, who hadn't said a word to anyone in over a week, only shrugged, like they were talking about another cow getting killed. But it wasn't a cow, it was Rachel, and it seemed that only he and his father knew what that meant.

He shuffled his feet in the grass and moved timidly toward the two girls. Carole would go with him. Or Bea. They had both done it before, holding his hand and smiling and handing the slip of paper to Mister Steed and somehow deflecting any comments into little jokes that made him laugh. That made him feel safe.

But when he stood at the head of the table and stared at them, they wouldn't look up.

"Carole?" He hated it when his voice sounded so small, so mousy. "Bea?"

Carole wiped her eyes with the backs of her hands and stared at him. "What." Flat. No recognition.

"I . . . I have to go get the lunches today."

"Who gives a shit," Bea said, suddenly taking a fist and smashing it hard on a sandwich. Timmy jumped, astonished at the anger that made the girl's tears glitter like polished steel.

"The lunches," he said, his hands fluttering at his sides.

Carole turned on him, squinting fiercely. "Go away, Timmy. Take your red ass and just . . ." She sighed and turned away. "Just go away."

Despite his promises, he felt the tears working like tiny claws in his eyes. He gnawed on his lower lip, blinking furiously as he tried desperately to understand what had happened to his friends. They shouldn't be like this, not at all. Didn't they know that Rachel was in a better place now? Didn't they understand her spirit was on the Mountain where it belonged?

A hand gripped his shoulder and he stiffened, the money envelope falling from his grasp. He fumbled for it, then saw a large hand lift it from the ground and hand it to him. He started to smile and turn, but held his breath when he saw Hardy Green standing beside him.

"It ain't right," the tall boy said, not to him but the girls. "He didn't do anything."

"Nobody ever does anything," Bea said to the air. "It's not anybody's fault, right? One of the best people in the whole world drops dead while shitheads like Ted Waters mouth off forever."

Surprisingly, Hardy clucked disappointment. "Incredible," he said. "All year you help this kid, and now you drop him like he was plague or something." He shook his head slowly. "Makes me think you only did it to get in good with the old woman."

"The lunches," Timmy said helplessly, knowing he would be scolded if he came back too late.

"It's all right," Hardy told him, reached down and took his hand. "I'll go with you. That is, if you don't mind."

Timmy stared up at him, wide-eyed, uncertain, but allowed himself to be led away. He returned in a daze that lasted throughout the rest of the school day, a daze that didn't lift until he found himself on the riverbank, crouched on a rock and watching the water. It sure was confusing, he thought to his reflection. People who like you one day turn around and hate you, and people who make fun of you turn around and become your friends. He decided to ask his father about it that night, but he was in no hurry to get home now. Only Charlie would be there, and maybe Dawn in her strange silence.

He tossed a stone into the water.

It was like some kind of monster, an invisible monster had taken hold of the town and shaken it until people's brains got all mixed up. Charlie suddenly working like a demon in the stables, and jumping every time someone knocked at the door or called him on the phone; Dawn grumping around and mumbling about running away to some place a million miles over the mountains; his mother still dying in her darkened room, nearly forgotten she'd been at it so long. Carole and Bea. Hardy. Like some invisible monster.

He sighed loudly and stood up. His father would take care of it, though. That much was certain. As soon as he came back from the MacKenzie ranch he would explain it all away and Timmy would be able to enjoy the sun again.

But when he turned around the monster was there, and Timmy never had a chance to do anything but scream.

(3)

Donna locked the far clinic door and held onto the knob as if it would give her some much-needed strength. For most of the day she had been making her regular rounds of the dude ranches, checking on the stock and tactfully warning the owners away from the slopes. None of them had seemed unduly alarmed; this wasn't the first time they'd been faced with such restrictions. At least once a season a bear, a rare cougar, an unidentified marauder took to the forest and made life miserable for them—and exciting for their guests. They did, however, demand she take water and feed samples back with her. Something was driving the horses into unquestionably queer behavior, and they refused to believe a single bear (or whatever) was responsible for that, especially at night. It made no difference that she told them they were wrong . . . they insisted. And her temper was long past the breaking point by the time she reached her office and dumped her bag on her desk.

To top it off, Jason was gone. Galen told her he'd driven into Blairs, and for a panic-laden minute she was convinced he was going to leave her. He was never coming back; after giving her a memory he was fleeing his own shadows. But the minute passed, and the fear was replaced by wondering if she were falling in love. And that, too, gave her pause and sent a series of icepricks digging into her spine. It was something she didn't want to think about, something she didn't dare consider until . . .

She shook her head and decided to have supper in the luncheonette. Eating alone had turned abruptly hollow, and she wanted to hear voices, to hear laughter, even to hear comments about the Perkinses' funeral this afternoon. Anything, as long as it wasn't the sound of her own chewing.

"Goin my way?"

She gasped and clapped a hand to her chest, wanting to explode anger and laughter simultaneously. Galen was just leaving Doc Vance's side of the clinic building, and she gave him credit for at least appearing contrite when he realized he'd scared her.

"Supper," she said, pointing down the street.

"I hate my own cookin. Mind a date?"

She grinned and took his arm, the two of them watching their shadows sweep long ahead of them.

"Have you heard from Jason yet?"

"Nope," he said, pausing at the curb to let a car take the corner. "He don't talk much. Not like some people I know," and he pressed her hand against his side with his arm. "You're the only two I know that can walk through a thunderstorm and not hear a thing. Makes me wonder what kind of thoughts . . . never mind, I'm gabbing."

At the luncheonette they were stopped when Charlie Sweetwater darted out, his hip smacking Donna's and nearly spinning her around.

"Hey!" Galen said.

"Sorry," the boy told them. "I . . ." He glanced up and down the street. "Mister Marsh, have you seen my little brother?"

"Timmy?" Donna shook her head. "What's the matter, Charlie?"

"Oh, the dope didn't get home from school yet. My dad's gonna kill me."

"Well, if I know Timmy," she said, "he's probably out in the fields someplace, stalking wild animals."

"Yeah," Charlie said, half fearful, half disgusted, "but it's late . . . I mean, my dad's getting worried."

He ran off without waiting for a reaction, and as Galen led her inside Donna found herself thinking of an afternoon a hundred years ago. A Connecticut afternoon on her parents' farm when she had decided she was going to explore the world, had discovered a quarry instead and had taken the slick sides down to a pool deep and black and utterly without movement. The glass surface fascinated her. She could see no fish, hear no wind, and she'd crouched on a rock ledge and stared until she'd heard her name echoing off the walls. She was positive she'd awakened some sort of creature living within the bowels of the water, and had been so frightened she couldn't move. There'd been footfalls and stones slipping off the edge. A clot of dirt landed on her back and made her yelp. She'd jumped to her feet and lost her balance, and the water was cold and deep and black and she was going to drown until strong hands had taken her back to the surface. Her father. Alternately shaking her violently and hugging her until she thought he'd crush her.

She'd been eight, the same age as Timmy. She understood how Aaron would feel when he found the boy at last.

It wasn't until Peg had placed a large wedge of peach pie in front of her that she realized she had eaten her meal in complete silence. When she looked up to apologize to Galen, he was grinning.

"You blush nice," he said. "Think a hell of a lot, but you blush real nice."

Suddenly there was a shout from outside, loud in the twilight, and she leaned out of the booth and saw people running. Galen wasted no time dropping a fistful of crumpled bills onto the table and sliding out to head for the door. She followed, slowly, the one sip of coffee she'd taken turning acid in her mouth.

Across the way the bar was emptying and people were lining the street and hugging the buildings. Jake Harmon was standing at the curb, and just as he stepped into the street the blare of the bar's jukebox was cut off in midmeasure. The only noise was the buzzing and popping of the neon in the window. Soft, Donna thought, like a snake dreaming.

"Jesus," Galen whispered as she came up behind him.

Standing in the intersection of Fieldview and the Pike was Aaron Sweetwater. His clothes were dark, dripping water slowly onto the blacktop; his face was running wet, his hair black and reflecting the streetlamp. Held close to his chest by his left hand was the limp, still form of his son. In his right hand was a silver-barreled pistol.

Harmon moved cautiously to the center line, keeping a good fifteen feet between himself and the Indian. Bill and Artie came out of Carosa's, and he said to them without turning around, "Get them off the street, boys. Don't take no for an answer."

"No!" Sweetwater said suddenly. His eyes were wide, his lips trembling. He looked to his right, and Timmy's head lolled on a broken neck. The revolver lifted. Donna heard a woman gasp behind her. "You, all of you, stay right where you are!"

"Aaron," Harmon said.

Sweetwater seemed to notice him for the first time. He

took an unsteady step forward, then pressed his cheek against his son's head. Despite the light, Donna couldn't see what injuries the boy had other than the neck, but she thought there were rents in the shirt and along the back of the trousers.

"What happened, son?" the sheriff said quietly.

Sweetwater aimed the gun at Harmon's chest.

"No!" Harmon snapped at the sound of one of his deputies pulling out a weapon. "Just clear the street."

"Yes," Sweetwater said. His voice was toneless. "Yes, you do that. You clear the streets, Sheriff, and then you and I will talk about who killed my son."

Donna couldn't help herself. She brushed by Galen to stand at the curb. "Aaron." He turned to her, and Harmon backed off as he motioned her into the street. She didn't hesitate and walked slowly, almost strolling, to the man in the intersection. The chill that had erupted in her stomach numbed her, but she managed to fight it.

"Aaron," she said, her voice breaking. "My god, Aaron."

Sweetwater rubbed his cheek into the boy's hair. "He came up missing this afternoon. Charlie came for me, we thought maybe he'd gotten lost. I looked. We all looked. I found him at the falls, Doc. I found him . . . wedged . . . reeds and . . . he was eight, Doc. One month and he would have been nine. I . . ." His voice trailed into a low, slow moaning that snared on his grief and twisted into anger. The gun moved from the sheriff to her, and she had to strain to keep from blinking. "I know what they think," he said, rasping, his gaze darting to the people on the sidewalk. "They think we killed the Perkinses, so someone"—his voice rose—"decided to teach us a lesson and take *my son!*"

She saw the knuckles of his gunhand whitening, saw the arm quiver with tension. "No, wait, Aaron," she said, one hand out. "You don't know that for sure, do you. He . . . dear god . . . he could have just fallen in. Fell. The river is still high, Aaron, strong, you know that. You *know* that."

"He swims, Doc."

"Aaron, even a grown man would have a time in that water now."

The man kissed his boy's forehead. "He could have been pushed."

Donna swallowed. "Yes." Sweetwater looked to her sharply. "Yes, he could have been pushed. That's a possibility. But you don't know that, Aaron. You can't know that. Please . . . let me help you."

Sweetwater suddenly seemed confused. "With . . . with what?"

"Doc Vance," she said, taking a step closer, close enough to touch him. "We'll take him to Doc Vance and he'll tell us what happened."

"I know what happened." He tightened his grip on the body, and the head rolled back to catch the light. The face was pale, the eyes closed, and she thought she caught a suggestion of a smile on the bloodless lips. Oh god, she thought, I'm tired, I'm tired.

"The men who beat Michael," she said quickly.

"What?"

She brushed a hand through her hair, a sideways glance noting Anthony Carosa slipping out of the stunned crowd into the street. "The men who beat Michael Wolf and hurt Little Star so badly. Do . . . do you want to be like them, Aaron? You don't, I know you better than that. I see the way you are, when we talk I hear the kind of man you are. You don't want to be like them, Aaron. You can't be like them."

A tear welled in each eye, and she saw him staring at them, shifting his gaze then to Carosa and Harmon, to Doc Vance, who was standing now behind the sheriff. His gun arm sagged and finally dropped to his side. Donna was by him in a step, her arm strong around him, until without warning he began sobbing and let the gun slip to the street and held the boy to his face.

"I don't think I can take much more," Vance said.

Harmon turned on him angrily. "Take him to the clinic. I don't care how you do it, Vance, but you damned well better find out what killed that boy before you go to bed tonight!"

Donna stepped away then as Carosa took the big Indian's weight and led him up the street. Within moments she was alone, shaking uncontrollably, hugging herself tightly and wondering what in hell had made her do a thing like that. It struck her that she could have been killed, that had she taken one more second to think about it she would have stayed there on the curb . . . and done nothing at all.

"Jason," she whispered, and Galen slipped an arm around her waist.

"Come on," he said, easing her toward the sidewalk. "I've got some brandy at home. I don't think Jason'll be long."

They paused at the gate while Galen whistled to warn the setters.

"Galen, do you think—"

"No," he said gruffly, lifting the latch. "Not even Ted has a soul that black."

(4)

The Studebaker cooled down like the ticking of a weary clock, and a sudden gust of nightwind made the chassis shudder. Jason held onto the steering wheel as if he were about to be tossed through the open window, tendons and veins bulging with the effort. He had only been sitting there ten minutes and already it seemed like hours. But he refused to step outside until his rage had worn off.

First had come the minor frustrations: twice getting lost in Blairs, then the humiliation of both front tires blowing out in the middle of the main street. Waiting for the tow truck. Listening to the garage attendant muttering about fools who drove without treads. Five minutes later the fan belt broke, then the radiator overheated. Galen was condemned loudly to eternal perdition.

He rushed, then, to meet the people Marsh had mentioned. The results (which cost him a bundle in under-the-table compensation) were fascinating, and confusing.

Then he had tried to call home. There was no answer, so he called Esther Lynn and learned about Timmy.

He was confused and enraged and decided to drive straight to MacKenzie's and take a chance with his head.

When he'd arrived, however, there were too many cars, pickups and grazing horses for him to go charging into the middle. The Shoshone, gathering for Rachel. He'd parked at the end of the drive's tree-tunnel and slipped through the shrubs toward the back. It was a fluke he hadn't been spotted. A pair of men talking by the house had forced him into the stables to hide. Just as he decided it was safe to slip away, circle around and make a proper entrance, he glanced into the now open stall at building's end . . . and saw the pinto, the one he knew was Gregory Thornton's.

His fury rekindled, and he'd slipped behind the wheel and stared at the house, hoping that somehow he would be granted the power to blast it to cinders with a narrowing of his eyes.

His right hand curled into a fist.

None of it made sense. None of it.

MacKenzie, he had learned, was a millionaire several times over. In the past few years he had sold all his holdings in Idaho and Montana parcel by parcel, in amounts that matched the selling prices of farms and ranches the Indians purchased in Windriver. Proof, then, of the suspicion of the deed: Simon MacKenzie wanted the Shoshone in and the white men out. He started with the ranches and it wouldn't be long before the houses went, too—though how in hell he intended to deal with the candy factory and the dude ranches was beyond Jason; MacKenzie had no land left now, no assets but his own home.

But where in hell did all this violence fit in? To force the selling? A deliberate fomenting of racial hatred just to disrupt the community?

And what in *hell* was that pinto doing in MacKenzie's stable? What did the man know about Gregory Thornton's running away, and why hold onto the horse, keep it hidden?

He felt the rage growing again and capped it as best he could. He needed to be calm to think, to sift through what evidence he believed he had to see where it would lead him. He took a deep breath and watched as a group of Indians left the house and made their way around its far corner, talking quietly.

All right, he thought. All right, let's assume for the moment MacKenzie really is trying to take over the valley for his people. Why? Why here and not someplace else? What's so special about this pocket of isolation that people and animals have to die for it? Somehow it just did not seem like MacKenzie's style.

He closed his eyes, left hand drumming on his thigh and tried to keep his mind in neutral while he figured out what he had: a definite (maybe) conspiracy to empty the valley, a pair of murders (maybe) or victims of a rabid or otherwise demented animal (maybe), the accidental drowning of a harmless little boy . . .

"Jesus," he muttered to the dark, "don't you know anything?"

He rested his forehead on the steering wheel, the plastic cool against his skin, and asked himself if he didn't think it was time for him to find the answers, and not run from them.

He slapped open the door and slid out, ignoring the perspiration that gave ice to the night.

(5)

There was a faint response to his knocking and he entered and closed the door behind him. The house was silent, no sounds of mourning. He dabbed at his lips with the back of a hand and faced around despite the sudden fluttering in his stomach. In the sunken portion of the living room MacKenzie sat in his chair, Palemoon behind him with her hands clasped at her waist. On the couch to the left were Sweetwater and Tallpines.

No running, Jason reminded himself; for god's sake, no more running.

"Jason," MacKenzie said solemnly.

"Simon." He declined a silent invitation to join the others because he wanted to stay near the door, to keep them all in sight, to gauge their reactions, to discover his allies. "I, uh . . . about Rachel—and Timmy, Aaron—I wish I were better with words."

Aaron nodded, a trembling hand shoving back through his hair. MacKenzie, however, only stared at him levelly. The room was warm, almost stifling, and Jason pulled down the tie he'd worn into Blairs. The cold he'd felt outside was gone, and what remained was the touch of a large open grave.

He cleared his throat and gestured vaguely at the door behind him. "I've been to Blairs, Simon," he said. "I'm sorry if this isn't the time, but I found out—"

"Everything," MacKenzie said, nodding as though he expected it.

"Except why."

"Well, Jason, that's something I don't think anyone outside this room knows."

He frowned and dipped his hands into his pocket. "Then tell me."

"Now wait a minute, Jason," Daniel protested.

"It's all right," MacKenzie said with a quieting sweep of his hand. "It's all right." He settled back, not quite able to hide the anguish in his eyes. "I take it you know about Chief Washakie and his move to the Wind River. He was a smart old bird, y'know. Kept his bucks from riding hell-bent for leather against the cavalry because he knew the army would beat the shit out of them. He wasn't stupid. He could see the future."

"And this is the future?" Jason said skeptically.

"Not quite. Did you also know that the Shoshone, as well as other nations, had women shaman? My great-grandfather married one, when his first wife died. So did my grandfather. When my father came along there were none and so the tradition was interrupted after only two generations. But the point is not that they did so, but why. It was a tricky thing, Jason, for a white to hitch himself up to an Indian in the first place. And to link up with someone who supposedly had powers . . . well, that was something else again."

"Rachel," he said, with a glance to the banded door at the far end of the room.

MacKenzie nodded. "You see, Washakie deliberately avoided this valley when he moved north from the Snake. Even before his time this was holy ground, used for ceremonies, burials, rites mostly forgotten. Great-grandfather, of course, didn't know that. And when he found out he didn't much care. He homesteaded the land and claimed it for his own. Washakie was in no position to argue. Smart chief, like I said."

"But it's still a holy place," Daniel said quietly.

"Then shouldn't it be part of the reservation?" Jason asked.

"Splinter groups are common among Indians, too," MacKenzie said. "And the Shoshone had their own places. This wasn't one of them. As far as I can tell, Washakie even threatened winter expulsion for anyone who came up here. Word is, he did it, too. It, all this land here, belonged to what we'd call today a bunch of hotheads, fanatics, shortsighted fools who in the old days believed the Indian was going to rise again, just like the South, and drive out the whites. The Ghost Dance. Tecumseh resurrected. This was what great-grandfather married into, and did not care about."

But MacKenzie, Jason thought suddenly, believed he had some sort of obligation; his harping on his ancestor's unconcern indicated he was carrying some burden of guilt, perhaps handed down to him by his father. With Rachel as his wife, however, he discovers a way to relieve that guilt, and he gives this minority a chance to fulfill the dream they've been thirsting after for over a century.

"He understands," Aaron said.

"Of course I understand," Jason snapped. "I'm not a complete ass, you know. And I might even sympathize, given half a chance. But that doesn't make what you're doing right."

"Obviously," Daniel said without rancor, "we don't agree."

"But this isn't one of those cozy little affairs where we can agree to disagree and go away like gentlemen," Jason insisted. "We're talking about too many lives, white as well as your own." He found himself standing at the edge of the pit, his hands fisted and pressed against his thighs. "I assume Rachel . . . was behind all this, that it was her idea."

"She told me how to do it," MacKenzie admitted. "Our friends here, and those few elsewhere, acknowledged her . . . guidance."

Jason saw the pain again, but refused to stop. Not now. "All right, I can follow you so far. But Simon, you could have tried to . . . I don't know, buy the most important land and leave the rest alone, right? Couldn't you have told them, Harmon and the rest, what you were after and why? I'm not sure, but it sounds like you would have been able to clear everything up that way."

"Ted Waters," Aaron said.

"There are always men like Ted Waters," Jason told him. "But I don't see how he could have blocked something like I suggested."

A silence, and the warmth grew. MacKenzie sank his chin to his chest and clasped his hands tightly in his lap.

"It was Rachel," Tallpines said then, and said it with such relief that Jason had to stare at him. "Rachel said it had to be done this way. I mean, how can you buy a spirit, Jason? We don't have churches; we have the land, the air, the mountains, the river. The whites in this country haven't been here long enough to value what's in the land's past. If they need a road it doesn't matter what's in the way. It gets torn down. It's progress."

"Killing people isn't progress," he said quietly.

MacKenzie shoved himself to his feet, the chair scraping harshly away. "We had nothing to do with that!" he insisted, his face mottling and a finger pointing. "We knew what we were doing, damnit, and we—"

"Simon," Tallpines said. "Simon, it's all right."

MacKenzie sputtered and dropped back into his seat. Tallpines nudged Aaron and stepped out of the pit to floor level. He took Jason's arm lightly and pulled him away.

"Listen, Jase," he said urgently, "this . . . this is what I wanted to talk to you about, even before Rachel died. That Town Meeting, I want to go there, Aaron and I. We want to tell what you heard tonight." He rubbed a hand over his face, back through his hair. "It isn't easy. It isn't the way Rachel said it should be done, but now she's gone and some of us aren't fools anymore. We learn, Jason. We want people to know what we're after, what we want."

"No matter what the consequence," Jason told him.

"Maybe, maybe not." He glanced back at MacKenzie, who was speaking low and earnestly with Sweetwater. "Jason, we've been trying all night to convince Simon of this, to tell him it's done and we want the air cleared. We don't need more Michael Wolfs in this valley. We don't need more Timmys."

Jason could think of nothing to say. He was no longer sure what to believe.

"Do me a favor," Tallpines said then. "Don't write about this yet. If you put it in the paper before we can explain, you'll tear the place apart. You know you will. People will read into it what they want to. They'll never understand. Never. There'll be more blood, Jason. There'll be more blood."

Jason faced him. "Then tell me about the pinto, Daniel."

Tallpines blinked. "What pinto?"

His temper stirred. He swiveled and said, loudly enough for MacKenzie to hear, "The pinto in the stable. Simon told me it was a late-foaling mare. I saw it tonight—a pinto with a red blotch on its neck. Simon, damnit, what the hell happened to Gregory Thornton?"

"I don't know what you're talking about," MacKenzie yelled. "You're crazy. You . . ." He rose and looked about him wildly, finally staring at Tallpines. "Daniel, I swear to you—"

Sweetwater cut him off with a grunt, rose and moved to the door. He opened it and Tallpines joined him without looking at Jason. "You've sworn to us before, Simon. You told us Rachel was . . . we *believed* you, Simon."

Aaron's voice sounded strangled. "My son."

"It was daylight!" MacKenzie said. "You know she—"

The door slammed, and Jason was alone with an old man who stumbled about the pit until he found the steps. Jason wasn't sure what they'd been talking about, why Aaron would think Rachel was somehow implicated in Timmy's death, but when Simon beckoned to him wearily he followed. He was led across the room and through the banded door, then down a dark corridor to another door as thick and as foreboding. MacKenzie pushed it open, stepped through and vanished into a wavering, bronzed dusk.

Jason stood behind a single tall chair while he gaped at the body on the bed.

Rachel lay atop the coverlet in a deerskin dress fringed and deep brown. Her hair spread whitely, weakly, over her pillow. The candles at the headboard flickered tall flames and danced gaps and shadows over a face he didn't recognize.

"You don't have to hide, Mister Clarke."

MacKenzie stepped out of a corner and stood beside the bed. He took hold of Rachel's left hand and held it in both of his, patting it, stroking, not once looking at her face.

"You should know something, Mister Clarke. Something Daniel did not tell you."

A wind picked up outside, ruffling the curtains on the French doors. A dead leaf scuttled into the room and ducked under the bed. It was full dark, and Jason could feel the presence of Kramer's Mountain.

"Rachel believed in things, Mister Clarke. Like all her people she believed in the spirits that inhabit all that we see. She knew them, spoke to them, and they made her content, helped her to understand. All her life she studied them, and the traditions of those who had come before her. She was related in some distant way to the woman who married my father's father, and his father before him. Nothing was ever written down. She heard it in stories, in dreams, and like the others she remembered. She was very religious. And she was very powerful."

Jason rubbed an arm slowly; he was cold. And he wasn't at all sure he wanted to listen anymore.

"It's not very hard," MacKenzie said, so softly the words were brushed aside by the wind that kept digging at the ashes scattered now from the hearth. "I myself, when I was younger, could walk with her anywhere and be what we looked at. *Be. Know from the inside* the difference between cottonwood and ash, between buzzard and kingfisher, between trout and salmon. It was . . . exhilarating. And humbling." He smiled, then. Devoid of mirth, filled with pride. "But Rachel could do so much more, Jason. So much more. *Being,* for me, was a mystical experience. For her . . . for her it was real."

Jason heard the silence, and the slam of his pulsing blood.

"She sought us out," MacKenzie whispered. "Me, because of my grandmother and such; Daniel and the rest because they'd been in the white man's world and found it . . . empty. Something inside them told them there were other things, told them they were missing something they could only find with her. She gathered them like children and told them stories and gave them promises."

"Like this valley," Jason said, needing to hear another voice besides the one fighting with the wind.

MacKenzie nodded.

Rachel's hair was feathered and drifted, covering her eyes, her mouth, while the fringe of her dress danced on the coverlet.

"She would stand here and say the words, Jason. I suppose there's a translation of them somewhere, but she never used English when she spoke them. They were . . . beautiful."

He fell silent, staring at the blackness beyond the open doors.

"Prayers?" Jason said.

MacKenzie gave him a look of slow pity. "She would say the words, Jason, and as I told you . . . she would *be.*"

He lifted an apologetic hand to indicate he was trying, but he could only shake his head when the understanding failed. "You mean she could turn herself . . . that she could become a . . . a tree or something?"

Simon's pity turned rapidly to disgust. "You're supposed to be listening to me, Jason! This is not the time for joking."

"But I'm—"

MacKenzie waved him silent and said nothing for several long minutes. Jason avoided looking at him, or the body on the bed, wanting only to leave this house and drive back to town. He would talk to Galen and Donna, tell them what he'd seen, what he'd heard, then walk over to Carosa's and get himself drunk. He started for the door, thinking he would leave the old man to his mourning, and his babbling, when MacKenzie whispered his name. He stopped. The old man had dropped his wife's hand and was running a finger through her hair.

"Every time," MacKenzie said. "Every time. She was old, Jason. It took her that long to learn. That long. Three, four times was all she could handle. Three . . . four . . . five times. Last year, and no more." He began weeping, and the wind blew futilely at the high-reaching candles. "I told her a hundred times, no more, Rachel, you'll kill yourself. She got sick. I told her, but she got sick. Old." He took a deep breath, another, and swallowed. "Winter broke and she wouldn't let me in. Wouldn't let me in."

The wind.

MacKenzie stumbled away from the bed, tripped on the dim hearth and grabbed for the mantel. "She came in here when it was time. The words. I . . ." He shook his head helplessly. His voice pitched high, a child imitating an ancient. "I don't know when the last time was." He snatched something from the mantel and threw it desperately across the room. It clanged against the wall and rolled, just out of the light. "Damnit, Rachel," he moaned, "what the hell's going on?"

(6)

Tallpines was waiting for him at his car. "Well?"

Jason looked at him glumly. "If you must know, I feel like shit." He slid in behind the wheel and started the engine, the sound welcome above the soughing of the wind.

Tallpines placed a hand on the door. "What did he tell you?"

The vehemence in the Indian's voice startled him, and stirred his temper again. "What do you think? Rachel was a werewolf or a weretree or . . . Jesus Christ, that man's crazy with grief! How do I know what he was saying!" He put a fist to his forehead, rubbed it in small circles. "Sorry, Daniel. I'm just—"

"Frustrated. You came for one thing, and you found something else."

Jason lowered his hand slowly. "Wait. Wait. You mean . . . you mean you believe what he told me?"

"How was the livestock killed, Jason? A goddamned rabid bear? What do you think killed Harry Felsom?"

"I don't . . . you're as crazy as he is!"

"Listen," the man said urgently, grabbing for Jason's shoulder and pulling away suddenly when Jason shrugged, hard. "It was only supposed to scare them off. It was supposed to make them nervous, that's all."

Jason batted at the air as though bothered by a fly. "You know, of course, you've just confessed the killer of—"

"I know."

"They won't believe you."

"They won't believe you, either."

He tilted his head back to rest against the seat, and looked at Tallpines from the corner of his eye. "I am supposed to sit here, Daniel, and believe that Rachel MacKenzie was able to turn herself, physically, into some sort of monster. That she killed Harry, drove Ellie nuts and knocked off a few cows and sheep and a couple of bulls? What the hell do you Indians take at a goddamned wake, for god's sake?" He held up a hand when Tallpines tried to respond. "Wait a minute. That means . . ." He looked at the house, back to the Indian. "That means you're saying the old woman did in Gloria and Billy, too. Are you—"

"No," Tallpines said quickly.

"Well, you can't have it both ways, pal. I saw the Perkinses, and I read all the reports. I'm surprised no one else caught it, but they were all killed the same way. And that means, my friend, that if your dear departed in there didn't do it, there's another monster roaming around here that's trying to put the blame on her. Isn't that right?"

"It won't do any good to make fun of it, Jason."

"I can see that," he said angrily. "But it won't do you any good to stick with that idiot story. Jesus!"

"We don't intend to. You're the only one who knows."

"Knows?" The urge to get out of the car and strangle him was overwhelming. "I don't know a damned thing, Daniel. All I've heard is a bunch of doubletalk from you, and madness from MacKenzie. But at least he can be excused. I don't know what your reason is for keeping this up."

He released the hand brake and popped the transmission into first. Tallpines grabbed hold of his arm. "Jason . . . Jason, I'm afraid."

My god, he thought, this isn't happening. But he didn't doubt the man was telling the truth. He struggled to remain calm, revving the engine several times and taking in the faint stench of exhaust.

"All right, Daniel, tell me. What is it?"

"Something is wrong. When she was ill after last year, Rachel was going to try again this spring. We talked to her, then, and tried to make her stop. She wouldn't. She was impatient. She wanted the sacred ground back before she died. And when the killing started again, we knew something went wrong. Jason—"

"But she's dead, right?" he said brutally. He realized with a sickening lurch that he would have to go along with the man for the time being, to soothe him so he wouldn't drive himself crazy the way Simon already had. A quiet, midnight sort of insanity had hollowed the man out and made him a shell. "She's dead," he repeated, gently this time. "What are you afraid of?"

"That . . . that someone will talk, that the people will believe we were involved in some weird, unnatural rites that called for blood sacrifices and things."

"Well, weren't you?"

"Damnit, Jason!"

"Damnit yourself!" he said, practically shouting. "You just admitted to me that Rachel MacKenzie murdered Harry Felsom! Now what the hell do you call that?"

"It was . . . necessary."

"For what, for Christ's sake?"

"To give her strength."

Jason swallowed a laugh.

"She never ate, you know. She didn't have to."

He slumped back in the seat and closed his eyes. He was beaten. He had no way to combat madness. "Daniel, what exactly are you asking me to do?"

"A week, Jason. There'll be a week of mourning, and there'll be a lot of our people here. Please don't write anything about Simon yet, and try to postpone that meeting until we can come in and explain everything. Rachel never understood the modern way, and we don't want any more blood. Please. Help me, Jase. Help us."

"And Harry Felsom?"

"We'll talk about it afterward."

It was too much. Jason told him he'd call in the morning with his answer, that he was far too confused—and, quite frankly, angry—to make any rational decisions now. "But at least you don't have to worry about Rachel anymore, do you. No more killings."

"I can promise you that, Jason. I swear it."

Sure, he thought, and pulled away onto the road, driving much faster than he realized until he nearly sideswiped the stone archway over Elkhorn Road. He slowed, then, and stared at his reflection in the windshield, the green tint from the dashboard reminding him too vividly of Rachel's dead face.

And of Daniel's drawn with fear.

He cursed the wheel for shaking so hard beneath his hands.

FIVE

(1)

The turkey sandwich was thick enough to make Jason's jaw pop whenever he tried to get his teeth around it. Nevertheless, it was worth the effort if he were going to do some serious thinking and drinking. He had left the car in front of Galen's and, when the editor proved not to be home, decided the little house was far too large to ramble around in. And when Donna didn't answer her phone either at the clinic or at home, he took the short walk to the bar and appropriated the table in front corner farthest from the entrance—shadowed by the backside glow of the window's neon, and the best vantage point for eavesdropping and just plain watching.

It was no consolation that the few others at the bar and the rest of the tables seemed also to be in moods that barely tolerated polite company. Most of them had been part of Harmon's hunting team, disgruntled, tired, complaining wearily about getting up the next dawn to do it all over again. A few, Jason understood, had stayed out; a few, but not many. A number of the men had reasoned that if the bear had taken Gloria and Billyboy right in their sideyard, it wasn't much of a jump to wonder if the streets themselves were safe.

The large number of guns in evidence made him nervous, and he had jumped when Carosa had thumped the sandwich and coffee onto the table.

"You ever get married, Jason?"

"Nope. I never had the means, or the time."

The bartender nodded his agreement. "Take my advice, don't. The only thing marriage gives you is kids, and they ain't hardly worth it, believe me."

Jason hid his smile behind an attack on his supper.

"I mean it," the man said. It had obviously been a poor night—his customary black bow tie was missing, and his large, hair-matted hands were twisting his half-apron as though it were someone's neck. "You take David, now." He glanced over his shoulder at his son polishing glasses behind the bar. "He gets himself a miracle and he don't do anything about it. Wants to work here, can you beat it?"

"What's wrong with that?"

"He's got college!" Carosa said. "He could do anything he wants and he wants to tend bar. Jesus. All that money so I got myself an educated bartender."

Jason managed a sympathetic smile.

"And Carole." Carosa lifted his face heavenward and waved a hand at the ceiling. "I never understand her, you know that? Tells me she can't wait to get outa here and into some goddamned city where she can get raped just goin to the drugstore." He shook his head slowly. "I don't know, Jase, I just don't know. You figure it." He sighed. "Southern Comfort?"

"Yes, please."

"Yeah, figure it. I take care of them all their lives, and he won't leave for a decent job and she can't wait to get out. Nuts."

He was halfway through the sandwich, the shot glass of Comfort daring him to eat it all before his first drink, when Stan Kelly wandered in. Jason tried to blend himself in with the wall, but the man saw him and waved. "Hey, reporter."

"Hey, yourself."

"You workin on a story?"

"Yep."

"Hey, Carosa, buy the reporter a drink!"

"Thanks," Jason said, "but I already have one." He held up the glass, even pointed to the coffee just in case.

"Have another. Gotta keep your strength up, y'know." Kelly peered at him through the gloom. "Got your back to the wall. That's good, Clarke. They can't get you by surprise that way."

Jason grinned and shook his head. The ex-rancher-turned-gravedigger had to be pretty far gone to carry his delusions into sobriety.

A handful of high school boys entered shortly after Kelly took his stool at the bar. They chattered and laughed their way back to the pinball machines, making the most of belittling teachers, school and Windriver. Jason wondered how many of them, in their middle-aged nostalgia, would remember the time when they couldn't wait to leave this place. He thought of Carole and winced, almost as if Anthony had overheard him.

Then he finished the sandwich and coffee and gathered in the glass of Comfort. He drained the liquor at a swallow and held his breath until the burning passed to leave him the powerfully sweet aftertaste. He grinned and made his way to the bar. "In a collins," he said, and laughed when Carosa grimaced. Bourbon, rye, a potent Wyoming scotch were the usual orders here, and Jason knew the man would never get used to his drinking something that had as much if not more proof alcohol, yet was sweet enough to rot a perfect tooth.

Back at his seat, he took a long drink and closed his eyes. He finished his drink and ordered another.

A few more customers came in and a few left, but none of them paid him much attention, and he maintained an expression to keep it that way. Without conscious direction his mind was jumping from one scene, one conversation, one hint to another. He made no effort to organize; it was a process he'd adapted from a professor's suggestion when he found himself continually bogged down by nonessentials. It often led to daydreaming and dead ends—but his success with it was frequent enough to keep doing it.

"Is that so?"

When he realized he'd nodded, he blinked rapidly and saw Donna pulling out the chair opposite him. Before she was settled Carosa had brought her a tulip glass of deep burgundy. He reached out a hand and she gripped it, released it and traced the humps of his knuckles.

"I tried to call you," he said.

"Galen told me where you were. When I got back from the ranch I buried myself in books. Rabies, things like that. Sweet stuff."

"Well?"

She shrugged, and sipped at her wine.

"You're right, then? There really is a rabid bear prowling around here?"

"Without the thing itself I can't . . . why? You look disappointed."

He smiled and leaned back. "Do I?"

"Jason," she warned, pushing at her glasses. "Jason, you're not telling me something. When I got here I must have stood there for five minutes waiting for you to notice me. What were you thinking so hard about?"

He tried to pass it off lightly. "God, Man, Nature, Evil, the Republicans, the—"

"Evil?"

An argument between Kelly and one of the high school boys erupted into a shouting match. Carosa quelled it, and the boys left. When they opened the door, the wind gusted in and fluttered the napkins on all the tables.

"Jason?"

He pushed aside his glass and rearranged the circle of moisture left behind. By speaking the word aloud he understood where his ruminations had been taking him.

"When I first got here," he said, looking up at her without lifting his head, "someone told me—hell, it was Galen—he told me he believed this town was turning evil. I'm not sure, Donna, but I don't think that's very far from wrong now." She set her glass in front of her, attentive, not smiling. "I'm not really sure what evil actually is, if it's some kind of active force in opposition to an active good, or if it's simply the absence of good, or what. I'm not sure. Some people say that *things* can be evil, like houses and bridges and things like that. I don't know. I don't think so. I . . ." He glanced around the room, at Donna, who had taken off her glasses and was leaning closer to him. Damn, he thought, and wished she had been with him at MacKenzie's. "A speculation, okay?"

She nodded quickly, and he wanted to kiss her.

"All right." He paused, waiting for the words to come. "Let's suppose that inside some people there's something that, if we let it, allows us to do absolute evil without any compunctions at all. We can control it, all right? This . . . this evil, it feeds on things. Like anger, fear, hatred. The more you feed it, the stronger it gets. It's not like Mister Hyde, something that can be artificially pried out. It's not Freud or Jung, not available to couch therapy or exorcism. It's part of us. As integral a part of us as, say, breathing. But we control it, see. Usually. But sometimes we can't, or don't want to, or don't realize we've changed."

"Hitler."

"Easy example, and I don't know if that's right. But let's suppose that this evil, for want of a better word, can be nurtured *and* controlled. It's deliberate, then. It has nothing to do with self-delusion or madness or anything like that. And let's say further that this *thing* we all have, let's say . . . let's say . . ."

He shook his head vigorously, once. He knew what he was trying to say, but he didn't want to be laughed at. No one should laugh at him the way he had wanted to laugh at Daniel Tallpines. He snapped his fingers, and Donna started, nearly toppling her glass.

"You have someone," he said, more urgently now, "who's spent time, a lot of time, understanding what it's like to live. Not just with himself, but with everything that's around him. So much so that he, or she, believes there can be a transference of experience, an exchange of places . . . and this someone is also carrying with him, or her, this fear, this anger, this hatred—all of it. All of it so powerful, so corrosive, that a combination of beliefs creates . . . I don't know, I'm not sure. A power. An ability. Do you know what lycanthropy is?"

She nodded, surprised. "Werewolfism." Then she frowned. "Is there such a word?"

"It doesn't matter," he said. "The point is this: from everything I've read, heard, whatever, those characters who get themselves involved with lycanthropy are involved against their wills. Nobody chooses to be a werewolf, you see what I mean? Nobody sets out to get bitten by a werewolf so he can go through the agony of the change every month. It's a tragic thing, doubly so because it's not only a horror to others, it's a horror to himself."

"Jason," Donna said, putting her glasses on again, "are you trying to tell me you think . . . you're fooling around with the idea there's a werewolf here?"

"No," he said. Then amended himself. "Not exactly."

"What. Exactly."

My god, he thought, almost in desperation, what the hell have I gotten myself into?

"The evil," he said, "was not in this town, it was in . . . it was in a person. It was an evil spawned from hatred and fear and anger and frustration and helplessness and . . . god knows what all else. And the creation that came out of it was deliberate. A werewolf is *driven* to kill, by its nature. This thing, whatever it was, did so with purpose. It did it without conscience. Without remorse or guilt afterward."

Donna stared at the table. "Evil's a good word for that, Jase."

"Yeah, I know."

A bottle dropped and shattered; Carosa and his son fell into a quiet, hissing argument.

"Jason, you keep saying 'was.' This person was this and this person was that—are you saying it's over?"

"That part of it, yes."

She studied him for several long seconds, and he could not help wondering what she saw when she looked at him. She gave him no clue, not even when he shrugged and smiled as if to say: well, Doc, is the patient bonkers or not? Finally he had to shift his gaze, to Anthony and David, who apparently had come to some kind of truce. He could tell by their expressions, however, that this truce was temporary, that they were feeling the tension that squatted outside the door.

"Jason?"

He sniffed, and brushed a hand through his hair to cover his nervousness. He felt not unlike a defendant whose jury had come in.

"How much of what you told me do you think is real?"

He spread his hands. "Who can say?"

"No, I mean it," she said. "Do you believe it? Do you really believe everything you just told me?"

"I said it, didn't I?"

"There you go again, not answering my questions."

"All right. All right . . . yes. About that evil in people. No matter what you call it—demons, devils, original sin, fall from grace—yes, I believe it."

She hesitated. "What about this . . . do you really think this creature of yours lived? Assuming, as you said, that it doesn't any longer?"

He forced himself to be truthful, and nodded. "For a moment, yes, I did. God, it was hard not to. But not now, not in—if you'll excuse the expression—the sober light of reality. It . . . I used it as a metaphor, a figure of speech, I don't know . . . a way to explain something I couldn't explain before."

She looked at him doubtfully. "Really?"

"Oh, come on, Donna! Do I have to run through the clichés like this is the twentieth century, we're not savages, things like that?"

"Then look at your hands," she ordered.

He didn't have to; he could feel them jumping against the table, could feel the drops of ice that slithered along his spine as he spoke. He reached for his glass and pulled his hand back when she stared at it, then dropped both into his lap and clasped them, tightly. Something—intuition, fear, it sure as hell wasn't reason—was telling him his speculations weren't all that far off the mark. It made no difference there was no sense in it, no logic—his hands trembled just the same, and his spine cringed to squirm away from the ice.

"Jason," and she reached over the table to touch his arm. He stared, and she touched him again, waiting until he had uncovered his hands for her to take. "Jason, what happened out there?"

"I don't know."

"Something frightened you." When he refused an answer, she squeezed his hands hard. "Jason, I've just been playing nursemaid to a few dozen animals that are . . . they're scared to death, Jase. I've seen how they react to predators down from the hills, but this is different. I didn't tell the ranch owners that, but it is. They're scared shitless." She stroked the backs of his hands lightly. "Tell me, Jason. Did something scare you?"

He bit at his lower lip. It was an effort to nod.

"Tell me."

He did.

(2)

She held his arm as they walked, not too tightly because she didn't want him to think she was being too proprietary, too pushy. As it was, he practically ignored her, talking in a low and soft voice about Donna Oldfield and how she was trying to snare his young cousin. Esther Lynn didn't see anything wrong with that, but she supposed Galen was getting his fatherhood up. She smiled to herself and moved a little closer, watching the shadows of the foliage cross and lace on the sidewalk in front of them. It had been his idea to get out of the house for a while, hers to stay away from the Pike and all those hunters. Eventually they would end up either at the river or the tracks, but as long as she was with him it didn't matter. The wind was pleasantly cool, the leaves talkative and the lights from the houses were both comforting and melancholic.

"You know something, Esther," he said suddenly, "I'm going to miss all this when I'm gone."

"Galen!" She said it quietly, fearfully, not liking to hear about the time coming closer. It bothered her, more so because he still hadn't told her about the clear capsules he kept in his pocket. Everyone knew, but he didn't know they did. And she wasn't about to say a word until he brought it up first.

"It's inevitable, m'dear."

"Oh Galen, shut up."

He looked down at her, amused, and she yanked his arm to wipe the grin from his face. He laughed and patted her hand. "Y'know, I'm not as dense as some people think."

"What are you talking about?"

"I mean, everyone's been awfully damned nice t'me these past few weeks. I suppose Jase opened his damned big mouth."

She heard the distant rush of the river.

"Galen, you know me better than that. You know I've—"

She blinked when he placed a hand lightly over her mouth, took it away slowly and slipped it into his pocket. "I know," he said. "And I was always gettin around to askin you, believe it or not. But it was always one of these days, and the days just kept on gettin by and . . . well, I never did."

"No, you didn't."

"Wanted to, though. Still do."

"You know, Galen Marsh, you're the only man in the whole world who can make a proposal sound downright morbid."

"Was I proposin?"

She would have answered him sharply and had the words already formed, but he suddenly stopped walking and was peering through the dark behind them.

"What?"

A moment passed.

"Nothing," he said. "A dog. An owl. Nothing."

She gripped his arm tightly then, not caring what he thought.

"You okay, Esther?"

She shuddered, and felt a staring at the back of her neck. "I'm starting to get chilly."

"All right. How about a quick look at the river, then a toddy at Carosa's."

She thought of dark water, dark skies, the clouds over the moon. "I make better ones."

"Do you, now?"

"Galen, stop that smirking!"

"Is that what I was doing?"

"You're impossible. Let's get it over with, shall we?"

"Funny, I thought you liked the river at night."

"I do, usually." A dozen paces, and she felt the staring again. "Galen?"

"What?"

"Did you hear that?"

"Esther, you're getting as bad as I am."

"Maybe, but did you hear it?"

"Yes."

"Forget the river. Take me home."

Whispersoft.

(3)

The temperature eased, and the valley was filled with the
hush of mindghosts. The hunters in Carosa's bar left in pairs,
in threes, never alone, checking the sky as they headed for
home and checked their locks once safely inside. Mutt and
Jeff, lying in the kitchen on the cool linoleum floor, sniffed at
the breeze seeping under the back door and whimpered in
their sleep, hackles half raised and tails switching.

Mac Felsom whipped his pocket watch into his plaid wool
vest and waited until the Casper Limited was out of sight
before he returned to his chair. Dumb crazy night, he
thought, scratching idly at a thigh and spitting on the floor.
Clarke and Esther Lynn come strolling by like they're in a
park, and wasted a lot of his precious drinking time talking
while the Limited unloaded a shitload of stuff for Waters to
pick up in the morning. Crazy. Artie comes by half in the bag
and tells him all the miserable details about the great bear
hunt on the slopes, trying to make it sound funny and
managing only to scare himself half to death and head for
home like there was a passel of Shoshone jumping for his
scalp. Dumb. Bunch of kids who oughta be home studying
start walking the track, he had to run near a million miles to
get them off before they got squashed. His face was still
drenched in perspiration from the exertion, and he mopped it
vigorously. Crazy.

He grinned for a moment at a passing gust of dust-coated
wind; old Rachel hunting around for someplace to light. Fool
squaw. Not bad for an Indian, but he couldn't remember the
last time she'd ever come into town. Simon or that crazy
Palemoon girl always doing the fetching and the carrying for
her. Like she was some kind of queen instead of just a
woman.

A whispering . . . a rustling.

"Ah shit," he muttered. Damned kids'll be the death of me
yet. What the hell's so exciting about walking the tracks,
anyways? He snatched up his lantern from beside the chair
and strode to the edge of the platform. The light barely
reached to the opposite embankment, and he squinted as he
held the lantern high over his head. It'd figure a night like this

wouldn't have a moon. Just like a woman—never one around when you needed her.

"Get the hell outa here!" he shouted.

Hell, didn't they knew he was in the movies? Damned kids.

The wind gusted again and grew steady, tossing the weeds from side to side, teasing the collar of his shirt to his cheek. He shook his head angrily, grunted and lowered himself to the roadbed, thinking that maybe Artie was right and he should start walking more to unload some of his lard.

"Come on, goddamnit, I ain't got time to fart around!"

The eight bulbs strung along the underside of the platform roof were unshaded, and their harsh white light folded his shadow sharply over the rails. The wind ebbed, and the shadows wavered. He let the lantern dangle at his side.

He whirled to his left at the sound of spilling gravel. The lantern held high, he crossed gingerly to the westbound iron with his free hand on his hip. It's what comes of letting them into Carosa's, he thought bitterly. Damned wop gives them anything they want to drink, even on a school night. Why the hell ain't they home studying?

He stopped and listened to the wind, the weeds, the faint crackling of the lights and the tired moaning of the station-house. He could hear the shifting of his boots, the brush of cloth across his chest, the wheezing of his lungs.

A stone landed, rolling just beyond the reach of the lantern. Mac willed himself not to flinch and held his face in check as he glowered down the tracks that vanished into the black of the night's throat. His arm was getting tired, but he kept it rigid, kept it high. Ain't no damned kids going to spook him, for crying out loud. Ain't they never seen him in the movies? Don't they know he got cops for sons? Crazy.

Something flew at him out of the darkness over the station.

He yelped as he hunched his shoulders and dropped the light. It clattered away from him, sliding and rolling into the low depression between the two lanes. Its beam speared at the sky, slicing without lighting.

A fluttering, and he stumbled backward, caught his foot on a rail and sprawled onto his back. He wanted to shout but his throat was too dry. He scrambled on his hands and knees toward the lantern, gravel splitting his trousers while he alternately cursed and prayed. He tumbled over the rail and rolled a few inches into the depression's hollow. On his back, he grabbed for the handle and held the lantern in front of him like a shield, just in time to catch the erratic course of a small bat as it passed over him and darted into the fields.

"Son . . . son of a bitch," he said slowly. "Sonofabitch."

He sat up and shook his head in shame, in relief. A bat. A goddamned stinking bug-eating bat nearly scares the living shit out of him. Maybe, just maybe, it was time he listened to Artie and stopped testing the sauce. At least while he was still on the job. A bat. A lousy little bat. Well, he thought as he pushed himself to his feet and slapped a dusting at his clothes, I sure as hell ain't gonna tell him about this. Laugh his ass off if he knew.

He reached the platform and leaned against it heavily, his stomach pressing into the edge, his breath still not coming easily.

Someone laughed.

Softly, Quietly. Dancing on the wind to tickle his neck.

His anger returned, and he spun around squinting. "All right," he said, lowering his voice to give it some power. "All right, you little bastards, now I'm gettin Jake over here. You hear me, you little creeps? I'm goin for the sheriff right now!"

The laughter returned, but distantly. But it wasn't the jeering or teasing kind he heard whenever the boys went on the prowl. This, and he couldn't help a swift and violent shudder, this sounded mean. Cold. Something he sure as hell didn't want to hear, out here in the dark.

He looked at the stationhouse, and the embankment, then eastward after the trail of the Limited.

The sauce, he told himself prayerfully; please, god, it's the sauce and Artie I swear to god I'll never drink on the job again. Just make it the sauce and I'll—

It glided toward him head high. There was no sensation of speed, no suggestion of sound. Just sinuous, fluid motion, and eyes that flared red.

(4)

Ted Waters loaded the last of the gear into the back of Arnold's pickup and rapped on the cabin's rear window. The engine sputtered to life as he swung to the running board and into his seat. Arnold was driving; they were going to meet

Chet Lancaster at just about midnight, near a spot where Ted used to fish before he could no longer take the time.

Arnold said nothing as they took the back streets away from the storehouse, and Waters was glad. For over two hours that evening he and Felsom had gone at it, arguing this and that and generally learning how to hate each other's guts. But he knew the result would be the same no matter how loud he shouted, how much reason he used: Felsom would not be deterred from sending him out to take down a bear.

"I don't give a damn whether it's male or female, long in the tooth or fresh on the ground. Just shoot the damned thing and bring it the hell back."

"Steve," he'd said in his best calm-down-idiot voice, "this ain't gonna work. It ain't damned gonna work!"

"Ted, you listen to me—if Jake ever finds out I've been in this with you guys, especially burning out that bastard Wolf, he's gonna toss me out on my ear. After he tries to take me apart. I don't want to fight him, Ted, he's an old man and he's goin crazy. So you take Arnold maybe, and Chet or Cy, and you go out to, say, Kramer's, and you shoot something. Big. Swear up and down it was foamin and moanin and you make it look damned good. And be sure to blast its head away so Oldfield can't tell about the rabies or not."

"Still can't understand why you can't figure a way to blame it on Tallpines."

"Because they may be bastards, but they're not that dumb. They didn't do it, take my word. Christ, don't you ever listen to what Doc Oldfield says?"

"Never thought I'd live to see you defend them, Steve."

"I'm not. Think what you want, Ted, but I'm not defending any one of them. It just wouldn't work, is all. I saw the bodies, remember? And I heard Doc Oldfield tellin about the bear. So you get yourself one, pal, and you take the heat off yourself, make yourself a hero and get me off the goddamned hook!"

"Y'mean, I get to be a hero?"

"Yeah. Yeah, you'll be a goddamned hero, Ted."

He thought about it until the rendezvous was made, and as the three of them skirted the sounds of the remnants of Harmon's men. He thought about being a goddamned hero every time he bumped into a tree or heard Arnold bitching or listened to Chet tell about the whore he loved in Blairs.

Thought about it—hard—and stumbled over a half-buried rock. He cursed loudly, mostly at himself for letting Felsom talk him into this nonsense. Only an asshole'd hunt bear in the dark. He heard Arnold grunt. Well . . . maybe two assholes.

(5)

A silence followed Jason's halting, sometimes stumbling recital. His attention was directed entirely at Donna, who had removed her glasses again and lay them on the table. Her curls shifted as though a breeze had crept in, and the dim light eased shadows across her cheeks and the folds of her skirt. Twice she opened her mouth to speak, and twice she changed her mind. She shook her head helplessly. He was on guard for anything that resembled pity, or despair, and would not begin to allow himself to believe that what he saw, briefly, was a thread of comprehension.

"Well?"

She took up her empty glass and twirled it reflectively. "I don't see . . . well, yes I do, but now that you've said all this, I don't know why you're still confused. It's grief, Jason, pure and simple. They're trying desperately to cover up for a fanatic who went too far. A fanatic, you should remember, they loved and feared."

"Yeah," he said. "I keep telling myself that."

"Jason," she said earnestly, her eyes dark with concern.

He pulled a roll of bills from his pocket and dropped several by his glass. "Let's walk, Donna. I need to breathe." He didn't wait for her to agree, but stood and made his way to the door. By the time she caught up he was already on the sidewalk, passing the barbershop. She said nothing to him, but after several yards linked her hand with his.

"Do you know," he said, "that one of my favorite courses in college was philosophy. Delusions of grandeur, toying with the foundations of the universe, working with puzzles that don't have any answers." He grinned quickly and looked at her sideways. "You bullshit in your room for hours at a time, and the only thing you can do is point out the window and say, 'That's real out there. I can't prove it to the nth degree, but it's real.' A faith, I guess. And I suspect it's why we lock away the insane—because they see something we don't, and there's no real way to put it in absolutes that our reality is the right one."

"You want me to argue?"

He laughed, and turned the corner toward the railroad tracks. "No. It's just that I can see how even someone like Daniel might believe that Rachel could do all those things. It isn't true—there are too many of us out here to refuse that faith—but it doesn't make Daniel crazy, either. Just a little sad."

"In other words—no monsters."

"Nope."

"Hell."

"You like monsters?"

"You know when Lon Chaney gets killed at the end of *The Werewolf* and all that fog covers him and that gypsy girl, the one who kills him—did she kill him, or was it his father? Claude Rains. Anyway, when he dies, I cry. Every damned time. Your're right, Jase—that's tragic."

"You feel the same way about Dracula?"

"The Jack Palance one, yes. That was a love story. He was what he was, but he sure didn't like it."

He stopped and put his hands on her shoulders. He wanted to say something to her—something profound, to seal the moment—but there was nothing. She tilted her face slightly and watched him, smiled and brushed a stray hair back behind his ear. Then she kissed his cheek and slipped her arm around his waist. "So, what are you going to do?"

He didn't know. He had managed to construct two parallel theories—one based on what he knew and what was possible, and one based on what he knew and could not believe. It had been so much simpler, he thought, for the man who'd lived a hundred years ago; so much simpler to accept things that did not seem to fit . . . or fit all too well. This kind of thinking was insane, but he had developed a very pat cosmic portrait back there in the bar, and he found himself falling in love with the image and ignoring the logic that was conspicuously, laughably, absent.

"Jason?"

Donna had stopped and was turned halfway around.

"What?"

"Did you hear something?"

"No."

The end of the block was washed in the glare of a streetlamp around which all foliage had been stripped. Beyond it lay the bleached rise of the railroad embankment, the curiously two-dimensional shapes of the storage shed and holding pens, and the wall of unyielding black that marked the start of the fields stretching silently to the mountains. There were no houselights burning. There were no cars at the curbs. He felt her hand tightening on his waist, felt the heat of her palm searing through his shirt.

The wind sent dust-devils blackly along the tarmac, trapping leaves, bits of paper, giving the street a voice he'd just as soon not hear.

The sound of paper rubbing across paper.

He licked his lips quickly, indecisively, unable to turn his head away from the blue haze that shimmered at the light's edge down there by the tracks. It took him several moments to realize something was moving through it.

"Donna."

Whispersoft.

Shadowfast.

He looked up, startled, laying one hand over hers, the other one grabbing for his belt.

The figure was black, indistinct, limbs almost like wings extending wildly from its sides. He found himself holding his breath, aware that Donna had moved a half-step behind him. He angled his right arm in front of her, and she took hold of his wrist.

He heard footsteps.

"Jase, who . . .?"

"I don't know."

The figure became a lurching man, became a boy, became Hardy Green in his high school baseball jacket. His face was pale, his legs barely keeping him upright. When he saw them moving hesitantly toward him he stumbled to a slow trot, one hand waving. "Please." He veered off the sidewalk and grabbed the nearest tree just as Jason lunged for him to keep him from falling.

"Hardy, what's the matter?" he said, feeling at once foolish and concerned. "Are you all right?" Drunk, he suspected, though he could smell no liquor on his breath.

The boy swallowed several times, his right arm over Jason's

shoulder as he gestured back toward the stationhouse. "Mac," he said finally. "Mister Clarke, it's old Mac."

"Is he hurt?" Donna asked briskly, her hands roaming the boy's face and chest for signs of injury, signs of struggle. "What is it, Hardy? What about Mac?"

"I . . ." Jason saw tears. "I think he's dead."

"All right, all right," he said quietly. "Take it easy, son, take it easy. It's all right." Donna cupped Hardy's face in her hands and told him the same. When the boy nodded, she released him and he swallowed again and brushed self-consciously at his jacket, trying to straighten himself. "Where is he, Hardy. Where is he, inside?"

"The tracks," Hardy said, fighting not to stammer. "He's . . ."

Jason urged him away from the tree, and, between himself and Donna, began walking the boy toward the tracks. Hardy did not protest, but kept his gaze on the sidewalk, his knees almost locked. Jason did not try to hurry him, but an exchange of glances with Donna told her not to let him lag.

"We were . . . we were foolin around, y'know?" the boy said, the words rattling under pressure. "We do it all the time. Then we ran. I didn't want to go home yet, so I went back to get him again. He's always chasin us away, always tellin us what a big movie star he was. Nuts, we knew that wasn't so. He's a lush, right? He . . ." Whatever courage the boy had found failed him as soon as they reached the parking lot behind the station. "I just found him there, Mister Clarke. Honest to god, Doc, I just found him there. We would never . . . we didn't . . ."

They climbed the platform steps and Jason moved ahead quickly, directly to the edge where he saw Mac lying between the eastbound and westbound lanes. He was on his back, a shattered lantern beside one leg. His arms were thrown up over his head, and the blood had stained the gravel around his shoulders. In the harsh light from the station the corpse didn't look real. Except for the blood, Jason didn't think it was real.

"Jase? Jason?"

"Stay where you are, both of you," he ordered, and jumped down. His stomach roiled and filled with acid, but he didn't need more than a single look to know that the gashes that had whipped the old man's face into more blood than flesh had not been made by the slashing claws of a bear.

Except for no evidence of devouring, the death was the same as the Perkinses'.

"Hardy," he said as he fell back against the platform, "get Harmon out here. Tell him what you saw, that we're here waiting, and get him the hell out here!"

The boy needed no further goading. He was gone before Donna could tell him not to say anything to either of Mac's sons.

"Jason, are you all right?" She walked out of the shadows, and saw Felsom's body. "Oh . . . god."

Jason stretched out a hand toward the dead man, but brought it back in a fist that punched hard at his thigh. Then, with a growl of angered betrayal, he climbed back to the platform and raced into the station. Mac's office door was open. He fumbled around in the lights' half-glow, found the telephone and dialed. He looked up in pale fury when Donna reached the threshhold.

"He swore to me," he said. "He . . . Daniel, is that you, you bastard?" He slammed his fist onto the desk. "Goddamnit, Daniel, you swore to me, you *promised* me there'd be no more killings! No, I am not drunk, damnit! Right now . . . right now I am looking through Mac Felsom's window here at the station, and do you know what I'm looking at, Daniel? Do you have any idea what the hell I'm seeing? *Mac* is out there on the tracks and he's all torn to shit and I want to know what the hell you think you're doing?" He put a trembling hand to his forehead, to his eyes. "Don't tell me she's dead, Daniel. And don't you dare give me that crap about . . . damnit, Daniel! Daniel!" He glared at the receiver, slammed it back on its cradle. "He hung up," he said. "I'll be goddamned, but the son of a bitch hung up on me." Jason stiffened, then started to bolt.

Donna caught him by the arms as he left the tiny room, her hands stroking his upper arms first hard, then gently. "Jason, come on, it's all right," she said. "Jason, take it easy, it's all right. It's all right."

He stared at her. Who . . .? Her face blurred, her voice droned, and he trembled and closed his eyes. Then he shoved her to one side and ran. He had to find the dark where the serpents couldn't find him, had to find a place where the boat didn't slip away from his grip and leave him floundering in the water. Where he wouldn't feel the bottom scrape against his face. Or see the woman standing above him—"Jason, please!"—grinning like a skull that had forced on a mask. There had to be a place where the woman and the serpents . . . where there was no such thing as people turning into . . . serpents and women and water and . . .

He was almost fifty yards from the station, stumbling and slipping over the gravel bed when he saw it.

"Jason!" Donna screamed.
Wingéd serpent.
The wingéd serpent.

It flashed past between him and Donna, who had run to the platform's edge and was crouched behind the last post. She had stopped screaming his name.

There was no sound at all, not even the wind.

He was unable to move.

Mac's body lay in the glare, a twisted mass of black laced with gleaming red.

Jason could not move.

It was a bird. No, a bird was a robin, a jay, a sparrow, an owl. This . . . this thing in the air had a dark beak curved and sharply pointed, feathers that rippled a deep tawny brown, and a smooth swept head that had turned toward him in passing with unblinking red eyes that knew . . . that *knew*. It was a bird. No! It was a dream. It was . . .

He could not move.

It had flashed by him as though it were taunting him. Slowly, its great wings barely riding the air, talons drawn . . . not a sound, not a sound.

And it had turned its head and it had looked at him squarely.

And vanished into the dark.

Donna was on the platform. The tracks were gleaming. Mac's body.

Jason lifted a hand to Donna in supplication, and almost screamed when he heard the laughter.

Soft. Quiet. Coming out of the dark and daring him to find it.

Soft. Quiet. Coming out of the dark as if to promise his dying.

SIX

(1)

There was a momentary shredding of silver-edged clouds, and the wind died as midnight approached.

The town ahead, etched in black ink and grey. From behind the poplars that separated houses from tracks it lifted into the sky, wings flexed. Coasting above the couple racing through the streets, it saw the men racing for the station; and swerved, and dipped, and coasted again and saw the empty bridge, the empty graveyard, the single light in the house that faced the river. A miniature car sped down the Pike. The neon in Carosa's bar flickered.

It soared and circled and sensed safety was ending, exposure near.

But right now it was hungry.

(2)

Esther Lynn climbed out of the bathtub and toweled herself briskly, wincing at the coarse cloth that reddened her pale skin. But she deserved the rough treatment. After Galen had brought her home, she had reneged on her offer of toddies and comfort. Suddenly, as he'd stood there awkwardly on the porch she'd had a vision of him dying while lying in her arms, and it had frightened her, and she'd stammered. The worst part of it was, the fool had understood. He'd mumbled something about walking the dogs before they ruined his kitchen, kissed her once on the cheek and strolled into the dark. Dapper. Assured. Turning in the flood of a streetlamp to wave and blow her a kiss. The temptation to call him back had lasted only as long as it took him to vanish. Then she'd slammed the door behind her and raced for the tub. The hot water scorched, and now the towel punished.

Afterward, she slipped into a bulky, quilted bathrobe, tied the red sash loosely and went into the kitchen to make herself something to eat. It didn't matter that her stomach jumped at the thought of food; she had to have something to keep up her strength. Because, she decided as she dropped bread into the toaster and set the kettle on the stove, she was going to get herself dressed as soon as she was done and march herself right over there to apologize. She had to. Otherwise she wouldn't be able to sleep a wink.

Maybe he'd think her brazen, maybe he'd refuse to let her in, but there was no question but that she had to try. She couldn't let him think she was afraid of him, and his dying. God knew he could last a week, or another thirty years; and if it were the latter, why, she'd never forgive herself for losing this chance.

The kettle whistled, the toast popped, and bundled in her robe she felt warm, the air stifling. With a sleeve she wiped her face, then opened the back door to get a breath of fresh air.

When she first heard the noise she thought it was someone shaking out a blanket.

She stepped back inside quickly and shut the door. Absently, her right hand turned the bolt while her left fluttered at the lapels of her robe. Blanket, she'd thought; then . . . wings. But either, considering the time, was clearly impossible, and as she wondered she poured the hot water into her cup and saw half of it spill steaming onto the table. Muttering chastisement, she hurried to mop it up, burning the tip of one finger that strayed into the puddle. The toast had already cooled by the time she remembered it.

Ordained, she decided, slapping off the light and heading for the stairs; it was meant that she should face Galen without anything in her stomach. Further punishment for her heartless behavior, and a reminder that compassion was an integral part of love. Not, she cautioned herself, that she pitied the man. He was too ornery, too strong, and his daily excitement about just plain living evoked nothing but admiration. She had to tell him that. Somehow she had to erase the impression she'd given him earlier that evening.

So she hurried, stopping only once when she thought she heard a fluttering in the backyard through the bedroom's open window. The wind in the trees, of course, or a tom making its rounds. Nevertheless, she closed the window and stared for several seconds through the pane, looking for something that would calm her imagination.

She kept all the lights burning when she returned downstairs and stood hesitantly at the front door, a trembling hand at her throat. It was foolish. She knew what the sound was, but suddenly, inexplicably, she didn't want to go out. She took a step back, her hands darting over her stomach. If it hadn't been for Galen and what she had done, she knew she would have turned right around and sat herself in front of the television, with the sound turned extra high.

"Silly old maid," she whispered to herself then. "When are you going to grow up? Galen needs you, fool. He needs you."

The unnatural calm of her voice pleased her, and with a bravado she didn't feel she opened the door and stepped out onto the porch. Her purse was held tightly at her waist, her fingers aching from their grip.

Her slow deep breath caught the scent of rain in the air, and she was almost to the steps when she heard it again.

A rustling. On the porch roof.

As if something she could not imagine was settling down to wait.

For her.

A few minutes later she was sitting in the living room, in the dark. Her purse was still in her lap. She was weeping without a sound. She wanted to call Galen, but she could not move. She wanted to scream for her neighbors, but all she could do was whimper.

And choke when she thought she heard something at the window.

Tapping. Scratching. Like a twig teased by the wind, or a dead leaf that hadn't fallen, or a fingernail, or a claw.

(3)

The laugh had been the final goad. Jason fell with small groans into the wide arms of panic, tripped into a drunken run and grabbed Donna off the platform. Holding onto each other like wounded soldiers, they stumbled away from the stationhouse, away from the tracks, passing Waters's darkened storehouse. As they dashed across the Pike, they looked up, skin cold and lips open in silent ragged screaming. By the time they reached the church they were running apart, eyes now determinedly ahead, their ears hearing nothing but the *crack* of their boots on the pavement. There was no thought of stopping; there was no thought at all. They ran in tandem with their quaking nerves on the reins, swerving left at the corner in so wide a turn that Jason stumbled off the curb and didn't bother to jump back on until they'd gone three blocks and turned left.

Terror rode on their backs, hunching their shoulders; and lurched inside their bowels.

Galen's house was dark.

Jason bulled through the gate, splintering the latch, and paid no attention to Jeff, who danced at his side until she smelled his fear. Then she fell back, puzzled, cowering on the grass when the front door opened, then slammed against the night.

"Light," Jason said hoarsely, lurching about the room, shying violently at each contact with curtain and shade.

Within moments every lamp was turned full. The windows lost their cold transparency and became black mirrors that reflected no color. The living room was ignored: its chairs were too comfortable, the hearth too wide; instead, they paced around the kitchen waiting for the kettle to boil and finally dropped into chairs while they watched their hands settle, while they stared at the ceiling.

Jason bit hard at the base of his thumb; he felt nothing until he took his teeth away.

"Harmon's going to wonder," Donna said at last, her voice cracked, and old.

Jason put his hands to his face; they were cold and it felt good, and he rubbed in small circles until his skin protested. He did not have to say that neither of them dared talk to the sheriff now; all they would do is present him with an hysterical, albeit controlled, story of some utterly impossible creature whose existence they had no evidence of at all. And whatever belief they might engender would be instantly dispelled the minute Harmon learned how long they'd spent drinking in Carosa's, and what had happened to Jason out at MacKenzie's ranch. He lowered his hands sharply when the kettle shrilled and drove the sudden ice from his lungs with a long trembling breath. He waited until Donna had poured them both dark steaming coffee before fixing her with a querying, almost terrified gaze.

"Yes," she said flatly, grimacing at a sip of the unsweetened liquid.

Still, they could be wrong. The shock of finding Mac like that, his own fears strangling him when he should have been strong, the incredible folly of calling Tallpines and accusing him of . . . they still could be wrong.

Donna was pale and haggard. Her hands ineffectually attempted to set her hair back into place. She had obviously surrendered her own prayers of denial.

"You're sure," Jason said. There was always hope.

"Yes," she whispered. Hope died to that as easily as to a shout.

The fear returned, and he gulped the scalding coffee and gasped. "You heard the—"

She shuddered and nodded.

No, he decided wildly; that's too damned easy.

"I was thinking maybe it was kind of a freak," he said, an apologetic laugh unsettling his voice. "It happens, right? Sometimes Nature takes a nap, looks the other way, and you get something that doesn't really belong. An outcast. God, it must happen all the time. Of course, it probably would have been seen long before this, I suppose." He was answering his own questions. Suddenly, he snapped his fingers. "Hey, condors! They're pretty big, right? Ten-foot wingspreads, big bodies. No, never mind. They're only in California, just a couple dozen left."

His foot tapped the floor until his hand clutched his knee.

"The laugh," Donna said, her voice breaking.

"Yeah," he said, swallowing. "Oh god, yeah."

They stared for a moment at the steam coiling from their coffee. Then Donna cleared her throat tentatively. "Jason, I refuse to ask you to pinch me, but if my arm should happen to come near you . . ."

His smile was wan. "I know how you feel." He looked to his thumb and saw the marks of his teeth.

"What do *you* think it was?"

He recalled the day he'd first gone to the MacKenzies'. What he had thought was a hawk stalking the sky Galen had told him was an eagle. There were golden eagles nesting on the crags of Kramer's Mountain.

"It was eight to ten pounds," he said, trying to be stern, trying to sound convincingly dogmatic. "Fifteen tops. What I saw was impossible."

"No kidding."

Yeah, he thought; yeah, no kidding.

"Okay, then let's assume for the sake of argument—"

Her hand slapped the table and made him jump. "Jason, damnit, there's no argument here! I, for one, am not crazy. The light was clear, I wasn't drunk, and that thing moved slow because it wanted us to see it. And we did. We did *not* imagine it. We saw it! There is no argument here, none at all!"

He held his breath until his lungs began to burn. To admit . . . to believe . . . the air whistled harshly between his lips as he felt his defenses crumble. He could not hold them back, could not help but see again that silent gliding thing whose red eyes pinned him and whose laugh in the dark promised him dying.

He shuddered violently.

Donna was right—there was no argument here.

"All right. Okay." So he carefully reviewed everything

Daniel and MacKenzie had told him, matching them and filling in gaps with speculations of his own. "So it was Rachel until now, until this year. It was only supposed to be a series of warnings and, I would imagine, a display of her power so the others would believe this land was truly sacred, and worth fighting for. But if they're right . . . if they're right and it took too much from her finally . . ." He stopped and shook his head, frowned and scratched his forehead. "But Rachel's dead, Donna."

"I know."

"Someone else?"

"It has to be," she said, with something less than conviction. "Except for vampires, dead is dead. At least I think so. I think that's the way I remember it."

He pushed away from the table and stood at the back door. The wind and the leaves moved, and were silent.

"Someone close," Donna said behind him. "A woman." He did not answer. "Someone else who cares about what Rachel was doing." She waited. "There's an easy way to find out."

He hesitated before walking stiffly into the living room to sit on the couch. The telephone waited on the end table, but he could not bring his hand to touch it until Donna had joined him, drawing her legs up beneath her and idly rubbing at her arms. She looked frightened. He didn't blame her. They were attempting to tackle the unreasonable with reason, make a leap of faith to a new system of logic. The leap was done; the logic was there; but the fear refused to wane. He dialed, then, and as he waited let his arm fall around her shoulders. She made no response, and he expected none—the bond that had been created between them had been forged from a scream.

"Aaron? This is Jason. Don't say anything, just listen. I'll explain later. But I need to know about . . . about Palemoon. Is she there? Is—"

The voice he heard was brittle with tears. "They all started comin already. They're gettin Rachel ready, dressin her and all, and that damned girl walks around here like she was a ghost. She's drivin everyone nuts. Listen, Jason, I appreciate your callin, but we got—"

"Aaron, wait a minute!" He closed his eyes, opened them. "You just said she's been around. Who? Palemoon?"

"Who the hell you think I meant? Christ, Clarke, this ain't no time—" There was muttering and keening in the background, and the line went dead.

"He could be lying," Donna said after he'd told her. "Do you really think he'd admit it with Mac dead like that?"

"Yes," he said, recalling the anger and fear on Sweetwater's face when he'd last seen him. "Maybe." He tilted his head to the back of the couch, chewed thoughtfully on his lower lip. "But if he didn't—"

"Who else cares as much for Rachel? What other woman?"

"Another possibility," he said quietly. "Supposing it was someone who didn't give a damn about Rachel at all. Supposing it's someone who's just the opposite, who hates, or thinks she has reason to. Someone who can get away for a few hours and not be missed. Someone—"

"Infected?"

Like a werewolf's bite. "Or taught."

"Jason, that could be anybody."

After a few moments' thought, he shook his head. "No. Not just anybody. Not just anybody at all." And he pulled the phone to his lap and dialed again.

"Mary? This is Jason Clarke. Listen, I'm sorry to bother you so late, but I was wondering . . . I wonder if I might have a word with Carole. If she's there, that is. It's about Rachel MacKenzie."

"It's a school night, remember? She's been here all the time. But I don't think it would be a good time to talk just now. She and Rachel were awfully close, you know, and she's still taking it pretty badly. If it weren't for those exams I don't think she'd go to school tomorrow. As it was, she had a hard time of it today."

"Yes, I can understand that. I really can."

"I know, Jason, I know. But look, I'll tell her you called and maybe you can see her tomorrow."

"That'd be fine. And I'm sorry for bothering you."

"No problem, Jason. She likes you, you know. She'll talk when she can."

Donna had moved away from him and curled herself into the corner when he rang off. "Strike one?"

He nodded, and smiled grimly. "But a man gets three, right?" He didn't bother to look at her as he dialed the second number.

"Kurt, this is Jason. I noticed you were open late tonight and I was wondering if Bea was there working with you."

"Damned hunters. Drink until they're stinkin, then they gotta eat. Bunch of them look like pigs at a trough, by Christ. You'd think they was back in the war or somethin."

"I'll bet. Look, about Bea . . . she was pretty close to Rachel MacKenzie and I was hoping—"

"Do you know what time it is, Jason?"

"I'm sorry. I know it's late."

"No kidding. And she's got exams tomorrow, y'know. She'd better have her ass home tendin her books."

"All right, thanks."

"Rotten thing, ain't it."

"About Rachel?"

"Oh yeah, her too."

The telephone at the Steed house rang eighteen times before Jason gave up. His palms were sweating and he wiped them roughly on his shirt. Then he called back the luncheonette and, closing his eyes briefly in a silent prayer for luck, talked to Peg, who whispered Bea was studying with her boyfriend and for god's sake don't say anything to Kurt or he'll string her up.

The Felsoms' line was busy, though he tried for fifteen minutes.

"Now," he said, "we have a strike-out."

"You sure?"

He hesitated before nodding. "Yeah . . . yeah." He punched his knee. "Damn! It's like the butler, I guess—too obvious, too easy. Carole's been home all night, Bea's at her boyfriend's and Ellie's gabbing on the phone with god knows who. Meanwhile, Rachel's being fussed over by a bunch of screaming women, and Palemoon's crying her goddamned eyes out. Now ain't that sweet."

She was startled at the disgust in his voice, the overlay of bitterness when he lashed out at the table with his boot and dropped the phone on the floor and made the bell jangle. She was not surprised, however, by the abrupt weariness that dropped over his face like a webbed mask. She felt the same. The adrenalin rush that had propelled them from the tracks had finally ebbed, and she could barely keep her arms folded over her stomach. There was no strength, and even thinking was beginning to be a chore. The only thing sustained was the fear that made her shiver.

(4)

The tapping ceased when Esther flung her purse wildly across the room. It struck a lampshade and set the lamp spinning on its base before it ricocheted to the baseboard. She listened to it, waiting, holding her breath in case the lamp should fall. When it settled with a thump, she sighed with hands pressed hard to her mouth and the house fell quiet.

The cushion beneath her was lumpy, and she could feel every rise, every rill, every tight fold of her skirt; her heart was still accelerating, and she could feel the pressure against her chest, as every beat threatened to pause, to stop; she could feel the air against her bare arms, the loose strand of hair over her right eye that felt like a moth trying to land. She could feel the ridges of her cold fingers on her dry lips, and when she finally lowered them into her lap her mouth was an oval that somehow failed to scream.

She had to move.

If she did not move now she knew she would stay there all night, waiting for the sun to throw patterns on the rug.

Slowly, infinitely cautious, she placed her hands on either side of her legs and pushed up. And when she was standing, trembling in the dark, she sidestepped around the coffee table, shuffling in painful inches while her hands took to the air in front of her and sought out the obstacles that would trip her or ensnare her. She knew where all the chairs were and she could picture the standing lamps, but the room had suddenly become alien to her, nothing the same as it had been for twenty years. She felt lost, and a bubbling began in her throat, as a scream tried to breech the barrier she'd erected. She swallowed several times and took a long step.

A harsh rapping started on the door.

Esther's sanity snapped: she shrieked and raced out of the room into the foyer.

Rapping. Harder, and insistent.

Her shin barked the newel post as she rounded the foot of the staircase, and she fell, sobbing, scrabbling at the risers while the sound filled the house and she thought she heard *Esther* her name through the thunder that deafened, the explosions *Esther* that spun her onto her back. She was kicking now, trying to climb the stairs and face the door. Her eyes widened as the pounding stopped and the door knob rolled slightly to the left, then to the right. Her hands groped for the bannister and the door knob rolled this way and that until a crack appeared the length of the doorframe.

She shrieked, and launched herself from the stairs and fell against the door, slamming it and locking it, then sliding to the floor and feeling her heart breaking through her dress.

A scratching by her elbow.

She crawled away and sat in the middle of the foyer, huddled, her eyes fluttering, dizziness showing mercy as she slipped toward a faint.

Until something tapped her shoulder.

Galen shifted uneasily on the edge of the mattress. He was a fool for doing what he did, but he kept telling himself he had no idea the woman had worked herself into that much of a state. After all, how was he to know she'd been sitting there all alone in the dark? He had tried the window, and the door, because he was positive she was home and was angry at him for his leaving. He should have stayed, as he knew she wanted him to; he should have accepted all her invitations—more in one night than in the past two decades—and buried himself in her friendship. But none of that had occurred to him until he'd gone home and fetched Mutt for a walk. Jeff, for some reason, had taken more to Jason and indicated by her reluctance that she would wait for him to return. He'd gone less than two blocks before guilt overwhelmed him and he hurried to Esther's home with every intention of explaining.

Now she was in bed, taking his cold compresses and

murmurings with her eyes tightly closed, while his own still found it difficult to take the sudden bright light. When he could think of nothing else to do, nothing else to say, he rose awkwardly and backed as quietly as he could toward the doorway. She had taken several stiff drinks once she'd stopped screaming—his hand brushed at his cheek in wonderment where she'd slapped him, several times—and had nearly passed out in the living room. No one, he thought, would believe he had carried her all the way up here, and he wasn't at all surprised that she showed him no gratitude. It had been a dumb thing, coming through the back door like that, sneaking up on her and touching her. A hell of a dumb thing.

He paused on the threshold. "I . . . I'll stay on the couch."

"You'll do no such thing," she said, the words slurring with liquor and exhaustion. "You'll leave me alone."

"Esther Lynn, please. I've told you—"

"We'll talk in the morning, Galen Marsh. Now get out of my bedroom."

He left without arguing. When Esther Lynn got into one of her moods he might as well try to level Kramer's Mountain with a spoon as try to make her see reason. He wondered how long she would begrudge him forgiveness, much less cold silence.

"Mutt," he said then, closing the front door behind him. The setter trotted to his side and they hurried to the sidewalk. Galen considered heading back home, but if Jason were there he didn't want to have to answer any of the boy's questions. Or see the knowing grin on his face, when there was nothing to know or grin at. Instead, he headed south toward the river, picking up a switch and snapping at his legs while the setter raced ahead to reach the water first.

There was another reason why he couldn't face Jason now: in just a few short days the young man had managed to unearth all the facts about MacKenzie that Galen had always known, and had always been afraid to learn firsthand. He had no idea why this was so—fear of antagonizing a man who'd given the town a firehouse and a clinic, fear of the man's power, fear of Indians . . . fear of himself, that he might in fact be all wrong and would subsequently appear to be an old man flirting with the first stages of senility, or a story-hungry editor of a two-bit newspaper.

He wanted to come to grips with his fear before he saw his cousin again.

So he walked and thought until the town fell behind him and there was nothing ahead but open space and the night. The river on his right seemed swollen and unruly, and he whipped the switch at the air, in anger and disgust. Mutt barked once. Galen smiled. It had been a miracle, he thought, that the animal hadn't run away from him years before this. He'd taken the two from a litter belonging to Cy Oaker, before Cy had given up raising setters and picked boxers instead. They had both been runts, both sickly, both impatient to get on with their living. He himself had no patience at all with them, and their training had been haphazard. But one way or another they had managed to survive each other. Mutt barked again, several times. His walking through the fields, along the river, with the auburn animals at his side had become, he knew with a wry grin, something of a town staple.

Mutt barked furiously.

Galen stopped.

He was almost a mile from the nearest house, and cursed at his wandering. One of these days, he thought, he would walk right off the edge of the plateau if he wasn't careful. Right off the edge, and into town legend.

He shivered. He was wearing only a worn cardigan over his thin white shirt, and it flapped against his hips when the wind resumed its keening.

"Mutt!"

His voice sounded hollow, distant, and in the near total darkness he could barely see his own hands.

"Damnit, Mutt!"

Suddenly, he thought of the bear. Did such a diseased animal sleep at night? Did it prowl? Was it driven down from the slopes by Harmon's men? Were those its footfalls he could hear just beneath the sighing of the wind?

He turned until the river was on his left. He could see the darker outline of the town and took a step toward it. "Mutt," he said weakly. No matter what enticements there were, his dogs always obeyed him. Something had happened to Mutt; he knew it, and he began walking. It would have been easy for him to walk toward the river, but the darkness was too complete, and it wouldn't do anyone any good if he tripped and fell in. All that would accomplish was his very swift drowning. And if there was something out there, something that had taken his dog, he wasn't going to play the movie hero and lay down his life. Not in the dark. Not when there were houses over there and all he had to do was rouse someone from their bed and borrow a flashlight and return with some help to—

Whispersoft.

He didn't have to look up. He knew the solid rush of air over his head wasn't caused by any bear. He kept walking. Whatever it was—bat, nightbird, anydamnthing—it would probably tease him and leave him alone.

Shadowfast.

He held his head rigidly, the switch rising and falling like a blind man's white cane.

There's nothing to be afraid of, he told himself. Just look at the house over there. If you stare hard enough you can see it through the trees. It's waiting. There's nothing to be afraid of. Just look at the house.

Whisper . . . shadow . . .

His left hand fumbled in his pocket for the plastic vial. When his fingers closed around it he sighed and pulled it out. His heart was racing, and perspiration dripped from his chin onto his breast. He stumbled once over an unseen burrow. The house; just look at the house. Only a few minutes more, only a few steps longer. The vial fell from his palm. He cried out and dropped to his knees, fumbling through the high grass. He couldn't lose them. But something landed heavily not five feet from where he knelt and he fell onto his side and curled into a ball.

Silence.

He opened his eyes slowly and struggled to his knees.

The grass was stiff, knife-edged, and he frowned and crawled forward. The switch served as a probe, and he didn't stop until it gave, nearly bent double. His hands reached out, and the dark shape in the grass caught the dim starlight and flashed it back amber.

He felt the soft fur, the familiar slant of the muzzle . . . and the dampness that matted the slope of Mutt's throat. He moaned.

Pretense vanished, and with it his false courage. He lunged over the dog's body and his momentum carried him until he was on his feet. He didn't care about the percussions that swept through his chest, didn't care about the tears that slipped from the corners of his eyes. The house. It had to be the house. Bobbing out there, dark against the dark. Someone daring to sleep inside while something out there dared to pursue him.

The house directly in front of him. Bobbing. Lifting. An ebony shadow that beckoned and taunted.

And it was curious, he thought, that the house had red lights.

(5)

"You ever think of becoming a nun?"

Donna's grin was crooked, and she wished Jason would stop staring at the phone as though he expected it to ring. What he needed now—what they both needed now—was a good healthy dose of Galen's unleavened cynicism. But the old man was still out, probably at Esther's, and Jason refused to take his gaze from that damned phone.

"I wonder what it's like to be a monk. All you have to worry about is keeping your robes clean and shooing the crows away from the crops."

"You're babbling," she told him, wearily, but smiling.

"No shit."

The base of her spine began to ache, and she shifted to find a spot on the cushion that would afford her some comfort.

"Maybe I'll try again."

"Why? You're not going to get new answers."

"Maybe they were lying."

"Who, Peg and Mary? Come on, Jase, you're reaching."

He crossed his arms over his chest and rubbed his shoulders monotonously, shaking his head in reluctant defeat and staring hard at the floor.

"Now what?"

He made a harsh, disgusted sound and grabbed for the copper bowl of peanuts Galen kept on the coffee table. One he popped into his mouth, another he flung into the fireplace without offering her a share. It became, then, a ritual: eat, throw, eat, and she winced whenever one of them pinged off the andirons.

"Are we going to just sit here?"

She pulled off her glasses and dropped them into her lap. Her fingers pressed circles tightly around her temples.

"Can you see without those things?"

"About four, five feet before it all starts to blur."

He grunted, and threw another peanut.

She said nothing. She knew both of them were waiting for one of two things: either a sudden confession of aberration (madness? reality?), or a moving to the door to begin a nighthunt. The urgency was there, the need to keep things in motion so there would be no time to think, but she was unable to find a way for it to affect the position of her limbs. It was as though they had managed to become detached, as if she were detached . . . a patron in the front row watching the actors trying like hell to make something of what was pure and simple imagination; the problem, however, with the front row was obvious—one saw the actors sweating, could see up into the flies, aside to the wings . . . the illusion was gone, intimacy in this case too great a curse. What was real, then, was what she saw, not what she was supposed to see, or wanted to see, or prayed please dear god to see.

She glanced at her watch.

Only a few hours ago the solution was at hand, the problem solved, all of it over except for the shouting that would have come when Harmon's men had returned with their trophy. A few hours ago it all should have been done. Despite her misgivings there had been no other answer than the rampage of a rabid bear.

It should have been over.

But she had seen Felsom, and the creature that had killed him.

She asked herself if the lighting had been all that good at the station. A glare like that could be just as tricky as twilight, just as deceptive as dusk. Lord, wasn't it possible that shadows and fear and revulsion and Jason had enlarged the thing in her mind to suit what had happened?

Its eyes . . . the silent windwhistle of its passing . . .

She shuddered and hugged herself tightly. It was so simple to lose it all. Just walk down the street and turn a corner and the world quite without warning suddenly tilts on its axis to

show you what it can do. It's the same world, but suddenly
there's no recognizing anything at all. Why . . . why the
hell . . .

Jason pushed himself into the couch's opposite corner, and
lifted his legs to the cushions. He groaned and stretched, and
stared at her blankly. "You know what we should do, don't
you?"

"Call the Air Force."

He stared, then grinned, and the chuckling deep in his
throat broke into a full-fledged laugh that brought tears to his
eyes. She waited patiently, a giggle breaking out once in a
while, a short laugh . . . and before she could scold, or
scream, her mouth flew open, and all the terror that had
clawed its way into her heart exploded outward in uncontrol-
lable laughter.

"It . . . damnit, it's not funny," Jason gasped, red-faced
and squinting.

She nodded, still laughing and slapping her legs. Her sides
ached. Her jaw ached, but she couldn't stop.

"Stop it!" he said, trying to glare at her sternly. "This is
serious, damnit."

"Sure," she said, and they were off once again.

Images of Gloria, of Billy and of poor drunken Mac ran
through her head and the tears she shed became tears of
weeping. Jason had rescued her, out there in the field, and
now she was caught with him in a blooded vortex of terror.
She saw his face when the eagle soared by him.

"You . . . you should have seen yourself out there," she
said, gulping for air.

He quieted, then nodded. "I damned near shit in my
pants."

It wasn't funny at all, but still she roared, bent over at the
stitching pain in her stomach and sliding helplessly to the
floor. She got the hiccoughs and threw a punch at Jason's feet
when he guffawed at her affliction. That, however, only
served to increase the laughter that tempted hysterics. Unable to think, the tears streaming down her cheeks, she
groped for the copper bowl and, without hesitating, dumped
the remains of its contents into his face. He sputtered and
grabbed for her, his laugh calming, but she scrambled to her
feet and raced for the door.

"Cheating!" he shouted after her without rising. "You're cheating, damnit!"

She flung it open, grinning.

A shadow on the porch lunged for her chest.

(6)

Jason leapt to his feet as soon as Donna screamed. He saw Jeff cringing on the floor, whimpering as Donna scolded him with a fist raised and ready. In less than a minute, however, she had regained her senses and was down on one knee, apologizing to the dog, stroking its coat until it relented and began licking at her face.

"Damned thing oughta be shot," Jason muttered, sweeping the peanuts off the couch to the floor.

Then the setter turned in Donna's hands and began a deep-throated growling.

"Jeff," Jason warned, and saw Steve Felsom in the doorway.

"Well," Felsom said. "Well, well, well."

Jason bit back a sarcastic retort and sat up quickly, dusting a peanut from his lap. Donna and Jeff backed away quickly, but the deputy strode by them as if they didn't exist. He was in his tan uniform, his hat pushed to the back of his head, the flap of his holster conspicuously unsnapped. His narrow face seemed leaner than usual, its skin taut and bristling with a blue-black shadow that marked his uneven beard.

"Well."

Jason gestured for him to have a seat, but he refused with an abrupt shake of his head. He scanned the room thoughtfully, his eyes half closed while he rocked on his heels.

"I'm sorry about your father, Steve," Jason said, folding his hands docilely in his lap.

Felsom jerked his head toward the porch. "So I heard. You was havin one hell of a wake."

Donna took a step toward him. "Steve, don't be silly. It wasn't what it sounded like. I mean—" She quieted suddenly when Jason warned her with a look and moved quickly to sit beside him as Jeff slipped into the hall.

After a few moments, Felsom nodded and sat on the table,

his hands draped between his knees. "You feel like talkin, or isn't the party over yet?"

"It wasn't a party," Donna said angrily; and when Jason glared at her she scowled. "Well, damnit, it wasn't!"

"What she means is," Jason said, trying to appear as shamefaced as possible, "we were a little hysterical there. We, uh, never saw anything like that before."

"I guess," the deputy said. "Should've stuck around, though. It ain't no fun chasin after witnesses." His face hardened as he swallowed. "You wanna talk?"

"Why . . . why didn't Jake send Bill Oaker?" Jason asked. "I mean, wouldn't it have been—"

"Yeah," Felsom said, "but I wanted to, okay?" He pulled a small notepad from his breast pocket, a pencil shoved through the metal spiral. He looked up, first at Donna.

Jason spoke for them. "We . . . that is, after we sent the boy back—Hardy Green, as you know—we figured there was something still out there, you know? I mean, whatever did that to . . . well, we didn't want any part of it. We waited on the platform, but we're not like you people, you know. We don't deal with this sort of thing, ever. It was dark, and it was quiet, and—"

"We scared ourselves," Donna finished quietly.

Felsom's look was meant to be withering.

"Hey," she said, with a glance to Jason, "you know where we're from, for crying out loud. You think we see bears and mountain lions and things like that every day of the week? Even doing what I do, Steve, I don't come across that kind of stuff. So . . . we heard noises, and there was poor Mac lying there and we . . . we . . ." She faltered and shrugged helplessly, groping for a fold of her shirt when her eyes misted.

"She's right," Jason agreed quickly, to keep Felsom from speaking. "We just let it all get to us, that's all. I'll tell you, Steve, I never ran so hard in my life. Then, when we got back here and Galen was gone, we had some of his brandy over there"—he pointed to the sideboard—"and it just caught up with us." He spread his hands. "What can I say? I've been a reporter long enough to know better, to know we shouldn't have run, shouldn't have left the scene. I know that, Steve. But . . . oh, hell, I'm sorry, that's all."

Felsom scribbled furiously for several seconds, then tapped

his chin with the pencil. "You see anything?" he asked without looking up.

"No," they said simultaneously.

"Shadows," Jason added. "Hell, you know what it's like out there at night. And I don't even know if we really heard anything except what was in our imaginations. And believe you me, they were working double overtime."

"You're makin a habit of this, it seems," Felsom said quietly. "Findin bodies, that is."

"Bad luck, what can I tell you."

The deputy nodded, almost as though he understood. "Did you check to see if he was . . . dead?"

"No."

"What?" Felsom stared at him, disbelieving. "You mean, you spooked yourselves and run off and he still might've been alive out there?"

"No!" Jason snapped. "No, that much I'm sure of. I'm no doctor, but your father was gone when Hardy brought us there. I got the closest look, and he wasn't breathing, moving, anything. He was . . . gone. You really think I would've run off if I thought there was something I could do to help him?"

Felsom didn't respond. Instead he snapped the notepad closed and stuffed it back into his shirt. Then, kicking at a peanut, he chewed on the pencil's ragged eraser. "You see any tracks?" he asked Donna.

"Not a thing," she said. "But all that gravel there would make tracks impossible I would have thought. Are you . . . are you thinking maybe that bear's come down to town?"

Felsom shrugged, but Jason caught the flare in his eyes.

"I doubt it," Donna told him then. "I mean, there's too many people here, right?"

"A bear's rabid, like *you* said it was, who's gonna tell what it'll do? Why'd you say that, anyway? Didn't you . . . it's got to be that bear, Doc, doesn't it?"

"Yes," Jason said, covering Donna's sudden confusion. "Steve, you have to understand we're not thinking straight just now."

"Yeah. Sure." He scratched across his jaw with the pencil, into his hair, and stared at the fireplace. Then he sniffed and rapped the brim of his hat. "Okay, yeah. So, you're sure you didn't see anything? Either of you?"

"Nothing," Donna told him.

"You was at Carosa's for a while," he said.

Jason frowned.

"Yes," Donna said firmly. "I met Jason there."

"You had a date, I take it?"

"Yes. I was late."

"Why?"

"I was out in the valley most of the day, then came home and did some reading. Then . . . I went to see Jason."

"Steve," Jason said then, "just what the hell is this?"

"Just askin, that's all, Clarke. No need to get ruffled." He rose, pushed the table back with his legs and walked to the door and opened it. "You drop by in the mornin, hear? In case I got something wrong."

They nodded and, just before the door closed, Jason called out the deputy's name. When Felsom paused he said, "And we're really sorry about Mac, Steve. Really."

"Yeah."

The door closed, just short of a slam.

Jason instantly fetched the decanter of brandy from the sideboard and poured them both a half-glass. He toasted her silently, drank and leaned back. "Great," he said to the ceiling. "This is just . . . great."

She put a finger on his knee. "Jase, what are we going to do now?"

"Well, I don't know about you, love, but I'm not moving from this spot until this damned bottle is empty."

"Is that going to solve the problem?"

"Nope. But it's going to help me get through the night without screaming, I can tell you."

She shuddered at his admission, emptied her glass and held it out silently. He didn't hesitate to refill it, then lay his head back against the armrest and closed his eyes slowly. He was cold, and the wind was making noises that sounded too much like whispering. Then there was a shifting, a slight coughing, and he moved over to give Donna room. It was cramped, but he didn't care; the warmth of her arms, her breath against his cheek, the scent of her hair kept him from trembling.

"I wonder where Galen is," he said after a while, for the sound of his voice.

"Catting with Esther."

His grin was forced. "Sure. And it'll snow on the Fourth of July."

"Don't underestimate him, Jason. You have to give the man his due."

He nodded, and felt the brandy inducing a drowsiness that both tempted and unnerved him. The lights were still on, but he wished there were more, he wished Galen were here, he wished the house were made of stone.

"Donna?"

"Hmmmm?"

"Jesus, I'm scared."

(7)

A single light shone from the second floor of the Harmon house, and its reflection on the river was little more than a glow. David Carosa watched it, wondering what Ellie was doing in there, wondering if she'd be mad if he made his way over and knocked on her door. He hadn't seen any movement for quite a while, not since the shade had snapped up some time ago, but he was sure she hadn't gone to bed. She stayed up late. Too late, he thought, and was immediately angry at Steve Felsom for not taking care of her better. The woman needed her sleep, and if he only had the chance he knew he could be the one to bring the rose back to her cheeks.

He shifted his weight on the canes and wished he'd brought the wheelchair. But as long as there was a chance they might meet, he wanted her to see him upright and mobile. The penalty in the morning would be aching hips and a sore back, but it was worth it. It was always worth it. No matter how stupid he knew he was behaving, it was always worth it for that one slender chance.

He shivered and scowled at the bat that suddenly flew overhead.

Part Four
WINGÉD SERPENT

ONE

(1)

Over a town like Windriver, and over mountains like the Range, the clouds that begin massing in preparation for an early summer storm would rumble first, just below the horizon. The western peaks would grow sharp in relief against the pale grey and white that rose solemnly above them, would blur as the grey darkened and would vanish when there was black. In the forest the birds from hawk to crow would rearrange that piece of nesting and this slap of mud; in dens and burrows and hollow-mouthed caves there would be restlessness, retreating, an endless frustrated pacing as the air charged itself and fur quivered and stiffened; elk and deer would test the deceptive wind and stay clear of those streams whose banks were too shallow, whose curves and twists would cause treacherous landfalls when trodden. On the eastern slopes and fields, where the new sun was still day-bright and the thunder a curiosity, cattle would begin lumbering reluctantly toward shelter, sheep would huddle and horses would paw nervously at the earth and snort their defiance.

And as the clouds darkened and swallowed the peaks, they

merged, spitting tentative lightning. Then, there would be a silence.

Not even the wind.

Just slender veils of rain falling in the distance.

Apprehension lasted as long as the ponderous approach, and the silence lulled the valley into believing the storm would pass in false warning.

The few cars that made their way toward jobs on the reservation were speeding, a race against the mudslides and rockslides that had been readied since winter. Those that moved west past the factory down to Blairs were slower, stoic and resigned, the only unknown the degree of force of their sure pummeling. Pedestrians, too, moved a little quicker, with heads ducked in anticipation and arms tight at their sides. The hairs on the backs of their necks reacted to the increasing static electricity, which gave an odd edge to the foliage and an odd tinge to the blacktop, making it almost green, with deep swirls of purple, ominous and fleeting. People at work and those left at home spent more and more time hovering about their windows, twisting rings on their fingers, wishing it would begin and be done so they could get about their living.

Lightning, then, and finally thunder that rolled and echoed, and windowpanes shimmered like bubbles ready to burst.

In the high school tempers shortened dangerously close to the flash point—the tension of the examinations doubled by the weather.

In front of the sheriff's office two dozen men gathered once again, distributing themselves into jeeps and campers. Slickers were passed out and instructions were issued along with walkie-talkies. Doc Vance scurried from group to group to remind them unnecessarily there was a very good chance the bear had infected other creatures it must have bitten. Take no chances. Look for the froth clinging to its muzzle. For the lolling tongue; the snapping at air; the dazed eyes. Take no chances. Blow the bastard away before it gets to you first. And save the head if you can. The head's the best way to determine the rabies. And how the hell should I know where Oldfield is? I'm not her keeper, just listen and pay attention. So they listened and nodded and patted their jacket pockets or reached under the seats for the flasks and the bottles that would keep their asses warm when the rains came and the temperature dropped and all hell broke loose and ruined this stupid expedition.

Not one of them mentioned the finding of Mac Felsom.

A single leaf in the gutter of T. Waters Farm Supplies and Feed Station leapt from the curb and clung to the base of the building. Inside, Lureen chewed her gum and played with the register and hoped to god Ted Waters had run away for good.

The sun was netted by the leading edge of the cloudbank and was shattered into brilliant white lances, a Hollywood design too perfect to last, spotlighting patches of green woodland, green fields, and spinning briefly through a prism display before vanishing as though a switch had been thrown.

One moment it was morning; the next, it was dusk.

One moment there was no wind; the next . . .

It made no difference that the storm might prove to be a bad one, or one that was spectacular for its lack of delivery; Windriver was relieved when the wind tunneled down the Pike. Patience had been rewarded; let nature do the rest.

And it did. With a vengeance.

It howled, it threatened, it postured cataclysm through the wires that hummed and the branches that rattled, the loose tiles that clacked and the loose shutters that banged; it raised dervishes in the fields and froth on the river, it trembled the bridges and deep-bowed the rushes and screamed to a banshee that drove animals to hiding. It roiled the clouds out of their thunderhead configurations, and formed a single black-grey mass that lowered the sky.

It would be an hour or more before the wind died and the processional ended.

All that was needed now was the first drop to fall.

Like a cathedral before a funeral, Windriver was hushed.

(2)

Daniel woke suddenly, a throbbing circling dully around his temples as though seeking a place to light. He was stretched out on the porch, a blanket tossed over his legs, and he could smell the bacon, the eggs, the coffee and toast drifting strong from the house. It was quiet. After Jason's call last night, the

Indians had gathered behind the house to begin their singing and their prayers, holding back the night with a bonfire whose girth might have engulfed the moon. But now it was quiet, the singing done for the moment, and all he could hear were the faint bell-sounds of children playing quietly in the distance. He pushed himself to his feet, not bothering to stifle a self-pitying groan, and Sweetwater came out to tell him Harmon had called about an hour before. Another group of men would be spreading across the valley to flush out that rabid bear. Most of the ranchers had donated hands of their own, and Aaron had taken it upon himself to order MacKenzie's people to borrow what weapons and vehicles they could and link up when the hunters reached the ranch line.

Daniel looked at him, uneasy.

"It's all right," Sweetwater reassured him. His eyes were red-rimmed, his mouth slack with fatigue and mourning. "I told the People to stay close until they passed. Ain't nothin that walks on fours gonna live out the day up there."

Daniel twisted and rubbed his neck. "Jason didn't tell them."

"Guess not."

A battered pickup parked loudly on the far side of the drive's circle. Visitors from the reservation, Daniel guessed; emissaries. Though virtually none of the Shoshone down below agreed with Rachel (laughing at her, mocking), they still held her in great respect. The ranchhouse would be crowded before the day was done. He glanced up at the sky, feeling the first of the wind's strong pushes.

"Have you been here all night?"

Aaron shook his head. "Timmy . . ." He swallowed, less in sadness than in the vestiges of his anger against Simon. "I had to bring him down to Washakie. The ceremony will be tomorrow." He hesitated, his beefy hands grasping at the air. Daniel waited patiently. "Charlie told me something last night," he said in a broken rush. "He told me he and some friends had done that thing to the druggist. He thought the man had done something to Dawn."

Daniel grunted, noncommittal.

"And Dawn has run away."

He looked at the large man fearfully.

"No," Aaron said. "I'm sure she's run away. Her clothes

are gone, her suitcase." He sighed and reached for the porch railing, strangling it. "Charlie cried when he told me."

"Did you—"

"No, I didn't touch him. I wanted to. I wanted to spread his face with my . . . no. I cried with him. When all this is done, Daniel, we will talk to the sheriff."

"And Laughing Sky?"

"She knows nothing. She never knows anything. A woman is staying with her, a woman from Washakie."

Incredible, Daniel thought, how the man keeps going. His whole family collapsing around him, and still he keeps going.

They watched as a group of horsemen rode away from the house. They were armed, wearing slickers and wide-brimmed hats, and were trailed for a hundred yards by a gaggle of laughing children.

Daniel thought for a moment, then held out one hand. "Let me borrow your car," he said.

Aaron frowned. "What for?"

"I want to talk to Jason. I must." He looked at his watch; it was just about ten.

"Why, Daniel? Why bother? They think it's been a bear, so let them do their hunting. It gets the heat off us, right? Why should you want to cause more trouble now? And if they do shoot something, so much the better."

"You forget," Daniel said, "Mac died after Rachel."

Sweetwater hesitated through a silent protest, then fished in his pockets until he found the keys. Daniel grabbed them and jumped off the porch.

"Careful, Dan," Aaron called after him. "You don't know him that well."

"You just watch Simon for me. The old man's going to need a shoulder. I don't think . . . I don't think he's going to make it."

He saw his friend nod, turned and walked until he found the dented, rust-streaked convertible Sweetwater had picked up for fifty dollars four years ago. That it ran at all was a miracle he had never stopped questioning. As he threw himself easily over the wired-shut door and slid his legs under the steering wheel, he hoped that Jason had not gone on the hunt. He suspected the whites were going to need his help whether they wanted it or not.

(3)

Waters hunkered down in front of the orange tent and held the tin cup close to his lips. From the way the sky had turned to slate and the tops of the trees were groaning eastward he knew there was a hell of a storm moving in on the valley. And like most of them this time of year, the clouds would probably hang ominously overhead until the middle of the afternoon before the rains finally decided to end the suspense. Great. Just . . . great. This fool expedition was already going down the tubes without it raining on him, too. First, they had all overslept; then Arnold had turned an ankle; and now Chet was cursing a blue streak trying to dig a shittrench off in the brush. He had half a mind to call it off right now, and let Felsom bitch all he wanted to.

He was about to decide just that when Arnold suddenly appeared in front of him.

"Christ, now what?"

"Ted, you'd better come over here and see what Chet found."

Ten minutes later they were back at the tent, all of them pale, all of them keeping their eyes on the sky or the slope up ahead.

"The way I figure it," Arnold said, scratching idly at the side of his nose, "he was caught back up there a ways, was dragged down here where it tried to bury him. Cover him up, anyways." He paused. "But I thought they was supposed to die pretty quickly when they got that stuff."

Waters shrugged. "I ain't no doctor, y'know. How the hell should I know?"

"He's been dead a long time," Chet Lancaster said. He had already thrown up at the sight of Thornton's ravaged and partially decomposed body and was waiting hopefully for one of the others to follow suit. "That bear got to be dead by now."

"Oh, yeah?"

"Yeah."

Waters finished tying off his pack, rose and hefted his rifle in his left hand. "We'll pick him up on the way back." Then he looked hard at Chet. "And you forgot somethin."

"What?"

"You think that there kid's the only thing that damned bear's bit in all this time?"

He kept to the rear as they climbed away from the treeline toward the caves that pocked the side of the mountain. He hadn't told either of them why Felsom had really ordered them out in the middle of the goddamn night. The talk of Oldfield's rabid bear had been the first thing that had popped into his mind. It didn't matter a damn that he didn't think bears could get like that, but it helped keep the other two close to him. No way, he thought, am I going to get nailed all by myself. Christ, but he couldn't wait to see that fool cop again! The choice words they were going to have—

Lightning scoured the air above the mountain, and all of them jumped.

(4)

Jason stood under the showerhead and let the water punish him. The steam helped somewhat to clear the fuzziness from his mind, but the water drumming against tile and tub only increased the pounding in his head. He held up his face and gasped, stood there for several long moments before stepping away to lather himself. Then, rinsing, he forgot for a moment the size of his hangover and reached out and switched the water over to cold. His yell made him grimace, but he stood his ground until the shower felt like needles. He climbed out, gingerly toweling himself dry while he mumbled imprecations against cops and Irish setters and decanters filled with brandy.

It wasn't until he was dressing that he heard the wind.

He walked over to the window and pulled aside the curtains. The willows were trying to tie themselves in knots, and the fragments of visible sky were gunmetal grey. A huge leaf slapped suddenly against the pane and he shied back toward the door.

And remembered.

Donna was already sitting down when he entered the kitchen. She smiled at him weakly, passing an eloquent hand over her forehead. With a sympathetic nod he went to the stove and poured himself coffee; and though its strong aroma repulsed him, he managed to down the first gulp without losing it. He sighed, refilled the cup and took a chair.

"Well," he asked, almost pleading.

"An eagle," she told him. "A goddamned golden eagle."

He nodded and spooned sugar into the coffee, stirring it absently while he retraced the night before until the last of his doubts had been crushed and scattered. When he looked up she blew him a kiss, and with a wan shrug looked to her own drink.

It began to rain. First a light splattering against the panes, then a thunderous downpour that made speech impossible, and thinking more so. Jeff crept into the room and squatted beside Jason. He scratched at the dog's head and pulled gently on his ears until she licked at his hand and lay her head across his lap.

The light seemed unnaturally glaring.

There was a split second following a lightning blast when the fluorescent bulb flickered and the refrigerator stuttered.

"If Vincent Price walks in that door," he said with a nod toward the back stoop, "I am going to shit."

Donna's laugh was delayed and explosive, and he felt his own tension slipping inexorably from his shoulders and his neck. He stroked a palm over the setter's muzzle until her trembling ceased and she pulled away to pad from the room.

Ten minutes passed along with another cup of coffee.

"If you're right," Donna said, "then we still don't know who we're looking for. All we can say is that it's a woman who's got a hell of a lot of fear and anger in her, and I'm telling you right now, Jason Clarke, that I'm not about to go around town knocking on doors. You can't tell just by looking, right? You . . ." She frowned. "Damn."

"Right," Jason said. "Unless we're overlooking something, all we can do is wait."

The wind eased and the rain settled to a monotonous thrumming that grew virtually silent. Time between lightning and thunder lengthened as the storm's vanguard drifted out of the valley and left the rain behind.

"Two grown people," he said quietly, smiling when Donna looked at him, puzzled. "Two grown people sitting around a cozy little kitchen actually considering the existence of a real, flesh-and-blood monster while a thunderstorm rages outside.

It should be midnight, not morning. And maybe we should be locked up so we don't hurt ourselves."

"Jason, I'm afraid."

"If you weren't, you'd be crazy."

"Are you?"

His laugh was more of a snorting. "Hell, yeah. If I had any brains at all I'd get the hell out of here."

"I want to."

He knew, and his look told her, and he reached out to let her hand slip over his palm. "If we had a race for the door, I think it'd be a tie."

She smiled, almost shyly, and squeezed his hand. "We're not going, are we."

The taste of escape was sharp on his tongue, but for the moment he could do nothing but swallow, and ignore it. "No," he said, the word rasping. "No."

He had considered, somewhere in the back of his mind where a small, shrill voice was screaming, blaming his cousin for the predicament he was in. If Galen hadn't kept in touch after his mother had died, if Galen hadn't played on his sympathy by playing the weary old man, if Galen hadn't pleaded with him (in so many words) to come out and help him . . . he would be hiding somewhere else. It made no difference that he wouldn't have been able to hide forever. That someone, at some time, would have eventually uncovered the graft and corruption he had spotlighted in New Jersey, and his fear would dissolve into shame. He was the one who had buckled to intimidation. And he was the one who had to live with himself.

He had also considered abandoning Windriver. He wasn't the only one capable of finding the answers, and doing something with them. Sooner or later someone else would spot the werebeast, and sooner or later Daniel would convince someone else that the werebeast existed. But how long would it take? How many others would be shredded and devoured?

He put his elbows on the table and clasped his hands into a double fist, lay the fist thoughtfully against his mouth.

But if he ran this time, where the hell else could he stop?

Donna rose from her chair and gently pulled his hands away from his mouth. She put her fingers lightly to his cheeks and kissed him.

"It's almost eleven," she said, her lips brushing his ear. "I'm going to make some lunch, then go out."

"Where?" A demand born of fear.

"I don't know, but I can't sit around here all day waiting for the roof to fall in. I'll pop in here and there, maybe find out who was where last night, things like that."

He grinned. "Things like that?"

"Sure, why not? You think you and Galen are the only ones who can report around here?"

The room darkened, and a wind gust rattled the windows in their frames.

"Galen," he said, and pushed out of his chair. "Donna, where the hell is Galen?"

The coffee in his stomach turned suddenly to acid. He ran to the front and picked up the phone. Donna stood beside him, but he didn't dare examine the look in her eyes, or interpret the soft stroking of his arm.

There was no answer at the office.

Bill Oaker at the sheriff's hadn't seen him.

After ten strident rings Esther Lynn answered her phone.

His eyes began stinging. He stood rigidly in the center of the living room floor, his hands fisted, waiting for fear and rage to separate within him. Fire seared his throat *Esther's voice . . . he was walkin that fool dog of his, scared the hell outta me,* and bands of spiked iron tightened over his chest *i thought there was something out there, jason,* the fear . . . the fear . . . *oh god, Jase, oh god, oh my god.*

He swallowed hard and started for the door, reaching for the raincoat hanging from its peg. Donna was there ahead of him, shaking her head, her eyes rabbit-wide. Her lips were moving, and somehow he heard her asking *how do you know, how do you know for sure.* He didn't, and for that reason pushed her gently aside, struggling into his coat and hat while he moved to the porch.

The rain drove in grey sheets; the wind smacking the trees.

The air was cold, but he was colder inside.

He heard the door close behind him, but he didn't look around.

Wingéd serpents.

"Fuck 'em," he said harshly. Taking the steps at a leap, he

strode to the pavement, kicking aside the gate he had
battered the night before.

For a moment he was overwhelmed, anticipatory sorrow
blocking his throat and stinging his eyes. But the rage was still
there, and he moved quickly toward the river, breaking into a
run. The houses were blurred, the streetlamps still on, and all
he could think of was Galen walking his dog. Nothing more
dangerous and nothing more clever than out in the fields
walking the damned dog.

He sprinted past the last house, his feet slipping on the wet
grass, squinting feverishly at the racing black river. Every few
yards he stopped to call Galen's name, his rage giving over to
panic. He fell twice as he slashed through the reeds at water's
edge, and again as he headed away from the river in a wide
circle toward the Pike. The wind sheathed him in ice, the rain
blinded him with stones, and he knew it was hopeless, that he
wouldn't leave till he'd learned.

No answer; only the wind, and the whipsaw of the grass.

He paused for a breath, a huge gulping breath while he
stared at the nearest house, not seeing, not feeling.

He could be out here forever as long as the storm kept its
lashing, but he didn't want to abandon the old man to the
rain. He couldn't. Not as long as he wasn't sure, not as long as
his greatest hope was that he was making a fool of himself
while Galen was somewhere warm, scratching Mutt's ears.

He wandered, wishing he knew how far Galen had walked,
how tired he'd been, what the dog might have chased. He
slipped down on his knees, his legs violently trembling, the
tips of his fingers turning blue. In desperation he tore at the
grass and ripped off his hat and crushed it between his palms.
Then he saw the vial in the grass.

He grunted, as the air took leave of his lungs.

He was unable to hold the vial still, close to his eyes to see
the capsules inside. He stood slowly, swaying, licking at the
water turning to salt at his lips, then stumbled forward when
he spotted the dark copper fur.

He knelt heavily, the vial dropping from his grip, and
stroked the dog's side while he searched for its master. But
there was nothing. Nothing but the rain, and the wind, and
the whipsaw of the grass.

It was an hour before he finally gave in, almost whimpering

when he discovered the sweater sleeve shredded in the mud. He picked it up and stuffed it deep into his pocket, then walked back to Mutt and cradled the setter in his arms. It was heavy, but he didn't feel it. He carried the body back to the house and lay it on the back porch, covering it with his raincoat before going inside.

Donna had been watching. He could only stare at her dumbly until she put her arms around his waist and drew his head to her breasts. Finally, he wept.

And in weeping felt the rage rekindle itself.

He pulled away and kissed her quickly, then hurried into his bedroom and changed into dry clothes. When he was done, in the bathroom, he stared at the mirror. A simple thing, he thought as he gripped the sides of the basin, to let the rage take him, and lead him, and . . . probably kill him. But what good would that do Galen? What good would it do the others? And in that moment he realized he was wondering what Galen would do if it had been Jason out there, lost and dead in the storm.

He scowled at his reflection. Thinking that way would only distance him again. It didn't matter what anyone else would do now; what mattered was him. For a change, it was him, not running but acting.

Donna was waiting by the hearth.

"Are you sure?"

"Yes," he said grimly, walked to his coat and pulled out the sleeve.

She turned away and placed her forehead against the mantel. "I feel like I'm going to crack," she said. Her fingers wiped her cheeks.

"Don't," he said softly. "For god's sake, I need you."

He moved toward her, one hand out, but the doorbell stopped him. He turned, as the door swung open, and Daniel Tallpines stepped in. He was soaked to the skin, and his shirt and hair were plastered to him darkly. Mud slopped on his trousers to his knees, and his hands were running grime.

"Sweetwater has a convertible," he said as he dropped uninvited into a chair. "It broke down four times coming in." Donna hurriedly fetched him a towel and he accepted it with a puzzled smile. He stripped off his shirt and began drying himself as best he could. By the time he was done he noticed her unease, and the redness of Jason's eyes. His hands slowed, and his chest swelled with a slow breath.

Jason pointed to the shredded sleeve on the coffee table between them. "Galen," he said. "And one of his dogs."

Daniel ground the towel between his hands, threw it hard to the hearth.

Jason watched without speaking, not daring to say a word in case blame might be leveled. And blame was something now to be avoided. When it was done and the horror was over and he could see straight again; maybe then. But, for the moment, something more had to be done than simply just sitting, or blaming.

Daniel began talking then, droning, his tone mournful, as his hands clenched and unclenched. He said nothing new, speaking mainly to Donna and taking his cues from her unquestioning belief.

Suddenly Jason looked up, his head cocked to one side. There was something . . . he rose and went to the window overlooking the porch. When he saw beyond the dripping from the gutter that the rain had finally stopped, he realized what he had heard was the silence.

The fingers of his right hand kneaded his chest as he turned slowly, knowing Galen was out there, and Windriver was still dying. He coughed away a single tear as he stumbled to the couch and let himself fall.

Donna looked at him quickly and saw his anguish. "So what you're saying," she said to Daniel, "is that we three here, and Simon and Aaron, are the only ones who really understand what's happened. What's . . . happening."

The Indian nodded wearily. "The rest of them, the New People, they think it was me or Aaron who killed the animals in some special way Rachel demanded. The people who died . . . they have their suspicions, but they don't think it was us. No," he said more quietly, "they don't know who."

"Neither do we," Jason said sourly. "Listen, Daniel, are you sure there's no way to tell? Maybe there's something you missed, something you weren't told. It's possible, isn't it? Isn't it possible there were secrets about this nobody told you?"

Daniel shook his head. "It's a difference in cultures, in beliefs. Your culture says such things are unnatural, are evil, and to protect the people there have to be signs. Not ours. We *are* the land and all that it implies. Nothing, from our way of thinking, could be more natural."

"But it's still just as evil," Donna whispered; and when he looked at her reproachfully, she bridled. "Well, damnit, it is! I don't care why it started, it's . . . it's . . ." She slashed the air angrily with the side of her hand.

"Damn," Jason muttered. "And you're sure it's not Rachel still, or that girl, Palemoon."

"Impossible," Daniel told him. "They were in sight all last night, Jason. All night."

"Then there's something else you have to tell us. If there's no way to pick out who it is, if we have to wait for it to show up again, we have to know how to kill it."

Daniel looked at him blankly; Donna turned to stare.

"Well?" he demanded, keeping hard rein to his temper. "Come on, Daniel, there's got to be a way! What is it, huh? Silver bullets, a crucifix, a stake, some special kind of bow and arrow? What?"

Tallpines put his hands to his face, dropped them and gulped as if he couldn't take in air. "I don't know, Jason. By god, I don't know."

"You . . . what?"

"I don't know, damnit!"

"Crazy! That's crazy. You know the stories, right? For god's sake, give us a clue!"

Tallpines reached out to him, but let his hand drop to the table.

"Daniel?" he said softly now, gently.

"I swear to you, Jason, I don't know. And I don't want to have to guess. I don't want to be wrong."

"Jesus!" Jason launched himself from the couch but ignored Daniel, who'd fallen back into his chair to avoid an expected blow. Instead he paced, and muttered to himself, his face dripping perspiration. Finally he returned to his seat and leaned forward earnestly.

"Daniel, you're the only one who can help us . . . the only one. You don't want to be wrong, but what the hell choice do we have? For god's sake, Daniel, give us something!"

It didn't take long for Daniel to decide, and Jason couldn't help flinching at the sudden fear he saw there. "A guess. All right, a guess from what I know."

Jason nodded.

"All right. Then I would have to guess . . . there's nothing."

Donna scoffed. "That's ridiculous, Daniel."

"How do you know?" he demanded. "You think you know so much?"

"I know myths," she retorted, leaving the hearth to stand directly in front of him. "And in every myth where there's a superhuman or monster, there's some way for that monster to be defeated. This . . . this werebeast, for want of a better word, has to have some mythology around it, Daniel. It just didn't pop into being out of thin air. In the stories. Think. In the stories, how do the good guys win?"

Tallpines looked so helpless he seemed ready to cry. "I told you," he said weakly. And he looked back to Jason. "I told you—as far as I know, the bastard can't be killed."

(5)

Kurt Steed watched a wood-sided station wagon glide past the window, but the streaks of rain on the glass prevented identification of the occupants. He tugged his lower lip thoughtfully and turned to Peg, who was checking on the level of the chrome coffee urn. "Peg?"

She looked over her shoulder and smiled.

He wondered, doubting, then made up his mind. "When Bea gets home I want you to take her into Pinedale. See your mother and spend the night."

She swiveled around slowly, her hands buried in her apron. "Kurt—"

"She ain't got an exam this afternoon. Take her, and I'll call you tonight."

"Kurt, please." She lay a hand on his arm, and he covered it quickly.

"Peg, there hasn't been anyone in here all damned day, and it's not because of the weather. Since Old Mac . . . you ain't been lookin, but I've seen a lotta shopping trips goin on, and it's only Tuesday."

"But Kurt, Jake and the others—"

He quieted her with a finger to her lips. "Peg, you've been as jumpy as a cat all day. And you know as well as me that with all that rain and stuff goin on they won't find an elephant out on those slopes if they walked under its belly. If that thing, whatever they're after, if it ain't died already on its own, it's hidin out in one of them caves on the Mountain, and nothin's gonna make it come out short of an earthquake." He hesitated, swiping with a cloth at the still shining, clean grille. "And maybe they missed it, went right by it. It's a big place out there, Peg. Maybe they didn't even see it."

She opened her mouth to protest, and he kissed her.

"For me, okay? Soon as Bea comes in." Then he turned around and saw Earl Carson walking past, head down, hands in his raincoat pockets. Kurt shook his head and looked away. Carson never left his store during working hours. Never. He looked at the clock and wondered what the hell was keeping his daughter.

Anthony Carosa was sitting in one of his brown leather barber chairs, watching colored static on the television set bolted to a ledge in the back corner of the shop. The floor was clean. The scissors and shears were clean. The variety of black combs were resting in their tall jar of disinfectant. Earl Carson came in and gave him a start.

"Hey, Tony."

He grinned and vacated the seat and dusted it with a flourish of an unsullied white towel. "My god," he said loudly, "a people!"

Carson laughed, shucked his raincoat and took the offered chair. With both hands he carefully smoothed his thinning, straggly hair back behind his ears. "Just a trim, if you don't mind."

"Business must be great, you comin out for an early lunch."

Carson shrugged and lifted his chin to accept the starched white sheet draped over his chest and pinned snugly around his neck. "Don't see David," he said, and cleared his throat.

"Out," Carosa said, flicking a glance toward the back of the shop.

"Lousy day to be runnin around, Tony."

"Yeah." David had been gone when he'd gotten up that morning, and neither Mary nor Carole had seen him leave. It worried him. David's wheelchair was still in its corner.

"Y'know," Carson said, examining himself in the mirror, "I'm beginnin to feel like I'm livin in a ghost town."

"Know what you mean," Carosa muttered as scissors snapped at the air over Carson's head.

"Next thing you know the dudes'll be runnin outa here like they were on fire or something. Damnedest thing. Goddamnedest thing."

"Yeah. Yeah, I know what you mean."

"It's crazy, Tony, but when I got up this morning I had the most powerful urge to toss Mabel into the car and drive down to Blairs. And maybe Pinedale. Just . . . out, y'know?"

Carosa nodded.

"Damnedest thing. If I didn't know better, I'd swear this place was jinxed."

"If you're bettin, Judge, I'm coverin."

Ellie wandered listlessly through the huge house, trying to shake off the effects of her previous night's restlessness. She knew she had to get into the office today and catch up on the paperwork that was going to drown her desk if she wasn't careful, but a fog seemed to have settled over her and she could not bring herself to function, or even get herself to move. She told herself it was partly the lack of proper sleep, and partly worrying about Steve out there on the hunt. She didn't want him hurt. But she kept having visions of monstrous grizzlies rearing out of some brush and swatting him over a cliff. It was foolish. He was going to be all right and she was only making it worse by dwelling on her fears. If she didn't do something soon, right now, her father would be furious. So she made herself the blackest coffee she could stand and took it out to the porch. The willows blocked the wind, but the damp chill was there, and the river raged with the feeding from the storm.

She smiled.

The water was black, the sky was angry, and far to the south the clouds split with dim lightning.

A miserable, bed-staying, mold-growing day.

She thought it was beautiful.

Ted Waters sat in the mouth of the deep cave and glowered at the rain. So far they'd been lucky; none of Harmon's idiot hunters had come across their path. No explanations, no new worries. But he had decided once the rain broke that he wasn't going any farther. The hell with it. The hell with the

bear and Felsom and all that other garbage. As soon as the
sky stopped its pounding he was dragging his ass back home.
And Felsom, the little weasel, could do his own dirty work
from now on.

(6)

They had argued for over an hour, but when it was over the
answer was the same.

"I don't think you can. I don't think it can be killed."

Donna groaned and rose, her hands hard against the small
of her back as she massaged the taut muscles that girdled her
with a throbbing. "I can't take it," she said, with half a smile,
half a frown. "I've got to get out of here, okay?"

Daniel said nothing to her, and Jason rose and walked with
her to the front door. His hand was pinching her arm and she
winced and pried it away gently.

"I'll be all right," she insisted quietly.

"I . . ." He could not say it, dared not nudge the shimmer
dark in his mind. Then he smiled and took off her glasses,
leaned back and studied her face until she was bewildered.

"Jason, what are you—"

"Nope," he said, and put them back. "Not like in the
movies."

Her teeth nipped at his chin. "You're babbling again."

"I can't do anything else," he told her. "If I really sit down
back there with Daniel and think—I mean, really think—I'm
going to scream."

"No," she said. "You're not." She kissed him, hard, then
opened the door. "I'll be okay. It's daylight. I'll be okay, and
we have to find out. You talk to Daniel, do whatever you have
to."

Where was she, he thought, fighting desperation, when I
was in New Jersey? "Where can I find you?"

She put her hands on her hips and grinned. "In a town this
size you're asking where I'll be? Hell, just stand on the porch
and holler."

He saw her image on the threshold long after the door
closed, long after her footsteps on the flagstone had been
swallowed by the storm. He refused to believe he was in love
with her; that kind of thinking only led to disaster. But he also

knew he wanted to give himself a chance to see if he could. And to do that he would have to . . . survive. Living, right now, was almost too much to ask.

When Daniel called to him anxiously from the kitchen he started, glanced out the window and saw that the rain had begun again, this time falling in a soft grey mist that reached in tendrils across the porch railing toward the house. He shuddered and rejoined the Indian, managing a thankful smile when he saw the sandwiches piled on the table.

"We Shoshone," said Daniel, "know our priorities. And no battle was ever won on an empty stomach."

Jason dropped into his chair, the heels of his hands scraping over his cheeks. "You think we're going to win?"

"Galen's out there," the man said coldly. "You going to leave him there for nothing?"

He jerked up his head as though he'd been slapped, his eyes narrowing and the rage rising from somewhere deep, somewhere cold.

"No," Daniel said, in his expression an obvious misinterpretation of what Jason was thinking. "Jase, I don't like this any more than you do. I don't want people to die. Not my people, not your people. Something . . ." He looked around the room as if the right words would fall from a cupboard or slide out from a drawer. "Something happened to Rachel. I know now she was after something more than she told any of us, but I don't know if Simon knew it. Now . . ." He lifted his hands weakly.

"Simon." Jason said it as if it were a new word in a new language, from a country he'd never heard of. "Simon. Surely now he'll—"

"He's gone," Daniel said sadly. "He's broken without Rachel. He doesn't care about anything anymore."

Jason frowned, his right hand pulling at his hair. "But Simon protected her, didn't he. He was sort of like her bodyguard." He looked at Daniel. "That means he knows how she could have been hurt." He smiled bitterly and rose. "So . . ."

"I'll go with you," Tallpines said. "They might not let you near him, otherwise."

Without thinking further, they each grabbed a couple of sandwiches and took Galen's Studebaker. Jason drove, and though they tried several times to speak during the trip out, their attempts at conversation faltered into silence. Tall-pines's face was impassive, but Jason could feel his own reflecting every passing thought. The fear he had accepted as a permanent companion now had at least lost its edge of unreasoning terror; what was left was a dull, exasperated anger at Simon and his wife—first for unleashing what should better have been left to fairy tales and ghost stories, and secondly for brandishing this weapon so coldly. It seemed to him MacKenzie's money should have been enough; there was no literal or metaphorical sense for all those deaths, or for making Galen leave him.

Again the storm shifted, and when he drove up to the house he was surprised at the number of cars in the drive, the children racing through the mud now that the rain had finally stopped. Their colors were bright, their laughter shrill and unfettered, and he couldn't help thinking that to most of them, Rachel's death meant little more than a day off from school. To them Galen Marsh and Gloria and Billy and god knew who else were nothing but names that belonged to the whites.

A dozen silent men stood on the porch as he and Daniel walked up; they were expressionless, hard-faced, moving aside only when Tallpines muttered to them sharply in a language he didn't know. Inside, the air was filled with cooking aromas, the soft voices of women, here and there a feeble death chant from a grizzled old woman. Sweetwater stood at the corridor door and looked at Daniel quizzically, receiving only a curt nod.

"Keep an eye out," Daniel said to him as they walked down the corridor. Then he turned to Jason. "Don't be too long, whatever you do." His voice was a whisper but Jason thought he was shouting.

When they arrived at the bedroom Tallpines knocked and waited, then turned the knob and ushered Jason in ahead of him. Palemoon was standing by the bed, her face serene and her eyes unsurprised. Simon, rumpled and bowed, sat in the tall leather chair facing his wife. Jason forced himself to look at the body and had to blink to assure himself she was actually dead. Her face was composed (*and old, so damned old!*), and her hair unruffled, as if her dying had been little more than a slipping, a gliding, away.

When Palemoon finally walked over to them, Daniel took

her gently to one side and began talking to her earnestly. It was apparent she didn't welcome the intrusion, but her confusion finally entrapped her and Daniel led her outside with a warning glance over her head.

The door closed and Jason hurried to Simon. The old man looked up, recognition slow but unpleasant.

"I've told you enough." It was the voice of a dead man.

"No," Jason said. He crouched in front of him. "I know, Simon. I know almost everything." The old man pushed back quickly, deeper into the chair. "I'm not going to try to make anyone else believe, if that's what you're worried about. But I have to know one thing—I have to know, Simon, what you were protecting Rachel against."

MacKenzie raised his chin slightly and looked at the body of his wife. He frowned and came close to shrugging.

Palemoon's querulous voice rose in argument from the hallway. Jason tensed. "Damnit, Simon, how could she die?"

"Old," MacKenzie said, the word matching his voice. "She was weak. Her heart—"

It was too much. All of it too much. He grabbed Simon's shoulders so suddenly the rancher whimpered and cringed. "You know what I mean, goddamnit. How can you kill them?"

MacKenzie shrugged off the grip, his eyes showing a brief glimmer, a spark, and his lips set tightly. Jason drew back a hand to strike him, snarled his disgust and shoved him away. Then he straightened and strode impatiently around the room, his eyes sweeping over the hangings on the wall. Eagles, all of them woven perfectly into backgrounds of mountain ranges and prairies, over villages and rivers . . . soaring, stooping, here holding a struggling animal in its talons, there gripping a dead meal on the ground and tearing at its throat. He looked around again and discovered that the one thing all the depictions had in common was an uncanny human quality about the eagles' eyes that gave them expressions otherwise impossible. Hauteur, disdain . . . hatred and superiority. Over the mantel was a scene of a village, the eagle above and the villagers surrounding an apparently composed woman. In all of their hands was a weapon of some kind. Near the door, an eagle grappled with a man—an evil man judging by the satanic fury in his face. The eagle had several feathered lances through its breast, the man's heart was exposed and torn. On the door's other side a similar scene, though here the eagle had a tomahawk buried in its back.

But it was the eyes. The eyes. Human, and red.

Jason whirled around, searching for a clue or a saviour, and his head began throbbing when he saw MacKenzie grinning at him. There was no grief-charged madness now; the man understood his wife had spawned a progeny of her powers, and he had no intention of instructing Jason how to destroy it.

There was silence.

He thought of Galen.

"God . . . *damn* you!" Jason shouted, and had taken one step toward the man's throat when the door slammed open and someone grabbed him by the shoulder. The touch was all he needed, after the talking and the wondering and the weeping and the remorse. He swung up his left hand and caught the unknown Indian on the side of his face. Unprepared, the man crashed into the wall with a cry joined by MacKenzie's.

"Jason!" Daniel yelled from the doorway. "Jason, what—"

Jason didn't know where they had been waiting or how long they'd been listening, but suddenly the French doors exploded inward and Tallpines was hurtled into the room in front of a rush. MacKenzie leapt instantly to his wife's bedside and flung himself over her. Jason kicked out at him as he passed, ducked a roundhouse and buried a fist into someone's taut stomach. He took a blow over his eye and gave one in return. A chair was swung at him; he ducked under it and butted the man into the nearest wall. A vase shattered. One of the totemsticks swayed. Hands pinned his arms to his sides, but he kicked back viciously and caught an unsuspecting shin, slipped loose and spun to one side to avoid a tree branch that split the air where his skull had been.

A large man stood grinning in front of him, a hunting knife in his hand. Jason put his boot into his groin, and the man shrieked, dropped his weapon and crumpled to the floor.

Another man took Jason's enraged kick high on his thigh but was able to club him with both fists across the forehead. Jason shook his head to clear the fire there and it was as if a knife sliced through the sudden fog in his brain. Suddenly he was clubbed again. His knees sagged and his legs wobbled. A brushing blow to his mouth followed. He tasted salt now, tasted blood. His arms were once again snared from behind, and someone was pummeling the back of his neck, the side of his face. He struggled weakly and moaned. His legs finally gave way and he felt the grip loosen. He yanked free, rolling toward the baseboard just as a kick skimmed past his ribs.

With his back to the wall he wiped a sleeve over his eyes and saw Tallpines wrestling with three men by the hall door. Sweetwater was lying motionless on the hearth.

"Stop it!" MacKenzie commanded.

A young man grabbed for Jason's shirt, and lost several teeth in the process; two more rammed their shoulders into his chest when he rose, and the air in the lungs left on the back of a torrent of fire. Feebly he tried to strike at their heads, but one of them finally put a fist in his stomach. A haze, black and red, slipped over his vision. He felt his right hand jab into some hair and he pulled, hearing an agonized grunt before his fingers were pried loose.

"Damnit, I said stop it, all of you!"

He fell and a kick aimed at his groin took his shoulder instead, snapping his head sharply into the wall. Sweat stung his eyes, and blood ran in and out of his mouth. It took him several seconds of gasping before he realized no one was trying to hit him anymore. A moment later he was lifted by his arms to his feet and held against the wall until he could stand. A cloth was pressed into his hand, and he dabbed gingerly at his face and eyes, until he could see. He looked at the cloth—it was stained dark red.

MacKenzie stood by the foot of the bed, flushed and quivering. "Take them out of here," he said, though he looked at no one but Jason. "Get them out of my house."

He was dragged through the building and out to the porch; then, without a word, he was dropped from the steps. He grunted as he landed on his hands and knees, kept his head below his shoulders to ward off the dizziness threatening to engulf him. The air was cool, caressing, and he gulped at it while he waited for control of his limbs. He did not look around when a body was dropped beside him, nor when another was dropped equally hard. He spat blood and sweat, and for the first time that day he wished it were raining.

Finally, he lifted his head and saw Daniel sitting cross-legged in front of him, wincing as his hands passed searching over his chest. He grinned, and Jason grinned back. Behind him Aaron was struggling to his feet. But when he heard a child laugh, the grin wavered, then faded, and he rose, gently, slowly, until he could stand without the earth spinning beneath him.

"You look like shit," Daniel said.

There was another laugh, muffled. Jason's heart pounded and he spun around without thinking. But when he stopped, the house and the children on the porch continued to revolve, the trees blurring, Tallpines and Sweetwater merging, the grey air and grey sky whirling as they faded to a comforting shade of black that was very much better than all that damned light. There was too much light. There was too much blood. There was too much laughter. The darkness that settled on him was much better.

The next thing he knew he was lying on the convertible's back seat, every square inch of him aching, every pore open to admit a slip of fire. Pins and razor blades found soft places to settle when the fire drifted away, and his knuckles felt as though they had been worked on with sandpaper.

He was alive, but he wasn't very grateful.

There were voices in the front, soft and anxious . . . but they deafened him. They bellowed and thundered, and he groaned and begged for the black to return.

And it did, and with it a silence, a warm summer's night silence that cushioned and suspended and encouraged dreamless sleeping. Unconsciousness. A faraway place that suddenly trembled and began slipping; and he was annoyed when he saw tiny pricks of white bobbing in the distance, obviously heading for him. He searched for a place to hide; he did not want to see them, did not want to hear the words that were filtering down through the black. The black haze lifted like a reluctant fog until he was blinking into the detached and wizened face of Doc Vance bending over him.

Jason groaned his disappointment.

Vance looked at someone standing behind Jason's head. "He'll be all right. I've seen worse when some of them dude hands can't take anymore and decide to rearrange Tony's place." He grinned and patted Jason's shoulder. "You'll be happy to know you're still alive, which is more than I can say for some of the souls I've been seein lately."

Jason did not dare smile; his face felt stiff, as if even thinking about movement would tear his flesh apart and start him bleeding again. The aches were still there, but they were dulled, and he picked out the pull of bandages taped under his lower lip, over his left eye, across his left temple.

Daniel floated into view, his crooked mouth puffed and a dark patch under his right eye. "Welcome."

Jason closed his eyes.

"MacKenzie called. Wanted to know if you were hurt badly. He said . . . he said he hadn't seen anyone take care of himself like that since your father let loose. He told me to tell you that. I don't pretend to know what it means."

"Get me drunk and I'll tell you," he said. His mouth, he was sure, had been flayed. His tongue probed each tooth he could find, and he was amazed not to discover new gaps, or any that were loose.

"Call me," he heard Vance say. "I'll be at the clinic for a couple of hours, then home." Then, in a whisper Jason wasn't meant to hear: "Would you mind tellin me what the hell's goin on?"

"Nothing," Daniel whispered back, his voice receding toward the door. "You know Easterners, Doc, and reporters. He said he was trying to get something for the paper's next edition and he . . . well, you watch TV, right?"

"Yes," Vance said doubtfully. "Well . . . call me if he comes up with something new. Those pills oughta help him sleep." He shook his head. "As if we ain't got enough trouble around here. Got one idiot in from that hunt already, thought he was shootin a snake. Was his own boot. Bah!" He left; Daniel whistled.

Jason waited until he was sure they were alone, then pushed himself gingerly up on his elbows. He was on the couch, a pillow shoved behind his head. Slowly, wincing and not caring if Daniel knew how much he hurt, he dropped his legs to the floor and waved away the man's silent offer of help. "Don't worry," he said, "I'm not about to get up. God! How they do it in the movies is beyond me."

"Stuntmen."

Jason looked at him sourly. "You have an answer for everything?"

Daniel took the rocker and stared at the hearth. "Nope." He crossed his legs. "Told Doc that Galen was missing, showed him the sweater."

"Oh . . . Christ."

"He wanted to know if you wanted to help with the looking."

Jason pinched the bridge of his nose. "I do. And I don't. I can't, Daniel, I can't."

"No shame in that, Jason."

The silence was almost soothing.

Jason glanced at the windows. The rain hadn't resumed, but it was considerably darker than he remembered it being. "Where's Aaron?"

"Charlie came for him a while ago. And Dawn."

Jason lifted an eyebrow.

Daniel shrugged. "No figuring women, especially Indian women. She was walking around Blairs, so Charlie says, when she decided she couldn't leave her folks just yet. So she came in and the two of them took Aaron away. He's all right. A dented rib and a mouse, that's all." He sighed, loudly. "I hate to sound like a bad movie, but I think the boy's grown up. Dawn, though . . ." and he shrugged again.

Jason couldn't think of a comment. The pills Vance had given him were making his brain feel as if it were floating just inches above the ground. Like a balloon, it drifted along sweetly, then touched down for a while, just long enough for a spasm of coherence before taking off again.

"What time is it?"

"Closing on five."

"Hell!" He nodded feebly when Daniel offered him coffee and waited silently until the man returned from the kitchen, then took the cup in two hands. He sipped to protect the cracks in his lips. "We didn't make it."

"Tell me about it, masked man."

Jason grinned as best he could. "What now?"

Tallpines hesitated in front of the rocker, then took the other end of the couch. "If you're really asking me, Jase—and I mean *really* asking—then I vote to stay inside until the sun comes up again."

It was tempting.

He shook his head. "And what about all the rest of them?"

"It's a bad night," he said reasonably. "Who's gonna go out?"

Jason slumped back, one arm crooked behind the pillow. He closed his eyes and considered, was about ready to concede when something stabbed him more sharply than his injuries. "Timmy," he whispered.

Daniel stiffened. "What about him?"

"If Aaron was right, Dan, and the boy was always too careful to get so close to the edge of the river, then this eagle of ours, this creature, it either knocked him in or frightened him into jumping."

"Yeah. Yeah, I thought about that. So what does that have to do with—"

Jason eased his throat into clearing. "MacKenzie denied everything. He wouldn't believe it, but Daniel, that happened during the daytime. That thing doesn't need the dark to move!"

TWO

(1)

As soon as she left the house, Donna turned without thinking toward the river. Water dripped from the leaves like ice-spiders seeking the slope of her neck, and she hunched her shoulders against them while berating herself wearily for not wearing her hat. She noticed little for the first hundred yards, thinking instead of how it would have been if she'd stayed in the East. There were dozens, thousands of communities where she could have set up practice and lost herself in work. The past would have passed, sooner or later; her stalking-ghosts would have faded into occasional nightmares and there was every possibility she would have met someone who would have exorcized her demons, just as Jason seemed to have done. But she hadn't. She had taken the path of least resistance, to a place she knew and whose people seemed to care, and now she was . . .

She ran a hand across her cheek to dash away a raindrop.

It was curious, she thought. In New York, or in most any other place in the Northeast, the idea of a werebeast would have been not only laughable, it would have been incongru-

340

ous to the setting. Here, however. Here in the mountains where the world was something better seen on television (and not always believed in spite of the pictures), there was something so utterly and completely natural, so frighteningly *right* about it, that her mind, instead of rebelling into insanity, had simply . . . accepted it. Based on the evidence of her eyes, of the deaths, and the whispersoft shadowfast sounds of passage, she accepted without question not only its existence but its right to exist.

She stopped in the middle of the block and saw the misty rain hovering in the foliage, the puddles on the sidewalk, the rivulets in the gutters. She heard nothing but the water slipping from the leaves, the gutters gurgling, the hum of the streetlamps. There were no radios muffled, no television sets mumbling, no automobiles hissing through the grey-light afternoon. She shivered and started walking again. She could have been in a cemetery for all the humanity she sensed near her, and decided at once that the river was too lonely. She swerved northward, toward the Pike, and stopped again.

Where am I? she thought.

The houses were unfamiliar, the air seemed different, the earth not level.

Where am *I?*

She was standing in the middle of a land bleached of color, chilled, streaked with rain, not the place she'd been living in where there was laughter, and caring, and voices that called her Doc even though they knew her first name.

A tic pulled at the corner of her right eye and she slapped a hand against it. She stood and stared at the nearest home until she realized she was looking at a woman sitting on the porch. An old, frail woman, wrapped in a worn black coat with a plastic rainhat over her grey hair and smudged makeup like a weeping clown, whose hands gripped a purse that even at this distance seemed crushed beyond recognition.

Donna took a hesitant step toward the walk, then hurried up the steps to stand beside Esther Lynn.

"I was thinkin'," Esther Lynn said, her gaze on the street, "that Galen and I were goin to be married soon. Took him damned long enough to ask me, y'know, but he did. He did."

Donna didn't know how the woman knew about Galen and was about to ask when Esther shuddered and looked up.

"I got all upset and bothered, y'see, when Jase called me

this mornin. So I biddied around like an old fart, then went over to the office. A call comes in. Bunch of kids who shoulda been in school were caught in the rain by the river."

"Esther," she whispered.

"He's over to Doc's, now. Wrapped up in a sheet. Doc is out somewhere, but word is the bear got him."

Donna put a hand on the woman's shoulder, feeling the tears she should have shed with Jason filling her eyes. Esther Lynn shook her off.

"They wanted me to identify him, but I wouldn't do it. I don't want to see him that way. They said it was a bear." Her eyes narrowed and became hard and dark and sparked a rage that forced Donna back. "I tell you, child, I am not gonna move from this spot until someone tells me what's goin on."

Donna shook her head helplessly, and when Esther Lynn turned away, she returned to the sidewalk.

"Girl!"

Donna turned as if someone had yanked her shoulder.

"You're a doctor and I'm a doctor's daughter, and I want to thank you."

"What? For . . . for what?"

"For not tellin me it was a bear."

A gust of wind made her duck her head. She did not look back when she felt her legs moving, felt her lungs trying to recapture their rhythm. One more word from the old woman and she knew she would go back and tell her everything. Let her know what had killed Galen, what was threatening to kill the town. But it wasn't because of pity. Esther Lynn had been around too long to expect land like this to hand her easy living; it was far too large, and the people far too small. And those, like Jason's father, who thought you had to conquer the land to live on it were the first ones to be driven off. Accommodation was the key, and compromise. And whenever something special arose you either figured a way to use it to your advantage, or you signaled defeat by moving out.

Esther Lynn wasn't moving out; she was only waiting to understand.

Good lord, she thought, I'm beginning to sound like the old-timers in Carosa's barbershop, the drinkers in his bar. The idea made her smile and eased her guilt, and when she reached the Pike she was reminded of the task she had set for herself—to snoop around a little, to see what she could so Jason wouldn't have to do it all on his own.

After all, he wasn't the only one who thought this place was home.

She had no idea where to begin, however, until she hurried by the sheriff's office window and saw a dim figure inside. She ducked into the luncheonette, ordering sandwiches and colas to go, thinking she would drop in on the law to find out if anything new had been heard from the men on the hunt. Not that she expected it; unless the storm let up they weren't going to get much of anything except, perhaps, a vicious cold or two.

Peg took her money glumly, and Donna held the waxpaper-wrapped sandwiches to her chest as she scuttled through the drizzle to the office. Once inside she straightened, and Ellie grinned at her from her place behind the front desk.

"I like your hair," Ellie said. "The rain does something for it."

"Thanks," she said, and held out one of the sandwiches. "Thought you might be hungry."

A telephone rang as Ellie accepted the offer gratefully, and Bill Oaker popped out of the cell block to pick up his extension.

With a disgusted wave toward the deputy, Ellie unwrapped her meal. "It's been like that since I came in," she said. "The folks who work in Blairs apparently spread the word, and now we got reporters callin in every five minutes, and people at the dude ranches tellin us about the herds of bears comin out of the woods—"

"Herds of bears?"

Ellie laughed. "That's what one of them called it. A herd of bears. All of them foamin at the mouth."

Oaker hung up, waved to Donna, then snatched up the receiver again before the bell had finished ringing.

"Madhouse," Donna said, still standing, chewing her lunch slowly and trying not to stare at the weariness laced across the younger woman's face.

"I know." Ellie stretched her neck, lifted her arms over her head and groaned. "I got to get vitamins or something, Donna. I've only been here since ten o'clock and I'm already wiped out."

Donna nodded, and half turned to look out the window. "Lousy day," she said softly. "Doesn't help the MacKenzies any, I'll bet." She looked back, and Ellie was watching her. "You knew Rachel pretty well, didn't you?"

"Yes," she said. "Back when, that is." She sipped at the cola. "Not since, uh, not for a while, though. I guess I outgrew her. Besides, she has . . . had her high school kids." Her voice turned flat. "You know, Kurt's kid, and Carosa."

"You going out there sometime? To pay your respects, I mean."

"Maybe. I don't know. Why?"

"Well, I thought I might, today or tomorrow, and I thought you might want to go with me. In fact, I tried to call you about it last night, but"—and she grinned—"you were gabbing for hours."

"Yes, I was."

Donna checked the storm again, if only to keep herself from examining the sheriff's daughter. Now, here, away from the house and Jason, she was beginning to feel foolish. In the flat office glare she'd discovered herself looking for a sign, a cabalistic clue; she blushed with guilt. For god's sake, she snapped at herself, you think she's going to sprout claws and feathers right before your eyes? Yet she could not refrain from noting the weariness again, how she kept rubbing at the back of her neck with one hand as though suffering through a cramp, how she held her pencil listlessly, almost as if she didn't know what to do with it. The answers the woman had given her meant nothing at all, and she couldn't tell if Ellie were lying or not.

Finally, with the sparse lunch over, she said, "What news from the front?"

Ellie seemed puzzled before she nodded. "Oh, I don't know." She glanced at the dispatch radio. "All that lightning gives us nothing but static. It's driving me—"

"Ellie," Bill said suddenly, "there's been a fender-bender out past the factory. I can't get Artie, so I'm goin myself." He mock-scowled as he shoved his arms into his raingear and slapped on his hat. "Jake always gets all the good stuff. Me, I gotta listen to a couple of dumb women arguin about who didn't signal where. Jesus!" He grinned and stomped out, and suddenly the office seemed larger, more quiet.

Two phones rang. Ellie, looking abruptly harried, appealed

to Donna, who shrugged and grabbed one, pulling a chair to the side of the desk as she did so. It was simple—no word, no panic, the sheriff will have a statement as soon as he's available. And once she'd taken the seat the calls kept coming for another twenty minutes.

"Hey," Ellie said when the last caller was begged off, "you're pretty good at that."

"Luck," she said, and would have risen to leave when the phones erupted again and Ellie turned her back. Donna found herself wondering at the edge in the girl's voice. She was tired, sure, but there was a trace of . . . what? Anger? Unrest? It bothered her. She jumped when the receiver slammed into its cradle. God, she thought. When Oaker returned Donna was on her feet, apologetically announcing her departure.

"I'm leaving, too," Ellie said then.

"Hey!" Oaker complained, half in and half out of his raincoat. "Damnit, Ellie . . ."

"I'm sorry, Bill, but I've got a headache that won't quit. I'm . . . really, I'm sorry."

"Yeah, sure." He dropped a clipboard onto his desk and glared at it. "What about you, Doc?"

"Errands. Office hours." She shrugged.

"You mean I gotta answer these things myself, *and* do all the paperwork, too? Christ, I'll be here to fu—to goddamned midnight."

"Then keep after Artie. He's supposed to be here, anyway," Ellie told him as she deftly swept a kerchief over her hair.

"Great. C'mon, Ellie, have a—"

"Bill, I'm not listening, do you hear me?"

Donna slipped out as the woman's voice rose petulantly, and almost smiled when she realized the rain had stopped and the wind had sighed down to a cool, lurking breeze. She continued west, telling herself she was not only jumping to conclusions, she was leaping at them with her eyes tightly closed. But she could not drive Ellie's voice from her mind, or the bitter look in her eyes, and by the time she reached her office her hands were trembling. She grabbed the phone, but there was no answer at Galen's. She stared at the wall, at the floor, looked through her front window and saw a bedraggled group of students leaving the high school.

Quit hiding, she thought as she pulled absently at her damp hair.

You've only talked to one; Jason had considered two others.

She hadn't seen Bea in the luncheonette, but that didn't prove anything; she might have an afternoon test. And so might Carole. She could always go to the school and find out.

She strode out quickly and crossed the street, angling to her right until she was in front of the bar. It was closed. There was no one in the barbershop but Anthony, standing near the back and dusting with one hand the arm of David's wheelchair. When he saw her through the window he waved, and she went inside.

"Need a shave?" he asked.

She laughed dutifully, trailing into silence when he didn't leave the chair. Glancing at the chair, she asked him where David was, and he sighed her a shrug.

"Should've been back by now," he said, kicking lightly at one wheel. "He's gettin worse, y'know. Worse."

Donna frowned, a hand raised to express her bewilderment.

"I mean, he's been takin these stupid walks at night and mopes around like his best friend died . . . I just don't know. He don't eat, either. He's gettin as bad as his sister."

She took off her glasses, pulled a handkerchief from her hip pocket and wiped at the lenses. "You know what it sounds like to me?"

"This a professional opinion?" the question stopped short of being completely bitter.

"A woman's opinion."

"Why the hell not?"

She felt nothing inside but a growing grave-chill, but she smiled when she said, "It sounds like he's in love."

Carosa looked at her, gaping, and exploded into a laugh that had him slapping at his legs. "David? My . . . David?" His laugh sobered a bit. "My . . . I'll be damned."

"The father," Donna said lightly, "is always the last to know."

"I'll be damned."

"Have to run. See you later, Tony."

"I'll be . . . damned. Never thought of it. I'll be damned."

She turned blindly to her left and walked swiftly, struggling to erect a barrier that would prevent her from thinking about the conclusion she'd already reached. David. Walks. Gone since last night. It was time to stop this feeble snooping around on her own. She was accomplishing nothing but a rubbing raw of her nerves. It was time to get Jason. On the other hand, he had enough problems without coping with a semihysterical woman who's supposed to be competent and rational. Be sure, then. Check it out and be sure. She walked as swiftly as she dared without running. Over to River Road, where she stood indecisively at the foot of the bridge.

She knew David well enough to understand the river would be his lure. Here is where he would do his thinking, his planning, perhaps even an indulgence in a little self-pity. Here. On the river.

The bridge's wood was rain-damp and slick, and seemed fragile enough to shatter at a sneeze. The river surged high and swift and dark; clumps of reeds in the shallows trapped leaves and small branches into temporary islands banked by white froth touched with yellow.

She walked to the center of the bridge and scanned the embankments as far as she could see. Maybe, she thought as she crossed to the other side, he didn't come here because of the storm. Maybe he found himself a woman and spent the night with her, was sleeping now in her bed with his hand over her stomach. A narrow footpath at the top of the steep southern bank was more stone than mud, and she walked it slowly eastward, hands jammed into her pockets, face averted from the slap of the wind. She wiped her cold nose with a sleeve and glanced across the river to Harmon's place. The day's gloom had deepened enough to show a light behind the front door. Upstairs, in the righthand corner, a window was open, and the tongue of a shade snapped over the sill. Ellie, she recalled, enjoyed the fresh air.

She walked, and saw nothing more, and four long blocks later reached the bridge at Middle Valley Road—steel, skeletal, built to last through the next century. She felt her cheeks grow stiff, her ears beginning to chap. The wind blew steadily now but enticingly soft. Two blocks later she reached Valley Ford Road and the town's third and last bridge. Iron and rusting, it rested on concrete blocks streaked with dull red and chipped blackly. Ahead of her the southern fields spread into a grey haze, a graveyard panorama, and the footpath stopped as if the rest had been sliced away. No further, it told her. The world ends here; go no further.

She shook her head in slow, thankful relief. No body. No sign. No nothing. She had done her part, and her hair was wet and her jacket was wet and she was going to catch pneumonia if she didn't get her butt back to Jason. No thought of her own home. Just back to Jason. She would let him decide. At least she hadn't been the one to find a body and confirm the fear.

It was bad enough about Galen.

She lifted her head as she turned around and judged another hour or so before the rain returned. She wanted warmth, and Jason to scold her for all this nonsense, to keep her beside him to battle the dragons.

She grinned, and had taken a step toward home when she saw it.

She stared, unmoving.

A clawed hand poked out of the clutch of reeds at the base of the near concrete piling. It was wrinkled, pale, veined with dark green slime. Swaying as it bucked the river's rush, torn between the current and the play of the wind. It seemed to beckon and she stepped off the path, dropping timidly into a crouch to keep herself from falling down the slick brown slope, squinting to get a better look. Beneath the surface was the glimmer of a white cuff. Halfway down she paused, arms outstretched, heels digging into the softened earth. She grunted, but she couldn't do it; she couldn't move any closer. The river pulled at her gently, molten dark glass sweeping by in soothing silence. She breathed deeply and turned slowly, her eyes fixed on the path. She grew afraid. The hand behind her moved closer—she could feel it and she became frantic, knees digging, toes pushing, hands pulling at clumps of weeds.

She slipped and fell several feet.

"No," she whispered, and slipped again.

The wind gusted and weeds slapped brittlely against her cheeks. Her hair darted like mothwings, blinding her.

"No," she screamed, grasping.

She flipped herself frantically onto her back and jammed her heels into the ground.

Her jacket had ridden up her back, her shirt pulled from

her jeans, and fingers of mud slid over her skin, needles of grass poked at her spine.

She could hear the river waiting for her, burbling and popping, boiling oil in a cauldron.

She had stopped moving.

She swallowed, took a deep breath, and slowly brought her right knee up and worked in the heel; then the left. Her hands shifted as she started to rise, and when she felt the ground threatening to give way she froze.

She could see the hand.

Her tongue pushed at her lips and she moved again, her palms and fingers testing for loose stones, for mud like viscous blood running down the banks.

Thunder.

Her protest was a whimpering groan, and she opened her eyes.

David's body had broken loose, for a moment buoyant enough to bring the shoulder to the surface, to expose the ravaged arm, the shredded sleeves of jacket and shirt. The arm crooked slowly, languidly, and the hand dove down to splash soundlessly into the sweeping black water. The elbow broke the surface, fleetingly, most of its flesh rubbed clean of the bone. Then she saw a leg—rags of dark cloth molded to glints of plastic and metal, springs and wheels, a brief glimpse of a shoeless heel.

Swimming, she thought madly; god, he's swimming; and she screamed in terrified revulsion. Her horror galvanized her feet, lashing them out, kicking them down and shoving her up. She flailed at the softened bank and moaned mindlessly until she felt the cold hard surface of the footpath beneath her back.

Her chest shuddered and a spasm arched her back as she collapsed in weary stages. She called herself a million kinds of fool. She wanted to laugh at the water, and at the hand she'd made a demon. She opened her eyes and greeted the lowering sky with a tremulous smile to prove she was all right now; even though she had managed to frighten a dozen years or so from her life, it was all right.

Oh, David, she thought; and there was no question in her mind what had chosen his grave. A tear rolled from her eye's corner, and she hastily, almost angrily swiped it away.

Then she rubbed them again with the back of her fist to

banish the speck that hovered below the clouds. But it remained. Came closer.

Oh god, not now!

Oh god

It sailed effortlessly above her, its magnificent wings spread to master the storm's currents. Dipping, and rising, circling black against the grey.

She scrambled to her hands and knees and was almost to her feet when she sensed the bird diving.

(2)

The streetlamps winked on just as the airhorn from the 4:50 out of Blairs sounded through the rainmist. The window of the luncheonette was speckled with diamond drops, flaring the right prism colors whenever a car passed with low-lights on, taillights dully gleaming. Kurt watched as one made a U-turn and headed east again, exhaust bluing the air for a moment before the wind took it. Then he pounded a fist against the counter, startling several customers in the booths —but they only glanced, didn't look or stare. They were grey shapes in the dim light, silent and sipping at their coffee and colas, placing their dollar bills under their saucers and slipping out quietly. Though none of them were watching, Peg smiled to excuse her husband's outburst, then maneuvered him expertly toward the register.

"But damnit," he whispered harshly, "it's almost five o'clock!"

"She's in love, honey, why don't you give her a break?"

He wasn't mollified. "Hardy knows better. She should have been home by now."

"Why?" she asked reasonably. "We didn't tell her any special time. Home for supper, as usual. Or call, right?"

"Yeah, well . . ." He sputtered into sulking silence.

Peg rubbed his back between the shoulder blades. "Look, if you're really that worried, I'll call the Carosas. Maybe Carole went with them, or knows where they went. If that doesn't work, I'll call Hardy's father." She kissed his cheek. "You're silly, you know."

"My baby," he said tightly, "is too young to be in love."

"I know, dear," she said calmly. "I know." She looked over her shoulder. "Stan wants another hamburger."

"Too young," he muttered as he turned toward the grille. "She doesn't know what she wants."

Esther Lynn wept soundlessly for an hour after Donna left her. Then she bustled off the porch and walked to her father's clinic. He was sitting behind his desk when she came in, but rose when she couldn't hold back a sob and took her in his ancient arms for the first time in thirty years. He wondered what in hell was going on in this town that men like Galen Marsh should be struck down by a crazy animal while fools like Ted Waters skated through life without so much as a sideways glance.

When Esther Lynn was done he gave her something to calm her and completed his report for the county medical examiner. There'd been no need to call Trumble in Blairs this time; the signs were the same as he'd seen on the bodies of Billyboy and Gloria, and rheumy Mac Felsom. Then he stopped writing in the middle of a sentence. Someplace in here he was going to have to mention Donna again, and the thought of her made him unreasonably angry. She was the vet, she was supposed to know about animals and why they did what they did; and if she was so goddamned smart why the hell wasn't she out with the hunters showing them where this . . . this thing that killed bulls and people was hiding? If she was so smart, why the hell . . . oh, what the hell. What the hell. He signed the form with a tired flourish, looked up and saw his daughter sleeping in the reception room. His eyes filled, his throat clogged, and he decided come the end of his summer he was going to retire. He'd had enough. He was too old.

The town he had lived in all his life had become, almost overnight, like something from another planet, like one of them shows on *The Twilight Zone* when you found out the Martians really were hiding in all the corners and running things from a little grey box chock with toggles and dials . . . when Windriver turns into something like that it's time to turn the diploma to the wall, pull the quilt over your head and wait for the rooster to tell you the night's gone.

From the bottom drawer of his desk, he pulled his bottle of

medicinal-purposes-only scotch into the light, twisted off the cap and drank without a glass. There was no getting around it. He was scared half to death.

The hell with it, thought Jake Harmon. When word of finding Galen had come to him he'd almost called off the hunt, determined to summon the state police or the National Guard or the goddamned Air Force. But sounds in the forest had deterred him, sounds of thrashing, running, and he'd urged his men on, letting them know of the new victim, playing on their newly fed anger to keep them from despairing, from grumbling, to keep their fingers on their triggers and their noses to the wind.

But it was darker now. The clouds had thickened, the 4:50 had wailed its way across the valley, and it would be pitch black in an hour.

"The hell with it." He lifted the walkie-talkie to his lips. "All stations, this is Harmon. The rain'll be back soon, we're callin it a day." He dropped his hand to his side and shook his head. His joints ached and his head throbbed, and if Steve told him one more time—

"Hey, Dad."

He turned around.

"I'm staying."

Harmon didn't want to argue. "Suit yourself."

"A few of the guys wanna stick around, too."

"It's your pneumonia. Just keep your head down."

Steve hesitated. "Tell Ellie not to wait up."

Sure, he thought. So what else is new?

Kramer's Mountain turned black before the rest of the slopes had even thought of greying. Sounds died quickly, the wind turned high-pitched and the rain came down sheathed in winter.

"Over there!" Arnold whispered suddenly.

"What?" Waters was angry. They had talked him into sticking around—the both of them scared shitless of Felsom—and now they were hearing bear around every damned rock.

"Damnit, Ted, over there!"

"All right, all right." He hefted the shotgun. Who the hell did Titus think he was anyway? Kit Goddamned Carson?

(3)

Jason lifted his head at the sound of the train. The daylong twilight seemed to deepen at the passing, and the rain dripping from the eaves fell in slow motion. Jeff was playing outside, chasing a tattered, striped rubber ball over the sodden grass; every few moments she would stop and shake water from head to tail, charge again with a yelp he couldn't hear.

"Damn."

He yanked his hand from the frying pan and sucked on it where a splatter of grease had landed. As he churned the eggs carefully with a fork, wondering if he'd added too much milk, he felt a curious sense of dislocation—just beyond the willows, he thought, was the Atlantic Ocean, the surf plunging in whites and greys to the beach while the gulls and terns, forced inland by the storm, were wheeling and crying, scolding their frustration until long after dark. The bite of salt air. The crunch of sand underfoot.

The bacon hissed, the ocean faded, and he grinned. Somehow, in all the novels that he'd read, none of the heroes ever took time out to eat, as if fear had squelched appetite, not stoked it. His own body, on the other hand, had long since run out of fuel and, as Donna had told him, it was better than sitting around waiting for the roof to fall in. He laughed aloud, and winced when his mouth and cheek protested the movement.

The pain reminded him of the call from Doc Vance. He thought of Galen lying on a cold metal table encased in dark green plastic, and thought of those same noneating heroes who took hold of their revenge and stormed into the night to do battle with their evils.

None of *them* seemed frightened.

He was terrified.

The wingéd serpents had come home to roost, and he knew he was hiding.

The scrambled eggs were done, the bacon ready, and he called out to Daniel before he could turn tail and run.

"I'm going back to the ranch after this," Tallpines announced as he walked into the kitchen.

"You haven't even tasted it yet, for god's sake."

Tallpines laughed. "It's Simon, not your . . . cooking. I'm worried about him, though I hate to admit it."

"But the others . . . won't they—"

"I don't think so. No salt, thanks. I'll do my humbled Indian corrupted by the whites routine and most of them will forgive me."

"And Simon?"

"Who knows? He's not the enemy now, but maybe . . ."

They ate without speaking, forks scraping the plates, cups rattling on saucers. Jason thought of Donna and only prayed that the woman had sense enough to stay on the main street.

Suddenly, a frenzied barking broke loose in the front. Jason was out of his chair and out of the room before Tallpines had jumped to his feet, kicking his own chair back against the refrigerator. The barking filled the house like a scream. Visions of that monster tearing at red fur propelled Jason to the door but made him hesitate for a moment before flinging open the door.

Donna fell into his arms.

Jeff was standing on the top step, yowling at the trees.

He shouted at the dog, slipped a hand behind Donna's knees and carried her to the couch. She was covered with mud, her jacket and shirt plastered with bits of grass blades and leaves. He called for warm and wet towels as Daniel raced into the room, then slowly peeled off the coat and tried to wipe as much mud from her face as he could with trembling hands. She was cold. Her complexion was pallid, her lips purple, and her attempts to fend off his ministrations were alarmingly feeble.

"Quiet," he told her, combing back her hair. "Later. Later."

There was no blood, no signs of gouging. He quickly muttered thanks, and pulled off her clothes, then grabbed a coverlet from the rocking chair, a patchwork and wool one Esther Lynn had made for Galen. Donna pulled it instantly to her chin, less out of modesty than from the shuddering chills that drew up her knees. Jason rubbed her shoulders softly.

Jeff was still barking.

"Jesus," Daniel said. He dropped the towels on the coffee table and ran for the door. Jason listened, tense and heard him scolding gently. The barks slid to threatening growls as

Daniel led the setter into the house and closeted it in the spare bedroom.

"She needs tea," he said, and Daniel nodded agreement.

Fifteen minutes later Donna was sitting up in the corner, trying to keep her damp hair from straggling to her eyes. Jason sat on the floor beside her, holding her hand and patting, rubbing, every so often squeezing tightly while she explained what she'd done since leaving the house. Her teeth began to chatter when she described the body in the river, her eyes clamped shut when she told him how it beckoned.

"And then," she said, neck muscles taut in her attempt to keep her voice steady, "I thought it was there, coming after me." She laughed quickly, a hollow deep sound. "What an idiot. It was normal. Just a dumb hawk going for a meal. But it was there . . . it was watching me . . . or I thought it was watching me and I screamed so loud my throat hurt and Jason, I couldn't run! God, I tried, but I kept falling, and once I almost went back down the bank. I was yelling and I fell again and cut my arm and . . . I kept on running. I waited for it to grab me or knock me down or . . . something! anything! and I looked up and it was, it must have been a good half-mile away, circling and waiting and I could see red on its wingtips and it was nothing but a hawk, Jason. A fucking hawk!"

Her eyes were wide open and filling with tears and she was staring around the room. Her mouth gulped for air, and she wept.

Jason held her hand.

She used the coverlet to wipe at her tears, smiling and weeping and her breath catching in a choke until she shook her head violently and started to cough.

"I'm going crazy," she said when she recovered herself.

"You were crazy for leaving town like that," Daniel said with a sympathetic smile. "And so saying I'm heading out to the ranch. But at least I've got a car."

"Just put the top up," Jason warned.

"Top? What top? You think Aaron would spend a couple hundred bucks for a top on a car he only paid fifty dollars for?"

Jason pointed to the gun cabinet in the hall. "Take something."

Daniel considered, then nodded and finally left with a

30.06 rifle tucked under his arm. He promised to call the first chance he had, and when Jason groaned while waving good-bye Donna noticed for the first time the bruises and the bandages. Forgetting her own fright, she grabbed his shoulders and demanded to know what he'd gotten into while she'd been fighting specters.

"And Dan called me crazy?" she said when he'd finished. "Jesus, Jason, that was a dumb thing to do."

He examined the scrapes over his knuckles. "Maybe. But it's given me the only decent idea we've had since this thing started."

"What?" she said.

"The victims."

She took a long, deep breath and shook her head. "I don't want to hear it. Not now." She flung the coverlet aside and stood. "First I take a shower. Then I'll listen. I'll think, too, and maybe get the same idea."

He wanted to leer at her kiddingly, but in spite of her disarray and nakedness, nothing at the moment could have been more neuter. "All right, but hurry."

She did, and when she returned she was wearing one of his dark shirts and a matching pair of corduroy trousers. Her hair was still wet, copper glinting through the dark, and she worked at it idly with a towel while he set a match to the fireplace kindling. "Summer," he muttered, "and here I am lighting a fire." He made a noise of sorry disbelief and rocked back on his haunches. The flames were low, the sparks snapping like skeletal fingers. Donna sighed in comfortable relief and told him, nervously, that she was ready.

"A connection," he said. "A small one, a minuscule one, but it's there."

When he paused she said, "Is this twenty questions?"

"We know how this started from what Daniel told us and from what I found out," he said after a moment's toying with the poker. "And we know why, now. But something Rachel didn't count on was that this disciple of hers has a mind, a will, a . . . a hatred of her own. Whatever control Rachel had was eventually lost—if there was any real control in the first place. And the people who died, even Gloria and Billy, they're all part of Windriver. The old part, as it were. Nobody, none of the new people, none who work for the candy plant or who came in after the Indians started their encroachment . . . none of them have been killed. It's the old families, the ones with ties."

Donna scratched at her knees. "So? That still leaves an awful lot of people, Jason."

"I know," he said glumly. "But it's also the first damned thing about this that makes sense."

"Huh? How?"

He leaned forward. "We know why Rachel was so determined to drive Windriver out. This other one, I think she hates it because she's forced to live here. Age, marriage, disability—something is keeping her here and she's let her mind be taken over by what she'd done. Her soul . . . I don't know if there's a real soul or not, Donna, but something inside her has blackened, has been corrupted, made so damnably evil you can reach out and touch it."

Donna tilted her head, frowning in thought. "It's all very nice, Jase, and I think you're right. But it still leaves us with the same question, doesn't it."

"Yeah."

He slipped into a musing silence, convinced he'd told her all he knew, and just as convinced during the telling that he'd missed a step somewhere along the way. He had a feeling that at some point over the past few weeks he had been given a clue, perhaps even the answer. He argued himself silently into a dozen different corners, and each time could see the partially open door on the other side of the room, a door through whose crack was a shadow demanding definition. But the more he circled it the more his head ached. He accidentally rubbed the back of his injured hand over his thigh, and his knuckles burned fiercely; his chest throbbed; his skull felt as though ice tongs had been implanted to pry out his brain. Finally he realized Doc Vance's medication had worn off, and action and thinking were beyond his strength now. When Donna headed into the kitchen for more tea, he asked for the pills the doctor had left behind.

And as soon as she was gone, he thought of Galen and stared at the flames.

I'm trying, old man, he said silently to the colors of the fire; just don't hate me if I don't have a white horse to ride on just yet. I'm trying. God, Galen, I'm trying.

Donna returned and offered him the pills. He took them, chased them with water and didn't protest when she told him to lie back. The fireplace warmth soothed him. The mortal reminders of his fight faded to dull red. He smiled, and he swallowed, and he never marked the point where the pills drugged him into sleep.

(4)

Donna grabbed his glass before it slipped from his grip to the floor. She did not try to wake him. Humming to herself tunelessly, she carried the glass into the kitchen, scooped the plates from the table and set them neatly in the sink. Then she washed and dried them, and placed them back in the cupboard. She returned to the living room where she picked up the wet towels still dark-streaked with her flight. She took them into the bathroom and hung them over the shower rod, then walked back into the hall and stood in front of the gun cabinet.

She heard Jeff whimpering in Jason's room.

Tallpines had left the glass door of the pine cabinet open, and after a minute's indecision she took two revolvers from their pegs, box of ammunition from the drawer at the cabinet's base, and returned to the living room.

The fire cracked at her.

Her nose wrinkled at the pungent sting of pinesmoke.

She kissed Jason's forehead and lay a gentle palm to his cheek. Then she pulled the rocker from the hearth and set it carefully at the carpet's edge. She sat and loaded the guns. The first one she lay on the thin cushion by her thigh, the second she held in her cold right hand. She faced the door. She curled her finger around the trigger and listened without thinking to the rising wind's keening.

She sat, and she listened, because she knew it was out there.

THREE

Danger.

She slipped away from the side of the house, pushing impatiently at the shrubs that barred her way to the lawn.

Danger.

At first she hadn't really believed the newcomer could cause her serious trouble. He was such a sad-looking man, such a short man for all that muscle he carried on his shoulders. She really hadn't thought he'd be able to do it, to make the leap from the improbable to the real. But she couldn't blame it all on him, that would be unfair. It was her own fault. She couldn't yell at anyone but herself. She shouldn't have done it, that much was obvious, but he had looked so confused, so *funny* out there on the tracks that she hadn't been able to resist. And god, how he ran! The two of them running like a couple of drunken Siamese twins. God, that was great. God!

And her laugh coming out of the dark. She had to admit it was a nice touch. She wished she had thought of it before.

But now there was danger and it was all her fault.

He knew, and she knew.

And it didn't make any difference that no one would believe them. There was danger because she'd played a silly game that wasn't silly at all.

No question about it—they would have to fall, both of them together, from their own Lover's Leap, and she was the only one who could push them. And for that she needed patience. Lots of patience, and no more mistakes like showing herself on the tracks, thinking it was a game. Patience. And they would be dead. She smiled to herself. They would go out tonight, of course. They had to. They were different. They weren't like the other farts who would stick close to home and wait for the storm to blow over. No. *They* would go out, because she was out here and they knew it. Here. *Here!* She was the bait, and she was the trap.

She shoved through the hedge that separated the Marsh property from its neighbor and ran to the picket fence and climbed over it agilely. The wind whispered love songs in her ear as she walked toward the Pike, and she clamped a hand over her mouth to stifle a giggle when Earl Carson's German shepherd whimpered and cringed on the porch as she passed. She wanted to turn around and shout *boo!* at it, but stopped herself just in time. That was kid stuff. And she wasn't a kid anymore.

Lord, Rachel, she thought then, you didn't tell me it would be like this!

She paused at the corner, for a moment somewhat indecisive. On the one hand she thought it prudent to let her father know where she was going; on the other, he just might try to talk her into staying close to home. Dangerous out tonight, he would tell her, and I don't think it's a good idea for you to be walkin around alone. She grinned to herself, then frowned.

They were watching her.

They were *always* watching her.

You couldn't walk ten steps in this godforsaken town without someone watching where you were going and whispering it to someone else who whispered it to someone else and sooner or later it got back and then all you did was answer stupid questions about where you were going and what you were doing.

And it had been so nice, too. Once upon a time.

She leaned into the shadow of a tree and studied the jeeps, the campers and the cars as they drew slowly away from the sheriff's office. Many of the wet, grumbling men had already walked across the street to the sanctuary of the bar; others had hurried right home. A number of them smiled at her as they passed, but none stopped to pass the time. That was all right with her. She wasn't at all sure she could carry on a decent conversation now, or answer the same silly questions, or smile the same silly smile.

She was glad they ignored her.

The way she was feeling—so good, so free, so far above it all—they might think she was drunk, and then the shit would hit the fan and she would have to pretend she was sorry and play the little girl until it all calmed again. That would be too much. More likely she would lose her temper.

They ignored her except for those smiles, but she was a little disappointed they hadn't shot anything out there on the slopes. That would have given her a little more time, another couple of days at least to weed out the bastards who made her life miserable, even if they didn't know it. Then she would have been content, she would have been able to work on her patience and only take care of things when she was feeling trapped, or cornered, or . . .

No; that was a lie. She would have gone on. And on. Slipping away from their stupid guns and their stupid hunts and their stupid traps because everything that had been given to her she had discovered was fun.

The kind of fun you dream about when nothing works right.

The kind you pray for, and it never comes true.

Except now. Except . . . now.

She smiled.

She would go on anyway and only the lovers would know what was really happening to this town. And *they*, poor things, wouldn't be around to tell anyone.

She ducked around the corner when the street emptied and there was nothing but the mist, the wind and the lights from the stores. Deep into the sidestreet shadows the dark took her and warmed her and called her its own. She wouldn't go home. The hell with her father. The hell with them all. She didn't need anyone's permission to do anything anymore. She was a big girl now, and she could take care of herself. And there wasn't enough time to take a chance on trouble.

Danger.

There was danger.

And besides, she was hungry.

FOUR

(1)

The grey hat had been on the back seat. In its prime the crown had been Hoot Gibson high, the brim stiff and upturned Aussie style. But that, Daniel thought, must have been a zillion years ago. Now its color was stained and faded, the crown battered, the brim floppy. He wore it without caring how foolish he looked because the mist was thickening to fog and he'd been soaked enough for one miserable day. He'd also found an army slicker with the sleeves cut off under the front seat; but again, considering the weather it was better than nothing.

He sat on the convertible's hood, a cigarette in his right hand. Less than fifty yards away was the turn to Elkhorn Road. He sighed loudly, stopping just short of an exasperated shout. He'd tried to locate a reserve of anger when the car had sputtered, bucked and died; he had walked around it in rigid fury, kicking at the bald tires and slamming open the hood. But it didn't last. Nothing he could see in the dim light was out of place. Resigned, he'd donned hat and slicker, dug a cigarette from his breast pocket and took his place in front of the windshield. He wasn't about to walk, not when he stood a better chance of getting help by staying where he was, and not when his ribs and legs still ached so much from the fracas in the deathroom.

All he needed now, he thought sourly, was a feather to stick in the headband, and a carload of tourists to come slithering by and take his fool picture. Though it could be worse: a flaming Eastern liberal could pull over and deafen him with platitudes.

He could always walk to Aaron's place, but that again entailed a physical effort he knew he couldn't sustain for more than a hundred yards. He'd never been beaten quite so brutally, and he was still astonished. There'd been fights, of course, and he'd had his share of black eyes and split lips, but the people who'd kicked him to the floor had been of a different breed than he was used to. The same color skin, but the inside was different. They thought they were protecting the sacrosanct grief of a great and humble man. They didn't know. None of them knew.

He wished he had Sharon with him now. He needed her. He needed to tell her at last what he'd gotten into, needed to tell her he was going to get out before he destroyed everything they'd worked for over the past eight years.

"Ah, *hell!*" and he tossed the cigarette glowing into the dark. It was no use. He felt guilty. He knew it was guilt. If he hadn't seconded the suggestions Rachel had made all those years ago, none of the others would have moved up here with him. As it was, he suspected ninety percent of them no longer believed in the old ways, no matter how much Rachel had influenced them then. All he'd wanted, all any of them had wanted, was off the reservation and onto a plot of land measurably larger than a man's noontime shadow. And they had gotten it. Each of them took the loan and purchased the property and put enough aside for them to live until Rachel told them it was all right to start ranching again. The land, the freedom, was a small price to pay.

He should have believed more thoroughly. He should have known that Rachel—indomitable, pigheaded, frighteningly wise—could do all that she said. Simon believed it, why the hell didn't he?

A car whispered out of the east without stopping. Daniel gave it a lazy middle finger.

And now Rachel was dead and there was . . .

He shuddered. The hood grew cold under his buttocks, and he slipped to the ground, stamped his feet and reached into his pocket for another cigarette.

Hell, he might as well walk. He drew the tobacco smoke into his lungs and coughed, wiping away the tears with the heel of his hand.

There was another pair of headlights. He stepped to the white-bordered blacktop and peered toward town.

The car slowed, then stopped. Daniel leaned to the passenger window and waited for it to roll down.

"Mister Tallpines," Earl Carson said.

"Evenin, Judge. You catch anything out there?"

Carson grinned sourly. "Pneumonia, that's all. Now I gotta go to Washakie to pick up some cloth."

"Ah." He waited. "I'm headin out to MacKenzie's."

"I don't know," Carson said doubtfully. "I'm not exactly—"

"As far as the entrance?"

Carson stopped debating. "Sure, why not. The only thing is, I might sneeze us off the road."

Daniel laughed as best he could. There was no conversation as they left the Pike for Elkhorn, and bored through the growing dark; and he thought it was just as well. It allowed him to concentrate on his fading aches, the warmth of the heater, Rachel . . . He grunted when the judge made a clumsy U-turn at the arch, and he thanked the man with a nod. He paused with his hand on the cold-damp door's handle, tempted to ask Carson what he thought about the existence of monsters in general, the supernatural kind to be more specific, and to pin it down further, . . . but he got out quickly and slammed the door, and stood in the middle of the road while the taillights shot over the far rise and disappeared.

It wasn't until he was alone that he realized how close to night it had grown. The clouds had thickened, and the wind rose as he stood there, dispersing the mist and leaving black behind. His skin felt clammy. He thought he could hear singing in the distance, a chanting, and he drew his arms into the slicker to put his hands into his pockets.

A story, he told himself; you need a story, Dan, or they'll scalp you for sure.

And then he heard them.

The sound of wings.

Lazy, using the wind, settling like the rustle of an old sheet dropped over a chair in a house long deserted.

He heard a light *scratching*, and a shifting of weight. Patiently waiting.

Daniel struggled not to scream. He felt it churning in his throat. It pulled the muscles of his neck into cold iron bands; and hollowed his cheeks. It petrified his jaw, gripped his lungs and spread ice in his stomach and lead in his feet. He swallowed and pulled his hands from his pockets. Slowly.

Scratching.

He would not turn around to look Death in the eye. If it happened (when it happened) he wanted to be facing the land he lived on. It was the only thing left he thought he deserved. A small thing. A very little thing, given to himself now because he had left Galen's rifle in Sweetwater's car, had been part of the terror since the terror began, had believed Jason and Donna and every word they'd said, except he could not believe it was real, it was now, it was waiting behind him because of his guilt. Payment; he thought he had paid with the nightmares he'd had and understood now he'd misjudged the price.

All in a split second while he decided not to scream.

Rustling.

He took off the hat with the Hoot Gibson crown and the Aussie brim and he scaled it to one side. Then he pulled the slicker over his head and dropped it to the ground. Slowly, cautiously, listening intently, he stretched his arms in front of him, his hands into fists.

He took a step toward home.

A step toward Sharon and the little girls, who were sleeping soundly, perhaps, and thinking about the way he'd been behaving.

He took another step.

Rustling.

Of all the ways he had thought he might die, this was beyond the reach of his imagination. But then, it was payment, right? It was what he deserved.

A third step.

Rustling.

Payment, Daniel.

He bolted straight down the center of the road and when he knew the pursuit had begun he veered sharply to his left and threw himself over the low stone wall. His shoulder struck the ground first and he groaned; and where he had launched himself from the gravel on the road's verge the air ripped apart like the Biblical temple curtains. He scrambled to his feet, and followed the wall southward.

He couldn't help it now; he looked up.

It was banking in a wide, slow turn . . . and he was heading directly for it.

He looked for trees. There were none.

The car, then, and the rifle on the front seat; but it would never let him get that far.

All he had was the wall and his legs.

He slowed to a trot, swerving whenever he caught sight of a possible tripping depression. No sense in racing. He had no intention of attempting close combat; all he could do was preserve what puny strength he had and try to reach the empty Perkins house. Even if there were no weapons inside, he didn't expect the eagle to try to follow.

Who are you, he wondered then; who the hell are you?

It climbed, but he didn't track it; he needed his eyes for the snares, for a possible shield or an improbable weapon. He heard the sweep of its descent, and just before it reached him it flared its wings back and up to cut its speed while its talons thrust forward and . . . he vaulted the wall again, slipping on the wet stone and falling to one knee. Trouser leg and flesh tore. He heard the passage, chanced a glance back and saw the wings rising and dipping, banking, climbing, keeping pace with him against the darkening background of the clouds. Not hurrying. Why should it? It had time and the dark and an ordinary man on its side.

He paused only once—when the lonely, tearing *screeee* of its cry settled over him in something less than a challenge. It wasn't a taunt, it wasn't a promise. It was nothing more than a simple marking of the quarry.

Goddamnit, who are *you?*

He used the wall to keep him upright, pulling to give his stride that desperate extra inch. The flesh between his shoulders tightened, anticipating a blow. When he slipped again he cursed and moved to the road. The sound of his boots was loud and oddly reassuring. It seemed as if he were moving more swiftly now, the wind coming at him from the west and buffeting him to the other side. Not hard, just a nudging. His mouth opened and demanded more air, his arms settled into a painful rhythm that matched each step. Head up, eyes partially closed. Up and over the rise.

He slowed almost to a halt and spun around, throwing up his hands as the eagle neared the killing point of its dive. His left foot plunged into a pothole and he fell backward, screaming at the ripping he felt at his ankle, at the breast feathers scraping over his face as it aborted its charge in bewildered astonishment.

Daniel rolled onto his stomach and watched the giant bird bank sharply. The game was over; the fun was gone. It would work as before, but this time for the killing.

He decided to take another chance with the wall, and darted off the road, and stopped, staring at the fence stupidly.

The game was over.

But still he ducked between the split rails, stumbled forward and threw out his hands to keep from falling. He grabbed a greyed branch half-buried in the tall grass and dragged it along behind him. He would use it if he had to, but the bobbing house seemed too close now to deny him.

It cried out.

He wanted desperately, fiercely to ignore it, but reflex turned his head.

His mouth opened, and it took a terrified long time before "Jesus" came out.

She was standing on the fence, one bare foot square on a post, the other curled slightly over the top rail. Her hands were on her hips, and the only thing white in that dusky grey light was the teeth of her smile.

His lips worked to form her name, but there was no air in his lungs.

"Peekaboo," she said sweetly. "I've got you."

Instinct made him bring the branch to his chest as she raised her arms and *lifted*. Fear froze him as she laughed softly and *changed*. Dumbstruck he watched the eagle soar over the land on the opposite side of the road. Wheeling indolently, then dropping and swinging about. It came at him chest-high, swiftly, wings undulating without effort, its eyes catching the last of the day's light and sparking it red.

He watched the body shift gracefully, saw the talons spread, and felt his tongue work uselessly at his lips as he hefted the branch to his shoulder and turned his side to the attack. Not at all brave, but with nothing left to do.

Sharon. And Rachel.

He changed his mind at the last possible moment and spun the branch into a lance, flinging himself forward and down with his arms stiff and out. The impact caught him before he hit the ground . . . and he screamed. Both shoulders were dislocated. He flopped on the wet grass, groaning and sobbing, then swayed to his knees to search for the body. He lifted his head and saw the eagle turn again.

The branch had been rammed through its breast. He could see a splintered portion of it protruding from its back. With his arms dangling at his sides, the agony a veil, he watched as the bird gave itself a shudder and the branch fell away, end over end to impale the ground.

What can kill it? Jason asked.

As far as I know . . . nothing.

His back began to sag as the eagle began to dive.

As far as I know . . .

Daniel wept as he looked his Death in the eye.

He was right.

He was

(2)

"My sweet lovin Jesus, will you look at that," Ted Waters said, shaking his head in admiration. Then he looked at Chet, who was holding the lantern aloft. "That there, m'friend, is the meanest fucker I have ever seen."

Titus Arnold preened silently, accepting the unspoken congratulations as his due. He wasn't about to tell anyone, however, that his eyes had been closed when he emptied his chamber.

"Blew his goddamned head to kingdom come."

Chet nodded. "Beautiful. Absolutely beautiful."

Waters laughed and slapped at his thigh. "Christ, Titus, I didn't think you could do it. Damn. Hot damn!"

Chet nodded his agreement, then kicked at the bear's rump. "Got a question, though."

"What?" Ted said, not caring at all.

"You really expect us to carry this sonofabitch all the way back to the truck?"

(3)

Jason woke with a cry, nearly throwing himself from the couch before Donna had a chance to call out his name. He looked at her, then fell back wearily while she mopped his face with a cooling damp towel.

"Bad one?"

He nodded.

"You going to tell me about it?"

"No."

"Then I have a bad one for you," she said. "Daniel hasn't called yet."

The last black shred of the nightmare faded when he saw the waxen sheen to her cheeks, and the tic that pulled at the corner of her mouth. Her hair was unkempt, and she kept pushing her glasses back with a thumb.

"Donna?"

She shook her head, looked away. "I called the sheriff's office and told them about David. I wanted to call Tony, but . . ." She squinted as though it had suddenly gone dark. "But I couldn't dial the number. It's silly. I had the phone right there in my hand, and I couldn't dial the number. I really couldn't." There were tears. "I tried, honest to god, I tried."

She fell against his chest, her hands grabbing his shirt, and there was nothing he could do but listen to the sobbing, feel the spasms down her back, feel the terror break loose that she had held back for a day.

(4)

The palomino shied at the grumble of the distant engine, and Simon had to talk to it urgently, soothingly, to keep it from bolting. Ever since he had left the house, just about an hour before, he had felt it—a curious ambivalence about the night air, a sensation more than a knowing that despite the storm's break-up the world was not yet quite right.

It was Rachel, of course. He knew now she was trying to make contact with him, using her powers to reach out from the Quiet Land, the Silent Land, to tell him what he needed to know. He wasn't sure exactly when he'd first known. Perhaps when he'd come out of the shower and had seen her coffin in the bedroom—a hand-carved rectangle resting on a brass bier, its sides and top varicolored with strips of wood from each tree in the forest, her likeness impressed in the gleaming coffin's lid. Or perhaps it was when he'd suddenly grabbed for some paper, had scribbled words on it, white words, that for no reason yet known to him gave the house and the land to the man, Aaron Sweetwater, should anything happen. Or perhaps it had been when the New People had stopped their singing and had left him alone, leaving him with only Palemoon to whisper his farewells. Yes. Yes, that was the time, that was the moment when he'd known she couldn't leave him alone with what she had left behind. That was when his weeping had ended because he'd known she was still here.

Palemoon, the poor mindless creature, had not believed him when he'd told her. Fearful as always, she had clutched at his arms and showed him the coffin again and again. And when he'd smiled at her patiently and tried to pat her anxious head, she'd backed away in a panic. Afraid of him. Imagine. Afraid of the man who had saved her from a life in a mental institution. Imagine that child afraid of her spiritual father. But she had been, she was. She'd started babbling to him about something—the words, a parchment, something incredibly foolish—and her voice had fluttered about his head like a startled and frenzied sparrow, chittering and scolding and making no sense at all.

So he had had to saddle the palomino and ride away from the house, away from the coffin that held the husk of his wife, out where he would be uninfluenced by the trappings of damned mortals.

That jeep almost spoiled it.

But it was gone now, and he was alone.

Listening to the wind as his mother had taught him, separating the hush of the trees from the rustling of the grass, the cries of the nightbirds from the creaking of dead wood.

No reins in his hands, his knees guiding the horse away from the house, away from the light, through an open gate and into a field that had lain fallow for ten years. Hooves fell softly in the soft earth, mingling with an occasional snorting; the bell-clinking of the bridle. Across the fallow field toward the slope of Kramer's Mountain, she would be there, waiting, beneath her favorite tree. A monstrous fir planted to mark the birth of his mother. How tall now? He frowned in estimation. Eighty feet? Ninety? It spread over its domain in almost perfect proportions, its needles as he approached it catching the increasingly frequent moonlight in darts of silvergrey, in sparkles of blinding white.

Here is where she would be buried in the morning.

And here is where she was waiting patiently for him.

Rachel, he spoke silently as the tree loomed ahead, so large its branches had swept clean its own clearing. Rachel, you're going to have to explain all this to me. There's so much I don't understand. What was Palemoon talking about? What did she mean?

He told himself it was the wind that brought back the tears, the slow drop in temperature that made his mount nervous. It stopped less than fifty yards from the fir, and would not move closer. Simon spoke to it softly, lovingly, and slapped its rump lightly. And still it wouldn't move. It sidled, edging away and backward.

"Damn," he said wearily. Wasn't anything going to work right today? "The hell with you, animal." He dropped from the saddle and reached out for the reins, but the palomino jerked its head away and broke into a thundering gallop, swinging wide of Rachel's tree and heading straight for its stall.

"Goddamn you!" he bellowed, raising a fist. "Damnit, you fool, she's not going to hurt you!"

He spun around toward the tree, still pointing at the horse. "Tell him, Rachel! Tell him to come back!"

Silence.

"Rachel!"

Silence.

". . . Rachel? . . ."

Silence.

His hand lowered and his shoulders sagged and his legs carried him beneath the low branches. He sat on the pine-ground, his back against the trunk, his hands in his lap, his chin tucked toward his chest. She wasn't here yet, but that was all right. Later. Maybe later. For now he would rest on the ground where she'd be buried. Rest, and think, and perhaps before dawn she would return to him, singing, and bring him all the answers.

And he never raised his head, though he heard the needles *rustling*.

(5)

Jake opened the front door and stood there in the dark. He was cold. He was hungry. And nothing about the house felt exactly right.

"Ellie? Ellie? Hey darlin, your daddy's home!"

The front door opened slowly and Peg switched on the foyer light. She walked nervously to the foot of the staircase and lay a sweating hand on the newel post's rounded top. She hated acting as the go-between. One of these days she would make Kurt take the first step. One of these days, when the town returned to normal. Meanwhile there was now, and halfway up she stopped. A light glowed softly from beneath her daughter's door. "Bea? Bea darling, do you think you could stop what you're doing and come with me back to the store? Your father . . . your father wants to talk to you for a while." She waited for a response. "Bea, when did you get home, hon? We were waiting for you, you know. You were supposed . . ." She waited. "Bea? Bea, are you there?"

"For heaven's sake, Anthony," Mary Carosa said, "why don't you go upstairs and talk to her, then?"

He stared at the empty fleet of tables, the lonely pinball machines, and nodded curtly.

"And darling?"

He looked down at his wife.

"Don't yell, all right? You can be awfully frightening when you yell. If you want some answers you're going to have to be nice."

"What?"

She laughed and hugged his arm. "See what I mean? You

don't remember what a smartass you were when you were her
age. But you were, believe me. Just be nice to her, for me. If
anything's bothering her, it's the only way you're going to find
out without starting another fight."

Carosa swallowed his temper. A hell of a thing when your
wife knows more than you do. And he grinned. "All right,"
he promised. "No yelling."

Five minutes later he was knocking politely on her door;
five seconds later he was pounding down the stairs. He was
yelling.

FIVE

(1)

Jason walked away from the telephone and stood behind the couch, his hands on Donna's shoulders. Palemoon had recognized his voice instantly and insisted rather coldly that Daniel had not been at the ranch all night, and no she would not pass on a message. Later, with considerably less rancor, Dawn Sweetwater told him that Daniel had not stopped at their place. Her father was still sleeping, she did not want to disturb him, but she would have him call as soon as he woke up.

He stared at a dying fire.

The notion that Windriver was dying had occurred to him before, though it had arisen in a different context, in the marking of time's passing when not all that was good and old and solid was able to withstand the new and the flimsy and the not necessarily fine. He had rebuked himself ferociously, recognizing it as a defense he had raised automatically; and had he not raised it he would have been on the 4:50 to Casper or wherever the hell, stopped at the far end and found himself a room. He would have called the bank the next morning and had all his money wired to him. He wouldn't have moved. And every time someone knocked on the door he would scream. He would scream until they took him away to a place that had no windows. And if it had no windows he wouldn't be able to see the sky.

And if he couldn't see the sky, he would never again see a robin or a sparrow or a jay or a crow.

"Jason, you're hurting me."

He looked down at his hands; they were clenching her shoulders, pinching the flesh. He snatched them away and rubbed them absently over his shirt.

"How do you feel?" she said.

"I don't feel anything."

"It's the medicine," she told him, and by her tone he understood she was talking only for the sound.

They were getting so good, he thought then, stalling. And he knew why it was: they were alone. And getting more alone the longer he stood there. A town that should be up in arms against the creatures of the night was waiting ever so patiently, ever so fearfully, for the hunters to return with the thing that had plagued them. While he stood here, stalling, because he knew what had killed them.

But how do you arouse people against madness?

"It's one of them," he said finally. He had to talk. He had to hear himself say it. He had to hear himself accuse three young women who only yesterday could reach out and be children.

"But we accounted—"

He looked down at the top of her head and touched it to quiet her. "We don't know for sure. We were so relieved when I called that we never bothered to check. Bea was *supposed* to be with her boyfriend, but we don't know that for sure. Carole was *supposed* to be in her room crying for Rachel, but we don't know that, either. Ellie's phone was busy. It could have been off the hook, it could've been Jake, it could've been Steve. We don't know, Donna, we don't."

"But they're only—"

"I know," he said. "I thought of that already. But it doesn't make any difference. You don't have to be old to want to be able to kill."

She pushed away from him and stood, hugging herself as

she stared down at the embers. "That's horrible." She turned to him, pleading. "Maybe what we were talking about the other night, about the werewolves? Maybe one of them was infected. Maybe she doesn't want to do it, Jason. Maybe she has to and can't help herself."

"The conditions—"

She darted around the couch and grabbed his arm, her face close to his and angry. "How the hell do we know what the conditions are? Full moon? High tide? What's the god-damned difference, Jason? She has to be found, and she has to be helped!"

She stepped away from him, frowning. "You don't believe that, do you."

His eyes felt cold.

"You know," she said, still retreating, "if Dan was right and there's no way to kill it, you'll have to trap *her*. You may have to *hurt* her. A *child,* and you'll have to hurt her until we can figure something out. Do you realize that, Jason? Do you know what I'm saying?"

He shook his head. "It dies," he said. "Remember what you said—in all mythologies there is some way for the monster to die. We just have to figure out what it is. We just have to."

"Oh, Jason," she said, "I'm getting so damned confused."

He walked to the front door and opened it. The wind bustled about his legs, took hold of his collar-tips and bounced them. There was a peculiar glow on the street, and he moved to the steps where he saw the clouds thinning. The moon was gaining, no ribbons of black and white yet but simply swatches and shades of variant grey. He barely noticed when Donna handed him his jacket, and slipped into her own. The gun that she gave him was heavy and cold and the box she dropped into his pocket rattled like rats' bones.

"Daniel would have called," she said.

He tucked the gun into his belt, held snug by the brass buckle, and leaned against the porch post. "I don't know if I can," he said, not taking his eyes from the shredding of the sky.

"The only choice we had we already made."

When she slipped her hand into his he wanted to drag her back into the house and lock her in his room, command Jeff to guard her and keep her from fleeing. But her grip was strong, and they stood on the porch while the air turned autumn chilly and the leaves glowed silver edges and the voice of the river was suddenly loud and mocking.

"All right."

His voice sounded strained, but he zipped the leather coat midway and started walking. Donna kept his pace, and by the tilt of her head he knew she was listening. She hadn't asked him where they were going first, but the pull of the river was much too strong.

They walked swiftly (much too loudly) down to Bank Road and turned right in tandem. After two blocks, she began pulling back on his arm. At the corner of Bank and River he stopped, looked both ways—it was deserted—and walked toward the bridge. Halfway there he stopped again and pointed to his left.

"Here," he said. The path was still there, but the brush had been cleared out and the trees thinned near to extinction. "Ellie and Harry took this way." He pulled her after him. "And just about here is where Harry was killed."

He sucked in his stomach as they pushed through the privet's gap. Lights were on throughout the Harmon house's bottom floor, and Donna's grip tightened so much he tugged and winced. Then she tapped his shoulder and pointed at an open window on the second floor. He understood what she meant and glanced down to be sure his gun was tucked out of sight. He wished he felt foolish.

The porch boards creaked loudly, sharply; behind them the river had dropped to a whisper.

The door opened suddenly at his first knock and Donna gasped. Jake stared at her a moment before turning to Jason.

"Sheriff."

"Evenin, Jase." He smiled. "Looks like you tangled with a wildcat. Evenin, Doc. Come on in outta the cold."

Before Jason could protest he found himself standing in the foyer, Donna pressed close beside him.

"So, what can I do for you folks?" the sheriff said. He was in his shirtsleeves and slippers, his hair slightly mussed as if a nap had been disturbed. Then he raised a palsied hand. "Never mind, I know. You want t'know how many dudes we potted on our expedition today, how many vicious chipmunks, how many men were lost to a rampaging fawn." He laughed and shook his head. "We'll be goin out again in the mornin, that's all I can tell you." He lay a finger knowingly alongside his nose. "But I'll be honest, Jason, if you promise not to print it."

Jason's smile was dutiful; he could not help looking up the dim staircase, at the dark at the landing where he thought he saw a shadow, and the glint of a red eye.

"Well . . ." Harmon leaned back against the door. "Well, I'm sold on that bear thing, you know that much. But no offense, Doc, when I say I've seen a few rabid critters in my time, and I tell you the truth, I don't think that bear's still with us. I expect it wandered up into the hills and found itself a place to die. Nope, I don't think we're ever gonna find a goddamned thing."

Jason opened his mouth, cleared his throat when he felt the stricture ready to choke him. "I see."

"Yep, that's the way I see it all right. But I gotta do it, y'know? For Artie and Steve, the others. We gotta go through the motions, if you know what I mean." He shrugged. "Besides, who the hell knows? We might get lucky."

There *was* a shadow up there, but when he glanced at Donna she was too busy smiling at the old man to notice. Damn! He began edging toward the stairs.

"Hey," Harmon said suddenly, and Jason froze. "I must be gettin senile, damnit. Here we still are here and I haven't even offered you two a cup of coffee."

"It's all right," Jason said. Donna looked at him then, and up over his shoulder.

"No it ain't," the sheriff insisted. "We got—"

They all turned to the door when they heard a pounding up the steps. The door burst open and Steve ran in, barely able to stop himself before the gaping trio. There was confusion— Harmon explaining why he had visitors while Steve was trying to get through them, talking about the state police and Cheyenne and wasn't anybody going to get the hell out of his way?

"Hold it!" Harmon shouted. "Now damnit, just hold it a minute!"

The shadow.

"That's no way to talk to guests in my house, son."

Felsom, angry and embarrassed, muttered an apology no one took seriously, then demanded to know where his wife was.

Jason looked at the stairs.

"Ellie?" The old man looked confused.

"Who else?" Steve said angrily, then relented. "Yes, Dad, Ellie."

Crazy, Jason thought; it really was true that Harmon was crazy.

A shadow.

He must have known it all the time, and threw up a mindblock so he wouldn't have to face it.

"Dad," Steve prodded, "where is Ellie, huh?"

Another glint of red and suddenly the shadow was—

"Here," Ellie said, hastening out of the living room and wiping her hands on a dishtowel. She kissed her husband solidly on his cheek, turned with a somewhat confused smile to Jason and Donna, then bent down to snap her fingers at the large black tom moving cautiously down the steps. "Fool," she said to it, "I've been lookin all over the house for you." Crooking the purring animal in her arms she rose and smiled again, still unsure at the company and the commotion. "Did I hear someone asking about coffee?"

"Yes," Jason said when no one else spoke. "But really, we have to be going. A couple more things to check up on, you understand." He shook Felsom's hand quickly, and Harmon's, and had the door open and Donna on the porch before another word was said. "'Night," he called brightly, and closed the door behind him.

He was nearly running by the time they'd returned to the street. His stomach had filled with bubbling acid, his lungs with water, and he could feel perspiration gathering solidly under his arms.

"I-I-I nearly shot that damned cat," Donna said, panting as if she'd been sprinting. "Jason, this isn't working."

He ignored her; he was too busy trying to coordinate his arms and legs and keep his bowels from loosening. He tripped over his shadow. His nose wrinkled at the sour odor of fear and sweat that rose from his chest.

"Jason, I don't think I can."

He wanted to be in a desert so there would be no leaves overhead moving contrary to the wind, so he would not hear the flapping of incredible wings as something—*not something, damnit, you know what it is*—waited for them to break into the open.

"Jason, please, I think I'm going to throw up."

The acid lurched, and he spat into the gutter, shuddering at an image of his insides peeling away.

"You'll be all right," he said then, hugging her shoulders, kissing her cheek. "You'll be all right. You just have to be calm."

"I will if you will."

He hugged her again.

They passed in front of the firehouse on one side, the town hall on the other. No lights. No people.

Only the wind.

At the corner they stopped, and he self-consciously tugged his coat down over his hips. He was positive anyone walking by would see the gun's bulge, would stop and demand to know why he was carrying that thing around when it was obvious it wouldn't stop a rampaging bear.

But there were no cars on the Pike, no pedestrians.

He refused to look up.

"Jase." His right hand stiffened when Donna pointed to their left. "Jase."

The luncheonette was still open, and Kurt Steed was heading back inside with his arms filled with unsold newspapers.

Jason looked down and saw his reflection distorted in a rippling puddle cowering in the gutter.

She took his arm and tugged gently, leading him into the fluorescent glare where all colors died or shaded to purple. The booths and stools were empty. Kurt was taking the day's grease off the grille. When he heard them at the counter he turned with a scowl, a scowl that eased to concern when he saw Jason's face.

"Jesus," he said, "you have a fight with a train?"

Jason smiled as best he could without grimacing and asked for some coffee. Kurt filled two cups and waved away an offered dollar with an "I'm closed, officially. Just waitin for Peg to get back with Bea."

"Oh?" Donna spooned sugar into the coffee. "She's been out on a school night? I thought you didn't like that."

"Not been out," Kurt said, returning to the grille. "She ain't been back from school at all."

Jason glanced at the wall clock; a few minutes past nine. "Nothing wrong, I hope."

Kurt shook his head. "Not that I know of. She's just late, is all. Damned late." The spatula slapped at the grille, scraped off the grease, and slapped again. "Women," he said in tired disgust. "Peg says she's in love, so she's probably out with Hardy. But I swear I don't know what she sees in him. I really don't."

A car backfired directly in front of the shop and Donna's cup rattled on its saucer.

"I think that accident had somethin to do with it, though." When Jason glanced at the man's peg leg, Kurt smiled. "No, not mine, hers. It was last year, just before the Felsom boy was killed. Bea and Carole—Carosa's girl?—they were at the MacKenzie place workin with Rachel on some kinda term paper. Turned out to be a damned windy night. Came up so strong, so damned quick, no one knew what hit em. Windows poppin left and right, you'd've thought there was a war on, for god's sake."

Hurricanes, Jason thought, recalling seaside warnings to keep one window open in the house to equalize pressure and prevent glass from shattering. When he said as much to Steed, the big man nodded.

"That's what happened, all right. Waters lost his plate glass, Green did, the town hall took it hard. On the ranch out there some kinda glass doors blew in. Caught Bea and Carole in the back, cut one of them women they got out there all to hell. Weird, Jase. A hell of a wind."

Donna frowned. "I don't get it, Kurt."

"Well, the kids got outta that with just a knock on the head and some bitty scars on their neck—but Peg she reads about these things and she says Bea thought she was gonna die, so now she's makin sure she don't waste any time." He scowled. "Shit, I'll waste her time if she wants, damnit. Next thing I know she's gonna up and elope or some damn thing."

Jason drank his coffee slowly while Donna chatted aimlessly about the weather, the killings, the unpredictability of the young and the foolish. He kept glancing at the window, at the empty street, waiting for something to move out there. He almost dropped his cup when a metallic crash rattled from the back room.

Donna's voice trailed off.

Kurt stared at the connecting door, the spatula in his hand and dripping grease. His breath released in an embarrassed grunt when Peg rushed in, her hands buried in a long white cardigan. Her hair had been blown wild by the wind and her cheeks were vividly flushed.

"Well?" Kurt demandéd.

"Her . . . her light was on, she was home before, but now . . ." and she shrugged helplessly.

Jason nudged Donna off her stool and headed for the door. "That does it!" Steed bellowed as the door hissed shut to leave them alone on the sidewalk. Most of the storefronts were dark, the streetlamps buzzing, and they walked quickly east to escape the muffled argument in the luncheonette behind them.

"Jason," she said.

Donna's voice was a reverberation of the strain that was weighting his shoulders. He felt as if he were a rodent caught in the path of a cobra, its hood spread to blot the moon, its eyes unblinking and daring him to make a move.

"Hey!"

Donna squealed and lunged for Jason's arm and cursed the air when Bill Oaker grinned from the law office door.

"Hey, either of you guys seen Artie around?"

They shook their heads.

"Damn." The deputy kicked at the pavement. "Fool's gonna keep me here all damned night. I mean, I know his father's dead and all, but Christ, the least he could've done was call in, right?"

Donna found her voice. "We were at Harmon's just a while ago. Steve was there."

Oaker grinned broadly. "Obliged," he said, spinning back inside and lunging for the telephone on the edge of the first desk.

"I am now ten pounds lighter than I was thirty seconds ago," she said weakly, sagging her weight on Jason's arm.

"Listen," he said, "if you were a kid, where would you go

in this town to be alone with your boyfriend? The theater's closed, you're not in Carosa's, and you're not at the boy's house."

They paused in front of Regan's, by tacit consent moving closer to the darkened store and huddling in the recessed doorway.

"A car," she suggested. "On a night like this fields are out, places like that. I'd guess . . . shit, a car."

Windriver expanded suddenly, became a nightburied city with too many streets and too many alleys, too many places for a couple to hide. Jason rubbed his brow hard, forcing himself out of the bonds that kept him from thinking.

In the dark, around the corner, a young woman laughed. Softly.

(2)

The jeep roared across the Pike without slowing at all, skidded around the corner into Station Lane and slammed to a groaning halt in front of the ramshackle Felsom house. Steve leapt over the passenger seat to the buckled sidewalk and stormed to the porch. The front door was open, the inside dark.

"Idiot!"

The house was empty, Artie's yellow raincoat gone from its peg.

"Goddamned idiot!"

He stamped and kicked his way back to the borrowed vehicle and stood by the hood with his hands firm on his hips, squinting into the wind. Then he yanked a powerful flashlight from its magnetic hold under the dash. He shouldn't be doing this. But when Oaker called, demanding Artie's appearance right now and don't tell me nothing else, it was Ellie who'd sweettalked him into making a search.

The fool's gonna ruin everything.

Ellie's smiling right for the first time in god knows when, Jake don't say anything when he hears about them moving out . . . and now this! He wriggled through the tightly packed trees and shrubs to the railroad embankment, slid down the slope on his heels and jumped to the rails.

Which way, damnit?

He started walking toward the stationhouse, the glaring light in front of him a white cane against the dark.

I don't believe this, Steve thought. I just don't believe this.

He kept his left hand to his throat, holding closed the fleece-lined collar. It was no use yelling and scaring half the neighborhood; if Artie had gotten himself stinking he wouldn't hear the last goddamned trumpet, for god's sake. Incredible. It was incredible. Though he supposed he didn't blame his brother all that much. Artie was the one who always kept it all inside, moping around when things went against him, sitting in the dark of his room until he figured out what to do next. Not to speak ill of you, Pop, but that's a hell of a lot better than growing a mouth around a bottle. But he was done with all that now. Artie was a grown man, and as soon as the funeral was over he and Ellie were getting out for good.

He stopped.

The far reach of the light had flared yellow back at him.

He frowned and took another step, grabbing his right wrist with his left hand to keep the flashlight steady. He trotted several yards before stopping again.

The coat was torn, blackened, ending suddenly at the waist. The man's mouth was open, a pencil-line of blood dried at his chin. Steve raised the light. A couple dozen yards up the line was the rest of the body. He lowered the light again.

Artie was watching him, wide-eyed and astonished.

He turned away and swallowed against the bile that jammed into his mouth. His spit tasted like metal, his tongue like ash, and he shut his eyes while his lungs worked for a calming steady breath. No, he begged his knees when they threatened to give way; but he was unable to stop the tears that burned past his eyelids and etched down his cheeks. Tears he had not shed for his father came now for his brother. Goddamned . . . idiot. It must have been a drunken wake that sent him blundering into the 4:50. And the train ground him in half. Steve dropped to the ground and vomited, listening to the splash and thinking how much Artie must have hurt inside, thinking how drunk he must have been to fall under a train that was moving at a crawl.

It occurred to him fleetingly that he might have seen the bear and had run the wrong way.

But it didn't matter. He was dead. He was dead.

And when his stomach was empty, the dry heaves tearing his insides apart, he staggered to his feet. He stumbled for several feet before his balance returned.

Ellie . . . Ellie . . .

A young woman laughed.

Softly.

His control snapped. Dragging up his coat to get at his revolver, he raced for the stationhouse and hit the platform in a single enraged leap.

The laugh again, from inside.

Revolver and flashlight crossed the threshold together. He couldn't believe what he saw on the floor. "All right, goddamnit, just what the hell do you think you're doing?"

(3)

Esther Lynn stood at her front door, key in the lock, her black coat flapping around her shins. She had gone to Jason's in hopes of some company, but the house was dark and the dog barking faintly inside had unnerved her. She had almost run home when the wind began playing tricks on her. It was doing it again now. The muted sound of a girl, laughing. Twigs scuttling. Leaves hissing.

The door opened, but she didn't go in.

They would think her foolish, Jason and Donna, for behaving so skittish, but she couldn't help it. Galen was gone for no reason at all, and the night was doing things to itself, things she could see reflected in Donna's doe eyes. It had infected her. And now she didn't want to be alone.

Carosa's or the Sheriff's Office; a stiff drink or some news.

Old woman, she thought as she pulled the door to and clasped her purse to her waist. You're nothing but a foolish old woman who oughta be home in bed.

Nevertheless, she didn't want to be alone.

Yet she didn't want to believe she wasn't alone on the street.

She stopped at the corner and clung to the lamppost. The Pike was only a block away, but the street that tunneled beneath the overhanging branches seemed a mile, two miles, a continent long. The wind took her hat off, and she reached after it feebly, dropping her purse in the same motion and shuffling toward it as it tilted off the curb.

Her fingers had just touched the clasp when she felt the shadow cross her back.

(4)

Jason had no idea exactly when it was that the struggling ended and the fighting really began. When the fear that had been a part of him became his partner instead of his shadow. What he did know was that a feeling of weariness had taken hold when he heard the laughing—a weariness born of disgust and impatience, a weariness that goaded rather than sapped.

Taking the gun from his belt he spun out of the doorway before Donna could stop him. He raced onto Fieldview . . . and stopped.

The street was empty.

Donna came up beside him.

"It's no good," he said, punching angrily at his thigh. "We can chase noise all night until she's good and ready to come for us."

"She knows, then."

He nodded. "Yeah, I think so."

"Jason, listen to me. I know you think what we've been doing is right, but that's different now. We've got to tell—"

They jerked around suddenly at the grinding roar of a vehicle, rushed back to the corner just as Felsom barreled his jeep past them. It shrieked to a halt in front of Steed's luncheonette, greyblue smoke from burning rubber lifting into the hazed streetlamp. Kurt and Peg were standing by the door when Felsom jumped out, reached into the back seat and dragged Bea to the sidewalk. She was wearing his coat, her legs and feet pale and bare. A moment later, Hardy Green crawled out and stood hangdog by the fender while Felsom gestured and Kurt's fists rose to his side.

"Poor kid," Donna said.

"Sure." He stared across the street at Carosa's.

"Jason, you don't have to, now."

"I have to know."

"Damnit, it isn't necessary!"

He whirled on her, knowing he wouldn't be able to explain,

frowning when something caught his eye at the far end of the
block. "Who . . . ?" He remembered the gun and clamped it
close to his side as he leaned forward slightly to peer through
the dark. A figure, black and hunched over, was plucking
something from the gutter.

He felt the blood drain from his face. "Jesus," he said,
"that's Esther Lynn."

Donna watched the stumbling helpless woman. "Is she
drunk or something?"

"I don't know, but we can't have her . . ." He pushed at
Donna's shoulder. "Get her before something happens."

"What?"

"Get her!" he said, his teeth almost clenched. "Bring her
inside someplace. Jesus Christ, Donna, just *do it!*"

He waited until she started to walk away from him, then
jammed the gun back into his waistband and rushed across
the Pike to the drive beside the barbershop. He paid no
attention to the grumbling of a truck winding down the road.
An urgency had gripped him, one that jerked his hand to his
face, his hair, his neck, his chest . . . a demented marionette
with nothing to guide it and noplace to go.

She knew.

She *knew.*

A rustling above him.

(5)

Donna watched Esther Lynn swing up from the curb and grab
onto the lamppost, her dark lips quivering, her grey hair
flailing at the wind.

Don't scream! she prayed silently.

She tried to keep to the few eddies of white light the trees
permitted, one hand raised to beckon and warn, the other
fumbling her weapon back to her belt. Esther Lynn's mouth
opened as her knees began to crumble.

For god's sake, don't scream!

She lunged to the curb and clamped her hand over the
older woman's mouth, feeling the scream's vibrations until
Esther Lynn recognized her and fell gasping into her arms.

"My Lord, girl," she said, panting.

"Later," Donna said, and pulled her away, lurching down the sidewalk toward the house in the block's center. Esther Lynn didn't argue and kept pace as best she could while looking fearfully into the trees for the shadow that had touched her.

She knew, Donna thought, *and she's playing a game.*

A low and gated fence guarded Esther Lynn's front lawn. Donna fumbled with the latch and had the woman through when a hissing shower of leaves and twigs hailed over them, the aftersound of a great weight crashing through the upper branches of an immense elm. Esther Lynn cried out and Donna pulled the gun.

"The porch!" she said, shoving the woman forward, almost sending her to her knees. "The door, Esther, for god's sake the door!"

She looked up, backing toward the house, trying to see something through the tangled foliage.

"I'll shoot," she warned loudly.

A young woman laughed.

She bolted, flinging herself to the porch and tripping over the hunched form of Esther Lynn on her hands and knees.

"The keys," she said, almost weeping. "I've dropped the damned keys!"

Donna's palms slapped the floorboards, a splinter gouged her knee. Above her on the porch roof she heard the *click-click* of talons on the slate.

Esther Lynn was sobbing, and muttering incoherently.

It was pacing above them, arrogant and patient.

It could kill us now, Donna thought, *it could.*

"Ha!"

Esther Lynn was on her feet, Donna's back against the wall.

Pacing, *clicking,* and a ruffling of feathers.

The door swung open and Donna spun to shove the woman inside, slamming the door closed and falling hard against it.

"What . . . child, what is it?"

Donna shook her head, swallowing and trying to breathe.

"Can it get in? What . . . can it get in?"

She pushed herself on her buttocks until her back reached the stairs. *It could have killed us,* she thought. And then she knew what it wanted. With the barrel of the gun she waved

Esther Lynn from the door. "We'll be all right for a while," she said, her voice small, her voice quaking. "Just leave off the lights. Please, Esther, no lights."

She sat. She stared. She heard the wind moaning.

(6)

Jason knocked impatiently on the kitchen door, shifting from one foot to the other, cursing the trees, damning the wind. Come on, Mary! He knocked again. Again. Come on, come on!

The light flared on inside, momentarily blinding him and he brought a hand up to shade his eyes. When he could see again, Mary was on the other side of the screen door, wearing a plain black dress. Her eyes were red and puffed, her cheeks flushed. The smile she gave him was a death's head grin, and he realized abruptly Oaker must have called about David.

But it was too late to turn away.

"Mary—"

"You want to see Tony, he's gone." Like a tracked doe she glanced behind her, a hand pressed to one cheek. "He was gonna talk to Carole, see, and she wasn't in her room like we thought. Her window was open. Then . . . a call . . . and he runs out to go find my boy and . . . I don't know, Jason, I don't know. Do you know where Carole is? I need her, her father needs her, but he run out and—" She blinked rapidly and gasped. "My god, Jason, don't tell me something's happened to my girl! Not my girl, too! Was there an accident? I keep hearing cars and trucks. Please, Jason, you gotta—"

"No, no," he said quickly, lifting a palm to calm her. "I haven't seen her, Mary, but I'm sure she's all right. She might have heard something about David and . . . ."

A horn was blowing, distant but coming nearer.

Mary caught her breath, put a handkerchief to her eyes. "It isn't fair, y'know. All in one day, it just isn't fair.

"Look, Jason, look." A pleading as she swallowed. "If you see her, would you . . . would you bring her home for me? She's gotta come home. I need her. Tony needs her."

A horn, blaring now.

"I'll tell her," he promised, and wrenched himself off the porch with a muffled groan, and ducked into the drive's shadow. Then he leaned heavily against the house and closed his eyes. The last doubt was gone; the only thing left now was the completion of the hunt.

And she knew.

He heard the horn again, shave-and-a-haircut blasts mindlessly repeated. He saw a filthy camper drive by. A man sat on the hood and waved a rifle triumphantly over his head, another waving an orange hunting cap from the passenger side window. A handful of men raced past. Across the street a gang of teenagers rounded the corner, whooping and laughing.

He moved cautiously to the drive's end and looked over to Harmon's office. A tow truck sat at the curb, and Aaron Sweetwater's convertible was dangling from its hooks like the half-eaten catch of a pathetic trawler. Behind it was the camper, and Ted Waters, Titus Arnold, and Chet Lancaster were all trying to speak to Steve Felsom simultaneously. They were grinning, the deputy was grinning, and within moments the street was afire with headlights of cars that stopped wherever there was room, at the curb or on the dividing line.

Waters pushed through the growing crowd, and with a grand and grinning flourish flung open the camper's rear doors.

There was a silence as he reached in and pulled out a flashlight.

A cheering when he turned it on and illuminated the dead bear.

Jason nodded to himself sadly, slipped out of the drive and darted diagonally across the Pike into Fieldview. The urgency grew; Windriver had its trophy, and he still had the hunt.

The cheers increased, and someone fired off a gun.

She wouldn't come now; there were too many people, too much noise. She would do what she had to do and be Carole again. She would join the others and Anthony would find her and tell her about her brother. He would weep; she would weep with him. Then he would be compelled to open the bar for the others' celebration because David's murderer had been caught.

The cheering sounded disturbingly like screaming.

He walked down the center of the street, his coat unzipped, and his right hand polishing the handle of the gun.

She would do all that, unless she had a target.

She was watching. He sensed it. She was nearby and watching.

And here we are, ladies and gentlemen, at the intersection of Fieldview and Laurel, midway between something called the Valley Pike and something called the Wind River. Behind me, and you don't have to listen very hard, you can hear the heartfelt, joyful sounds of a town that has just been rescued from extinction by a man who strove like hell to kill it; and ahead of me, beyond all those marvelously stately trees at the end of the street, is by god the future.

"CAROLE!"

A series of gunshots was fired, sounding like the hollow rattle of Chinese firecrackers.

Dozens of horns blared, driving back the dark.

Doors opened, lights flashed on, and people ran past him grinning like fools.

"Hey, Jase, ain't this somethin else again?"

"Clarke, you jerk, you're goin the wrong way!"

"Hey, man, ain't you *heard*? Waters got himself a fuckin goddamned giant!"

Earl Carson, struggling into a suit jacket and trying to knot a tie at the same time, slowed and took hold of his arm. "Never thought it was them, y'know," he said, looking Jason over for notepad and pen. "Sold Michel Wolf a suit just a few weeks ago, in fact, before he got himself hurt. Never thought it was them all along."

Then he was gone.

Jason walked. His smile that of a man who knew no need to hurry, and no need to laugh.

He walked, heading for the river, the gun close and heavy at his side, the wind tagging at his heels. Into the shattered spill of a streetlamp, out to the sea of black beyond. Listening to the stamp of his boots against the tarmac, the leaves pacing him in the gutters, the bellowing of his blood echoing in his ears.

Houselights were on, and all the houses were empty.

He was cold, but it had nothing to do with the wind. It was the moon. It had finished the job of slaughtering the storm and was waiting full for him above the southern fields, showing him the lunging ripples of the river, the silvertips of the reeds, the greyhaze that clung like dying fog to the crowns of the trees. It showed him movement in shadows, the slithering, the sweeping, the whispering of black.

The gunshots; and horns and hoarse cheering faded behind him.

Hedges became tombstones, a sagging rose bush a ghoul.

Now he could hear it.

Keeping pace above him.

The *hush* of the wind through its golden brown feathers, the impatient *click* of its beak, a slashing sharp beak snapping impatiently closed, a slashing sharp beak impatient for his throat.

A harsh guttural warbling, a young woman laughing.

Hush.

Click.

Keeping pace above him.

Its deathcold shadow shrouded him for a dozen yards, reaching for his own and gathering it in. It was black weight, taunting him, filtering the light. Then it climbed to a blur that became grey with the street, and veered off sharply with a harsh guttural warbling.

He shifted the gun to his left hand and saw the River Road bridge stretched before him.

Here the water slapped and rushed, and surged around the pilings.

Here it was quicksilver.

And here it was black.

He stood in the center of the bridge and faced the town, his mouth open and trembling to taste the sharp air, his left thumb pulling back the revolver's hammer. There were no lights in the sheriff's house, and the rest of the homes were buried by the trees that still lined the bank.

He hoped Aaron would recover, and recover his family, and perhaps bring to the town the unity it needed. He could do it. He was strong enough, and by saving the others he might save his children.

For a moment he listened to the river below him, and remembered the night on the bay when he had nearly drowned because of a self-confident man and a naked confident woman and the temptations offered and the temptations refused; he heard the bridge creaking, rocking itself to sleep, and remembered the branches outside his bedroom, scratching to get in while his mother fought his father downstairs in the kitchen.

He hoped Donna had kept her wits about her, and kept Esther Lynn inside. He knew now he loved her and it pained him to think that she had been through two hells: the one she'd left behind, and the one he'd brought with him. He hoped her glasses would never stop sliding down her nose, that the copper in her hair would always find the sun. He hoped she was inside. He hoped she was alive.

And when memories and notions and thoughts jumbled to incoherence, he looked up at the sky. It was a clear, washed, black spring sky. He looked at the moon, waiting, and at the stars, unseeing.

At the fire-eyed eagle that glided steadily toward him.

Over the water now, just high enough to clear the railing on the bridge . . . high enough, if he didn't move, to take off his head.

He spread his legs and raised his arms, both hands clutching the revolver's butt. He did not try to use the sights, only tried to keep the barrel's mouth from wavering too violently. Sweat blinded his right eye while his throat snapped dry and one leg began to jump, the other to cramp. His gaze fixed on a point just to the right of the creature's head, away from the firestare that was insolent and unmoved.

He pulled the trigger.

He gasped at the pain in his wrists and lowered left shoulder, at the deafening roar that rang in his head. He fired again and saw breast feathers ruffle. A third time almost blindly, and his rigid stance broke. He threw himself forward, rolling against the bottom rail as the eagle swung up, and over, its outline momentarily swallowed by the darkshadow of the trees over Stan Kelly's graves.

His ears sang, and he spat thickly several times to keep his stomach from ripping through his mouth.

With forearms and elbows he raised himself to his feet just as the eagle dove at him again. Twice more he fired, the last time at point-blank range, and dropped with his arms wrapped tightly around his head. His teeth were chattering uncontrollably, his fingers refusing to do their work as he sat up and pried the ammunition box from his pocket and jumped open the chamber. He shook the gun to empty the shells, and dropped it. He scrambled for it and cursed, and nearly laughed. Then he had it again and shoved in the new cartridges, sighed and rose a third time.

It was gone.

He waited, scooping in air and shaking his head to clear it. Then he straightened to his full height and felt the bridge sway beneath him. The banks rippled. The moon blurred. He turned in a tight circle, but the eagle was gone.

No. It wouldn't do this to him. It wouldn't dare. All this time, and it couldn't just leave him.

His terror was shunted to a place where it waited while frustration thrust his jaw like a club at the night.

Suddenly, the width of the river and the length of the bridge and the silverblack wash of the sky made him feel terrifyingly vulnerable. After another swift scan of the target range he'd occupied he ran in a half-crouch to the far side, dropping heavily to the ground with one arm linked around the endpost. He was cold. Sweat stained his shirt, his trousers, and his hair clung to his neck like the hands of a wet corpse. A hundred yards ahead, the iron fencing of the cemetery broke the plane of the fields.

And in the middle of the road a young woman stood, waiting.

There was no conscious order given to his legs. He just felt himself moving, slowly, warily. His fingers flexed stiffly around the gun's beveled grip. Hair blew into his eyes, and he shook his head once to free them. The ringing in his ears had faded, and despite a desperate need to spit his mouth remained dry.

The wingéd serpent in the shape of a woman; the wingéd serpent naked in the shower of the moon.

Her skin was dark and writhing over with shadows, her breasts large for a woman so young, her nipples nearly black and distended with excitement. Her hair was wind-blown, her eyes sparking yet sultry. She stood with one hip cocked, her hand splayed over it, and she would have been erotic had she not looked so deathly cold.

He stopped.

"Hello, Carole," he said.

"Mister Clarke?" Her voice was broken, and there were silver tears in her eyes. "Mister Clarke, what am I going to do?" Plaintively, softly.

A girl, not a woman.

She brushed a fiercely trembling hand back through her hair, her head twisting from side to side in unending despair. "I . . . I don't know what to do. I don't know what to *do*." Then she turned away from him abruptly and when she turned back, silver tears were cascading down her cheeks.

A girl, Jason. For god's sake, she's a seventeen-year-old *girl*.

She crossed her arms over her breasts. "She . . . she never really liked Ellie or Bea, you know," she said, close to whimpering. She touched one finger lightly to the back of her neck. "She liked me the best, and I kind of liked her. But when that wind came and the glass broke all over the room . . . she said words to me and she touched me! I didn't know what I was doing, Mister Clarke, you have to believe me. Hell, I thought she was really crazy, y'know?" Her voice rose slightly, and Jason moved a step closer. "Jeez, she *touched* me and she *talked* to me, and I thought it would be fun to learn . . . to learn all that stuff. I mean, I thought she was crazy, just crazy. I didn't know . . ." She swallowed, touched her hair and looked up to the moon. "Oh *God*, I don't know what to do!"

Jason knew there had to be words he could say to the child. There had to be something, just look at her, for god's sake. There was no directed, conscious evil here, just a foolish, bored girl who had fallen into a nightmare made real. There had to be help, then; there had to be help. But the words would not come while she wept silver tears.

Unable to bear her pain for her, he looked down at the ground and bit his lower lip. He had thought he'd known what to do; from the hanging in Rachel's room, over the fireplace where the villagers surrounded the young woman with drawn weapons. But Donna had told him *if Daniel is right, you'll have to hurt her, Jason, hold her until you can help her*. But how could he hurt her? How could he hold her?

Her sobbing grew louder, and he pushed his hair angrily out of his eyes. Maybe he could get Donna out here; maybe Donna would know the right things to say.

"Mister Clarke?"

Maybe if he had had a daughter, or a young niece, he would know what to tell her and save her more pain.

"Carole, listen . . ." He looked up, hoping she could see the mirror of her pain. "Listen, I don't . . ." Rope, he thought. He should have brought some rope.

She covered her face with her hands while he cursed his ignorance, and the dead myths of his race. Damnit, Donna!

She lowered her hands slowly as he began to walk toward her.

"Carole, listen," he said urgently. "If you can just—"

Her eyes were bright . . . a deathfire red.

"Mister Clarke . . . help . . . me . . . ?"

He almost staggered backward.

The voice was dark, it was night, it was the slow and bloody grinding of blasphemy into something once white.

"*Help . . . me . . . ?*"

He took another weak step before he realized what was happening. He halted, his free hand pinching his nose hard to stop the cold stench of blood, of death, of rotted waiting flesh.

With her hands on her hips, she laughed again . . . softly.

"Help me, Jason?"

It was mocking.

A girl, he thought desperately; for god's sake, man, a seventeen-year-old girl!

"Oh Jason, honey, did little Carole fool you?" Sweet, like the lilac and lavender that line a demon's coffin.

She's just a girl, he thought wildly; please, God, she's just a little girl, *but he knew he'd been right all the time.*

He jammed his knuckles into his eyes and relished the pain, then fumbled with the gun and brought it up, aiming.

A flicker of time, a vision, of wind-driven night . . . and the eagle was hovering, red-eyed and hungry.

A flickering, a whispering, an echoing of laughter, and Carole was smiling, posturing proudly as she fingered the medallion slung between her breasts.

"You can't kill me, you know," she said brightly. "Daniel tried, lots of them did." She shrugged. "Really. You can't kill me."

wingéd serpent

He nodded his defeat, and kept on nodding while the

young woman walked toward him. One hand held the hammered copper eagle, the other reached out in respectful admonition.

"You're right," he whispered harshly, damning the weak sound. "You're right, Carole. I know. I can't kill the eagle."

And her eyes widened in fear and fury and disbelief as he pulled the trigger and *heard her screaming;* and pulled the trigger and *heard it shrieking* pulled the trigger until the hammer kept clicking

and clicking

and clicking

until he whirled around with an anguished cry and threw it in the river.

He dropped to his knees and waited for the quaking to stop, for his throat to stop burning, for the sound of her enraged screams to die in the wind.

Then he staggered to his feet, and mindless of the blood lifted her body into his arms and carried it gently to the water. He watched the sweeping silverblack until he could no longer hold her and let her slip into the cold where the currents took her under.

Epilogue
THE NESTLING

(1)

The station wagon was so loaded down and packed to the roof that Steve was unable to use the rearview mirror and would definitely not be able to travel as fast as he'd like. But it was a hell of a small price to pay, he thought with a grin. Windriver was a full six hours behind them, and he had half a mind not to stop until they reached their destination. It was good. Damn, but it felt so good to get the hell out!

"Darling?"

He glanced at Ellie and suddenly leaned over the parcel jammed between them and kissed her cheek wetly. She giggled, and he said, "What can I do for you, love?"

"You . . . are you sure you don't mind?"

"Hey," he said, spreading his hands, "I'm just as glad to get the hell out of that ghost town as you are." His fingers drummed the wheel for a moment. "You know, I wasn't gonna say this—you know what an ego I have and all—but I have to tell you straight out, Ellie m'love, that you were right. Dead right. Everything you've been sayin about that place was damned straight right on the barrelhead. If I'm ever gonna make something of myself, I got to get to a place that's growing. People comin in, people settlin down, a place with a hell of a future is exactly what I need." He grinned wryly. "Of course, I didn't exactly have someplace like Arizona in mind."

She smiled tightly. "It's just as beautiful."

"Oh, I know that," he said quickly.

"Mountains, deserts, cities."

"I know, I know." He scowled at the glare rising from the road. Why the hell did she have to rub it in like that? Damned woman. Now there I was admitting something real close to her, and she has to go and . . . ah, the hell with it. The hell with it.

An hour later the sun began to slide behind the peaks to their right. Ellie squirmed uncomfortably and tugged at a lock of hair.

"We'll have to find a place to stay soon," he muttered.

"All right."

He laughed. "Long as they ain't got no Indians."

She glanced sideways at him. "There are Indians in Arizona, you know, Steve."

"Sure, sure, I know that," he said. Jesus, don't she ever stop? "But I'll bet dollars to doughnuts they're a lot more civilized than those stupid Shoshone."

"Steve!"

He set his jaw and clenched his teeth. But he would not look behind him, to the woman in the back seat. It had slipped out, that's all, and there was no taking it back. If she didn't like it, she could get the hell out and walk.

Ellie sighed loudly, and he scowled again, squinting through the congealing twilight for signs of a motel. Brother, he thought; ain't there any people out here?

(2)

When Jason walked into the sheriff's office, Bill Oaker was the first to grab his hand and pump it enthusiastically. "Hey, Kent, you sure you're comin back?"

Jason grinned. "Damned straight, m'man." He looked over to Jake, who was sitting quietly at his desk. "I just have to get away for a little while. God knows I need a vacation."

"What? Hell, you ain't been here much more than a month."

"Yeah." He laughed. "But you people pack more into a month out here than New York has in a year. I'm wearing myself out before my time."

Oaker laughed, slapped his back heartily and returned to his desk to pick up the phone. Jason hesitated a moment, then walked over to Harmon and looked down at him.

"Jake?"

Harmon shook his head. "You gotta learn to slow down, boy. Galen never got to his age like he did by tearing up the roads like you. Probably would've gone on another twenty, thirty years."

"I know, but what can I tell you. My cousin was something special."

The old man pushed his chair to one side and peered out the window. "Givin Doc Oldfield a lift?"

He smiled and pulled at an earlobe. "You could say that."

"Just don't keep her away too long, hear? Vance's a fair vet, but he don't have the touch anymore, if you know what I mean." He paused. "We need her." He looked to Jason, and said nothing beyond the echo in his eyes. Then the phone rang and he snatched it up, then frowned and motioned for Oaker to take it. When the receiver was back in its cradle he shrugged an apology. "Expectin a call from Ellie. She said she'd ring when they settled down for the night."

"She'll be all right," Jason said softly. "Steve will take care of her."

"I know, but . . ." He smiled weakly. "A father, I guess." His expression clouded over. "At least . . . well, at least I should be thankful I still have a daughter. Poor damned Carosa. It's been two weeks already and I still stay up nights with him. A hell of a thing, Jase, when a celebration like we had ends up like that. And there ain't no way we'll ever catch the guy what did it. A bunch of drunks shootin off guns into the dark like that—I'm surprised no one else got hit."

Jason fussed with his belt buckle. "Does he still want to leave town?"

Harmon nodded. "But he won't, y'know. We're his family here. We took him and Mary in when they come, we'll be here to see them raisin another batch of kids before the spring comes back. He's just . . . it's just the way it happened, that's all. He's a good man. He'll settle it down where it belongs before long."

"And Aaron? Have you heard from Aaron?"

"Nope. He's got his hands full, goin from a stable to a big place like that. Charlie . . . I think that kid'll do fine once he grows up some. Dawn, on the other hand, who the hell knows."

Jason tried a knowing nod, then shook the man's hand. "Well, Jake, I gotta run. When I get back, you'll have to take me hunting."

Jake laughed. "Make a westerner outta ya?"

"Something like that."

Harmon rose unsteadily, then pulled open a desk drawer and fished out a clear plastic envelope. In it Jason could see a folded brown feather. "Here," the sheriff said, handing it to him. "Find a deep canyon."

Jason's back stiffened, and his skin grew cold. But there was nothing in the man's eyes that told him a thing. He took the envelope and shoved it in his coat pocket, hesitated before nodding and waved to Bill and left.

"Jason!"

He turned and saw Esther Lynn huffing down the street toward him. He laughed, and Donna poked her head from the car and waved at the woman impatiently.

"Jase . . . god, let me get my breath . . . Jase, I know we said our goodbyes last night, but I couldn't . . ." She whipped a handkerchief from her sleeve and daubed at her eyes. "You're what I got left, and I didn't want you to go without seein me again."

He put his hands gently on her shoulders and gathered her to his chest. An amazing woman, he thought as he hugged her, knowing what she does and still able to take a walk after sunset. She had only shed one tear at Galen's funeral and had spent the following day in the office with him, parceling out responsibilities before he'd known himself that he would be the new editor. And once the thought had lodged, it felt as though it were home.

She leaned away and patted his cheek, standing on her toes to search his squinting eyes. "You're leavin again," she said.

He had told her why'd he come here.

"On my own this time, Esther. I'll be back, that's a promise."

She took his hands and held them tightly, then grabbed him in an embrace that lasted just long enough, and not long at all. Jason felt his lips trembling at her ear.

Then: "You end it." The whisper barely audible. "End it, Jase, for god's sake."

Ten miles later Donna poked his thigh and said, "So?"

"No," he said sadly.

"Why? I'm not attractive? I'm not sexy enough? You think I can't cook or something?"

"Yes, yes, and probably," he said, laughing.

"So?"

"So . . . I can't."

"It's not your fault, Jase. It isn't."

He inhaled deeply. "Yeah. Yeah, I keep telling myself that."

"Listen, Jason Clarke, I've never proposed to anyone before, you know. This could ruin me for life."

He took her hand and squeezed it tightly, then brought it to his lips and brushed the back softly. "We'll talk about it . . . after."

"You're that sure?"

He watched the road slip by him, and heard the engine and the wheels and the muffled roar of the wind.

"It was the infection and the teaching both. And it all fits, love. From the time she was attacked Ellie hated this place. She was fine during the winter, but when . . . when it was spring she started acting funny. Jake said so. Artie said so. I think Steve must have noticed, but he wouldn't admit it, at least not to outsiders. The infection happened when Harry was killed. She was reacting without knowing what to do about it."

"And now you think she does?"

"I doubt it," he said after a mile's consideration. "Carole was the last. There isn't anymore, that much I'm sure of. Simon himself told me nothing Rachel knew was ever written down."

"Then why are we going? How's Ellie going to learn something no one else knows?"

"I'm not *that* sure," he told her. "And god, I've got to know."

She shifted until she was pressing against him, her head on

his shoulder. "And Esther Lynn's going to let us know if Bea starts acting . . . funny."

"Something like that."

She sighed and held his arm lightly. "I thought it was over."

"It is."

"Promise?"

He almost nodded.

(3)

"A cigarette," Steve demanded as they passed the fifth motel in two hours Ellie didn't like. "Come on, a cigarette."

She frowned but said nothing, only pawed through her purse to find the crumpled pack.

"Ellie, for god's sake, you want me to have a fit right here on the road?"

She shoved aside a gold-edged brown envelope that crackled like parchment and found the matches. She put a cigarette in his mouth and lit it.

"Hey!" he said, pulling away from the flame, the station wagon swerving crazily toward the verge. "Hey, damnit, watch it!"

He puffed angrily, his gaze flicking to the rearview mirror and he saw the woman sitting back there smiling at him blandly. Great, he thought. And it had been great, in the beginning. Ellie had convinced him they could use some help in the new house, and who better knew about being a servant than the retarded bitch who used to work for MacKenzie? But the way she smiled at him, the way she fussed over Ellie . . . well, sometimes it gave him the goddamned willies.

"Steve?"

He wrenched his gaze away and back to his wife. "What."

"Would you mind pulling over, hon? Please?"

"Jesus," he said as he applied the brakes and slipped onto the shoulder. "Jesus, you gonna be sick?"

"No," she said, opening the door and sliding out. "No, but I'm hungry."

Palemoon smiled.

And Ellie laughed.

Softly.